John Thompson's adaptati tribulations of city management is as entertaining as it is insightful. His fictional approach conveys a very real sense of the realities facing today's local government administrators. A great supplemental balance to any public management text. I would suggest that each and every one of you interested in the day-to-day life of a city manager read this book. If I didn't know better, I'd think John was a fly on the wall in my office when I was a city manager. A good read with great insights. This certainly would be a great supplemental text for those of you who teach urban-management related courses.

—Stephen G. Harding,
Former City Manager Instructor, Master of Public Policy &
Administration Program, Northwestern University

I really believe this will do well in many classrooms for state & local, public policy, economic development, and public administration - both at the undergraduate and master's levels. UNDERGRADUATE teachers are desperately looking for something interesting like your book. I have been looking for years for a good novel like yours to help immerse my students into the reality of city management. It is especially helpful for my pre-service, younger students in the MPA program, as well as our graduate certificate in urban and regional planning. I know of other faculty who are looking for a reality-based novel about public administrators at the local level, with gripping attention to these ethical dilemmas.

—Bradley S. Chilton,
Ph.D., J.D., Professor & Director,
Public Administration Program,
University of Texas at El Paso

On rereading your book, I am struck again by how much you convey in it. One could construct an entire course around its content and themes. Very well done!

—Rod Gould,
Retired City Manager and Adjunct Professor,
Price School of Public Policy,
University of Southern California

I am a big fan of using the story to illustrate and support the academic material we teach. I would recommend the book to the students who are in the Local Government Specialization and pursuing the City Manager career.

—Masami Nishishiba
Ph.D., Chair, Department of Public Administration,
Mark O. Hatfield School of Government,
Portland State University

When The Dam Breaks is much more than a fascinating novel. It is an insightful and instructive primer on the day to day operations of local government. Students of politics could learn a tremendous amount about the inside workings of small cities from the experiences of Brad Jacks, the city manager of the novel. Most enjoyable!"

—Elizabeth F. Moulds,
Professor of Government Emeritus,
California State University, Sacramento

A highly enjoyable read, woven into a story of the city management profession from a highly regarded retired city manager. The story provides insight into development issues from the public and private perspective, along with very interesting stories about some little-known California's history. I wish I had read this before becoming a city manager.

—Sean Quinn,
Retired City Manager

After serving as a city manager for 25 years and then working in a consultant capacity with public agencies, it is encouraging to see a leader in the profession translate his experience into an interesting book featuring the city manager craft. Thompson has a thorough understanding of the issues, concerns and challenges faced by city managers everywhere. Everyone should read it for entertainment and for the window it provides into the exciting field of city management.

—Jack A. Simpson,
"Trackdown Management" Newsletter

A fun and engaging read. The story sheds light on the common struggle people face reconciling workplace demands and personal pressures with their own ethics and values. This is a book for the general public as well as those in interested in local government or considering a career in that field.

—Kevin O'Rourke,
retired city manager, MPA Adjunct Professor &
Co-chair, California Chapter, International
City Management Association Ethics Committee

What a read! The diverse and complex challenges city management professionals face daily come to life in Thompson's page-turning story.

—Nat Rojanasathira,
Past President, Municipal Management
Assistants of Northern California

WHEN THE DAM BREAKS

When The Dam Breaks

A novel

by

JOHN P. THOMPSON

Adelaide Books
New York / Lisbon
2021

WHEN THE DAM BREAKS
A novel
By John P. Thompson

Copyright © by John P. Thompson
Cover design © 2021 Adelaide Books

Published by Adelaide Books, New York / Lisbon
adelaidebooks.org
Editor-in-Chief
Stevan V. Nikolic

For any information, please address Adelaide Books
at info@adelaidebooks.org
or write to:
Adelaide Books
244 Fifth Ave. Suite D27
New York, NY, 10001

ISBN: 978-1-955196-45-1

Printed in the United States of America

To Diane

CHAPTER 1

"Shit!" Brad Jacks stumbled over a rut in the decomposed granite track at the park. Why hadn't they fixed that thing? Maybe because "they" was "he." As city manager of Santa Ynez, California, the buck stopped with him. But there were not enough bucks stopping these days to make the track a priority. In nearly forty years of doing city budgets, he had never seen a picket sign clamoring for more preventative maintenance. He expected the city would not get to the track maintenance until settling a trip-and-fall claim at far greater cost. That kind of government decision-making made as much sense as Dolly Parton singing "The Muleskinner Blues," but somehow, she made it work, too. For a city manager, "making it work" was the name of the game.

Brad sighed as he always did when faced with a problem he could not solve and jogged on. Shouldn't a paunch be okay on a sixty-one-year-old? Not according to those taunting, ideal-weight charts, apparently created by anorexics, telling him to lose thirty pounds from his six-foot, two-hundred-fifteen-pound frame. The doctor's warnings about high blood pressure combined with his poor family health history were sobering. After five career moves, Brad and his wife, Marie, had finally found paradise on California's Central Coast. He better take care of himself, physically and professionally, or he would never attain a happy retirement here. God knows he owed Marie that after what she had been through early in their marriage. Happy. A loaded word. Could they ever be truly happy after what happened? He would settle for a day without being reminded of the trauma. Listening to his eclectic music playlist usually distracted him from his aching knees. But the distant wail and occasional yelp of approaching sirens reminded him that he had put off the fire chief's request for a citywide emergency preparedness drill. He sighed again.

Now fully into work mode, even ZZ Top's "La Grange" could not bring him back to the moment. Screw it! He took out his earbuds, turned off the iPod, rubbed his throbbing left knee, and set out again to organize his thoughts for the day, accompanied only by the soft squish of his cross trainers on the damp track.

The chilly gray late January morning mirrored Brad's mood as he plodded along. It promised to be a busy day full of meetings with staff, councilmembers, and citizens. Common denominator: they would all want something from him. The city manager served like a circus plate-spinner at the fulcrum point between the community, its politics, and the city organization. The city departments handled the routine. Brad got the exceptions.

He slogged around the moist path and scouted for more trip hazards. A long-haired Golden Retriever bounded across the wet grass right at him. The dog had the lumbering gait and dopey, tongue-waving smile that marked the breed. In other circumstances, he might have thought it endearing, but right now man's best friend was only another violator of the city's leash law. Goldie—or whatever clever name his owners picked—jumped up on him playfully. He pushed the dog off and discovered streaks of mud on his jogging pants. Damn it.

"Yah!" he yelled and flung his hands at the smelly canine. "Go on!"

Goldie stared up at him with his big, brown, sad orbs, dropped his haunches, and deposited a steamy pile of last night's Alpo at Brad's feet. He took a mock swat at the dog, yelled "No!" and "Stay!" and trundled off again. He had nothing to clean up the mess with, and it was not his responsibility anyway. Goldie's owner was AWOL, but Brad's foul mood did not extend to sentencing the dog to a visit from animal control.

An elderly woman with her dog passed him in the opposite direction. She had her Cocker Spaniel on a leash and a plastic bag in hand just in case. She scowled at him as they neared.

"Not my dog," he said defensively.

She still scowled. Her lotion, or whatever she had on, was more nauseating than Goldie's pile. How did her Cocker tolerate it with its keen sense of smell?

Brad sensed the woman recognized him and would likely spread the word about the public official who could not be bothered to enforce the city's leash ordinance. What did she expect? For him to pick up the poop in his hands and hogtie Goldie with his drawstring until animal control showed up? He sighed. Being unfairly judged was another occupational hazard.

He paused at the park entrance to remove the small baggie of soy nuts from his sweatshirt and popped them into his mouth. They tasted like roasted sawdust, but the crunch entertained his teeth and the little bit of salt tingled the front of his tongue.

The woman still spied on him as she walked her dog. Brad imagined throwing the baggie on the ground and jogging off. Might as well give her something good to gossip about. His common sense won out, and he walked over to the garbage can and bent over to pick up a Styrofoam cup and potato chip bag along the way. *See, lady, I'm a diligent public servant after all.*

Brad acknowledged the public's right to critique him, but like anyone who serves the public, there were times it chafed. He occasionally fantasized about doing something outrageous just for kicks. He smiled remembering a colleague's story of getting a call at four in the morning from an irate citizen who had been awakened by a garbage truck. She held her receiver out the window so the city manager could hear the crashing metal and the truck's back-up alarm as it serviced the office building behind her. The manager called the garbage company that day and worked out a route change. That night he set his alarm for 4 a.m. the next morning and woke the lady up to tell her he had taken care of her problem. Brad lacked the guts.

Brad plodded out of the park into his older neighborhood, trading the scent of leaves and grass for wet asphalt streets, car exhaust, and chimney smoke. Last night's rain came and left like a cat burglar. He breathed in the oak and pine scents from neighborhood fireplaces that still hung in the morning's heavy air. The smell reminded him of the blaze his grandfather always built in their huge stone fireplace on Christmas Eve, all the grandkids gathered around for his reading of '*Twas the Night Before Christmas.* The memory warmed him momentarily.

The dull gray of the morning suddenly glowed with a figure in the distance running toward him.

"Excuse me," beckoned the hard-bodied young woman in lime green spandex who stopped in front of him. "Aren't you Mr. Jacks, our city manager?"

He halted his forward progress and jogged in place. She seemed friendly enough. "Yes. Brad. Is there something I can do for you?" He hoped it would not be much.

"Yes, you can get rid of all this smoke in the air. Lots of other cities have banned wood-burning stoves and fireplaces entirely. This air is not healthy."

So much for the sweet memories of the fires of Christmas past. People had different perspectives. No point in challenging them unless it required only a clarification of facts. Brad continued to bounce as he commiserated with her and told her how to write a letter to the city council. She thanked him and raced off like the green flash he had seen once over a Maui sunset, a welcome contrast to the grayness of the morning.

Not far away, a car backed down the driveway, spewing white vapor from the tailpipe. Brad waved at his neighbor as he jogged by. *Enjoy it while you can, pal. They'll probably outlaw gas engines soon, too. We're getting regulated to death in this country.*

As often happened, his lousy mood found a source—the controversial Green Valley Village active adult community being developed by SoCal Communities—the most exciting project ever proposed for his city of 5,000. Brad coveted the financial benefits and image boost the project promised. A majority of his bosses, the city council, were likely supporters. But while still in its formative stages, the proposal's sheer size had already polarized the small community. Brad's experience told him it would only get worse. Agitated local politics endangered his goal of retiring in Santa Ynez.

Brad's thoughts shifted to the meeting later this morning with his fiery Planning Director, Megan Cain. What a perfect way to kick off a dreary Monday. Distant screaming sirens amplified his annoyance.

Megan Cain: young, smart, principled, courageous, and spirited. In short, a pain in the ass to manage. Brad liked her anyway. Outside a tense situation, she had a terrific sense of humor. Something about the Green Valley Village project set her off. It could not be SoCal's rep, Scott Graves. Brad had never worked with a more congenial, competent, and polished developer—Cary Grant in Birkenstocks.

Brad suspected the problem was the land seller. Hubert "Hubie" Nettler was the octogenarian patriarch of the Nettler clan, who first settled in the valley over a hundred years ago and now had their name on buildings and signs all over the area. Hubie and his son, Hank, lived on the family cattle ranch in the hilly land to the northeast of the city. To Brad's misfortune, they had optioned some of that land for the Green Valley development. Brad got along fine with Hank but his father, Hubie, could rile Buddha. In his long career, Brad had never thrown anyone out of his office. Hubie Nettler was the odds-on favorite to be the first.

Brad's mind stayed focused on the Green Valley project until he saw the fire department engine and ambulance turn off the arterial and into his development four blocks away. Wait! They entered the second cul-de-sac. His street. Five houses. Twenty percent chance. Too high. He broke into a sprint, gasping for air as his mind assaulted him with nightmarish images of what had happened nearly forty years before and what might be going on at home right now.

"Oh, God!" he cried as he rounded the corner and saw the flashing red lights at his driveway. Now in full panic, Brad spotted a firefighter emerge from his neighbor's door and his wife Marie and their son, Dillon, talking casually to Fire Captain Lopez next to the engine. "Thank you, God," he gasped, as he slowed to a fast walk.

"Lilly fell," Marie announced as he approached. "Lee is in with them."

"We see it all the time in elderly people, Mr. Jacks," Captain Lopez volunteered.

"Call me Brad, Joe. The Andres are pretty spry for their age. I don't think of them as frail. I took Lee out a couple months ago for a round of golf to celebrate his ninetieth birthday, and he hit the ball fine."

His statement evoked Marie's grilling for facts after the round that Brad had failed to gather. "How can you spend five hours with Lee and not know anything about how they are doing?" she had scolded.

"Is Mrs. Andre going to be okay?" seventeen-year-old Dillon asked the captain.

"Well, as your dad knows, we can't talk about a patient's condition except to a family member. But let's say I like coming on a call where the patient's vitals are strong," Captain Lopez winked at Brad.

"You go ahead to school," Marie said. "And drive carefully. No more fire department visits today."

Marie and Brad waited outside until Lilly emerged from her front door on a gurney. Lee held her hand.

"What happened, Lee?" Marie asked as the paramedics hoisted the gurney into the ambulance and continued to minister to her.

"She fell," Lee said, a bit distracted.

"Where'd she fall?" Marie probed further.

Brad ground his teeth. *Leave the poor guy alone.*

"She slipped in the bathroom. She said something snapped. She has osteoporosis, you know."

"My mother has it, too," Marie said. "It must have really hurt."

"Lilly doesn't complain much about aches and pains," Lee said. "But she sure did this time. I called 9-1-1 and didn't move her."

"I'm sure she'll be fine, Lee," Marie said. "Come on, I'll drive you to the hospital."

"I'll take a quick shower, call the office, and meet you there," Brad said. He tried to act calm for Lee, but dreaded going to the hospital, knowing it would unleash the fear and guilt from that incident so many years ago.

CHAPTER 2

Brad Jacks made the short drive to Valley Community Hospital. He switched the car's satellite radio to the old-time radio classics, hoping for a snippet of *Dragnet*. Better yet, *Gunsmoke* came on. The baritone voice of the macho lawman Marshal Dillon, played by William Conrad, concluded the show's opening with, "It's a chancy job, and it makes a man watchful—and a little lonely." That always evoked a wry smile. Brad could relate.

He easily found Lee Andre and Marie in the hospital waiting room. Lee stared straight ahead, paying no attention to the news broadcast on the small TV in front of him. The elderly man slowly rose and accepted Brad's guy hug—a quick embrace and a couple light back slaps.

"How's she doing?" Brad asked.

"She broke her hip. It left her left leg shorter and turned at a weird angle. They gave her an IV and a little morphine for pain. She's settled down some. Just waiting for the doctor."

They endured a constant barrage of indecipherable buzzers, bells, and coded announcements over the PA as they passed the time together. Marie asked about Lee's family. Brad mentioned how colorful Lee's chrysanthemums were this year and joked about bringing in a bouquet to kill the hospital's antiseptic odor.

After twenty minutes, the doctor entered and confirmed that Lilly had broken her hip. She advised that the best course of treatment would be to transfer her right away to the larger regional hospital in Santa Maria for surgery tomorrow. She explained that they wanted to get older patients into surgery within twenty-four hours if their EKG, chest x-ray, and labs indicate they could handle it.

"They've had splendid results with hips, even in patients of Lilly's age," the doctor advised. "It mostly depends upon the patient's temperament and whether they have the will to get up and moving again."

"Oh, you don't need to worry about Lilly, doctor," Lee said proudly. "She's been through tougher scrapes than this. After all, she's a survivor, you know."

"What do you mean, Lee? A World War II survivor?" Marie asked.

Brad smiled, grateful this time that his wife did the prying.

Lee lowered his head. "No. It happened when Lilly was little. A big dam broke and flooded everything. It killed hundreds of people, including her parents who were staying at a construction camp when the wave hit. They died saving her." Lee shifted his gaze to the doors leading to the Emergency Department. "Lilly doesn't talk about it much."

"That sounds terrible," Marie said. "Where did it happen?"

"You know where Castaic Junction is at the bottom of the Grapevine on I-5?"

"Sure," Brad responded, "just as you go over the mountains from the San Joaquin Valley on southbound I-5 and drop into the LA Basin."

"You know where that big amusement park is down the road from Castaic?" Lee asked.

"Yeah," Brad nodded. "Magic Mountain, right along the west side of I-5. I've driven through there a million times."

"Well, Los Angeles built a big dam in the mountains near where that amusement park is now," Lee said. "Back in the 1920s. The dam broke and a wall of water came down, flooded Castaic, and turned west toward Santa Paula along Highway 126. It took everything in its path all the way out to the Pacific Ocean. Dead bodies from miles away washed up on the beaches at Oxnard. Lilly's family was in the path of the flood."

Brad cocked his head and squinted. He had grown up in Camarillo, over the hill from the valley where this flood supposedly occurred and took California history while at the University of California, Santa Barbara, not far from the dam site. How could he not know about this incident?

"Was it an earthquake or something?" Brad asked.

Lee paused. His words became more measured. "A lot of factors caused that dam to break. I'd say the biggest was greed."

Brad was curious about what his neighbor meant by "greed" but Marie was quicker.

"I've never heard of that," she declared.

"What happended to Lilly?"

Lee stiffened. "I shouldn't have said anything about the disaster. Maybe Lilly will tell you some day."

Brad got the message and glanced at Marie, giving her "the look." She turned back to the TV news.

Ten minutes later, they wheeled Lilly back to the ER to await transport to Santa Maria.

Brad and Marie offered to go with them. Lee declined, saying his son from Salinas would be there soon. They waited a bit longer until the ambulance came, hugged Lee, patted Lilly's hand, and promised to check in.

They walked out of the hospital into the crisp wintry air to their cars. An ambulance pulled up to the ER, its red strobe lights signaling another life in danger. Brad reached over and took Marie's left hand, the soft plastic compressing slightly. After all these years, it was natural for him to treat her prosthesis the same as her right hand. She turned and smiled. He was relieved to leave the hospital without Marie mentioning anything about how she ended up with a prosthesis. In fact, he was glad they almost never brought it up.

City Manager Brad Jacks guided his politically correct, locally purchased, white Ford Fusion into the parking lot of the small single-story City Hall building off Highway 246 and walked into the lobby at 9:40 a.m.

Kerry Fenton, Executive Director of the Santa Ynez Tourism Bureau, trudged behind with a box in both arms. Brad held the door.

"Hi, Kerry. Bringing us doughnuts?" Brad chirped.

"New brochures, hot off the press," she said, hefting the box slightly. "Your public dollars at work."

"Nice going, Kerry." He smiled and walked away to avoid any potential request to do something. But seeing Kerry straining a few paces got to him. Brad turned back and took the heavy box from her over to the tourism racks.

"By the way, Kerry, you're doing a helluva job. You sure capitalized on *Sideways*. Loved that movie."

"Yup. The adventures of Jack and Miles have done great things for our wineries, hotels, and tourism in general," she observed.

"Don't sell yourself short in that. I know how hard you've worked to make that happen. Before *Sideways*, people only stopped at Santa Ynez for gas."

"Hah! You're forgetting that we were once home to the Leader of the Free World." She gestured at the mountain range to the west. "When the Reagans lived up there, we had visitors like Queen Elizabeth, Mikhail Gorbachev, and Margaret Thatcher."

"Maybe so, but I know that since you took over the Visitor's Bureau, our motel tax revenue jumped to one point six million—twenty five percent of the city's total General Fund. I give you credit for a large chunk of that."

"Thanks again, Brad. It's a team effort, as you know."

"Sure. See you later." He turned to walk away, and an impulse hit him. "Oh, I didn't mean to imply that I'm going to support a big increase in your budget. Just wanted to let you know you're appreciated even if we can't afford to pay you more."

"God forbid you should be so reckless with the public's money." She laughed. "Nobody can ever call you a spendthrift."

"Nah, they have choicer terms for me. Oh, since you brought it up, how about giving Marie and me a tour of Rancho Del Cielo? I read that Reagan said the panoramic view of the Pacific Ocean fed his soul. Mine is starving."

"That would be fun. Let's email some dates."

"Great. Gotta go," Brad said. "I have urgent, unimportant things to do."

Kerry smiled. "Understood. I'm a Stephen Covey fan, too. Hope you can squeeze in some important, nonurgent stuff."

Mission accomplished. Kerry Fenton was Public Works Director Dipak "Dee" Sharma's sister-in-law and tight with most councilmembers. Brad was plagued by a back-channel pipeline between City Hall and the Green Valley Village supporters. Kerry was a likely coupling. Rumor had it that she was seeing the developer, Scott Graves. Regardless, she had some political juice. Marshal Dillon would have kept his eyes on her, too.

Brad paused outside the glass wall off the lobby with "City Manager's Office" painted in gothic gold lettering. His assistant,

Jane Stanar, was hunched over her keyboard. Jane's official title was City Clerk/Executive Secretary. She was so much more than that to Brad, but "Aide-de-Camp/Partner/Organizer/Guardian/Confidant" did not fit on a business card. He was comforted watching Jane doing her job so competently and felt a wave of sadness. Jane deserved better cards than she had been dealt. Her husband had been killed in an industrial accident five years ago. It had to be a struggle just getting through each day with her young daughters, let alone have a social life in this small town.

She had a new hairdo with gold streaks. Brad also noticed her turquoise turtleneck and recalled a Rotary program on color analysis. He and Jane had fun deciding their "seasons." They concluded that with her strawberry blonde hair, hazel eyes, and pinkish skin tone, she was a "spring." He glanced down at his camel hair sport coat and smiled, anticipating the grief she would give him again about it. "Winters" should not wear beige.

Brad put his hand on the chrome door handle and paused to take in the Spartan waiting area. The office furnishings looked like refugees from an H&R Block office, circa 1972.

"Morning," he said, heading to the swinging half-door to the left of the light walnut veneer counter that ran across the entire room.

"Oh, my favorite brown sport coat," Jane teased. "You know, if it had a burgundy lining, you should wear it inside out."

"I wore it for you. I know how much you love it."

"Right. Why don't you hang it out here? A drab coat blends right in with my view."

Brad had barely enough time to skim a technical study about consolidating countywide communications and safety records management. Santa Ynez had its own fire department with a single station but contracted with the county for police services and emergency dispatch, then argued every year about the city's fair share of the costs. Because his city was a minor player in public safety compared to other agencies in the county and the draft report was so filled with technical jargon, he planned only a token review to show he had read it. He learned early in his career that he could never be proficient in all the issues that came his way. He relied on his staff but asked them penetrating questions to ensure they were on top of things. His "bullshit meter" vibrated when sensing only superficial knowledge.

Two pages into the report's executive summary his phone buzzed.

"Chief Powell," Jane announced.

Brad picked up the phone. "What's up, Barry?

"Wanted to let you know we're on a wildfire that's looking bad."

"Wildfire? In January?" Brad asked. "I stopped worrying about *them* and was getting ready to start worrying about floods."

"In our business, disaster can strike at any time."

Brad rolled his eyes. "Of course."

"It's that damn drought," the chief added. "The moisture content in the grasses and chaparral is still really low. We've usually had enough rain by now to lower the danger assessment, but we're still in moderate."

"Okay, so what's going on?"

"Looks like it started along the road in the grass behind Nettlers' rental yard. Probably a tossed cigarette. It spread to their redwood fence and then to a stand of dead oaks. We've got a line on it, but the high winds are blowing some good-sized embers all over hell. Right now, it's blowing them to the unincorporated area across the road."

"Sounds serious. Did you call for mutual aid?"

"Yes. County fire has a team setting up. I've established an incident command post in the parking lot of the rental yard. The county chief is on his way."

"Anything you need from me?"

"My biggest worry is that those embers could start fires anywhere. I'm especially worried about Chumash creek. Have you heard about Black Tuesday, maybe twenty years ago, when a wildfire got into the creek and raced along behind all those houses for more than a mile? We had only limited access points back there and ended up losing nine houses."

"Yeah, I heard about that, Barry. What do you need from me?" he asked again.

"Just a heads-up for now. I suggest you put everyone on alert that we might have to activate the emergency operations center protocols if the fire gets into the creek or the embers blow back to town."

"Will do. Anything else?"

"Not now. Oh, crap. Here comes old man Nettler. He looks mad. Better go. I'll update you later."

Brad chucked the report on the desk and got up. "Jane, I need you to call the EOC team and put them on alert that we may need to activate. We have a wildfire out by Nettlers' rental yard that could get ugly fast."

"Ugh," she moaned. "Most of us feel like fifth wheels in those situations. It's mostly police and fire's show with public works sometimes. The people from finance, planning and the rest of us feel like window dressing."

"I know. But if this thing gets bad enough, all the safety folks will be needed in the field. The rest of us will have to pick up the slack providing food, shelter, pet care, and other support. I learned an embarrassing lesson early in my career that in a real disaster you're going to make some big mistakes, so you better at least follow best practices in how you organize for the response."

"Embarrassing? Give me the dirt," she prodded eagerly.

"It was my first manager job. I activated our EOC when a wildfire in the hills threatened houses in the city. A fire department battalion chief, acting as incident commander at the command post near the fire, received a damage assessment report from a fire captain on the fire line. To make a long story short, I hit the panic button after I was told six 'houses,'" he made air quotation marks, "had been destroyed. I directed the opening of the community center for a relocation center, had them call the Red Cross, SPCA, county emergency services director, the whole shebang. It turned out to be six *structures*. Sheds, chicken coops, and fences. No houses at all. You could say we overreacted."

"Oops. Was it cool in the hole you crawled into?"

"Yup. But I took more flak from the Monday-morning quarterbacks for not conducting any emergency plan training for three years. I know the emergency operations center is a pain for non-safety folks but doing it by the book is important when they pick you apart afterward."

Jane sang, "*Paranoia strikes deep. Into your life, it will creep.*"

"Yeah, I suppose I do worry about job security. Especially lately with Green Valley Village. But remember the old saying, 'just because you're paranoid, doesn't mean people *aren't* out to get you.' So, as my grandmother used to say: 'quit yer belly achin'. I'm going to head out there. I'll call the mayor on the way over. Will you try the rest of the council and tell them I'll get back with more info when I can?"

The musty, stuffy air attacked his nostrils immediately upon leaving the building. It conjured images of his family sitting around an open campfire eating s'mores. But the plume of dirty yellow-white smoke rising over the trees to the east was more ominous than he expected. Brad called the mayor and reminded him of his limited role if the EOC became necessary.

After being waved through the roadblock by a public works employee who recognized him, Brad pulled into the rental yard and walked toward the trailer being used as the command post. A large cluster gathered around the trailer—mostly men wearing white uniform shirts bedecked with badges and insignia. The scene was more chaotic than he was used to seeing at an incident command post. Instead of police and fire professionals poring over maps and talking calmly with each other or on radios, this looked more like a muddle of angry men waiting to see who would throw the first punch. Hubie Nettler and his son, Hank, were right in the middle of it. Brad recognized Santa Barbara County Fire Chief Terry Comerford in the mix, who seemed to be distancing himself from the fray. Brad stood back to observe.

Hubie, towering over Fire Chief Barry Powell, had one hand on his hip and stabbed the air with the other, first at Chief Powell then toward the plume then again at the chief. Chief Powell shook his head and barked right back at Hubie. The county chief interjected something that made Hubie nod and Chief Powell angrier. Brad noticed Hank Nettler moving closer to his father.

Hubie wagged his finger in Chief Powell's face. The chief backed up slightly and said something to the Nettler patriarch. Hubie took a step forward and poked his index finger into the chief's chest. Powell swept the hand away aggressively like a boxer blocking a jab. Hubie clenched his right fist and threw down his dirty green and yellow John Deere cap. Hank grabbed his father in a bear hug and pulled him back. Hubie struggled and swore at Chief Powell until finally being led away.

Brad approached his chief. "I know Hubie is a tough old guy, but I had ten bucks on you in the third round. You okay?"

"Yeah, but that son of a bitch jerked my chain pretty hard."

"What was that all about?"

The chief nodded toward Hubie Nettler who stood outside the office gesticulating wildly with Hank nodding in synch with his raised, open palms. "That asshole thinks he runs this town and everyone in it."

"Suppose he's used to that. What happened, Barry?"

"Well, since the fire started in the city limits, I'm the incident commander even once it spread to the unincorporated area. This thing is moving fast, and we need a quick, coordinated response, not everyone doing their own thing."

"Makes sense. Where's the problem?"

"Captain Lopez was first in and set up for an attack on the fence fire from inside the rental yard. It was a good decision since there were good-sized embers landing all over a big wooden storage garage back there. If that had caught on, it would have likely spread to other structures and over that masonry wall to the creek around the side of the yard. We can't get an engine back there."

Brad glanced over his chief's shoulder and saw the mayor's blue Mercedes pull into the lot. He watched Hubie Nettler stomp over to the car.

"Got it. Good decision. Go on."

"When I arrived, I took command of the incident. Shortly after that, the first team from county fire arrived with a battalion chief. They had an engine and a brush rig. I assigned the engine to the other side of the fence to cut down the embers and told the brush rig to hold at the road in case we needed a quick attack into the creek."

"As the guy who jumped off the skyscraper was heard to yell on the way down: 'so far, so good,'" Brad joked, hoping to calm his chief.

"Yeah, but it went to crap when the second county team arrived with Chief Comerford. I told him I wanted to keep his second team in the staging area to protect the city until our call-back team got here. He wanted to turn all his units onto the wildland fire rather than coordinating our resources. I argued that the risks were much greater if the winds shifted again back to the city versus the potential damage from a wildfire in the hills."

"Sounds sensible." Brad sneaked a peak at the mayor, who was getting an earful from Hubie Nettler. "Better make it fast."

"Chief Comerford and I were still arguing the strategy when Hubie and Hank walked up. Hubie was adamant about stopping the wildfire before it spread to his land. He went on and on about the old days when they ran the volunteer district and knocked down wildfires without all this conversation. He said the engine at the yard was enough to protect the city and we should deploy everything we had to the wildfire. Right about then, Captain Lopez radioed screaming: 'It's in the creek, it's in the creek!' All I could think about was Black Tuesday all over again. On my watch!"

Brad nodded toward the Mayor and Hubie. "Better hurry up, the mayor will probably be coming over soon."

"Okay. To sum up, with the creek threat, I got more forceful with Chief Comerford and told him to send one of his brush rigs along the creek and leave his second engine at the staging area to respond to a structure fire in the city. He disagreed and we got into it. Hubie was still butting in, arguing tactics like it was his decision. Eventually, Hubie said 'screw you guys' and stormed off with Hank."

Lopez put his man on a ladder over the masonry wall and helped him with the inch-and-a-half line. They fought the creek flare-up from there. Somewhere along the way, Hank drove over with his own water tanker and directed *his* inch-and-a-half over the fence also."

Brad's attention was drawn to bright red embers wafting high over the trees, thankfully to the east, toward the unincorporated area. The smoky air stung his eyes and kept his breath shallow. He thought about his meetings today and wondered if he would have to change clothes before going back to the office.

"Sounds like Hank helped saved the day. Why were you arguing?"

"When Hank emptied his tanker into the creek, Hubie, without telling anybody, drove back out to the street hydrant and hooked into the two-and-a-half-inch outlet to refill. We already had the engine hooked into the four-and-a-half. Sometime in there our firefighter slipped on the ladder and lost his grip on the hose. Lopez held on, but the nozzle was whipping around pretty good. Could have knocked them out. The engineer left the engine to give them a hand. By the time he got back to the engine he saw that the pump pressure had dropped way too low."

"So, Hubie connecting his tanker to the hydrant nearly cavitated our pumper?"

The chief smiled for the first time. "Hey, not bad for a city manager. As you know, we have low water pressure at this end of town. We're all looking forward to getting that fixed with the Green Valley project. But I'll tell you, if the engineer hadn't gotten back when he did and made quick adjustments to the valves, we'd have lost the engine. I guess Lopez gave it to Hubie pretty good about butting in."

"Gotcha. Finish up, here comes the mayor."

"Hubie came back to bitch at me about Lopez and I told them to get out of my face or I'd have him arrested. Looks like we have things nearly contained here and the county has lines on the wildfire."

"Good going, Barry. Let me try to head off the mayor."

Brad left the command post and met Mayor Buddy Murray halfway, bracing for the attack. He listened passively as the mayor spewed Hubie Nettler's perspective for a couple minutes. Then Brad told him the rest of the story and convinced the mayor it would be wise to not get positioned on this incident.

"You're probably right, Brad, but Hubie's watching us. Just stand there and look worried. I'm going to wave my arms around like I'm chewing you out then get out of here."

Safely back in his car a few minutes later, Brad chuckled about the mayor's performance. He clicked with Mayor Buddy and was warmed by the official's willingness to cover him in a tough spot. He drove back to City Hall thinking about his upcoming meeting with the planning director about the Green Valley project. Brad wondered if his collegial relationship with the mayor would be enough to sustain him with what was coming their way.

CHAPTER 3

Planning Director Megan Cain was late for their eleven o'clock meeting. As usual. Brad pushed his coffee mug away, drummed his gold Cross pen on his desk and launched into a mental bitch session about his young department director. Megan should care more about Green Valley Village's financial benefits and the movers and shakers who supported the project. She had to know how much heat her criticisms were generating…for both of them. Couldn't she be a team player?

At 11:19 Megan finally strolled into his office. "Hi," she said. She took her customary upholstered chair across from Brad's usual spot and plopped her stack of papers on the dark wood coffee table. She didn't bother to apologize for her tardiness.

Brad didn't return the greeting and pivoted around his cluttered desk to his chair at the coffee table across from Megan. Her movements seemed quick and stiff. Her black slacks and canary yellow sweater accentuated her bright blue eyes and athletic body. She appeared ready to pounce.

"What's up?" he asked.

"This Green Valley review from public works," she said disgustedly.

"What's your problem with Dee now?" he asked. Megan Cain and Public Works Director Dipak (Dee) Sharma, were like fire and ice, sparring all the time. They were both competent and hardworking but had far different styles. Megan was fire.

"He's deliberately understating the impacts on Green Valley's environmental assessment."

Brad flinched. "Come on, Megan, why would he do that?"

"Easy," she continued, undaunted. "I think SoCal has Dee in their back pocket. Do you know about their big donation to Dee's pet cause?"

"Now hold on, Megan. Dee's vice president of his daughter's soccer league. I want all the department heads to be active in the community. It's great that his board got SoCal to donate the new fields. But I'm sure Dee was careful not to make the 'ask' himself or offer anything for it besides the same recognition they'd give other sponsors."

She sneered. "I'm glad you defend your department heads—"

"*You*, of all people should be! You do know people call you Megan 'Cain't,' don't you?"

"Yeah," she said, softening her demeanor.

"You know," he continued, "a city manager is like a boxer. We can only take so many shots before we go down. I've taken more body blows over you and your relationship with Kay Nance than all the other department heads combined. It's part of my job to shield department heads from political pressure, but you don't make that easy for me. I'll keep at it until I can't get off the canvas anymore." He managed a quick smile, hoping to ease the tension.

She leaned forward slightly. "All of us appreciate how much you protect us and let us run our shops. But as to Councilwoman Nance, her views on community development and environmental protection make sense, a lot more than Mayor Buddy and his let's-break-some-ground-today cronies. I've never compromised my integrity for Kay Nance or anyone else. And I've never been disloyal to you, Brad. I'm not so sure you could say that about your public works director."

"You need more evidence than a soccer field to back that up."

"Well, how about this?" Megan leaned over to pick up two reports from the table.

He glanced back at the pile of paperwork on his desk. "Just summarize, will you?"

For the next ten minutes, Megan shuffled through the stack of reports. She focused on two traffic studies prepared by the department of public works. She claimed they were inconsistent and projected an unrealistically high "level of service" for several intersections that she expected would be more degraded by the Green Valley Village traffic.

He made a point of staring again at his messy desk.

She caught the cue. "Give me a couple more minutes, Brad. There's an even more serious problem with the draft Water Supply Assessment."

Brad sat impassively for the next ten minutes as Megan pointed from one table and chart to another, arguing that water demand for the residential units and golf course were understated and the city's total water supply was overstated. He yawned.

"I can see I'm losing you," she said. "I'll cut to the bottom line. Public works' analyses of Green Valley traffic and water impacts is fishy. Dee is deliberately glossing over major issues." She sat back, jaw set.

"I assume you haven't shared any of this with Dee."

"I tried and he blew me off."

He pondered a moment. "Did you even try to use our communication training to talk to him in a way he'd listen? You and I tend to be pretty abrupt. Dee is hypersensitive to criticism, so you can't go right at him and expect him to engage."

"Oh, but it's okay for him to treat me like I'm just some little girl right out of college? I'm supposed to adapt to him?"

"Well, you are female and you ain't been out of college that long," he smiled and instantly wished for a delete button.

Megan stiffened. "So, this is about my age and gender?"

Brad slumped backward at his mistake. "Of course not. You have a habit of casting any legitimate disagreement with you into some epic battle between good and evil." The reprimand was for her own good, but the force behind it came from his anxieties. Maybe he should tone it down.

He leaned back in his side chair and laced his fingers. "Look, Megan, almost from the time we first got wind that SoCal optioned Nettlers' land, I've had complaints about your sniping at the project. Sure, Hubie's a son-of-a-bitch, and I wish SoCal hadn't picked his land, but we both have to deal with it and get the project done."

"Get the project done?" she objected. "Do you mean give it a thorough review?"

"For your information, Megan, there are a lot of people, likely a majority of my bosses, who want it." He crossed his arms. "Now, I'm willing to look at your information, but you need to lighten up a little. Stop parroting Kay Nance's antigrowth biases. People question your objectivity."

She scoffed. "I don't care what people say about me."

"*You* might not, but I do. I have college tuitions to pay and hope to retire in this town, even if you're long gone. I'm not going to let you turn Green Valley Village into some personal crusade at my expense."

She recoiled and stared at him with wide blue eyes.

Her reaction startled him. She almost seemed vulnerable. A lawnmower made a pass outside the window and broke the silence.

"Megan," he said quietly, "you're a smart person. When it comes to city planning, you know your onions, as my grandfather used to say. I admire your tenacity and courage. But dial it down a little, would you? Everything isn't as black and white as you make it seem. Public policy comes in shades of gray."

"I know that, Brad." She sat serenely for a moment. "And I also know that I'm in a lot of gun sights in this town. I'll let you worry about what your public works director is or isn't doing. My main concern is with the environmental assessment. That's my responsibility."

"Actually, it's the *city's* responsibility to lead the environmental assessment," he corrected. "Not yours alone. Other city departments and agencies have a role in that, too. Everyone might not see things the same way you do."

"True, but the environmental review process is pretty detailed. There's not much gray in it, Brad. And with Green Valley Village sprawling out on rolling range land and jumping our population by some sixty percent, you know there's going to be formidable opposition. They're going to be all over the EIR, so we better not give it a wink and a nod, or the courts will throw it out."

Brad shook his head. "I understand, but I don't have nearly the reverence you do for the whole environmental process. It has morphed into a multi-billion-dollar playground for biologists, archeologists, geologists, traffic engineers, civil engineers, civil service bureaucrats, and lawyers. It's hard as hell for anyone, including the city itself, to build something these days without undergoing a NIMBY attack."

Megan set her jaw. "If I were about to get a big project like this in my backyard, I'd want to make sure I understood the likely impacts. And I'd be pretty pissed if I knew the city rushed it through."

He sighed and tossed the report she gave him on the table. "Rushed? Rushed? Megan, give me a quick rundown on the main entitlements Green Valley Village will have to get before it can be built, will you?"

The planning director held up her left hand and folded down a finger with each milestone in the process from preparation of a specific plan for the development through annexation of the site, and the environmental impact report. After folding her thumb, she opened her hand and started anew with additional steps.

Brad smiled and interrupted the countdown. "Stop there. You made my point. Nothing about this project is going to be rushed. A plethora of government agencies will weigh in throughout the process with all sorts of technical requirements and the public will have numerous chances to take a whack at it for maybe the next two years."

"The EIR is a critical component of that process," she argued.

Brad shook his head and scowled again. "You know as well as I do that the real fight is over the project itself, not the environmental impacts. The EIR is a battleground. Smart opponents know it's the best place to attack a project. They may not be able to convince the elected councilmembers to kill the project even with picketing, tears, anger, and threats of recall. But challenging the EIR gives them access to the courts. The threat of a delay is the weapon, not the environmental impacts."

"Exactly!" she replied. "And that's *my* point. The more thorough we are with the environmental assessment, the better the chance of getting a quick summary judgment to throw out a legal challenge. Leave too much unstudied and the court will be more likely to send the EIR back. You know Scott Graves and SoCal won't like that."

"Sure, they'll want to see a defensible EIR. But you can study things to death and opponents will still sue. I'm not going to stand by and watch a project that's clearly in the public interest bottled up in an endless, futile process."

She jerked to attention. "I don't know how you can say Green Valley is clearly in the public interest when we haven't studied the impacts yet."

He sighed again. "Look, we have different roles. Yours puts the emphasis on process. My role requires me to consider other realities, including the council majority's position, and yes, the city's financial situation, whether you care about those factors or not."

"I care about those other things too, but you're right, my primary function is to follow the law."

He exhaled fully through his mouth, took a sip of his coffee, and frowned. Thanks to Megan, it was now cold. "What I'm trying to say is that sometimes the process runs amuck from common sense. Just do a fair review, not overkill."

"Message received," she said. "Better make sure Dee gets it, too. These reports don't add up."

"I've managed to spend my entire career without having to study an EIR. I don't intend to start now. If you and Dee can't get on the same page, I'll set up a meeting and listen to what you both have to say."

"If that's what you want to do," she shrugged. "But if you're going to stay on the schedule we set with SoCal, we better meet soon to complete the IS."

"IS?"

"Initial Study. It's a notice to the public and responsible agencies describing the project and possible impacts. It gives them a chance to comment about what should be included for study in the DEIR, sorry, Draft Environmental Impact Report. It gets everything officially kicked off."

WHEN THE DAM BREAKS

"Okay, I'll ask Jane to set up the meeting ASAP." He raised his finger for emphasis. "Oh, that means, As Soon As Possible," he said, smiling.

"I know." Megan did not smile back. All business.

"Megan," Brad said, "I can see you're worked up about the Green Valley entitlements. Just remember, at the end of the day, it'll be politics that'll decide whether the project will get built, not the EIR."

"So, you want me to pencil-whip our environmental assessment, Brad?"

He pounded the arms of his chair. "Stop making this black or white. Let me make this easier for you. Yes, Green Valley's 3,000 senior citizens will generate more traffic, require more water, and add some air pollution and run-off. Some people won't like it at first, but they'll get used to it. It'll also be an attractive project with stylish homes for people who'll contribute their cash to the city, including your own salary by the way, and contribute their energies to the community in a hundred ways. There, I saved you a ton of work." He crossed his arms over his chest, leaned back in his chair, and smirked.

The planning director fell back in her chair heavily. "I'm sorry you have so little regard for the work I do."

"Okay, Megan." *Call her by name. Tone it down. End on a positive note.* "I'll have Jane set up a meeting with you and Dee to get to the bottom of your concerns."

"Fine," she replied abruptly, corralled her reports, and got up to leave.

"Have a nice day," Brad said after her, wishing he had not. Probably sounded dismissive.

She tossed him a strained nod on the way out.

He needed a friend and went out to talk to his assistant, Jane Stanar, under the pretext of giving her some of the finished paperwork off his desk. "Here's some of the pile," he said flatly.

"It's none of my business," Jane volunteered, "but from how Megan stormed out, it must have been a rough meeting."

"Not a career highlight for me. She pressed my buttons and I put her down."

Jane smiled. "But not like Hubie would one of his cows. She *did* walk out."

"Hah! Truth is I admire Megan. I'm trying to protect her from herself. She's a pistol and may go off on both of us."

Jane nodded. "Hubie and SoCal aren't going to sit by and watch her shoot down Green Valley. I mean, Scott Graves is a great guy and all, but he has bosses, too. They'll get to her if they have to. You, too."

"I know," he said, dropping his head.

Neither said anything for a few moments. He glared through the glass wall in the direction of the lobby where two men were laughing loudly.

"Damn it, developers go through hell these days in order to bring people jobs, places to live, shop, or play, and keep the local economy afloat."

"The average citizen has no idea what it takes to get a project approved," she agreed.

Brad pressed his point. "I've dealt with a lot of developers in my career. Some were jerks with no appreciation or finesse in managing the public processes. Others, like SoCal, hire solid people you can trust, like Scott Graves, and are more win/win. Scott and SoCal are in the upper percentile of developers."

"Agreed," she said, turning back to her screen. "Well, back to work."

Brad wondered about the quick cut off and kept the conversation going. "Scott must get hit up for donations all the time. He's become a pretty popular guy, especially since he rented that house."

"Yeah, some house and some view," Jane agreed, not looking up.

"It's convenient to his other projects in Ventura County and Santa Maria," Brad added. "But the poor guy must have to entertain stakeholders from someplace every night."

"Uh-huh," Jane responded flatly.

"He's good at it too," Brad continued. "So personable. And you gotta admit: a handsome devil. He dresses so GQ, and that blond hair is never out of place."

Jane grinned. "Is this a budding bromance?"

"Okay, okay. He's just so polished. I'm more like George Gobel, who said on the Johnny Carson Show, 'Did you ever get the feeling that the world was a tuxedo, and you were a pair of brown shoes?' Now, don't you agree, Scott's the most eligible bachelor in the area?"

Jane stared straight ahead at the computer screen and said, "He does throw a helluva party, I'm told."

Brad heard Marshal Dillon's warning again.

CHAPTER 4

Brad busied himself after lunch with emails and paperwork until leaving for the high school to do his annual "City Government 101" talk for the government class. This one would be more stressful. His son, Dillon, was in the class. Last night's dinner conversation had not helped.

"Just don't be boring," Dillon piped off through a mouthful of hamburger.

Brad's wife, Marie, a former middle school English teacher smiled. "And don't talk down to them."

"I get that," Brad replied. "So, I guess I shouldn't hand out those plastic firefighter helmets, police stick-on badges, or water conservation coloring books?"

Marie ignored him. "Be yourself. They can spot a phony like you can a maple bar." Her comment did little to calm his nerves.

"Just don't be boring," Dillon urged again.

"I know! I'll do the organization chart in rap."

Marie rolled her eyes.

"Forget what Mom said about being yourself," Dillon taunted with mock disgust. "Be somebody cool."

"Hey, who's cooler than a city manager?" Brad asked, leading with his chin.

"That would be everybody, Dad," Dillon retorted. The teenager shoved the last bite of burger in his mouth and gave his dad a fist bump. "Gotta go," he said. "Library."

Dillon had been a surprise to Brad and Marie, coming twenty years after his sister, Kristen. Marie was forty and Brad forty-four. Raising a child at that age was sometimes exhausting for Brad. But he enjoyed the more relaxed relationship he had with Dillon that was absent the fear and protectiveness that so often crept into his thoughts about Kristen.

Brad turned into the high school parking lot and smiled, remembering the cold sweats and nausea every time he had to give a formal presentation in class. He took a visitors' spot in the lot and sat in the car a moment. A shrill buzzer went off and the benign scene erupted in an explosion of noise and movement. Girls screamed somewhere. A couple boys wrestled in an apparent noogie attack.

Way back when, Brad would have been another face in that crowd, hoping to get through the day without being picked on or doing something embarrassing. He had been late hitting puberty and was one of the smallest boys in his class. He would have gladly traded a full point from his GPA for some height, a deeper voice, and a girlfriend.

Brad walked through the parking lot in a fantasy about returning to high school with his adult confidence and abilities. Oh, to have those high school years to do over now. He spotted Dillon in a corridor talking freely with some friends, both girls and boys. Thank God, the boy got his mother's genes. His son was roughly the same size as his friends, started shaving in his junior year, and had a steady girlfriend. Dillon likely ranked nearer the in-crowd than Brad had ever dreamed of getting. Brad's gut spasmed in a worried clinch about being boring today.

He checked in at the office then jostled his way through the bustling hallways to the classroom and held the door for two girls behind him. They were in an animated conversation and walked past him like he was part of the door frame. Ignored by girls in high school. Déjà vu.

Mr. Heldt, Dillon's government teacher, met him at the door, shook hands, and said, "Congratulations for running the gauntlet. I sometimes lose guest speakers at the parking lot."

Brad laughed. "The whole scene *is* a little intimidating. It reminded me that high school wasn't a fun time for me."

Mr. Heldt nodded. "You're not alone. They say that most of us spend our adult years either trying to live up to, or down from, whatever we were in high school."

"I guess I'm in the latter category," Brad said. "I'm trying to get through this without embarrassing my son."

"Don't worry, I got your back." The teacher turned to greet the students.

Brad watched the teacher fist bump students as they arrived. *I got your back.* Shouldn't a high school teacher rise above the students' level of jargon? Or maybe it's more important to him to be worshipped by these acne-faced impressionables rather than imparting adult authority. He scanned the teacher's outfit critically, a red Tabasco t-shirt and blue jeans. Heldt could put on a pair of slacks and a dress shirt, for God's sake. It's high school, not a beach party.

Brad caught himself. Had he become so old that he sounded like the cranky men he rebelled against? He had to envy Mr. Heldt's connection with these kids.

The room filled with commotion and the competing fragrances of Right Guard, Clearasil, and buckets of drugstore perfume. Gas built up in Brad's lower GI. He regretted that third cup of coffee. The buzzer was nearly drowned out by the din.

"Ladies and gentlemen," Mr. Heldt said in a loud voice that carried throughout the room, "we are honored to have Mr. Brad Jacks, our city manager, with us this morning."

Several students turned to Dillon.

"Yes, he's Dillon's father, and he's an important man, so I want you to give him your fullest attention."

Brad put his right hand in his pocket and leaned on the lectern, the coolest stance he could come up with. Dillon gave him a quick, but encouraging, thumbs-up. Brad squeezed back another gas cramp and stared out at the young faces. Most of them stared back blankly. A few were oblivious to his presence, too busy flirting or clowning around. One lanky young man in the back row seemed asleep already. Had kids been this disrespectful when he was in school? Probably.

"Good morning," Brad said. *Snappy opening, Brad*, he scolded himself. A few students returned the salutation.

"I'd like this to be a conversation rather than a lecture. So please ask questions as we go along." He got a head nod from Mr. Heldt. All righty then, an endorsement from Mr. Popular.

"I'd like to start with a short quiz."

A chubby, acne-faced boy on the left side of class shot his hand up. Brad acknowledged him.

The boy leaned to address Mr. Heldt. "Does the quiz count for our grade?"

The rest of the class groaned at the question. Brad suspected he had uncovered the class dork and rescued him.

"No, it's not a test. I just want to ask you a few questions. If you know the answers, shout them out."

He asked some questions to sample their knowledge of city government, such as the mayor's name and how many people were on the city council.

A cute girl in the second row had all the answers. Everyone else had stopped trying. Brad nodded at her and said to the teacher, "You have a sharp one here, Mr. Heldt."

The teacher made a tight, forced smile in return. What did that mean?

Brad hoped to draw in more students. "Does anyone know the term of office for the city manager?"

He overlooked the raised hand of the same girl in the second row but snuck a closer look. She had on denim jeans, a red and white plaid long sleeve cowboy shirt, and boots. Brad had taken his children to all the "Toy Story" movies. This girl could be Jessie in the flesh. He called on an eager boy.

"Four years?" the boy guessed.

After a few seconds of ignoring "Jessie," Brad broke the silence. "Okay, that was a trick question. The city manager isn't elected at all. I serve at the pleasure of the mayor and city council. That means I don't have a specific term. Some city managers serve the same city for twenty years and some don't last a year. It all depends."

Brad scanned his audience hopefully. Oh, God, he was boring them. His gut tightened. He wiped his hand across his forehead. Where was he going next? Ah, his "importance of local government" shtick.

"I'm not surprised that, except for the young lady over here, most of you don't seem to know much about your local government. But it's the level of government that has the most impact on your daily lives."

Quizzical looks.

"Look, you got up this morning and nobody burglarized your house, and it didn't catch fire, partially because the police, fire, and building departments watched out for your family's safety. You showered in safe water the city treated and delivered to the faucet. Your shower drained or you flushed your toilet, and the city treated the waste in a healthy way that won't hurt the environment. You drove here on streets built and maintained by the city, and some of you will play soccer or basketball at a city park after school. But you'll learn very little in school about local government. It's a pet peeve of mine and why I'm here."

No shouts of "Horrors! The injustice of it all!"

He had hoped for more reaction than the boy up in the third row digging into his nose. Do they care about anything besides what is on *Access Hollywood*? Mr. Heldt moved stealthily to the rear of the room, came down the center aisle, gave Sleeping Beauty's huge sneaker a kick, and gestured to him to sit up.

"In the time we have left, I want to give you some information that'll help you understand the level of government that you'll most likely be able to influence."

He clicked through a few slides describing the origins of the council-manager form of government, the dominant municipal governance structure in the USA and popular across the world.

Brad liked his little history lesson. But as he surveyed the class, he noted he was a cult of one. A few of the kids were writing, apparently interested. A giggle from the back of the room suggested another possibility. Had somebody drawn a caricature of him and written *boring* on it just like Brad had done in high school?

Brad stifled another gas cramp and leaned on the podium with fake confidence. "Luckily, I've got more fascinating stories about the council-manager form of government." The joke did not go over.

He clicked to the next slide and got a whiff of his own deodorant. "Only one more picture left of an old guy, I promise. This is Charles Ashburner who's considered to be the first true city manager. He was appointed to that position by the City Council of Staunton, Virginia in 1908. In the early 1900s, the country was growing rapidly and needed roads, water lines, and other things built. So, most of the city managers of that era, like Ashburner, were engineers."

Silence.

"A funny story: Ashburner came to the City of Stockton, California in 1923. The local paper heralded his arrival as the man who would get things done. He's quoted in his first interview saying, 'By God, I go into a town to build! When I can't build, I get out!' The same excited newspaper soon nicknamed him Charles 'Cashburner' after he built too much. Sometimes you can't win."

Jessie smirked. The others did not get it or did not care.

"Like Ashburner, building things like streets and parks or helping to bring in new restaurants or stores is my favorite part of the job. And, like Ashburner, the local newspaper picks on me, too."

Some grins. He clicked through more slides comparing the council-manager form of government to a McDonald's Board of Directors and CEO. They were still with him. Mr. Heldt gave him a nod. He liked this guy after all.

"Remember, we said that our mayor, Buddy Murray, who is like the chairman of the board of a company, works in real estate. A lot of people call City Hall to speak to him and are surprised to learn he isn't there. The council expects the city staff to take care of operations."

Jessie raised her hand as she said, "So, you're a bureaucrat? My dad said if you want something from City Hall, don't waste your time with the bureaucrats, talk to the politicians."

Brad cleared his throat. "Yes, I'd be considered a bureaucrat since I manage a bureaucracy. But I don't consider that a pejorative term."

Mr. Heldt shook his head slightly.

"I mean, yes, a bureaucrat is an appointed official of the government, so that fits me, but some people also use the term to mean somebody who is all hung up on procedures and maybe uses the power of their office to make life difficult for people. I hope that doesn't describe me. If it did, I'd expect the council to fire me and hire someone else."

Apparently, his passion to serve the city with excellence did not impress them. "You see, councilmembers get reelected if the voters see their city government doing good things for them, not being obstructive."

"How much money do you make?" Jessie blurted out.

The question jolted Brad like a five-gallon dousing of ice-cold Gatorade. He had been on a roll. Mr. Heldt merely shrugged at him.

"You have a right to ask that question, young lady. It's public information, but here's a tip: don't try asking that same question to the guy who runs the casino or the Chevy dealership. They might kick you out." He smiled.

She did not. Charming girl.

"My annual salary is about a hundred thirty-eight thousand."

That got their attention. There were some oohs in the crowd.

Mr. Heldt said, "I picked the wrong profession."

Jessie continued her assault. "My dad says city employees are overpaid and that their pensions and healthcare will bankrupt the country."

Geez! Who is this kid? He launched into a hurried justification of his salary and compared his responsibilities to the McDonald's CEO. She stared at him, unimpressed. The moment he finished counterpunching, the girl raised her hand. Brad braced for the next blow.

"Now Jenny," Mr. Heldt broke in, "let's let someone else ask a question." Then to the class, he said, "Remember, ladies and gentlemen, we will have a quiz on what Mr. Jacks told us today, which will count for three-quarters of this lesson. The other quarter will be based on class participation. So, let's have some other questions."

Jessie, AKA Jenny, sat there smugly.

"Where did you go to school?" asked Sleeping Beauty.

"I have a bachelor's degree in political science from UC Santa Barbara and..."

"Yes!" Sleeping Beauty cheered. Brad could not imagine this young man aspiring to such a desirable institution. More likely, he had crashed the annual Halloween street bash in Isla Vista and tossed his cookies all over the street.

"...and a master's from University of Southern California." They were not impressed.

The rest of class went as expected. Jenny sat patiently seemingly waiting for another opening. The questions were benign. What is being built in the lot next to the Shell station? Why does the water taste funny? Why don't you heat the swimming pool? Do you get free backstage passes at the casino? Are we going to get an In-N-Out? Brad fielded the questions crisply and even occasionally with humor that hit its mark.

With what must have been his last ounce of wakeful energy, Sleeping Beauty raised his hand slowly. "Would you please tell us what you do in a normal day?"

Other students turned from the boy to Brad, apparently interested.

"Excellent question," Brad said enthusiastically. God bless Sleeping Beauty. He filled most of the remaining time describing his daily routine, keeping it light so they could relate. A glance at the wall clock revealed it was time to wrap up.

Jenny shot her hand up.

"Yes?" Brad said warily.

"You didn't say anything about the Green Valley Village project. It's a lot more important than a stupid In-N-Out. Aren't you in favor of it?"

This kid had to be a narc posing as a student. Her questions reeked of an agenda that went beyond a grade.

"Yes, young lady, Green Valley is hugely important. It's still early in the CEQA process. We're only starting the EIR, so it's a little premature to talk about."

Blank faces.

Mr. Heldt stepped in again. "Mr. Jacks, we haven't talked about city planning. Maybe you could give the class a quick overview on what you mean by CEQA and EIR."

"Oh, sure. They are required processing to study a project's effects on the environment. We use lots of acronyms in government."

"Maybe you should tell them a little about the project," Mr. Heldt prompted.

"Sure," Brad said, casting a glance to Jenny. "Green Valley Village is being planned as an active adult community for residents fifty-five and older. SoCal Communities is the company trying to develop it. They do high quality, large residential projects all over Southern California. Green Valley will have about 1,400 living units, mostly houses with some duplexes and apartments and even an assisted living facility for old codgers like me. There will be seven acres of neighborhood commercial—things the residents will want nearby like a small market, beauty shop, coffee shop, bakery, that sort of thing."

Some head nods.

Okay, stay at that level of explanation. "There will be a community center, pool, and other meeting and activity rooms, an

RV lot and storage lockers, a park a little smaller than Sunny Fields, and an eighteen-hole golf course." At the mention of the golf course, a boy in the back slugged the guy in front eagerly.

"The project will also help the city with police and fire protection, increase water storage and fix the low-pressure problem in much of the city. It is being planned on 550 acres on the east side of town past Meadowvale Road off Highway 246, as you head toward Lake Cachuma."

He observed Jenny smile and others in the class turn to her.

"Why did you want them to build that project there?" asked a girl from the back row innocently.

"I didn't," he said. "By the time I learned about SoCal's plans, they had already optioned the property."

Mr. Heldt shook his head again.

"Oh, in real estate development, the developer doesn't want to purchase property until they are sure they can build what they want on it. So, they'll pay the landowner a smaller amount of money for the right to purchase the land at the agreed upon price later, usually after they get their entitlements." Pause. "I mean once they have all of the approvals they need from the city and other agencies to start construction."

He glanced around. Better. "The environmental impact report for Green Valley is in process now. It could take as much as two years before the project could begin construction."

The classroom sat silently.

"Are there other questions about Green Valley?" Brad asked, avoiding eye contact with Jenny.

"Why did SoCal pick Santa Ynez for that kind of project?" Mr. Heldt asked.

"Santa Ynez has some advantages for a senior citizen development. We are far enough from the high land prices of the more urban areas, which is better for people on a fixed income.

Yet we're convenient to a lot of attractions that would appeal to seniors like art galleries, wineries, museums, community theatre, boutique shopping, Solvang, golf, fishing, and boating. And the beaches and ambience of Santa Barbara are over the hill."

"And the weather is so perfect," Mr. Heldt added.

"It sure is and that's a major attraction."

A few more students showed an interest in the topic.

"Being ten miles inland from the Pacific and protected by the California Coast Range mountains, we get cooling breezes in the summer and moderate temperatures in the winter without as much fog as more coastal areas get. And, like the rest of the Central Coast, it doesn't rain much, so most of the days will be fine for active adults to golf, swim, bike, and whatever."

"It sounds great," Jenny said without being called. "But what if they find some kind of rare plant or something on the property? Do you side more with private property rights or protection of endangered species?"

What the hell? What seventeen-year-old knows about endangered species or cares about private property rights? The way she asked the question and waited expectantly for his response gave Brad the sense that her interest was more than academic.

Heat burned up his chest and neck. Normally only belligerent constituents or the state legislature in session evoked this level of anxiety.

He stared at the girl, momentarily dumfounded. "Yes, I believe in property rights. I own a house myself. And, as to endangered species, there are lots of laws and processes in place to balance private and public interests. Our time is about up and I want to get to this last slide. Maybe we can chat after class if there's something specific you're interested in."

He clicked through listings of various city jobs and the qualifications required. He urged them to come to Career Day to talk to city representatives.

"Will you be there too, Mr. Jacks?" Jenny asked with a grin. She delivered it more like a dare than a plea.

"Absolutely! That is, if you want me back, I'm happy to help you."

The class applauded. Even Jenny joined half-heartedly. He beamed and gave them a little wave. He had connected. Ah, popular in high school at last. The students filed out. Some thanked him politely for coming.

Brad motioned to Jenny as she passed. She walked over warily. "You asked some tough questions, Jenny. You seem to have an interest in government. I want to invite you to do some volunteer work with the city, maybe even in my office. You would learn a lot. Who knows, you may be city manager of Santa Ynez someday. The profession could use more women."

Jenny seemed taken aback. "Hmmm," she said, "maybe I'll take you up on that, Mr. Jacks. Thank you. In the meantime, I want to do some research on endangered species." She smiled and walked out.

Mr. Heldt came over. "Sorry about Jenny, I should have warned you. She's smart, strong-spirited, and has a bit of a rebellious streak."

"Yeah, she put me on the spot a few times."

"You did fine, Dad," Dillon said as he joined them.

"Thanks, son. But do me a favor, don't bring Jenny home to meet mom anytime soon."

"Jen Nettler?" Dillon said. "She's all right. Don't you know her father, Hank?"

Brad shook his head. There was no avoiding that family.

CHAPTER 5

The stress of high school behind him again, Brad drove back to City Hall in a reflective mood. He took in the panoramic views of the Santa Ynez Mountains to the south, the San Rafael Mountains to the north, and the rolling, oak-studded hills and meadows in between. Beautiful Santa Barbara and the Pacific Ocean were only thirty minutes away. He so much wanted to live the rest of his life in this picturesque valley. Did Marie truly share that desire? They always talked about it, but his wife never seemed as expectant as he.

Since her amputation, Marie had a hard time making new friends when they moved for new jobs. Brad did not think it was self-consciousness over her prosthesis. It was more about the backstory. Only a few family members and lifelong friends knew most of the truth. Others, including Marie and Brad's children and newer friends, heard a sanitized story of Marie losing her arm in a car accident with a few fictional details provided for credibility. More casual acquaintances who asked just got "car accident years ago" in a dismissive enough delivery that made most people uncomfortable about probing further. Brad's response to those brazen enough to ignore the signal has been: "Look, Marie has worked hard to put that behind her and doesn't want people to focus on her injury so long ago.

Her *friends* don't even notice her arm." That admonishment had proven effective in changing the topic. Brad suspected that keeping the secret about what happened was a barrier to Marie's building close friendships. He could not actually remember ever asking her about that.

Marie was clearly happier at their last job in West Sacramento. Living in proximity to her roots in the nearby Stockton area was comforting. She loved their house and enjoyed adding her own touches. She joined a women's bridge group and a book club and got active in church. However, none of those interests carried over to Santa Ynez. Brad was annoyed that Marie spent so much time on the phone with her West Sacramento friends and periodically visiting her family three hundred miles north instead of making better friends here.

He felt the familiar pain. Is this all their relationship would be from now on: Brad letting his wife down and Marie adapting stoically, making him feel even guiltier? Sometimes he wanted to just have it out with her. Clear the air. But he was no Christopher Columbus. Dealing with deep emotions was uncharted territory. Brad preferred more certain outcomes. Besides, he had hurt her so much already. Why re-open any wounds? Better keep things on an even keel. He sighed as he parked in his stall at City Hall.

"How'd it go at school?" his assistant, Jane, asked. "Standing O?"

He put his thumbs to his armpits and puffed out his chest. "None of the boys picked on me and only one cute girl rejected me. I'd have to say *this* high school experience went a lot better than my last one."

"Please tell me you didn't try to hit on those girls. I was just getting you broken in," she teased.

"Nah, I got sandbagged by a cute little girl who looked like Jessie from *Toy Story*. Dillon says she's a Nettler."

"Which branch?"

"Hank's daughter. She must have had a full glass of Hubie's Kool-Aid for breakfast."

"Hank's daughter, Jen? She's a sweetie."

"Wasn't sweet to me. Think she got too many of her grandpa's genes and not enough of her father's," Brad cracked. "I've never had any real problem with Hank except his raspy voice makes my skin crawl. He must smoke three packs a day. Makes me clear my throat whenever he talks. But we're in Rotary together and friendly enough."

"He's not as rough as his father," Jane said. "I've known the family all my life and went to school with Hank. They're a lot more bark than bite. They do a lot of good in this town, especially Hank."

"Yeah, Hank's okay. Wasn't Hubie in his seventies when he punched that building inspector less than half his age? I'm glad I wasn't around when the city tried to buy a patch of his property for the well."

"I was," Jane said. "A lot of that hassle came from Hubie's attorneys. They're a hard-nosed bunch."

"Hubie has plenty of money and I'm sure he hired mean pit bulls to fight the city over that well. It's like only an acre or so. No big deal. But I'm told they put the city through hell and finally settled at an extortionist price."

She smiled. "Like I said, the whole family has done so much for people and this town for years. But I guess Hubie can get his back up if he gets pushed, especially by government."

Brad struck another pose, now sticking his thumbs in his belt and standing ramrod straight. "Now listen and listen tight. We got no use for your fancy law books in these parts. We settle things with lead."

Jane laughed. "You do a horrible John Wayne. It *was* John Wayne, wasn't it?"

"My daughter likes it," he protested. He thought of the times watching *The Man Who Shot Liberty Valance* with Kristen doing Jimmy Stewart to his "Duke" Wayne.

"I hope Hank's little girl wasn't too hard on you, tough guy."

"I'll survive," he said. "But I'll tell you the crab apples don't fall far from that family tree. She basically called me a worthless bureaucrat and grilled me about my salary, pension, health benefits, and made some out-of-the-blue reference to endangered species on the Green Valley Village site. Cute kid."

"That'll teach you to volunteer to help our youth. Aren't you the guy whose favorite slogan is, 'no good deed goes unpunished?'"

"If I only had a competent assistant who would remind me of that ahead of time," he shot back from the coffee machine.

Brad zipped through the League of California Cities weekly legislative report. More bad news for cities. Bewildering that so many state legislators, most of whom cut their political teeth as local government elected officials, forgot their roots when they got to Sacramento and became captive to statewide politics. He plowed through some of the in-basket until boredom won out.

He leaned back in his high-back leather chair and stuck his nose into the large mug of dark roasted black coffee. After savoring the distraction, he remembered failing again to inquire about Jane's mother's health. Or was it her former mother-in-law? He did not make time for inter-personal niceties as often as he intended or as often as some of his staff seemed to want.

He sighed, threw down his pen and rose from his desk, prepared to deliver some TLC.

"Knock, knock," came a voice from the door. Human Resources Director Jackie McCall took a tentative step into the office, followed closely by Public Works Director Dee Sharma. "Got a minute?" she asked.

"They say you're in for a long day if the *60 Minutes* crew shows up at your office. Why do I have that same feeling right now?" Brad asked.

"Suppose I am sometimes the grim reaper," The HR director said.

"What's up, Jackie?"

Brad noted that Dee Sharma looked down and had not said a word.

The HR director took a deep breath. "We had the disciplinary hearing last week for Rick Burnham. And as these things go, it's another case of turning over a rock. Burnham basically ratted out the entire water plant."

Burnham was a water plant operator assigned to the graveyard shift. He had been arrested for driving under the influence two weeks ago. The arrest occurred near a bar at 2:15 a.m. when he was supposed to be working.

"We won't go into too many details in case you end up as the hearing officer," Jackie explained. "But the investigation so far corroborates much of Burnham's allegations about wrongdoing at the plant. This is likely to be embarrassing when it comes out."

"Here we go again," Brad groaned. "Doesn't anybody ever say 'yes, I screwed up and will take my medicine?' Does everybody have to try to scuttle the ship on the way out? Tell me what you can."

Dee Sharma sat with his head bent like a scolded child. He still had not said a word.

"Employees playing poker on the job, watching porn on TV, and falsifying water quality reports. Apparently, plant supplies and tools are routinely 'borrowed,'" Jackie said, making air quotes.

Brad swallowed back a wave of nausea and turned to his public works director. "Talk to me, Dee."

"She's right. It's a mess," Dee Sharma confirmed, shaking his head. "I've submitted budget requests the last few years for a utilities director to oversee both the water and wastewater plants. I'm kept so busy with development issues, capital improvement projects, and everything else here at City Hall that I can't get out to the plants much. I've had to rely on the chief plant operators."

"Oh, so this is all my fault for not approving that position?" Brad snapped.

"I didn't mean that Brad," Dee said meekly. "The chief operators report to me and are my responsibility. All I'm saying is that if you run with so little supervision like we do, things like this can happen."

Jackie looked from one man to the other. "Sure, in a small city like ours, we have to put more faith on a smaller number of staff. We can't afford lots of layers in any of the departments. But we haven't had evidence of such severe mismanagement up until now. We have to deal with it aggressively to send a message."

Dee cleared his throat. "We need to be careful. The entire city could end up with a black eye if this thing goes public." He looked directly at Brad. "And there could be ramifications up the chain of command."

Brad tensed, understanding the threat. "Tell me more about the falsified reports, Dee."

"Burnham claims a lab tech has been dry labbing."

"Dry labbing?"

"Basically, faking the water analysis at one of the wells and plugging numbers into the water quality reports."

"Oh, great!" Brad moaned. "Which well?"

"Well 2."

"The site we acquired from the Nettlers? I smell a rat! Why would the lab tech do that, Dee?"

"We don't know yet. I'd only be guessing at this point."

"Then guess, damn it!"

The public works director stiffened. "We had a tough time acquiring that well site from the Nettlers before you came. Your predecessor got political pressure to back off. We were told to do whatever we needed to do for an agreement without legal action. We ended up giving Nettlers unrestricted, unmetered water from the well for their agricultural use on the property and had to give them access through the gate to get to the well."

"What's that got to do with not taking the samples?" Brad growled.

Dee Sharma cleared his throat. "Again, I'm only guessing here, but I know there have been problems with the gang lock on the chain link gate at the well. The city's lock gets vandalized a lot. Twice it was shot. Our tech would have to track down one of the Nettlers to open *their* padlock, so he could get the samples. Maybe he got tired of hassling with the access and entered data that was close to Well 1 right down the road."

Brad noticed that the HR director grimaced and sat back in her chair. "You seem skeptical, Jackie."

She leaned forward. "It could be as simple as that," she said guardedly. "But there might be more to the story. Apparently, the tech threw big barbeques at his house, living way beyond his means. Maybe he was getting free meat or something from the Nettlers to not take the samples, for whatever reason."

"You don't know that Jackie!" the public works director grumbled.

"You're right. I don't. I'm just inclined to think more sinisterly in this case."

Brad felt the blood coursing through his body. "What if the lab tech, and maybe other city staff at the plant, discovered there's something wrong with the water at that well and have been covering it up?"

Dee Sharma folded his hands calmly. "We dodged a bullet on that one, Brad. We just tested Well 2 and there's nothing significant we need to report."

"That's a relief," Brad said. "You know that ridiculous water quality report we're mandated to mail out to everybody annually? Nobody but a chemist can understand it. People throw it away and bitch about the cost to send it. But if we had to send out a revised version highlighting some problem, *that* would sure get everyone's attention. So, everything's fine, huh?"

"No problems to report. The test did show a spike in iron but it's below the MCL."

"MCL?"

"Maximum Contaminant Level. It's a health standard set by the feds and state for drinking water. We are below the MCL for iron, so we don't have to do any special reporting or treatment. Iron isn't a health issue, anyway."

Dee's calming assurances did not match his body language. Brad's BS meter kicked on. "What's the problem with too much iron?"

"Oh, nothing much. We need iron in our bodies. People take iron supplements." His smile was too tense.

"What's the problem?" Brad pressed.

"Oh, customers closest to that well might get a little metallic taste and there could be staining on laundry and plumbing fixtures. It's common in the unincorporated areas to have high iron in wells. Water from rainfall seeps through soils and rock with iron in it and gets dissolved into the water table. It's natural. You can't avoid it."

"Have you been getting complaints about iron?"

"A few," Dee said. "We get taste complaints once in a while. But you always have people who imagine things in the water that aren't there. And we still have people who swear the fluoride we add for dental health is killing them. But our water is fine." Dee leaned back in his chair, as if that should be the final word.

Brad's BS meter kept pinging. "Are you getting stain complaints, too?"

"Some," Dee said vaguely. "Probably associated with that higher iron reading at Well 2. Well 1 doesn't show a spike."

"What could cause that all of a sudden from one well?" Brad asked impatiently.

"The most likely thing is that the water table is dropping from the drought. And remember that we had to give Nettlers unrestricted connection to Well 2? It looks to me that they have a lot more of their land planted in alfalfa for their cattle business. They could be drawing down the well much more than in the past, and the strata we are now drawing from has some different constituents, including higher iron, than we get at Well 1."

"What's the worst that can happen?" Brad asked.

"If the well doesn't go back to drawing from better strata, and the iron builds up at our customers' homes, they can experience ongoing staining, and their dishwashers and sprinklers could clog."

"What can we do about it?" Brad was getting nervous.

"You can treat the wells to remove most of the iron. Right now, we give the wells a little shot of chlorine and fluoride and put it right into the distribution system. Adding an iron treatment process would be expensive. Or we could drill a test well somewhere else."

"What if Well 2 is a harbinger of things to come, like the entire aquifer getting too high in iron? We had these big studies of our water supply for the Green Valley Village project and are telling the public we have plenty of water for it. Megan wasn't convinced about that and that was before any potential of a well having problems. Should we be sending a different message to the public on water availability for Green Valley based on this?"

Dee Sharma stiffened. "That's not necessary at this point, Brad. We'd be inviting more trouble. All we need is a couple normal rain years. That should bring the water table back up to the strata where iron wasn't an issue. I wouldn't abandon a well or spend a ton of money right now for a few people who don't like the taste of their water or see some rust stains in their sink. We'd be better off buying them bottled water and Bon Ami." He laughed like a scared boy hoping the bully was only teasing.

Brad leaned forward and glared at Dee. "Is that it?"

Dee cleared his throat again and looked down at the report in his lap. "Oh, the lab picked up an elevated chromium reading. But it's below the MCL, too."

"Tell me about chromium," Brad said, tensing.

"Chromium-3 is an essential element in our diet. It's in many of the foods we eat. Chromium-6 is toxic. Looks like the chromium-6 increased some since the samples taken before the lab tech was hired and they're higher than at Well 1. No big deal since they're still below the MCL," Dee added hastily.

HR Director Jackie McCall snapped to attention. "Chromium 6? Like in *Erin Brockovich*? My cousin had a bit part in that movie. That's based on a true story. Very scary."

"Sounds familiar," Brad said, "Remind me, Jackie."

"Julia Roberts played a legal clerk researching water quality problems out in a small town in the Mojave Desert. The residents sued, alleging high rates of cancer from chromium-6 in the cooling water from a utility power plant outside of town.

The company dumped it into unlined ponds and canals where it got into the groundwater. There was a huge settlement."

"Oh, great! Cancer. So, we might be on the verge of poisoning people from that well?"

"Not at all, Brad," Dee said too calmly. "Actually, there are trace elements of arsenic, lead, chromium, and all kinds of other toxins in drinking water all over the state, and always has been. A lot of it occurs naturally, not the result of industrial pollution. But, like I said, the chromium is still within the healthy range at that well."

Jackie shook her head. "I'm out of my league here, Dee. But won't the public be alarmed about any increase in chromium even if it's still in range?"

"It's not a problem. We don't have to alert the public unless there's an exceedance of the MCLs. It's a nonissue."

"Bullshit, Dee," Brad barked. "This place leaks like a second-hand air mattress." He glared at his public works director. "The problems at the plant are going to come out once the discipline gets appealed to the council. The chromium issue is bound to be mentioned. It will scare people and maybe derail Green Valley's water supply. We need to get ahead of that."

"The discipline actions won't get to the council for weeks," Dee said, still appearing unfazed. "We have time to study the iron and chromium problem, so we'll be in a better position to address it. If we bring it up now while the whole Green Valley environmental study is getting underway, without having more facts, it's going to fan the flames. Both sides will go nuts if it seems like there's a question on the reliability of our current water sources when it'll probably turn out to be fine."

Brad grasped the dilemma and frowned.

Dee leaned forward and spoke softly. "Like I said, Brad, iron isn't a health issue, and the chromium-6 is within healthy range. We shouldn't mention it right now. It will get everyone unnecessarily panicked and that won't be good—for either of us."

Brad saw the fear in his public works director's deep brown eyes. It hit close to home. "I suppose you're right," he said. "Stay on it and keep me informed." He paused. "And no sense rushing the disciplinary process right now, Jackie. We have people on paid administrative leave, but that's a cheap price to buy some time on the water quality issues before the disciplinary appeal hits the council and things go public."

"Right, Brad" Dee said, letting out a long breath.

After his department heads left, Brad sat alone in his office brooding over the potential ramifications of the water plant problems and the vague sense that he was participating in a cover-up of important information the public had a right to know. He felt himself sinking into depression and got up to brief his assistant Jane on the iron and chromium situation and use her as a sounding board. She listened dispassionately to what Dee Sharma told Brad, but she seemed skeptical. Her simple question set him back: "Do you trust him?" Brad stood at her desk pondering his answer when he spotted Councilwoman Kay Nance through the glass wall approaching the outer office door. Now what?

CHAPTER 6

Councilwoman Kay Nance. There she stood in her customary loose fitting, bright, floral moo-moo dress that concealed most of her considerable body. Her name evoked a stream of associations from everyone, whether they had ever met her, or not. Her entire persona screamed "1967 San Francisco Summer of Love." Brad marveled at the braid of gray hair stretching beyond the small of her back. While you could not say Kay was pretty, she had a pleasant, open, and unwrinkled face that radiated quiet confidence and a mercurial nature that belied her sixty-seven years.

Kay was Brad's polar opposite. He dressed conservatively, chose a house and car that would not raise gossip, was careful about who he was seen with, and tried to be everyone's friend, or to at least reduce his enemies list.

By contrast, Kay's mantra could have been: "Here I am. Deal with it!"

Brad caught the first whiff of Kay's musk oil when she entered the outer office lobby. The scent reminded him of his college years at University of California, Santa Barbara – one of the few things Kay and he had in common. While usually frustrated with Councilwoman Nance's politics and feeling dull in her presence, Brad liked her and enjoyed their banter.

"When are they putting in my moat?" Brad asked Jane loudly, pretending not to have seen the colorful councilwoman dressed like a flowerbed a few feet away. "Oh hi, Kay. What can I do for you?"

"Many things, my friend," she said, her confident smile filling her face.

"I mean that wouldn't clash with my Puritan values," he teased.

"Relax, Brad. Won't stay long," she said. "Just wanted to drop off our petition talking points for you."

"Fine," he said, smiling insincerely.

"Do you mean 'fine' that I'm not staying long or fine that I brought our League materials?" Kay teased.

"Yes," he smiled again, leaning on the counter next to Jane. "How goes the battle?"

Kay and others were seeking an endorsement from the League of California Cities, the primary membership association for cities, for a ballot initiative to strengthen regional planning. Brad had misgivings.

Kay shook her head. "We're up against 482 cities, 58 counties, and nearly 5,000 single-purpose special districts all trying to maximize their own provincial interests. We need to wake people up that the lack of coordinated regional planning is ruining this state."

Brad glanced longingly past Kay, through the glass wall, and out the City Hall lobby to the front lawn. He fantasized about escaping to the haven but realized his boss expected him to respond. "You trust regional government to make good decisions for Santa Ynez residents?"

"Don't be so black and white, Brad."

He flushed at the identical rebuke he recently leveled on his planning director, Megan. Jane pretended not to notice and turned to her computer.

"Sure, truly local decisions should stay local," Kay continued. "But issues like air quality, watersheds, and traffic aren't local. You can't manage complex issues for the forty million people in California with thousands of agencies doing their own thing."

"I agree there should be better coordination of development in this state," Brad replied, attempting to recover some standing. "It's pretty much a hash right now. But you're bucking strong inertia." He peeked at his watch, mostly out of habit.

"Okay, I get the message, Brad. I'm on my way."

"What do you mean?" he asked, panicked by his boss's sudden annoyance.

"I shouldn't have expected you to care about our petition drive," she huffed.

"I do," he lied. He did not need Kay displeased with him.

"No, you don't. You'd be drummed out of the city manager corps for even suggesting that it may be time to consider stronger regional planning." She turned to leave.

"No, no, no," he said hastily. "Don't hurry off, Kay. I've got a lot going on right now. But I can always find time for one of my five favorite councilmembers. Can we get you some coffee?"

She turned back around, softening her manner. "No thanks, I don't do stimulants…this early," she joked. She walked past him into his office, a contrail of musk oil scent in her wake.

Brad rolled his eyes at Jane and followed his boss into his office.

Kay sat on her crossed legs, yoga style, in the chair to the right of where Brad usually sat instead of across from him. She raised her head to accept the rays streaming through the open vertical blinds.

"So, how many mayors and councilmembers do you have signed up?" he asked.

"Oh, Brad, you're such a linear thinker. It's all about numbers for you. An artist sees a deeper reality."

"Hah! Not doing too well, huh?"

"We have close to thirty. It's a start. We're also reaching out to some county supervisors." She handed him the papers.

He accepted the stack but immediately tossed it on the table.

"I can see you're not impressed, Brad. But this is either going to result in legislation or we'll take the fight directly to the public and put it on as an initiative."

"*I* wouldn't want to get in your way." He smiled.

"Why don't you join us? We could use some help from a seasoned city manager. We're not talking about cutting cities' balls off with these regional land use plans. You and Mayor Buddy will still have your share of groundbreaking ceremonies to strut around at."

"Whew!" he said, sarcastically wiping his forehead with the back of his hand.

"All we want is local development decisions better tied to preservation of the natural resources in the nine planning zones. That includes promoting infill of the urban areas instead of sprawling on ag land and open space, more efficient long-range infrastructure planning, and sharing the costs and benefits of development more fairly across an entire region."

"Oh, that's all?" he scoffed. "You're up against a century of local government tradition and a huge power base that will fight to the death to protect the status quo."

"It's a noble fight worth joining, Brad. Back when you woke up every morning hoping to find some armpit hair, I was marching for civil rights and peace. It's in my blood. You have to be willing to accept setbacks and realize you're in it until you win it."

Brad gazed out the window and followed a military cargo plane, most likely on final approach to Vandenberg AFB.

"… failing the people of this state on the growth issue like they did in the '60s and '70s on the property tax problem." Brad became conscious again of Kay's voice and snapped his head back to her to avoid another scolding.

Kay continued lecturing. "History shows that we either deal with our problems sensibly or the public, courts, or federal government will eventually take control. That's where you come in."

"Go on," he said warily.

"Relax. All I want you to do is give me a city manager's take on these talking points."

"Not an easy sale." He frowned. "Those of us who've been in this business a while remember how frustrating things got after the feds took away our ability to regulate cable TV. Moving decision-making up a level or two isn't necessarily an improvement in governance. The devil's in the details."

"Tell me how we can convince fair-minded, concerned officials that the status quo isn't working. They have a professional and moral responsibility to engage on the issues, not just hide behind the home rule veil."

He maintained the frown.

"Look at it this way, Brad, would you rather have me working on a statewide campaign like this or applying all of my time and energy on city business—right here—with you?" she chuckled.

He opened his arms widely. "Putting it that way, I'd *love* to help you with your talking points."

"Great, I'll email everything to you. Can you get back to me tomorrow with any suggestions?"

For a split second, Brad imagined himself shouting "No!" He might as well have some fun with it. "I'd love to work on it for you, Kay. But you know the council's policy on that. It takes a majority vote to direct the city manager. Should I call the other councilmembers to make sure they're okay with me working on your statewide regional planning initiative?" He grinned.

Kay didn't bite. "Yeah, right. And while you're at it, tell them you intend to have the staff spend as much time on projects that will protect the public's interest, like my proposal does, as you do on projects like Green Valley that don't. You *are* supposed to be neutral, right?"

He ducked his head behind his raised arms in a fighter's protective stance. "Okay, okay. I'll have time tonight to work on it. Sleep is overrated. I'll have to tell Marie I can't take her out for dinner like we planned."

"Tell her she can come to my house for dinner tonight while you work on this. I guarantee she'd have more fun. My 'no stimulant' policy ends at five." She turned to leave. "Thanks Brad. I owe you. I'll be a good girl and won't give you, Mayor Buddy, or Scott Graves any grief about Green Valley." She gave her braid a flip and added, "for the rest of the day."

Brad sat alone in his office at 5:30 still stewing about how he handled his public works director's revelations about the iron and chromium-6 spikes at Well 2. Was it truly as benign as his public works director made it seem? Or was Brad covering up a potentially critical health threat? He rose from his desk and stood at his window gazing up at the Santa Ynez Mountains to the west, toward Ronald Reagan's former home, Rancho Del Cielo, overlooking the Pacific Ocean. From out of nowhere, he recalled the former president saying, "Trust, but verify." It had been one of Reagan's signature lines, describing his approach to the former Soviet Union at the end of the Cold War. Message received. Brad picked up the phone and called Quinn O'Rourke, his friend and former city manager colleague, who retired and now did business development for the Payton/Carlisle engineering firm under the lofty title Executive Vice President. Brad knew O'Rourke would offer a free and discreet second opinion.

Driving home after 6 p.m., Brad's heart sank as it often did when his house came into view. The two-story ranch house was stylish enough and the neighborhood well-kept, but not nearly the house they left behind in West Sacramento to take the Santa Ynez job. Selling during an economic downturn resulted in a loss that damaged Brad's financial forecast nearly as much as his pride. But he had to leave. His city was emerging from the shadows of the much larger City of Sacramento, across the Sacramento River. Brad worked long hours at breakneck pace, drank too much to relax at night, put on weight, and snapped too often at Marie. She insisted that his health was more important than his spreadsheet and urged him to find a less stressful situation. She never grumbled about leaving her family, friends, and nicer house. Marie was always a trooper. Brad was increasingly aware of his annoyance at feeling like the cause of her suffering.

Brad walked in from the garage and flipped his keys into a wicker basket by the door.

"Wait 'til I tell you what I Googled about Lilly's dam disaster!" Marie yelled from the living room.

Brad scowled. "Crap, I forgot all about that and was looking forward to checking it out tonight." He walked to the kitchen to make a bourbon and water and reconsidered his attitude. "Lemme change and you can tell me about it over dinner."

The disaster story got side-railed when Dillon announced at dinner that he'd like to join his best friend next year at Colorado State. The snowboarding season is so much longer there. Brad's financial plan assumed Dillon would attend Sacramento State University in the fall, and live with their daughter, Kristen. Twenty-thousand dollars a year *more* for out-of-state tuition could tilt Brad's financial game plan. Brad and Marie thrusted and parried with their son through dinner. Dillon scored some solid hits with free room and board with his friend's aunt in Fort Collins in exchange for yard work and pet sitting and a promise to work part-time. Then he delivered the coup de grace, how Colorado would still be less expensive than what his parents had spent for his sister's education at her private university. Dillon had done his homework.

Brad finally said, "Okay, Mom and I will talk about it."

Dillon jumped up, hugged his mom quickly, high-fived his dad, and bounded up the stairs. Brad's forced smile dissolved into a scowl as he stared at his empty plate.

"I'm happy to see him finally excited about college," Marie offered.

"Yeah. I guess."

"I know you're worried about the money, hon. I'll cut back. I'm willing to sacrifice to give him this."

Shit, Marie. Enough with the martyrdom. He got up for another bourbon and water. "Tell me about the dam disaster," he said from the kitchen, hoping she would not notice.

"Go easy on that," she warned, as she walked to the family room for her laptop. Brad hid his drink as casually as he could and took his normal position on his leather recliner across from her.

"Ok, shoot," he said.

"I Googled 'California dam break.' And there it was. Wikipedia had a big article about it."

Marie scrolled down her screen. "It says that the St. Francis Dam break was the second worst disaster in California history, second only to the San Francisco Earthquake and Fire of 1906, and ranked as the worst US engineering disaster of the Twentieth Century. It happened in 1928. Some 450 to 600 people were killed. Like Lee said, the flood washed people, livestock, and everything else all the way out to the Pacific Ocean between Ventura and Oxnard."

"Holy crap! Tell me more." But seeing her laptop reminded him that he had to review Councilwoman Kay Nance's regional planning talking points tonight. "Quickly," he added.

"The dam was built under the direction of the Chief of the Los Angeles Department of Water and Power, a man named William Mulholland."

"Sure, Mulholland. There's a winding street in the hills above LA named after him. It's a popular place for couples to park. Great views of the city lights." He stopped short of mentioning the time he and his girlfriend drove from UCSB to park on Mulholland Drive, just to be able to say they had.

"Why'd it give?" he asked, reluctantly picking up his own laptop.

"It says here that it was a concrete gravity dam, which I think means that the water in the reservoir was held back by the sheer weight of the thick concrete. Apparently, the hill next to the dam gave way because the rock the dam was anchored to wasn't stable." Marie punched a couple more keys. "Here it is. They called it 'schist.'"

"No schist?" he smiled proudly.

"Very funny," she replied.

She read a few sentences to him about likely causes of the dam break. He looked back and forth between her and his own screen, tapping his fingers on the laptop.

"Look, hon, what you're reading is more interesting than what I have to do. But I promised Kay I'd work on something for her tonight. So, let me get through it first, then I'll take a break and see what else you learned. Okay?"

Brad opened his email and skimmed Kay's talking points hoping for a few spots where he could insert some pithy margin comments. He wanted her to see that he had put in some effort on what he regarded as tilting at windmills. Ever since its admittance to the union, California has suffered numerous attempts to carve the state into more manageable chunks. None had gone far and no reason to think this one would either.

Marie's periodic "hmm's" and "that's interesting's" were like Siren calls luring him to put down his boring work and join her with the dam disaster research. He concentrated harder on Kay's missives for another half hour until Marie's "oh my God" put him over the top. He glared at her, plopped the laptop down loudly on the table, and stomped to the bathroom. Taking an indirect route back, he went through the living room to the kitchen and quietly mixed another bourbon and water.

"Back for more?" Marie grumbled. She had rabbit ears.

He gave up trying to be quiet and changed the subject. "I take it from all your 'oh my Gods,' you discovered something interesting."

"I think I just read about the construction camp where Lilly was when the water hit," Marie exclaimed. "It says the camp was along a railroad siding called Kemp, close to the Los Angeles and Ventura County borders. Southern California Edison power company was building a transmission line through the valley. They had a tent city with 150 people living there. Eighty-four people were killed that night." She turned her computer around. "I found these before and after pictures of the Edison tent camp. Lilly must have been there."

She handed him her laptop. Brad examined both images on the split screen. The "before" shot showed kids playing at the tent city. He clicked on some links and reported what he found. Eventually, Marie got up from the couch.

"I'm going up to read." She gave him a peck on the cheek and motioned to his glass. "Remember, you have Rotary in the morning."

"Night, hon," he said, deflecting the admonition.

Brad took another pass at Kay's project then set down the computer and went into the kitchen again. The bourbons were doing their job. Another would really mellow him out for bed.

He returned to his recliner. The piercing chime of the mantel clock activated his constant time pressure stress. He cursed silently, took a sip of his elixir, and typed "worst engineering disasters" into his laptop. St. Francis Dam made the list. All the other incidents were familiar. Brad knew someone who was staying at the Hyatt Regency Hotel in Kansas City in 1981 when a skywalk collapsed, killing 114 people. He re-watched old newsreel footage from the '40s of the new Tacoma Narrows Bridge that vibrated from heavy winds. Giant rhythmic spasms eventually brought the structure down. Fortunately, the only loss of life was a dog in an abandoned car.

The St. Francis story was so much more compelling, yet mysterious. He was absorbed in the topic until startled again by the annoying clock chime on the quarter hour. 11:15 p.m. He clicked back to the pictures Marie showed him of the Kemp construction camp and did a double take at a little girl in the "before" photo. Could she be Lilly?

CHAPTER 7

Six fifteen Tuesday morning came too early for Brad. He might have been tempted to blow off the weekly Rotary Club meeting, but Scott Graves was scheduled to speak about his Green Valley Village project.

"Good morning, sunshine," Marie said when he came downstairs. "You put quite a dent in the bourbon last night."

"Yeah, I stayed up late reading about St. Francis Dam," he said, shifting the conversation away from his hangover and a potential *I told you so*. "I need to get going."

"You know, what kills me is how fast the dam was built," he said, wrestling on his sport coat. "Mulholland personally selected the site. Incredibly, his staff designed and built the dam in two years with no oversight from anybody. Hell, it would take twenty years now before you could even put a shovel in the dirt. That was definitely the golden age for city managers and engineers."

"Maybe so," Marie said, "but I'll bet Lilly wished it hadn't been *that* easy in those days."

Brad rolled through two stop signs hurrying to the Red Barn restaurant for the 7:30 a.m. start of Rotary. He imagined a headline, *City Manager Cited for Reckless Driving*, and slowed down. City managers had been fired for lesser offenses than a moving violation.

Brad was proud to be a Rotarian for all the club did internationally and locally. He exchanged "good mornings" with many of his club friends as he moved through the receiving line, picked up his badge, and filled his plate. He willed himself to pass up the fried potatoes but went extra heavy on the scrambled eggs and bacon—a questionable diet trade-off. The bacon bouquet was particularly irresistible. He filled up at the coffee urn and stared at the pastry tray. Screw it. He sneaked a bear claw, waivered a moment, then added a small cheese Danish. Cheese was protein, right?

He walked slowly toward the main room and perused the framed, yellowed photos of riders on horseback lining the walls. Brad liked bringing guests here and telling the history depicted in the black and white photos.

The Rancheros Visatadores social club went back to 1930. Seven hundred prominent people from all over the USA converged on the Santa Ynez Valley every year for a sixty-mile horseback ride to honor the Old West and raise money for charity along the way. Clark Gable and Ronald Reagan had participated. Walt Disney rode his horse, Minnie. Having rich dignitaries from all over choose his adopted city for this celebration endorsed his decision to retire here.

Brad looked over the crowd as he always did in any social gathering with community movers and shakers. He spotted the mayor and two councilmembers and noted who they talked to.

"Morning, Brad."

Brad flinched and turned. Developer Scott Graves stood behind him with a plate that looked like it came from Old Mother Hubbard's Diner. Brad glanced guiltily at his own impressive mound and sucked in his belly. "Welcome to Rotary, Scott. You probably hated having to get up so early for this meeting."

Scott nodded his head in the direction of a small group to their left. "Yeah, too early for me. But, hey, the opportunity to breakfast with Hank Nettler? How could I resist?"

"You think Hank is tough, you should meet his teenage daughter. The cute little girl tried to castrate me in her government class yesterday."

"I can imagine," Scott said. "Quite a family. Did I ever tell you about the option negotiation with Hubie? Now *that* was a career experience."

Brad confirmed that the coast was clear and whispered, "Tell me."

Scott stepped closer and lowered his voice. "I made several approaches to the Nettlers about SoCal's interest in their land, but they played hard-to-get, like they had no interest in selling at all. Then, out of the blue, Hank called and said his dad was willing to talk. Hubie always wanted our meetings at his house. I'd sit on one side of their huge oak dining room table. Hubie and Hank sat on the other side with their attorney, a frothing bull."

Brad smirked. "Doesn't sound like western hospitality. I guess Hubie never watched *Bonanza*."

"Nope," Scott laughed. "Hank did most of the talking, but he was on a short leash. Hubie mostly leaned back in his chair with his hands crossed behind his head and eyes closed. He acted like he wasn't interested at all, but he tracked every word."

"I imagine so," Brad said. "You know I'm surprised Hubie ever agreed to sell. The Nettlers are known for *buying* land, never selling."

"Tell you the truth, I was never sure we'd make a deal. A few times, after Hank and I agreed on some deal point, Hubie opened his eyes, leaned forward and said something like, 'Bullshit, Hank, here's how we're going to do it.' He'd completely undercut his son. I genuinely felt sorry for Hank."

Brad was not convinced. "Maybe that was their negotiating strategy. How did you ever get it done?"

Scott smirked. "After our fourth half-day meeting, and after Hubie reneged on a previous deal point I had with Hank, I stomped out. Hank called me the next day to see about another meeting. I bitched about the way Hubie was negotiating. I told him my boss—you've met Jeff Simpson—was ready to throw in the towel. And he was. We agreed to have one more 'make or break' meeting, but this time it would be Hubie and Jeff leading things."

"I've met Jeff. He comes on like a Sherman tank. Must have been an epic face-off."

"Spectacular. Hubie met us at his front door and right off the bat they were like two boxers sizing each other up. Hubie's entry hall walls are lined with heads of deer, wild boars, mountain lions, and other game he and Hank bagged. As we walked toward the dining room, Hubie pointed to the animal heads and said to Jeff, 'If we don't get this deal done today, there's a spot up there reserved for you.'"

"Wow! What did Jeff do?"

"He told Hubie to go fuck himself and turned to leave. Hubie gave him a big slap on the back, let out a belly laugh, and said, 'Now here's a sonofabitch I can make a deal with.'"

"I can picture it."

"Jeff and Hubie cussed their way through the final points of the agreement until they both finally stood up and shook hands on the basic points. They went off to drink Tequila while Hank and the attorney and I tweaked the final language. By the time we were done, they were smashed and arguing over recipes for tri-tip rub. Hank grilled steaks and we were there most of the night eating, drinking, playing poker, and smoking cigars."

Brad laughed. "I'd love to have the Norman Rockwell painting of that scene."

"We got it signed. But I'll tell you, we ended up with the strangest land deal I've ever done."

"How so?"

"I can't share all the details with you. We all signed confidentiality agreements. So, this is just between us. But you know how normally the land seller wants his money right away?"

"And the developer wants to postpone paying much of anything until all the entitlements are in place," Brad added.

"Well, sure," Scott smiled. "That's just good business. Trying to manage risk, you know. But this deal with Nettlers was different. They made a point that they didn't want to sell their land unless we were going to develop the project because of the value it will bring to their adjacent lands. So, we ended up with a phased purchase agreement with a bunch of milestones, each with nonrefundable progress payments."

"Interesting," Brad mused. "Can I ask how that's going?"

"So far, we've made progress payments when we accepted the prelim title report and the public works draft water and traffic reports showing no major problems and when we got a clean report on the biologicals. The next big milestone is our acceptance of the EIR Initial Study when we'll have a draft specific plan and development agreement and a comfort level with what's going to be studied in the EIR."

"Why a big payment *then*?" Brad asked. "Why not wait until at least the Draft EIR comes out?"

"That was my argument. Nettlers' attorney was sharp. He knew it would be a year or more until the IS would go out and another year to get all the entitlements in place. There was quite a back-and-forth between Hubie and Jeff at that point. Hubie said something like, "If you want to control my property that long, you're going to pay for the privilege.' Jeff countered with, 'We *will* be paying. Big time. We'll have hundreds of thousands of dollars in engineering, design, legal, and market studies just getting to a draft plan that can be studied in the EIR.'"

"For sure," Brad agreed.

"Hubie basically said that was our problem. If we didn't expect to make a good return for our risks, we wouldn't be there today. He added that there's other things the family could be doing with that land, so we'd have to pay for the privilege of tying it up."

Brad recalled something the girl, Jenny Nettler, said in class yesterday. "Any endangered species on the property?"

"We only paid for a records search on the biologicals at the beginning. Looks clean. A full field survey will be done later, as part of the EIR. This was another touchy issue in the negotiations. Their lawyer drafted language that specifically stated the Nettlers were making no representation about haz-mat or endangered species. Jeff settled for language that if something turns up later in the full field study, our cost is capped at one hundred thousand dollars. Nettlers are on the hook for the next hundred thousand. If it goes beyond that, there's a reopener in the contract to negotiate it out." Scott paused. "Well, to be more precise, either to reach a deal on the mitigation costs or either party can terminate. But if Nettlers terminate, they have to reimburse us a hundred thousand dollars for our hard costs to that point."

Brad frowned. "Won't you have a whole lot more than a hundred thousand into the project if they terminate?"

"Right. But Jeff and Hubie had been banging each other pretty hard for hours at that point. Jeff finally went along with that compromise to get Hubie's concession on several other sticking points so we could wrap up. In fact, I think reducing the amount of the progress payment to Nettlers at the IS stage was one of those points. Jeff thought it was a reasonable risk. After all, the land was never developed. We might find old barrels of diesel or pesticides that won't be tough for Nettlers to clean up, but that's probably all. If something big is found down the road and they balk at the cost-sharing, we'd come back and offer to split the cost with them, or something, to get it resolved. In our experience, by the time we are that close to the finish line on a long land deal, the seller has already spent their sale proceeds many times over in their mind. We aren't worried about that."

Brad started to press again about the endangered species contingency, but Mayor Buddy Murray walked up with Vice Mayor Tim Mullikin in tow. "There's the man of the hour. Welcome, Scott," the mayor said, extending his hand.

"Welcome, Scott," Mullikin echoed. In fact, echoing the mayor was Mullikin's M.O. He was a retired sergeant from the Santa Barbara Sheriff's Department and used to patrol the Santa Ynez area. Mullikin lacked the mayor's political skill but had lived in the community all his life and knew everybody.

"Come on, Scott," the mayor said, "let me introduce you to a few people." He grabbed the developer's arm and led him off with the vice mayor on their coattails.

Brad stood there a few moments longer watching Scott work the room in full glad-handing mode. Scott could have been a suit model in the Nordstrom ads, with his trim, thick blond hair, a little gray peeking through at the temples, clear blue eyes, big smile with perfect teeth, and an easy-going air. Today, Scott had on his business casual uniform for this crowd. No sport coat or tie, but a tailored plaid dress shirt and khaki pants that said, "I'm successful, but still one of you."

Brad sought out the third councilmember in the club, Reverend Al Landon, sitting at a table at the other side of the room. "Can I join you, Al?"

"Please do, Brad. I saw you talking to Scott over there until the mayor whisked him away. Everything going okay with Green Valley Village?"

Brad was prepared to answer the question when the mayor, vice mayor, and Scott Graves approached the table.

"Al, say hi to Scott," the mayor urged.

"Welcome, Scott," Councilman Landon said. "Looking forward to your program." They shook hands. In contrast to the mayor and vice mayor, Al Landon held his cards close. Always. He was cordial to Scott Graves, but the councilman remained seated until the trio moved to the next table rather than standing up to be conspicuously seen with the developer like the mayor and vice mayor.

"To answer your question, Al, yes, the project is moving along." Brad waited expectantly for his boss's reaction.

"Hmmm," was all the councilman said.

Brad exhaled and slumped slightly. Councilman Landon was tough to read. He could count on Mayor Buddy Murray and Vice Mayor Tim Mullikin to take the pro-business, pro-growth perspective. Councilwomen Kay Nance and, to a lesser extent, Claire Schmitz had a left-leaning environmental perspective. More correctly, Claire Schmitz leaned, Kay Nance fell over.

This usually put Councilman Landon in the powerful position of being the third, deciding vote. Even more powerful in this case because the city attorney had already advised Mayor Buddy Murray that he would have to disqualify himself from voting or advocating on behalf of the Green Valley project due to his many business ties to the Nettler family. The project supporters now had a taller hurdle. They had to lock down Councilman Landon and pick up Councilwoman Schmitz in addition to Vice Mayor Mullikin to get their majority vote. Forget about Kay.

Brad leaned over to the councilman, nodded toward the head table and snickered, "Looks like the mayor isn't going to let Scott sit down and eat."

Al Landon whispered back, "Buddy better be careful. He's not supposed to be advocating this project. And Mullikin shouldn't wear his support on his sleeve. I can give you a lot more bargaining power if Scott still wonders if he's got enough votes lined up."

Maybe not a bugle call from the heavenly host, but this was the clearest indication Brad had so far that Reverend Al Landon was a Green Valley supporter.

"Gents?" Hank Nettler greeted, as he pulled out the chair across from Brad and Councilman Landon. "Hand me a program, would you, Al?" he added with a voice as rough as his big, calloused, cracked hands.

"Morning, Hank," other members at the table said in unison. *Toadies.*

"I forgot Scott was the program today," Hank said, tucking his napkin into the collar of his flannel shirt. "You got the votes lined up for Green Valley, Brad?" Hank asked, scooping up a mouthful of potatoes.

Brad blanched. *What a stupid question to ask right in front of Councilman Landon.* "Al can certainly speak for himself. But the answer to your question is 'no.' It's illegal for me to poll the councilmembers on something that has to be decided in public."

"And I suppose you never do that, right?" Hank scoffed.

Brad squirmed. Hank had blundered into one of his core challenges, his obligation to carry out the policy wishes of the elected officials without coordinating their positions and, at the same time, to conduct municipal operations based on sound management practices, not politics. Politics and management made strange bedfellows. That is why, for many years, the logo of the International City/County Management Association, a square peg in a round hole, reflected this dichotomy.

"Like I said, Hank," Brad said with a wink. "There are laws about this. My official answer to your question is that a city manager has to learn to read the tea leaves."

"Come on, Brad," Hank teased in his raspy cigarette voice. "You can't tell me you make all of your decisions or recommendations in a vacuum." Hank turned to Al Landon. "He's got to be talking to all of you all the time outside council meetings, right, Al?"

"Sure, we can talk outside the meetings," Brad jumped in, "and we do. But I can't legally try to build a consensus position. Like I said, you learn how to read the tea leaves to know if you can go hard on something or if you should back off." He tried to change the subject. "My wife says I drive the same way, constantly alternating between the accelerator and brake. She calls it 'city manager foot.' I argued with her about it until I rode in another manager's car and got carsick."

That elicited some chuckles from most of the breakfast mates. Hank brushed them off and pressed his point. "You guys do some dumb things. We'd bankrupt the family businesses if we had to operate like you." Hank pointed his fork at Brad. "So, what do your tea leaves tell you the council will decide on Green Valley?"

"You tell me, Hank," Brad challenged. "I'm not allowed to poll them, remember?"

Hank smiled confidently. "Okay. I'll do your job for you. We'll get three votes. Of course, we'll never get the bitch, but

Claire will come along. I hear she's interested in moving into Green Valley's assisted living facility."

Brad smiled and said straight-faced, "You must be referring to Councilwoman Schmitz, but I have no idea who the other reference applies to."

"Keep lickin' them boots, Brad. I'd hate to have your job. I'd probably punch somebody out on the first day."

"Yeah," Brad replied, "I get that a lot." He tried again to change the subject. "This bacon is awesome. Is the Red Barn still buying your family's meat, Hank?"

"Yup," Hank said proudly. "We supply most of the restaurants in the area. A lot of Rotarians are in our meat club. It's a lot fresher and tastier than the crap you get at the store, and cheaper too, if you buy in bulk. Why don't I set aside some steaks and ribs for your family to try?"

The other members at the table looked at Brad. He was not sure if Hank was offering him a gift or just drumming up business. He punted. "Thanks anyway, Hank. I'm planning to go vegan." He took another big bite of bacon and grinned.

"You're missing out. Our family has been in the beef business for generations. Whether this Green Valley project goes or not, we're expanding and even looking at a dairy operation."

"Good luck, Hank." Brad said, turning away.

"It's not a matter of luck," Hank persisted. "We'll get the votes for Green Valley. It's your job to get the paperwork done fast. SoCal has some milestones to hit. And we have some ideas to help them do it." Hank Nettler shoved a whole piece of bacon in his mouth, smiled conspiratorially, and, seemingly as an afterthought, turned to the councilman and added, "Oh, yeah Al, my guys will be over with the lift this afternoon and change out those bulbs in the church parking lot. No charge."

Brad picked up the weekly club bulletin and pretended more interest in the contents than whatever scheme Hank may be hatching. Fortunately, the club president rang the bell to begin the meeting. Brad paid no attention to the president's announcements as he mulled the conversation with Hank. What was he cooking up?

He stole a glance at Councilman Landon. Brad liked him, despite his peccadillos. Landon was the senior minister of a medium-sized Protestant church in the nearby city of Buellton. He was educated, principled, and attentive to his council role. His day job made him the leader of his organization, which Brad expected would make him more understanding on the organizational issues Brad faced. But Al Landon, like everyone else, viewed things through the filter of his own experience. The minister's organization was small, collegial with loose policies, and dependent upon volunteerism. Brad's was larger, procedurally based, legalistic, and unionized. He got annoyed any time the minister tried to tell him how the city should be managed.

The President finished her announcements, gave another pitch to everyone to invite new people to the club, and turned it over to the fine master, a dentist and legendary extractor. The fining or "recognition" period was usually a highlight of the meeting. Members were fined for all manner of trumped-up offenses. There was no escape. The fine master nailed a female florist $10 for having her name in the paper. He fined a chiropractor $10 on a rumor that he'd been spotted in a new car and bumped it to $20 after he got the doctor to admit to a Porsche.

"Brad Jacks," the fine master announced.

Brad was easy game in this crowd. He stood up grudgingly.

"Brad, I know I fined you last week. But your city did something truly stupid. In accordance with Rotary's Four-Way Test, it wouldn't be 'fair to all concerned' to let you off the hook." He held up a piece of paper. "I have here my city water and sewer bill. Just came in yesterday's mail."

Brad felt instant embarrassment. He knew where this was going.

"Now, Brad, I know you do things a little different in government. And I appreciate that you included a return envelope with the water bill. But wouldn't it be beneficial to all concerned if the return address part of the bill stub that you send back actually lined up with the little window?" The fine master put the detachable portion of the bill into the return envelope to demonstrate that the city's return address was halfway outside the clear window.

The room exploded in hoots and claps. Some must have already discovered the colossal screw-up. Brad was busted but not going down meekly.

"Well, Mr. Fine Master, we contracted with a new print shop and got a heckuva deal from the low bidder—a local business by the way. It was an add-on alternate to have the full return address appear in the window. We passed. Always trying to save you taxpayers some money, you know."

More laughs.

The fine master played along, "You aren't going to get a lot of checks delivered if the Post Office can't see where they're supposed to go. Isn't that what they call 'false economy?'"

"That's the genius of it," Brad protested. "See, if we don't get their payments, we'll shut off their water and collect penalties to turn it back on. We'll make a killing!"

The room erupted in boos. "Twenty bucks!" the fine master ordered.

At 8 a.m. sharp, the club's program chair went to the podium to introduce Scott Graves, reading a blurb that had obviously been prepared by SoCal Communities. The bio mentioned Scott's MBA from UCLA and his experience building high quality living environments around Southern California.

It covered his charitable activities and closed with a short statement on the Green Valley Village project now being reviewed by the City of Santa Ynez.

Six-foot tall Scott Graves strode to the podium to loud applause. "Thank you for the lavish introduction. It's like I wrote it myself."

A courtesy laugh ensued. The members had heard that one.

"I'm happy to be here this morning, and I want to tell you how excited we are to be working on such a great project with your outstanding city council and city manager. I can assure you our company's interests line up a whole lot better for this community than Brad's envelopes."

Real laughs this time. Brad gave Scott a little salute from his chair.

The developer went on to tell everyone how much he loved Santa Ynez and how it reminded him of his hometown outside Austin, Texas. Score. Most people are proud of where they live and pleased by an outsider's envy. The object was to not seem like an outsider. Brad imagined Scott pitching his Santa Maria project a half hour away, a community dubbed by Sunset Magazine as "The West's Best BBQ Town." He would probably be talking about his boss's beef rub by now. Once again, Brad acknowledged Scott was a capable representative for his project.

Scott Graves spent twenty minutes walking everyone through a PowerPoint presentation showing the layout of the Green Valley Village project, attractive renderings of the streetscapes and buildings, and the amenities. The last slides had deal points from the draft development agreement that proved Green Valley would be a valuable partner for Santa Ynez.

"We've received a warm welcome from *most* of the members of the city council and city staff." Scott added with a smirk.

There were some more chuckles and whispered comments. Many of the members understood who would *not* have been included in that praise.

Brad glanced to his right at Al Landon who was smiling and nodding, and to his left to see the mayor and vice mayor sitting up straight to catch any ambient praise in the air.

"But I can assure you," Scott continued, "they aren't push-overs. There are times I leave City Hall feeling like Jack from *Sideways*. You remember the scene where his new girlfriend beats the stuffing out of him with his motorcycle helmet?"

More laughs. Hank leaned over and said a little too loudly, "I hate hearing that, Brad."

Brad shifted in his chair.

After his presentation, Scott opened himself for questions from the audience, which he handled adroitly.

The president headed toward the podium. Scott was about to get the hook. Mayor Buddy noticed it and elbowed the vice mayor who rose to his feet hastily. "I'd like to add something."

"Make it quick, Tim," the president warned. "Time to adjourn."

"I wanted to pick up on Scott's last point. SoCal is a great builder. I know other cities in the area are jealous that we're getting this project. They've given them tours and offered incentives if they'd build something like Green Valley Village in their towns. SoCal isn't asking us for anything special. In fact, the development agreement Brad and his staff are negotiating with Scott has them giving the community all sorts of extra benefits we wouldn't ordinarily get from a new development. We're lucky to have Scott and Green Valley here. I know I speak for the council majority saying we should expedite the approval process."

"Damn straight!" Hank blurted from the audience.

Brad glanced at Councilman Landon who merely smiled and raised his coffee cup to his mouth.

The mayor, vice mayor, and Scott stayed behind after the meeting to talk with the half dozen Rotarians lined up to shake hands and wish Scott the best with the project. Brad joined the line.

"Nicely done, Scott," he said.

"You heard what the vice mayor said, Brad," Hank said, walking over. "Don't let Megan Cain't chase this project away. Where are you with the IS?"

"IS?" Brad smiled back at him. "Well, it depends on what your definition of 'IS' is." He chuckled at his little joke but saw that only Scott got the reference to the Bill Clinton/Monica Lewinsky scandal.

"Initial study for the EIR, smart guy." Hank snarled. "Otherwise known as bullshit process."

"Should be ready soon, Hank, I've been meeting with staff about it."

"How 'bout less meetings and more action out of City Hall?" Hank scowled. "Are you going to let Megan Cain't process this thing to death?"

"He won't," Mayor Buddy assured the small group. "Brad'll take care of city staff."

Brad squirmed and made a mental note to remind the mayor of his legal prohibition from participating in the project. He thought of an up-beat exit. "I have to get back to the office. We're meeting with the water bill printer to see if they want to take over paramedic services, too."

Scott laughed. Hank merely grinned menacingly like the crazed Jack Nicholson in *The Shining*. Brad forced a smile to hide his tension over Hank's suddenly harsh behavior, so contrasting with his normal, more affable ways. *What's up with that?*

Mayor Buddy stopped by later that morning, still ebullient from the Rotary meeting.

Buddy Murray was easy to like. In his early 70s, above average height, thick wavy gray hair parted on the side and perpetually sprinkled with dandruff. He was the top real estate professional in the region. Some of that, no doubt, due to his public stature.

"I see the banner's still up," the mayor complained. He had mentioned a real estate competitor's illegal banner twice to Brad who followed up with Megan to investigate the zoning violation.

Brad slumped in his chair. "Yeah, sorry about that. I sent Megan a note about it yesterday. I'll give her another nudge."

"She's a tough person to nudge, Brad. You may need to give her a boot in the butt," the mayor advised. "And that goes for the Green Valley project, too. I hear she has it in for Scott about water."

Do the walls really talk? "She's doing her job, Buddy," Brad responded. "She wants to make sure the project is sufficiently analyzed. We both know Green Valley will likely go to a referendum challenge if the council majority approves it. It's better to have Megan find the weak points up-front instead of the opponents afterwards, right?"

"Don't let her drive SoCal off by creating so many extra hoops for them to jump through that they decide to cut their losses and move down the road. We need this project, Brad. Agreed?" It was more of a decree than a question.

Brad saw his opportunity. "Oh, and a gentle reminder. Remember that you are disqualified from participating in anything with Green Valley. Be careful. The opponents would love to catch you violating the law."

"The hell with them. Got a meeting," the mayor said, turning to leave. "Get that banner down today, will you? Otherwise, I'm going to put one up." He paused and smirked. "Now, I'm not saying you should support Green Valley," he added with a wink, "but it would be a shame if Megan screwed up the project and we don't end up with the money we need for the raise you deserve."

"Smooth as coarse sandpaper." Brad made a mental note to re-run his family financial plan to factor in his son's Colorado out-of-state tuition and a looming five percent raise. The spreadsheet projections gave him the illusion of control over his future.

CHAPTER 8

Later that day, Brad lumbered back to the office after a get-acquainted lunch with the new school superintendent.

"You don't look so good. How was lunch with *Doctor* Deborah Downey?" Jane asked.

"Ugh," he groaned, rubbing his stomach. "Gave me gas."

"But you love Moreno's," she protested.

"The enchiladas were killer. The company churned my stomach. I was hoping to connect with a new kindred spirit like I did with the previous superintendent." He set a pack of papers on the counter. "Paul and I accomplished a lot because we got along so well. Not going to be so easy with Deborah. She and Paul are as different as they could be."

"Sounds like you at least are calling her by her first name, not *Doctor* Downey, as she introduces herself. A little stiff, was she?"

"Stiff? You'd need a whole can of WD-40 just to get her to stiff. I tried to order some wine, to loosen her up, but she made a big deal out of being a non-drinker. I ordered my Tecate anyway, and she sized me up like I was Otis on *The Andy Griffith Show*. She had this annoying way of squinting at me with her head tilted. I was my usual dazzling self, trying to warm things up between us, but she seemed suspicious of anything I said."

"Well, it's her first superintendent job so she's probably cautious to begin with, or maybe awed by being in the presence of your radiance."

He smirked and rubbed his stomach again. "I never ate Mexican food so fast in my life. I wanted to say, 'check please' as soon as the plates hit the table."

Councilwoman Kay Nance walked through the outer glass door. "Hi, Kay," Brad said, picking up his papers from the counter. "I was telling Jane about my meeting with the new school superintendent."

"I haven't met her yet. What's she like?"

"Not me, apparently. You wouldn't like her, but you sure could help her."

"How so?" the councilwoman asked.

"She's even more uptight than me, and you know how much you always loosen me up."

"Yeah," Jane chimed in. "He's always happy every time you leave his office."

They all laughed at Jane's double entendre. Brad invited Kay into his office.

Despite her pungent musk oil scent, Kay was a welcome breath of fresh air compared to Brad's lunch partner. They sat across from each other at the coffee table and talked awhile about her petition drive. He offered some arguments for selling her concepts to city officials.

"Thanks, Brad," Kay eventually said. "We can make some minor modifications to our proposal without sacrificing the goal."

He simulated a tipping of the hat. "Glad to be of service, ma'am."

"So, Scott Graves charmed them at Rotary this morning, huh?" she said.

"Yup. He can do that." Brad wasn't the least bit surprised that Kay had received a report from someone in the club.

"Did he talk about where the water is coming from?" she asked, narrowing her eyes.

Brad tensed. Had she been talking to Megan? "That's going to be a main topic of the EIR. Dee says we have plenty of supply to serve it, but Megan has concerns," he responded.

"We can't keep approving sprawling development in this state. We don't have the water," Kay scolded.

That was another of those 40,000-foot elevation perspectives that Brad had no time for. His responsibility was right here in Santa Ynez, not statewide issues. He squirmed in his chair, wishing he had just talked to Kay briefly at the counter.

Kay must have picked up his restlessness. "Listen a minute. We're writing checks all over California that we can't cash. New development is being approved based on contracted water that the state will never be able to deliver. You remember your Oglethorpe, don't you? California began as a myth and we are still living it."

Brad got the Oglethorpe reference, a popular professor at UC Santa Barbara who taught a California history class they had both taken fifteen years apart. A chance to show off.

"Sure, California was named by Spanish conquistadors in the early 1500s after a mythical island from a popular novel of that time. Queen Califia ruled the island of giant Black women warriors who rode their griffins—part lion and part eagle—to support Muslims trying to take back Constantinople from the Christians."

"*You* must have actually gone to your classes," she said. "What was wrong with you, anyway?"

He ignored the taunt. "The virgin Queen was stunning. Her warriors used weapons and armor of gold, the only metal they had," he added. "Queen Califia ends up being taken in battle, falling in love with her captor, and converting to Christianity."

"Bravo, Brad! That's the way I remember it, too. Back in the Middle Ages, myth and fact blended in popular wisdom."

"Kind of like my kids used to do," he noted. "They had no problem moving between fantasy and reality in the same sentence." He had an image of his daughter, Kristen, wearing her homemade princess tiara as she read to her "class" of dolls.

"If you remember the lectures," she continued, "the Spanish had no problem with that either. They came to believe that California was a land of gorgeous giant women warriors covered in gold and waiting to be converted to Christianity. That belief funded a lot of Spanish expeditions. And that mindset has been played out for over half a millennium. We still are living the California myth. Only now the myth isn't about gold, it's about water."

Brad slumped a little. Kay was about to launch into one of her anti-growth tirades. He took a deep breath through his mouth.

"Have you ever heard that in California, water doesn't flow downhill, it flows to money?" she asked.

"Don't know about that," he responded, not wanting to appear too meek to his tough-minded boss. "I do know we wouldn't be the fifth largest economy in the world without the State Water Project. My father idolized Governor Pat Brown for building it."

"Hmmm. What did your father do?" Kay asked.

"He was an engineer with the old State Department of Highways and Bridges, like his father. He got disgusted with government waste and inefficiency and joined a big construction company."

"Humph," Kay responded. "I can see why your father would love Pat Brown. The State Water Project is still the largest public works project in the nation. Back then, everyone wanted growth. We didn't begin to worry about the environmental consequences of these huge projects until the late '60s and early '70s."

Brad flicked his hand at the insect buzzing in his left ear. He picked up the fly in his peripheral vision and watched it do touch-and-go's on the coffee table, Kay's chair, and his arm. He started to take a swat at the nuisance but held back, unsure of Kay's reaction.

She seemed oblivious to the contest between hunter and prey playing out right in front of her. "Sure," she continued, "the State Water Project was massive, but built with lies to satisfy the big-moneyed interests. You can trace a lot of the state's problems today to that project."

Brad's right foot tapped involuntarily. He envied the fly's freedom. Kay always had interesting perspectives, but he had work to do. The phrase "not my monkeys, not my circus" came to mind.

"Lies?" he asked weakly.

"You got it, Brad. Where water's concerned, it's always about money and power. Remember that. The big water contractors have always used legal maneuvers and deceitful public relations tactics to serve their purposes."

"That's pretty cynical, Kay."

"Cynical? Read Pat Brown's interview for UC Berkeley's Oral History program at the end of his political career. He admitted they lied about what the State Water Project would cost to get the initial construction bonds approved. I'll email you an article to read tonight."

He sat up in his chair. "Great, Kay! I was afraid I was going to have to go home and relax."

"You are a major player in public policy around here, and you should know more about the implications of what you're doing," she scolded.

"Teasing," he back-pedaled. "I'd love to read your article. Pat Brown could never get away with those tactics today with our stronger laws, independent career civil service, the Internet, and so many watchdog groups."

Kay shook her head in disgust. "Don't kid yourself. His son, Jerry, followed in his footsteps. Your daughter is studying the Delta, right? Ask her about the Water Fix plan. They want to build huge tunnels to carry Sacramento River water around the Delta to be sure the land to the south has plenty of water. This is the modern version of the LA water grab of Owens Valley at the turn of the Twentieth Century—ruin one region of the state so that an area that God didn't want to have water can use it wastefully."

"I've read a little about that plan," he said sheepishly, "complicated stuff."

"It's a re-do of the Peripheral Canal Jerry Brown tried to sell during his first term as Governor in the '80s that got trounced by the voters," she said. "It's a horrible plan and has been discredited by anyone who cares about preserving the Sacramento Delta. Yet, state government is trying to ram it down our throats on behalf of the water contractors."

"Hmmm," he said, faking interest. The fly was back. Brad waited for it to come nearer. "Like you said, water has always been controversial in California. Was it Mark Twain who said, 'whiskey is for drinking, water is for fighting?'" He tried again to bring his boss back to *his* reality. "We are fortunate to have plenty of contracted water here so that shouldn't be a problem for Green Valley," Brad observed. "And since we're at the end of one of the state's pipelines, I'm glad there are projects being planned that will protect our deliveries."

"You believe you have a state water commitment now since it's in your supply contract? Hah!" Kay warned.

"What do you mean?" He sat forward, alert for a possible threat.

"The state oversold those commitments to make the State Water Project costs seem more reasonable. In fifty years, they've never been able to deliver more than half of that contracted supply. The EIR for Green Valley Village should take that reality into consideration."

"Interesting," he said, daring another furtive glance at his in-basket.

She leaned forward and wagged her finger in the air. She didn't miss much. "Now this is important, Brad. What's going to happen when—not if—long-term drought, climate change, over-pumping of groundwater, pollution, endangered species, degrading water quality in the Delta, and everything else, further reduces water supplies around the state?"

"I would have to say I never thought about it," he said, looking down from Kay's gaze.

"Well, you should! It really worries us. People will have to let their lawns go brown, no more swimming pool permits, and severe rationing will be permanent. At that point, the populace will link arms with the water contractors and demand more dams and other projects that'll further ruin habitat and cost the taxpayers through the nose. The people will vote to protect their own comfort and property values. They'll get hustled. They'll be told California has a water problem. We don't. There's plenty of water to serve reasonable agricultural use and projected population growth for many decades, *if* we use it wisely."

Okay. Okay. Okay. I get it. What the hell do you want from me? "I see your point, Kay. I don't know what you expect me or the city to do about this whole situation. Santa Ynez is such a small player in all of this."

"And I'm sure every other sprawling development could say the same thing, 'Let me have my water. I'm just a little guy in the whole scheme of things.'"

"I suppose," he said meekly.

The councilwoman ran a hand down the long braid of hair falling to her lap, her countenance serious. "We all share a responsibility for the environment. We owe it to future generations. We need to take a stand somewhere, and Green Valley is as good a place to start as any. We aren't convinced that there will be enough water available for Scott's project without putting the rest of the city in jeopardy."

Brad's antenna twitched with that comment. Who is *we*? Did that include his own planning director who may be working hand-in-glove with Kay and her crowd? No point trying to get Kay to reveal her sources.

"Your perspective is always interesting, Kay. And I'll quiz my daughter tonight about the Water Fix plan." Brad smiled, thinking about talking to Kristen. So smart and dedicated. In a millisecond the warmth was swept aside by a familiar wave of worry. He despaired from the realization that what happened so long ago would stay with him forever. He would do everything in his power to prevent it from engulfing his daughter, too.

"Thanks for your help on the petition," Kay said, heading to the door. "But you better tell Scott to gird his loins. We're digging into the water issues."

Kay's parting shot unnerved him. Councilwoman Nance was sending a message that she fully expected Brad would relay her conversation to Scott. And yet, she was friendly, as though everyone was playing out their predesigned roles in the unfolding drama. While Kay's politics and lifestyle were so different from Brad's, he respected her and appreciated that she could disagree with people, including him, without being nasty about it. Not all councilmembers had that maturity.

Kay's assault on big government and corporate greed exhausted him. What he mainly cared about regarding water, right now, was ensuring there would be enough for Green Valley Village. Wasn't that what the council majority wanted him to do? Wasn't that his job?

The tormenting fly landed on his desk. Brad slammed his hand down and turned his palm up to examine the squishy aftermath.

CHAPTER 9

Brad got home at about 5:30 p.m. to pick up Marie and drive to the hospital in Santa Maria to visit their neighbor, Lilly, after her surgery that morning.

"I have a sandwich, apple, and Diet Coke for you for the road," Marie said, as he entered through the front door. "Ready to go?"

"Can't you at least let me change my clothes first?" he grouched.

"Bad day?"

"Sorry. Let's talk in the car. I'll be right down."

Marie did the driving in silence as Brad gobbled the tuna sandwich and washed it down with soda. After a few miles and deep sighs, Brad was ready to bring his wife into his inner world. He briefed her on his recent meetings with Planning Director Megan Cain and Councilwoman Kay Nance.

"They raised some points that got me thinking," he admitted. "Early on, one of my city manager mentors told me, 'This job is a lot easier if you keep the budget balanced, the reservoirs full, and don't try to regulate cats.' So, I always concentrated on finance and economic development. Never had much use for the environmental assessment process. It's always been something to check off to get a project approved. After talking to Megan and Kay, I can see another side."

Marie glanced at him quickly as she drove. "Why should that be so upsetting?"

"You remember the slogan from the '60s, 'If you're not part of the solution, you're part of the problem?'"

"Sure. It was groovy," she smiled at him.

"Cute. I always considered myself part of the solution, driving hard for economic expansion - beefing up the tax base to pay for better services, creating jobs, and giving the people new places to shop and eat. I'm starting to wonder if I'm part of the problem." He paused a moment, the sting of those words burned in his chest. "Am I just another wimpy bureaucrat taking the easy way out by responding to money and power without fully considering the consequences? What *is* the public interest anyway? Lately, I'm not as sure as I was."

Marie turned back to him. "You're not wimpy. You got some information that's caused you to examine what you believe. That's one of your strengths. Being open to different perspectives makes you more effective."

Her assessment comforted him. He took a huge bite of the crisp, cold Gala apple and wondered if it would neutralize the tuna odor on his breath. "Sometimes I wish I held stronger opinions, though," Brad admitted. "It would make decision-making so much easier. It's like my favorite scene in *Midway...*"

"Oh, God. You watch that movie every time it comes on," she interrupted.

"My favorite scene is when Glenn Ford, as Rear Admiral Ray Spruance, visits Admiral "Bull" Halsey, played by Robert Mitchum, in the hospital. Spruance confesses his misgivings about his own bold plan to attack the Japanese fleet at Midway Island, a surprise move against an enemy with far superior forces that could either even the field or imperil the West Coast to invasion. Halsey blasts back, 'When you're in command, command!'"

"If you say so," she responded. "I've never sat through the whole thing."

"I wish I had more Bull Halsey in me."

"Or William Mulholland?" she dangled.

"Yeah, maybe," he replied warily. "They were macho leaders who got things done—damn-the-torpedoes types."

Marie frowned. "There's a time and place for strong-willed leadership. Commanding the fleet in the most important naval battle of the war would be one. But, as we've learned from St. Francis Dam, it's usually better to have a leader who reaches out for other opinions."

"Hmmm." He stared out the windshield, watching the buildings slide by as they drove toward them. "Thanks for boosting my ego."

"You're too hard on yourself, Brad. You never give yourself enough credit. Your staff likes you because you *aren't* a Bull Halsey. You're open to their opinions and try to find compromises to resolve conflict rather than asserting your own will. Instead of seeing that as a plus, your mind distorts it to a negative, like you aren't measuring up to some fictional, macho standard that wouldn't be as effective in your situation anyway."

"Geez, you're not just a pretty face, are you?"

She smiled. "I wish you could relax more and stop worrying so much about everything. You work way too hard attempting to control everything. That's impossible."

He smiled back at her. "You're right. That's my pattern."

"And if the situation calls for a command decision, you'll be a Bull Halsey. Right now, you're struggling to do what's right amidst competing perspectives and pressures. There are too many people in leadership positions who wouldn't even consider challenging their beliefs, especially if it jeopardized their own security. The fact that you are, I find to be macho. Better than that, sexy."

He inhaled her cologne. "I'm going to remind you of that when we get home." He reached over and turned on her favorite satellite station featuring love songs. Her smile confirmed that the message was received. It was a rare moment of intimacy. There had not been enough of those lately.

Marie and Brad were relieved to see Lilly awake as they entered room three of the ICU. She looked frail but sat up in bed wearing a dark pink housecoat over the top of her hospital gown. Her husband, Lee, leaned over the metal side rail of the bed to deliver a spoonful of lime Jello.

"Hey, you look great!" Brad said cheerfully.

"She does," Lee responded. "They've already had her out of bed walking a little."

"I guess I'm a lucky girl, all things considered," Lilly said softly. "They were able to screw me back together. I didn't have to have a new hip."

"Yeah," Lee said. "She has more titanium in the plate they screwed in than I do on my three-wood. They said she had a simple fracture, and with the plate, she'll heal faster." He set the Jello on an end table. "They said she'd be out of here in a day or two and moved to a rehab facility for a week or so."

"That's great," said Brad. "You really are a survivor, Lilly." He winced as he remembered how Lee shut down about the St. Francis Dam break. He cast an apologetic grimace to Lee.

Lilly caught the silent exchange. "It's okay," she said. "Lee told me he mentioned the dam break to you. It happened a long time ago. I don't talk about it outside the family. I don't want to seem like I'm after some personal status from having been there."

"I understand," Brad said. "The important thing now is that you're going to be patched up and out of here."

"We expect to see you out of here in a day or two," Marie added. "I'll have a plate of brownies for you to celebrate."

Lilly cocked her head slightly as though digging deep for a distant memory. "It's funny," she said. "I have trouble remembering what I had for breakfast or why I went into the other room. But I get memories of things from long ago." She turned to Marie. "When you said 'brownie,' it reminded me of my favorite toy when I was little: a hobby horse. You know, one of those sticks with a horse's head on it that kids ran around with, pretending they were riding a horse?"

"I had one of those, too," Marie said.

Lilly smiled. "My father made one for me out of an old broomstick. He painted it pink, my favorite color. Kind of silly now that I think about it. I named the horse 'Brownie,' can't remember why now. In fact, Brownie was pretty close to this color." She pinched the lapel of her housecoat. "Father had somebody burn Brownie's name on his neck."

"That's a sweet memory, Lilly," Marie said with a smile.

"My father worked for Southern California Edison in the construction crews. That's what brought us to the Santa Clara Valley where the flood from the dam break went." She smoothed down her blanket and laid her frail hands neatly on top of her thighs. "I didn't have many toys. I slept with Brownie. And I lost him in the flood," she said with a weak, trailing voice.

She closed her eyes and lay still for a time before getting a second wind. "Oh, what a silly old lady I am!" she cried. "All those people who died, including my own mother and father. And I'm getting mushy about a wooden horse."

Marie took Lilly's thin, nearly transparent hand etched by blue veins.

Lee caressed her shoulder lightly.

Brad regretted raising the dam break. The folded copy he made last night of the "before" photo of the girl in the Kemp construction camp screamed to come out from hiding in his coat pocket.

"I'm okay," Lilly said, "a little tired maybe. But if you don't mind an old lady's walk down memory lane, I'll tell you what I remember about the dam disaster next time I see you." She looked at Brad. "Something tells me you should know more."

As soon as they got home, Brad went upstairs to change into his lounging attire: cotton sweatpants and a nonmatching flannel sweatshirt. He settled back into his black leather recliner with a dish of chocolate peanut butter frozen yogurt and turned on the basketball game he'd been waiting for all day. The local cable company covered the Lakers, but tonight they were playing the Sacramento Kings, his team. Life just got better.

After catching up on the game, he picked up his laptop and found the email from Councilwoman Kay Nance with the article she mentioned earlier today written by a nonprofit public policy advocacy group. The second quarter of the game still had five minutes left, which gave him at least a half hour through halftime to read Kay's article. In truth, he could take an hour since it seemed like ninety percent of NBA games were decided in the last two minutes anyway.

Brad whizzed through the write-up on the Central Valley Project and State Water Project which supported what Kay had said about the cozy relationships that have existed between state government and the water contractors they are supposed to be regulating. Then he read the interview with former Governor

Edmund G. "Pat" Brown that Kay mentioned. Governor Brown was water development's tireless champion and cracked the whip with the state agencies to build the water facilities that enabled the state's rapid expansion. Brown's director of the then new Department of Water Resources went around the state saying, "We must build now and ask questions later."

Brad noted the amazing oral history quote from Brown near the end of his life that Kay referenced: *I loved building things. I wanted to build that goddamned water project. I was absolutely determined I was going to pass this California Water Project. I wanted this to be a monument to me.*

He read on and found everything Kay described about the State Water Project of the '60s. And more. State officials deliberately understated the cost of the project to get the voters to approve a first bond issue. They planned to return for another bond to finish it once it got going. The most critical component of the massive project, the giant Oroville Dam, wasn't even included in the costing for the bond measure. Neither were the aqueduct branches to San Luis Obispo and Santa Barbara counties, which supplied Brad's region. They contracted to deliver twice as much water as storage and delivery facilities were able to provide so the cost per acre-foot of water seemed more reasonable. Brown also convinced the Legislature to divert the tidelands oil tax revenue paid by big oil companies to subsidize the water project and further drive down the cost to the users. The oil companies did not object since they owned so much of the southern San Joaquin Valley land that would jump in value once the state-subsidized water arrived.

Kay had the story correct.

Brad finally closed the document and stared at his computer screen in disbelief. The conniving between state government and the water contractors disgusted him. Where were the checks and balances on government? Weren't there courageous people with power somewhere in the bureaucracy who tried to get the truth out? What did Kay expect from him?

He sighed and sought refuge in the basketball game. Halfway into the fourth quarter, the Lakers were up eight points. Anybody's game, usually. However, the Lakers had already achieved the 100-point threshold. If Ralph Lawler, the play-by-play announcer for the LA Clippers was right, the game was as good as over. "First to a hundred wins" was true ninety-four percent of the time.

The phone rang. Marie answered. He hated taking calls at home. This was either work-related, or his daughter, Kristen. Those were the only calls they got past 9 p.m.

"Hi, hon," Marie said into the kitchen phone.

Brad relaxed. Marie and Kristen were talking about something related to the cheesy potato dish Kris was supposed to make for the upcoming gathering of Marie's family. He smiled. Kris was bright but not much of a cook. She and her Schnauzer lived in a small condo in Mid-Town Sacramento. He pictured the little efficiency kitchen in complete disarray from her latest foray into the culinary arts.

He left them alone to talk for a few minutes and later gave Marie a wave to get her attention, gesturing with his thumb straight out to his ear and his little finger to his mouth.

"Just a minute, hon," she said to her daughter. "Your dad is giving me a hand signal. He either wants to talk to you or he's telling me to hang loose. Considering the source, I'm assuming he wants to talk to you." She brought the cordless phone to his chair.

"Hey there, you watching the Kings game?" he asked.

"It's on, but I'm not watching. I study all night, remember? Lawler's Law strikes again, huh?"

"Yeah, but of course, you wouldn't know that since you're studying, right?"

She laughed. "It's called multi-tasking, Dad. My generation is better at it than yours."

"No doubt. Were your ears burning today?"

"Why? Somebody you know want to give me a job for a hundred thousand?" After getting her bachelor's degree in environmental studies, Kristen held several jobs with consulting firms doing EIRs and now worked for a public foundation doing research on statewide policy matters. She was ready to move on and decided to pursue her MBA on nights and weekends.

"If you want more money, you could always come home and take over as my planning director. Dillon's off to college soon and I'd like you closer. We'll make his room a nursery, you can have your old room, Mom will help with the baby, if you ever get going in that department, hint hint. How you gonna beat that?"

"You're way ahead of me, Dad."

He eventually got down to business. "One of my councilmembers hammered me about state water policy and claimed the Water Fix plan is the latest example of a corporate-driven government boondoggle. I've read a little about it, but since it doesn't affect me, I haven't studied it. How about an overview when we get together so I can hold my own next time I talk to her?"

"Well, Pilgrim, that plan does affect you," Kris said in her best John Wayne impersonation, no better than her father's.

"How so?" he asked.

"Doesn't most of your water supply down there come from the State Water Project?" she queried.

"A lot of it. Okay, that water comes through the Delta. I got it," he said.

"And the Delta is the largest estuary west of the Mississippi. What happens in the Delta ripples across most of the state?"

"So I gather. My councilwoman painted a pretty bleak picture about the current conditions of the Delta and how the state is promoting major plans on behalf of the big water contractors that'll make it worse."

"That's true. Are you becoming a Greenie?"

"Hardly. But I am surprised by an article she sent me. I'll forward it. I guess the state has always had a cozy relationship with the big water contractors."

"That's an under-statement" she replied. "Hmmm. I wonder how many of your citizens think your City Hall is too cozy with developers?"

Brad flinched. "Yeah," he responded with a nervous chuckle and changed the subject to his daughter's job before saying good-bye. Kris' innocent, likely rhetorical question, hounded him the rest of the night. Was he guilty of kowtowing to powerful interests just like the state officials he had been disgusted by? Is that how his daughter thought of him? He was so lost in his head, he hardly cared that the Kings fought back and broke the law at the buzzer.

CHAPTER 10

Brad's eyelids drooped as he drove home from work early Wednesday afternoon. He planned to nap while Marie drove the first leg of their trip to Stockton for the annual gathering at her family ranch. However, Dillon pleaded to drive. They relented to their son's pestering in exchange for his help packing the car. Dillon would take the wheel for the forty-minute trip to Santa Maria to visit Lilly in the hospital. There would be no rest for his parents.

Driver's training was one of those important, potentially frightening rites of passage a parent must help their teenager survive. Dillon and Kristen still laughed about their father's first lesson for each of them. He took them to a cemetery in the evening. Brad liked the solitude and not-so-subtle message the venue offered. As they approached the hospital, Brad rallied in anticipation of talking to Lilly about the dam disaster. They all entered the hospital. Dillon veered off to the cafeteria as Marie and Brad navigated the floors to Lilly's room—a regular room, not ICU. They embraced Lilly gently and got an update on her condition. They exchanged small talk about families and hospital experiences.

Brad stole a glance at his watch and steered the conversation. "We did a little Internet research on the dam disaster. If you're up to it now, Marie and I would be fascinated to hear from someone who lived through it." He had the Kemp camp photo of the little girl in his pocket.

"Yes, I'd like to. Now," Lilly said.

"We're all ears," he replied, earning a glare from Marie for his abruptness. He cleared a place on the padded window seat for the two of them.

Lilly took off her glasses, closed her eyes, and seemed to be praying. She opened her eyes and nodded her head resolutely. "Okay, keep in mind that I was only two or three at the time. I only have bits of memories of the night it happened. Most of what I know I got from other people who were there, or things people wrote." She swallowed a sip of water through a straw. "You probably know that Los Angeles built that big pipe to bring water from a lake on the Nevada side of the Sierra mountains that allowed the San Fernando Valley to be developed."

Marie and Brad nodded.

Lilly continued, "They built the St. Francis Dam to store some of that water in a canyon a few miles east of Highway 99."

"I-5," Lee interjected.

"99 at the time. It's my story, don't interrupt!" Lilly scolded.

"Okay, okay," Lee said. Then he turned to Marie and Brad. "You can tell she's her old self again. I'm going to take advantage of you being here and go to the cafeteria. Can I bring you two back anything?"

They both declined and Lee walked out.

"So, Highway 99?" Brad prompted and regretted sounding impatient.

"Oh, yes, like I told you before, the Edison electricity company had a tent city along the Santa Clara River at a railroad siding called Kemp, ten or fifteen miles west of the dam near the Los Angeles/Ventura county lines."

"I know the area," Brad said. "I grew up over the hill in Ventura County and just read a little about that camp."

Lilly nodded. "The men built power lines through the area. The families pretty much stayed in the camp all the time. There were lots of kids to play with."

Brad thought again about the photo in his coat but did not want to break Lilly's flow. "Did people at the camp worry about being downstream from the dam?" he asked.

"Oh, they used to joke about it," Lilly responded. "They'd say things like 'see you tomorrow— if the dam don't break.'"

"Was there any warning?" Marie asked.

"None." Lilly said emphatically. "It happened in the middle of a cold, dark night. Everyone was asleep. People heard the roar and felt the ground shake long before they saw the wave. They say it measured sixty feet high at the camp."

"Whew," Brad whistled. "That's like a five-story building slamming down on you. It's amazing anyone survived." Brad remembered a ribbon-cutting ceremony for an office building he helped attract to downtown West Sacramento before he left and what it felt like to look up to the top at a five-story building.

"Now that I think about it," Lilly continued, "the man who my father got to burn 'Brownie' on my horse was Mr. Locke, the night watchman who became a hero. He was awake and must have heard a terrible crushing noise like maybe a train derailing nearby. They say that as soon as Mr. Locke got his first glimpse of the water, he ran through the camp waking people up and yelling to run to high ground. He kept yelling until he got swallowed up by the floodwaters himself. He never even took a moment to remove his heavy topcoat. If he had, he might have been able to outrun the wave, slowed by every manner of wreckage, or at least have a chance to swim to safety as a few men did." She paused, let out a long exhale, and stared into space. "He was nice to me."

"That's horrible, Lilly," Marie cried. "What did *you* do?"

"Well, I learned this part later. Remember I said it was a cold night? Father must have tied off the door flap of the tent we lived in to keep more warmth in. A lot of other families did the same thing that night. At first, we were all swept away by the wave, but the water hit a big rock outcropping where the valley narrows. Some of the water doubled back on itself and it created a whirlpool. The tents that got to that whirlpool and had their door flaps tied up had some air trapped inside. They bobbed to the surface and rode out the flood on top of the water for a while."

"How scary!" Marie exclaimed.

Lilly paused again and dabbed her eyes with a fresh tissue. "I don't know how much of this I remember and how much I imagined or learned. When our tent bobbed to the surface of the whirlpool, my father pulled back the door flap of the tent and threw me into some brush on the hill. As soon as he did, water rushed into the tent and they went down again. Mother and father were found dead later that morning downstream wrapped around each other inside the tent at the bottom of a huge plug of trees, pieces of barns and houses, cars, and all sorts of junk. They died saving me."

"Oh, my God!" Marie cried again. "I can't imagine. You were so little. You must have been terrified."

"To tell you the truth, about all I can remember from the rest of that night was the cold and being driven to some building for the night in the back of a truck. Everyone was crying. Some woman wrapped me in a blanket and held me tight all the way there. She stayed with me all night and the next day until Dad came for me."

Marie and Brad exchanged quizzical glances. She said her father had died in the flood. Was she losing some of her faculties or was she getting mixed up by the meds?

"It took a long time to discover how many people had been killed. Bodies turned up everywhere." Lilly appeared to still be back at that dark early morning of March 13, 1928. "They didn't have the methods to identify bodies that they have now. There were hundreds of people who were reported as missing and some bodies that were never identified. But I learned that of the 150 people at our camp, eighty-four were officially identified as dead. Many of those who died were found wrapped inside their tents. Some had literally torn off their fingernails trying to claw their way out through the canvas as the water rushed in."

Marie gasped. Brad was both fascinated and guilty for encouraging Lilly to relive such a trauma.

"When I got older and started asking questions about the disaster, my dad told me about the Los Angeles Coroner's Inquest hearings. I'll never forget some of those stories."

Marie and Brad glanced at each other again at this second reference to her father whom she said had been killed.

Lilly told poignant stories of unimaginable horror, of the mother who ran from the wave and had to make a split decision about which of her three kids she could carry to safety, of the father and son in Castaic Junction who clung to life on a telephone pole, the man using his own body as a human shield from the onslaught of debris until he was dislodged and never seen again, and of the family of seven who tried to outrun the wave in the family car that became their coffin.

She also told stories of great bravery. Volunteers plunged into the raging water to rescue victims, both human and animal. Some perished in the effort.

"It took a long time to get the alert out," Lilly said. "The landslide at the dam took out phone and power lines that served a wide area. When the siren finally sounded in Santa Paula, people came out half asleep in their night clothes to see what was going on. Word spread about a flood. A hundred mostly Spanish-speaking gawkers congregated on the bridge over the Santa Clara River. A Highway Patrolman named Edwards roared up on his motorcycle and yelled, 'mucho agua.' People were confused because it hadn't been raining and the riverbed was dry. It isn't known what Officer Edwards said next, but it put the fear of God in the people. They ran off the bridge minutes before the flood wiped it out, snapping the gas lines that hung from it. They say the gas explosions and noise from the bridge ripping apart were deafening."

"I can imagine," Brad said, recalling the complete destruction of a small apartment building in a previous city where he worked caused by a leak in the gas wall heater.

"Officer Edwards wasn't done. He continued his motorcycle dash through the streets of Santa Paula with his siren blaring. He took a fast turn from one street downtown to another and ran smack into the wave. He got inundated but lived and became the first man in CHP history to receive a gold medal for bravery."

Lee came to the door with a Styrofoam cup of coffee. Brad signaled to his wife to stay with Lilly and motioned for Lee to join him in the corridor.

"We appreciate Lilly opening up to us about her experiences," Brad said. "But she seemed confused."

"Oh?" Lee said.

"She talked about how her father was killed in the flood while saving her, but later she talked about things her father told her years following the incident. I figured it would be normal for her to be disoriented about such a traumatic event when she was so young. Or maybe it was the pain killers. Just thought you should keep an eye on her."

Lee smiled. "Her mind is sharp, don't worry about that. What she didn't explain was that after her father was killed in the flood, his brother, her uncle, adopted her. She refers to her birth father as 'father' and to her adoptive father as 'dad.' I can see why you'd be confused."

"Okay, good," Brad said. "What an admirable thing for her uncle to do. It must have been tough for everyone involved."

"I never met him," Lee said. "He did a fine job raising Lilly. But there's more to it. That's another very painful part of the story that Lilly might want to tell you sometime."

"If she feels like it," Brad said. "We better rescue the cafeteria from the 'Attack of the Ravenous Dillon' and get back on the road." The men went back into the room.

Marie hugged Lilly. "I am so happy your surgery was successful. You'll get stronger every day."

"Yes, and thank you for sharing all of these stories with us," Brad added. He bent over the bed to give Lilly a hug also and pulled back. "Oh, I almost forgot, we have something to show you." He reached into his coat pocket and handed her the photo. "Marie found this picture of the Kemp tent camp on the Internet. Did you know the girl in the picture by any chance?" He held his breath. How would Lilly react to seeing herself as a child before the disaster?

Lee helped Lilly on with her glasses and adjusted the gooseneck of the bed light. She held it closely, then even closer, scrutinizing it.

"Oh!" she gasped, clutched the photo to her chest and sobbed. *Just like I thought—it was her.* Brad was excited to have sleuthed out the connection in the photo then remorseful for allowing his ego to overshadow the obvious pain of the frail, grieving woman.

Lee caressed Lilly's arm and handed her a tissue. She continued to cry softly, accompanied by the whirs and beeps of the instruments attached to her body.

Marie took her hand and waited for her to calm down. When Lilly's eyes were dry, she said, "We're so sorry, Lilly. We wondered if that was you in the picture."

Lilly inhaled deeply and pushed herself up in the bed. Her demeanor changed from a weak, elderly patient to a determined survivor. "That's not why I cried," she said softly. "It's beautiful. God works in mysterious ways."

"Yes," Brad agreed without understanding.

Lilly looked at Brad directly. "The last time you visited, I somehow sensed I was supposed to talk to you."

"I see," Brad responded, trying to mask his skepticism and confusion. How could something be so beautiful and upsetting at the same time?

"Maybe you do," Lilly said, "maybe you don't. Or maybe you will. I believe He made this the right time for me to talk to you about the disaster. It's a blessing to sense His presence, especially in my current situation."

"We all need that at any age, Lilly," Marie said.

"Because I told you about the dam break, you brought me a picture I've never seen before that means a lot to me. A picture of pleasant memories from the worst time of my life. God is reminding me that He's always here."

"The little girl *is* you, isn't she Lilly?" Brad asked softly.

She shook her head slightly and held the black and white photo in her bony fingers, pointing to a tent in the background behind the girl. "Look here."

Brad leaned over the bed rail and studied a gray image of a tent. A shovel and long-handled axe leaned against the side of the tent astride their pal, the valiant steed Brownie.

CHAPTER 11

Marie drove the next leg of the trip from Santa Maria to allow Brad a quick nap along northbound Highway 101 before the turnoff on eastbound Highway 46, then over to northbound Interstate 5. She liked to drive. It was one of the competencies she regained completely with her prosthesis. But two-lane Highway 46 could be slow and scary, slow if you got stuck behind a big rig or a huge RV pulling a jeep piled high with camping gear, scary if you dared to pass. The highway had plenty of straight stretches where passing was permissible but dicey. The James Dean Memorial at the junction of Highways 46 and 41, the site of the head-on crash that killed the Hollywood icon, was a grim reminder of the danger. Brad wanted to be awake to help her through that stretch.

"Thanks for the rest, hon," he said as they approached Kettleman City on I-5.

They made a quick pit stop and Brad took over driving. Traffic moved at a decent clip. The clear weather treated them to picturesque sunset vistas of waterways and farmland as they skirted the southeast edge of the Sacramento-San Joaquin River Delta in the upper middle part of the state, east of San Francisco Bay.

"Pretty, huh?" Brad observed.

Marie nodded. "I never appreciated it growing up."

They rode the next hour in relative silence. The soft jazz rhythms on the radio moved in harmony with the changing landscape as they approached Marie's family home in the rich agricultural area east of Stockton near the community of Linden. Eventually, they pulled off the paved county road onto the family ranch's graveled driveway past at least a hundred acres of walnut trees, vineyards, and cherry trees. Next came huge vegetable and herb gardens, assorted fruit trees, the barn, and stable areas, followed by several oversized garages. The rambling, single-story brick home appeared with two little guest houses peeking out from behind.

"Funny," Marie said. "The sound of rocks crunching under the tires feels like home." She busied herself by picking up the things from around her seat and primping in the lighted mirror on the back of the sun visor.

Brad pulled around the circular driveway and stopped under the porte-cochere. Their daughter, Kristen, was the first one out the front door. She walked briskly to hug Marie and Brad as they emerged from the car. To Brad's surprise, and apparently Dillon's, she also gave her brother a quick hug.

"Hey, Scoot!" Tanner bellowed, plucking his sister Marie off the ground for a bear hug.

"And Crat Man! My favorite Superhero." Tanner always teased Brad about working for the government, although his brother-in-law clearly respected him. Tanner was a generous spirit who was not diminished by propping somebody else up. Brad suspected Tanner was not a frequent visitor to the self-help section of the bookstore.

Tanner bounded around the car, extending his bulging right arm out like an alligator rushing at game. Brad braced for it and jammed his own hand deep into the big man's. Strong pumps. A manly embrace. Tanner put his powerful left hand on Brad's shoulder and gave him a couple thumps.

Brad put an arm around his daughter's shoulder as they all walked to the door.

Inside, Tanner's twin twelve-year-old girls sprawled on the carpet in the living room with the television blaring and honored the new arrivals with a wave and quick "hi" before turning back to the TV.

The entourage proceeded to the kitchen where Tanner's wife, Bridget, took off her quilted oven mitt and met them with a tray of piping hot, cheesy jalapeno poppers in one arm and an embrace with the other.

Marie's mother, Beva, known to the family as Nana, got up from her jigsaw puzzle on a round maple table in the kitchen with outstretched arms that begged for a Jacks member to enter.

Once everyone caught up Nana called them to a dinner of Sloppy Joes. Following a long day and drive, the steamy tomato sauce and ground beef looked like a pot of gold at the end of a rainbow. The whiff of garlic and onions made Brad salivate and recall childhood family dinners featuring his mother's signature meatloaf.

Tanner left the table and came back with two bottles of wine. "This is our latest Zin. You're going to love it," he proclaimed proudly. "You know San Joaquin County is one of the top Zinfandel producing areas in the world, don't you? The combination of rich, fertile soil, and hot temperatures transforms the black-skinned grapes into a robust red wine." Tanner had a twinkle in his eye that suggested he was performing an act.

Tanner gushed about the wine like the father of a newborn. He deftly removed the cork and poured the juice into a decanter to let it breathe. He swirled the decanter and dribbled a sample into a large goblet then swirled some more. He raised the glass to the light and showed the results to his audience. "Nice legs," he pronounced.

Tanner continued swirling and stuck his nose into the glass. "Ah, fruity."

Finally, he took a sip and let it stay on his tongue a while, finally swallowing slowly with a look of pure contentment. "Hmmm, notes of blackberry, anise, and pepper." He smiled mischievously. "Who wants a snort?"

Tanner could pull off the transition from Master-Somme-lier-at-the-Ritz to good-old-boy-at-the-bar without seeming fake in either role.

Most of the adults partook. Nana, whose longevity secret was two cigarettes and two shots of Scotch every night, stayed with her Cutty Sark.

After dinner, Nana, Bridget, and Marie shooed everyone from the kitchen so they could clean up. That was code for "leave us alone so we can talk about you."

Kristen, Tanner, and Brad migrated outside to the covered porch that ran the width of the front of the house, each holding a full glass of Zin. The trio settled into the comfortable padded white rocking chairs on the redwood deck. A waxing moon played peekaboo with the scattered cumulus clouds over the walnut grove. Tanner set a bottle of wine down next to him and handed Brad an expensive looking cigar.

They engaged in a bit of small talk until Brad turned to Tanner. "I have a councilwoman who's a big environmentalist and is all worked up about the Delta tunnels. If you don't mind, I asked Kris to fill me in. I'm interested in your take too, Tan Man."

"Sure." Tanner said. "We could use more government types from south of Tracy to give a damn about the Delta."

"Okay, Kris, make me smart for my councilwoman."

"I'll try. First, you should understand that the Delta has been described as the Gordian Knot of the entire State Water Project," she began. "It's an absolute tangle of conflicting interests."

She went on to describe the hydrologic history of the region before and after the Gold Rush, the richness of the silty soils fed by major rivers from north, south, and east, and the fragility of the peat-based levees struggling to keep the fresh river water in and the salt water of the San Francisco Bay out. She talked about the importance of the region to the entire state. Two-thirds of all Californians, and millions of acres of irrigated farmland, get their water by way of the Delta. She briefed her father on the uncertainties of the Delta tunnel plan regarding water quality, endangered species, agricultural production, habitat restoration, fishing, and tourism.

Tanner punctuated the lecture with snide comments about the state government being in bed with the big water contractors south of the Delta. His voice became louder and thicker with each successive glass of Zin.

Kristen had seen how worked up her uncle got with alcohol under his belt. She looked at him uneasily before continuing. "The basic scheme is to divert water that would flow to the Delta into these massive tunnels and take it around the Delta to the pumping plants and then into the concrete aqueduct to the Central Valley and Southern California. It's a precaution to protect the fresh water from saltwater intrusion in the event of a levee breach. Proponents even argue it will improve water quality in the Delta."

"Bullshit!" Tanner slurred. "The governor's point man for the tunnel plan even admitted that it isn't, and never was, about saving the Delta. He said, 'The Delta can't be saved.' He was forced to resign for telling the truth." Tanner flicked ash into the sand-filled abalone shell ashtray and gulped down the rest of his wine. He was no longer savoring the blackberry and anise undertones of the Zin.

"The whole tunnel project is so complicated, it's impossible to fully understand the impacts," Kristen said. "Originally it was called the Bay Delta Conservation Plan that, along with the EIR, was over 40,000 pages."

"Forty thousand?" Brad cried incredulously. "*War and Peace* was the longest book I've ever read at about 1,000 pages of tiny print. It took me an entire summer after college to get through it, but I wanted to be able to say I read it. I can't imagine reading a technical government document equivalent to forty books that size."

"Well, those experts who have tried to wade through it have pretty much debunked much of the touted benefits of the project. It drew so much fire that the backers replaced it with two separate plans. California Water Fix is the same idea to take water around the Delta in big tunnels and Eco Restore is the habitat restoration piece. It's another 8,000 pages. I haven't read it either. I understand that the conservation portion went from seven billion to only three hundred million. And, in fact, most of the 30,000 acres left in the plan for habitat is already required to be restored under an endangered species agreement with the federal government. It's not new habitat at all."

Tanner pounded his rocking chair. "See? Same ole, same ole," he snarled. "They don't care about Delta conservation. They want to grab the water. They aren't going to stop until they've destroyed the Delta. That's why we keep our shotguns loaded." He refilled his glass and sat back heavily.

After rocking quietly a while, Brad blew a smoke ring, winked at Kristen and nodded toward Tanner. The big man's eyes were closed and his mouth open, a nearly empty glass barely balanced on his lap.

"I guess my lecture put him out," she whispered.

"I'm not far behind," he admitted. "What was that study you were working on about the tunnels?"

"I was part of a team studying the plan's economics. The supporters peg the construction and operations costs over a fifty-year life at twenty-five billion dollars. But factor in interest on the bond issues and a bunch of other huge costs that should be included in the analysis and seventy billion is a more reasonable estimate. The state seems to be deliberately understating the environmental impacts and ignoring the financials that argue against construction."

"Holy cow!" Brad exclaimed upon making a connection. He rocked faster. "This sounds like what I just read about…how the state leaders deliberately understated the costs of the State Water Project in the '60s to get it built. If the ratepayers are supposed to pay the load, that's going to be some expensive water."

Kristen nodded. "There's also a problem with the demand estimates. The plan assumed five million more people in Southern California than the State Department of Finance is forecasting. It doesn't tie to the city and county General Plans on what the local communities are preparing for. Urban water use is dropping thanks to local conservation practices and declining population growth. The cost of the water will be much higher if there isn't a bigger population base paying for it."

Is this really happening again? "Geez, again, like when they contracted for twice as much State Water Project water as they'd ever be able to deliver to get the per-unit cost down. 'Déjà vu all over again,' as Yogi Berra said."

"And the heck of it is," Kristen added, "that seventy billion doesn't supply *any new* water. It mainly is about reducing risks for the big water contractors south of the Delta."

Brad sighed deeply. "The whole thing seems like a scam. I can see why my councilwoman is so worked up about it."

"Yup. Too much money, too many unknowns, and too many people dug into their positions. I think even the big water contractors who were driving the tunnels have lost the faith. I read an article in the paper that LA water agencies are hedging their bets by buying land in the Delta and along the Colorado River to get control of that area's water rights. The Metropolitan Water District that provides most of the water in Southern California is now the biggest property owner in the Palo Verde Valley farming region at the Arizona border. The local farmers are worried they plan to dry it up to wheel the Colorado River water to Southern California for more development."

Brad sat forward and shot out a stream of smoke. "Really? Like they did in the Owens Valley a century ago? Incredible." He leaned over to carefully remove the glass from Tanner's lap.

"I'm fading, too," Brad said. "Let's end on a hopeful note. I attended a meeting on the new groundwater management plan law. It took a terrible drought to get it through the Legislature, but we're finally on the path to stopping the big water contractors from pumping the aquifers dry."

"Too little, too late, Dad," Kristen complained. "We should be managing *all* of the water now. Today. That groundwater regulation Sacramento politicians are crowing about is so lame. It only calls for *plans* now. The law doesn't require the groundwater basins to achieve sustainability until around 2030. Meanwhile, the contractors sink their wells deeper as the water table drops, and they go right on planting new arid lands until the groundwater finally runs out. It's a race to the bottom. State officials know all about it, but there's not enough political will to reform. The corporate interests in the Valley have the legislature in a noose. Not a single legislator from the Central Valley voted for even the wimpy groundwater planning law."

"It's complicated and real reform seems like a pipe dream," he said, ruefully.

Kristen laughed. "Nice pun. The state has a pro-build bias for the tunnels because of the money and politics. But the EPA weighing in with their opposition over water quality and endangered species impact was a game-changer. They can't do the tunnels if the feds oppose them. The water lobby controls state government, so we better hope the feds and courts force some restraint."

Brad mulled her comment. "I guess I'm guilty on that pro-build bias myself. Thanks for the education. Worth every nickel I spent on it."

They rocked to the tune of chirping crickets and creaking wood. Brad gazed over the walnut trees to the moon and sky above, searching for answers. He took a pull on his smoke and watched Kris savor the final sip of her wine, deep in contemplation as well. Through the haze of his cigar smoke, his daughter melted away and a colleague now sat before him.

His heart swelled first with pride, then dread. Was this very capable young woman strong enough to cope with their past?

CHAPTER 12

At least twenty of Marie's relatives descended upon the family home for the annual reunion. Babies cried, little kids ran around the house screaming, and adults gathered around the dining room table to drink coffee, graze, and catch up. Basketball blared in the background on TV all day. The elders held court between naps.

Dinner kicked everything into an even higher gear. Plates and platters swirled around the table. Mothers instructed children to take the green beans, not so much Jello salad. The women talked over each other about recipes and what minor changes they tried this time. The men concentrated on eating.

Tanner was the MVP of the feast. He raised the pig that gave its all for the main course, grew the green beans and the pecans for the pie, grew and arranged the chrysanthemums for the centerpiece, handled the carving honors with aplomb to the rapt attention of the salivating crowd and, of course, made the Zinfandel they enjoyed again.

After the house quieted and most of the family left, Brad stretched out on the big leather sectional couch and opened his Golf magazine. Nap position.

"Why don't we lay out our gear for tomorrow morning?" Tanner urged.

Dillon leapt to his feet. Brad sighed. Nappus interruptus.

Tanner deemed that Dillon was ready for the big time—an outing at his duck club on Lower Jones Tract, a manmade island in the middle of the Delta due west of Stockton. On previous visits, Tanner had taken Dillon to a sporting clay course to familiarize him with handling a shotgun and shooting at a moving object. Tanner was a patient teacher. He showed Dillon how to determine his master eye for aiming, lead the target, keep his movements smooth with a slight forward lean, concentrate on the target with his head on the stock until the shot, and take his time, do not jerk. Tomorrow was Dillon's big day.

Brad was jolted awake by an annoying noise. Cell phone. He grabbed it from the side table and fumbled with buttons trying to make it stop. "Hello? Hello?" It kept ringing. He finally figured out it was his phone's alarm and groaned. Was it 4:30 a.m. already? He shook Dillon awake and plodded to the hall bathroom. As he donned his warm clothes, Brad gave Dillon a "hurry-up" and joined Tanner who was already in the kitchen pouring black coffee into a gallon thermos.

"Afternoon, Crat Man!" Tanner said in a chipper voice as if he habitually beat the dawn by two hours.

"Morning, Tan Man," Brad replied. "Hey, I appreciate you bringing Dillon along and all. And I know you'll make sure he's safe. But we don't want to mess up the experience for anyone else and have Dillon get all embarrassed. You know how self-conscious teenagers are. So, make sure you tell us if either of us is about to do something wrong. It will be important for him to fit in with your friends."

"No sweat," Tanner assured. "These are good guys. They come in all shapes and bank accounts. Out there everyone is only a duck hunter and a friend. They don't get all stressed about making their limit. They'll make Big D feel welcome."

"Okay," Brad said. "And I'll do my best to make sure the pointy end is toward the ducks."

Brad and Dillon loaded the gear into the rear of Tanner's truck cab while Tanner fetched his hunting dog, Blab, a Black Lab. Blab nearly jumped out of his skin with anticipation. The hunters climbed into the cab and drove slowly down the gravel driveway in the early morning blackness.

"Why don't you break out the coffee?" Tanner suggested to Brad. "And, Big D, there's a package of bear claws behind you."

They spent most of the thirty-minute trip to Lower Jones Tract in silence. Brad relished the hot coffee, sweet pastry, and emerging views of the Delta as dawn heralded a cloudy, blustery morning.

They took a right on westbound Highway 4, then headed north on a narrow, rutted slough road and reached the driveway to the club around 5:45 a.m. Light from the open front door exposed the primitive surroundings that hadn't improved since Brad's last visit. The club was a house like he might have drawn in the sixth grade, a no-frills, one-story rectangular building with inexpensive T-111 plywood siding and cheap asphalt composition shingles. Duct tape secured aluminum foil over one of the window frames. Several spindles of the wooden porch rail were either missing or hanging atilt. This was a place that got hard use by hardy men, not some prissy showplace. They parked on the gravel, gathered their gear, climbed the three warped and squeaky wooden stairs to the porch, and prepared to enter the hubbub inside.

"Tan Man!" somebody yelled as soon as Tanner hit the threshold. Brad recalled that it was here that he first heard his brother-in-law's nickname. A few guys came over to shake hands with Tanner and meet Brad and Dillon.

The large red picnic table off the kitchen was covered with cards, poker chips, crinkled cans of beer, spaghetti strands, half-eaten containers of dip, and open bags of chips and Oreos.

"The guys had a good time last night," Tanner noted to Dillon and Brad.

"Come on, assholes. Get movin.' We gotta get out there," shouted a burly man from the kitchen. The tantalizing aroma of frying bacon permeated the club, and the man continued to shout orders to his helpers who plopped down platters of scrambled eggs and toast for the dozen or so men who were slowly getting into motion.

One of the other guys, dressed only in a flannel shirt and boxer shorts, yelled back, "I'm already movin' quick, Doc. Your cookin's gave me the trots!" The cook smiled and flipped him off.

Tanner nodded toward the cook and whispered to Brad and Dillon, "That's Doc Tompkins. You'll like him."

"What kind of doctor is he?" Brad asked.

"Actually, he's a Superior Court judge in Calaveras County."

"Why do they call him Doc?" Dillon asked.

Tanner thought a moment and replied, "I heard his real first name is David. The story goes that his parents wanted him to be a doctor, not a lawyer. He graduated from law school with a Juris Doctor degree and his dad called him 'Doc.' He's the most laid-back judge you'll ever meet."

Under Doc's goading, the guys picked up their pace. Some attacked their breakfast while others put on their waterfowl gear. An obviously hung-over gentleman staggered out of a back bedroom wearing only his tighty whities and stood at the hall doorway trying to absorb the scene.

Doc motioned Tanner over to the table and said, "Welcome boys. Grab some food and suit up. We leave in ten."

"Wind's comin' up, Doc," Tanner said. "So's the clouds. Should be a pretty good shoot."

They bolted down breakfast, put on their gear, grabbed their guns, and walked down the levee in the pre-dawn light to a small pier where Tanner kept his duck boat. Nobody bothered to clean up the mess they left behind. That could wait. The ducks wouldn't.

The threesome piled their gear into Tanner's twenty-foot aluminum boat camouflaged in mossy brown. Blab jumped in, his tail whipping at allegro tempo. Tanner yanked on the pull cord and the small outboard motor came to life. They putt-putted to the farthest duck blind on the east edge of the flooded eighty-acre cornfield to a grassy area below the levee. The blinds, concealed shooting platforms, had been laid out in north/south rows on the east and west sides of the pond so the hunters did not have to shoot into the sun in the morning or evening.

The club was perfectly situated along the Pacific Flyway, the path stretching from Alaska to the tip of South America that millions of migratory birds travel during the spring and fall. To attract some of the ducks their way, the club had shaved the corn stalks after the harvest and opened the levee gate to flood the field. Ducks prefer the high carbohydrate diet offered by grain fields to build their energy for the remaining flight. But by the time the ducks reached them, they had already been hunted for two months or more and were wary. The hunters had to be skilled in their calling, blind construction, decoy placement, and camouflage to draw the birds in.

"Good job with the decoy pattern, Sluggo," Tanner said to a man in the next boat through his cupped hands, his voice barely audible over the motors.

Sluggo tipped his greasy Husqvarna-logoed cap.

Brad started to ask about Sluggo's nickname but let it pass, his fear of committing a faux pas with unnecessary chatter being stronger than his curiosity.

Once settled in the blind, Tanner concentrated on mallards since they were the best eating. He scored a double in his first shoot. Blab bounded through the thick Johnson grass and corn stalks and returned the first duck. He stood on the platform wagging his tail like a metronome on fast forward. Tanner stared at Blab holding up his index finger as if to say, *wait for it, wait for it.* Blab was raring to go. "Fetch!" Tanner finally commanded, pointing in the direction of his second bird. The retriever was off like a shot, returning with his prize carefully nestled in his soft mouth.

Tanner patted Blab and set his Browning down to help his guests. With his coaching and calling, Brad got a mallard and a couple of pintails. Dillon had taken a few shots but had nothing to show for them. Even Brad could tell he was shooting too jerkily. His son glowered.

A cold north wind blew the drizzle sideways making whitecaps on the pond. Lovely weather for a duck, indeed!

Brad's anxiety grew with each of his son's missed shots. The conditions were perfect. Sluggo's decoy pattern proved enticing and the ducks must have been hungry. He worried that the other guys would be ready to leave soon. He motioned to Tanner and nodded toward his son. Tanner picked up the signal and leaned over to give Dillon a little more coaching.

"Remember, Big D, aim small, miss small, and keep the gun moving in front of him," Tanner reminded Dillon. "Relax, be smooth, and stay on the gun," he added.

Another hunter nearby blew his call. It got the attention of a gigantic flock of passing pintails that came in for a closer look. Tanner pointed up, gave Dillon the okay sign, but waved his hands to signal for the boy to wait. The birds came closer.

"Easy," Tanner cautioned, barely over the cacophony of the flock directly above. Brad held his breath. Shotguns erupted all around them.

"Now smooth, Big D, take your time," Tanner urged.

Dillon stood up, his twenty-gauge in perfect firing stance and, this time, slowed down his shot. Blam! A moment later, he pulled the trigger again. Blam! The second shot scored. Feathers sprayed in the sky and a large pintail fluttered into the stalks. Blab was up with the shot, his head darted back and forth between the falling bird and his master. Finally, Tanner gave the command, and the dog was off again.

When Blab returned, Brad gave his son a hearty pat on the back and pulled out his phone from the protective plastic bag. Dillon posed, holding his trophy in the air with an ear-to-ear grin and Tanner's strong arm on his shoulder.

Dillon got off two more shots later. One missed, but the other may have caught a wing. However, judging from the bird's trajectory after impact, Tanner thought somebody in the next blind got the kill. Dillon was fine with letting it go. Blab was not so understanding. Brad suspected that's how it was with a group of friends in a private club. People took care of each other and shared the day's bounty. The legal limit was seven ducks each. With conditions like this, they could limit out in the morning shoot if they wanted to. But these guys were in it for the sport. They did not want to overshoot the flooded field and make it tougher for the evening hunters. They were content to harvest a little of what nature provided for their own use now and leave the rest for another time. It occurred to Brad how different this mindset toward nature was from the greed and exploitation he had been learning about that characterized California's water practices.

Despite the cold, windy conditions, Brad was warm inside. He studied his son as they sat in silence on upended buckets in the duck blind. How excited Dillon was about downing a duck on his first hunt. Brad spied small, black whiskers sprouting from a face that was becoming more chiseled. Wasn't it just last year they were in the cul-de-sac playing Home Run Derby with whiffle balls? And soon Dillon would be off to college.

Brad shifted his gaze to his brother-in-law. Tanner had pivoted on his bucket ninety degrees directly into the harsh north wind. His face was red raw from the wind that buffeted his thick brown hair sticking out from under his camo hat. The sun ducked in and out of the clouds, alternatingly shrouding the vista and bathing it in vivid color.

Tanner was not looking at anything in particular. He was not scouting to set up the next call or shoot. He stared ahead serenely, his chin raised to catch as much of the climate on his face as he could, the picture of contentment. His wife, Bridget, called it being in his "Puddy" mode, after a character in Seinfeld. Brad always joined the laugh over the Puddy crack. Now he got it. Tanner was not zoned out at all. To the contrary, he was completely *in* the moment. *God, will I ever know such peace?*

The hardest place for Brad to be was right where he was rather than in the past or future. But at this moment, he, too, was close to present. No more worries about his son getting his duck, someone getting hurt, blundering with some faux pas, or any of the other dozen calamities that had crossed his mind. Instead, Brad reveled in gratitude and connected with nature in a way he had never experienced. He forced himself not to analyze it and to breathe it in.

"Thanks, Tan Man," Brad said, sweeping his hand at the view.

"Pleasure, Crat Man," Tanner replied, contentedly.

The three relaxed in the blind until an outboard motor came to life nearby. Others soon joined the chorus. The threesome, and Blab, loaded into the boat.

"Take us home, Big D. Or should I call you Buffalo Dill now?" Tanner cranked the motor and moved over to let Dillon pilot the boat to join the flotilla. Some of the guys held up their bounty for all to see as they chugged along the pond. Tanner gave them a thumbs-up and raised Dillon's hand as the boy displayed his bird. Some of the guys returned the thumbs up or clapped.

With Dillon steering them home, Tanner removed his cap and let the wind whip through his wavy hair. He leaned back in the boat with his head on a sideboard and raised both arms to the sky as if giving thanks for nature. "It doesn't get any better than this, Crat Man," he said.

"Amen," Brad said, wondering where that came from. Brad could not recall ever having a serious discussion about theology with Tanner. He suspected he knew more about the Bible and the dogma of the world's leading religions, but Tanner had a closer connection to God.

The group finally sputtered up to the small dock by the house, tied their boats up, and passed around the iced beer from the cooler at the dock. The frigid fog made hot coffee a better choice, but beer is the de rigueur quaff for a manly activity. The guys toasted each other's success. Dillon looked questioningly at his father who nodded assent. By the way Dillon handled the can, Brad could tell it was not his first.

Tanner took Brad and Dillon aside. "Hey, guys," he whispered, nodding at a man still in a boat, "Marty over there's a helluva a cook but he just got laid off, and his family could probably use the meat. You okay with giving him some of the birds?"

With their quick concurrence, Tanner threw a can of beer to Marty and said, "I helped Big D here get his first bird. But you know I hate to clean 'em. Would you be willing to do the honors and give him a mallard to take home? You can have the rest."

"Cool. I got my special marinade in the fridge," Marty said, "I'll throw some of that in and tell them how to cook it."

The men finished their beers and headed back to the house to store their gear and relieve themselves. Many of the guys took care of the latter task from the levee rather than bothering to use the bathroom.

Inside, Doc Tompkins was back in the kitchen wielding the whip. Some of the guys pitched in for a half-hearted attempt to clean up the mess. Somebody turned on a college basketball game. Guys lined up at the large coffee urn. A bottle of Jameson Irish whisky sat next to it.

"Outta the way, assholes," Doc said gruffly. "I made it, me first." The judge went to the front of the line, filled his mug, added a healthy shot of whiskey, and gave the bottle to Tanner.

Brad held back. Better not have any whiskey. Early morning. Fresh air. It is warm in here. I am already sleepy. Tanner will probably drink too much, and I will have to drive his over-sized truck on that narrow levee road. He caught himself reverting to pattern. *Loosen up!* He got in the coffee line, added a generous shot of whiskey, and shook his head at Dillon.

The trio took their drinks outside to keep Marty company as he cleaned the birds. The wind had died down and the light drizzle of the early morning was turning into a thickening ground fog. Tule fog could hang over the Central Valley for weeks at a time, sometimes causing horrendous car pile ups on the freeway. He worried again about having to drive home on the levee roads and remembered the image of a head-on wreck on the narrow, foggy roads leading out of the Delta. Once again, he caught himself, shook his head, and took another sip of his spiked brew. *Get out of your head.*

Two large propane barbeques stood next to an open fire pit of mortared cobbles. One guy grilled Italian sausage and warmed a pot of the leftover spaghetti. Marty built a fire using manzanita for kindling with larger oak logs on top. The fire hissed and popped already providing warmth and an antidote to the grayness engulfing the area. Doc Tompkins and two other men came out of the house and plunked down on folding chairs next to the fire with their ducks, buckets, pans, and utensils.

The Irish coffee hit its mark. Brad relaxed deeper. He ignored the dreariness of the ground fog and the hazard it posed for the drive home and leaned his head back on the red plastic mesh chair as full breaths expanded his chest and pushed anxieties out. It truly was relaxing being here. In this place. Nowhere else. Right now.

He held up his cup to the other men. "Nice to be here, gents. Thanks for having us."

The men sat quietly for an hour or more. They talked sparingly. Brad observed that when Marie was with other women, they often talked over each other, the words like energy pellets propelling them onward. These guys were happy to sit and stare at the popping blaze and enjoy the quiet camaraderie. That is, until one of the guys brought up the deteriorating condition of the club. That sparked an animated discussion about whether it was a waste of money to repair it considering the precarious future of the entire Delta. Brad sat silently. He wasn't in the mood to be serious, preferring to enjoy his buzz and the crackling fire.

The fire snapped. Doc poked it with a long stick and settled back. "You should know, Brad, a lot of people and businesses up here are discouraged. The Delta is in dangerous condition and all the money and votes are against us."

The topic was a downer, but Brad felt he had to engage. "Yeah, I've learned a lot lately about water issues in this state and especially the threats to the Delta. I'm afraid to admit that my city receives Delta water through the State Water Project. Don't lynch me."

The other men nodded without taking their eyes off fire watch. Doc threw the remnants from his cup on the fire. It hissed and shot up sparks. "No need to apologize, Brad, most everyone in this state gets something out of the Delta, whether they know it or not."

Doc motioned back to the building. "Some of these guys farm here. One guy sells marine insurance to clients with boats docked all over the Delta. Marty here was a cook at Al the Wops restaurant in Locke until he got laid off. Tourism and fishing employ thousands. But with so much power lined up to exploit the Delta to its ruin, we're worried for the next generation."

Another man Brad had not officially met added, "Yeah, it's no crime to use the water wisely. The crime is to waste it. That's the biggest difference between us and the Big Ag conglomerates who take the most from the Delta. We want the area preserved for future generations. Do you think the big shots with the corporations that own most of the land in the south valley care about a thirty-year horizon on their balance sheets? They want to take the water and run."

Brad was surprised to see Dillon following the discussion with interest rather than texting a friend or otherwise absorbed with his cell phone.

"Right. Look at how they fought fracking regulation," Doc added.

"What's that?" Dillon asked.

"That's where oil companies inject water and chemicals into their wells under high pressure to break up the shale and extract more oil," Doc said.

"What's wrong with that?" Dillon asked.

"It uses a lot of water, for one thing, Dillon," Doc responded. "About 100,000 gallons per well. There are thousands of oil wells in California and hundreds more being added every month. Nobody knows how much potable water is being used since it isn't metered."

Marty threw a handful of feathers into a bucket with authority. "It's not only the water waste from fracking. My uncle farms down by Bakersfield. With the cutbacks on state water deliveries through the aqueduct, he's pumping the hell out of the aquifer. He's worried about all the wastewater from fracking being dumped back into the ground. Nobody has a handle on what that's going to do to the aquifers."

"He should be worried," Doc said. "The state is giving the oil companies a pass. They're approving new injection wells like crazy. They got their hands slapped by the EPA for allowing the wastewater to be injected into a federally protected aquifer. But even the feds didn't stop the process immediately. They're giving the oil companies a few more years to get into compliance."

Tanner banged his right fist into his left palm. "Jerry Brown's backing of the oil companies was so out of sync with his support of solar, wind, and other renewable energy. I remember a quote from him pounding his chest about maximizing the state's resources, including drilling new oil wells. He said there will be screw-ups, indictments, and deaths. Then he said, 'But we're going to keep going. Nothing's going to stop us.' Pretty strange stance for a supposedly environmentally sensitive governor who's so worried about climate change."

"And remember," Doc added. "Brown fired the top two state officials in charge of regulating the gas and oil wells after the oil companies complained that their environmental reviews slowed new drilling permits. State officials now hardly even use the word 'fracking.' It has farmers and environmentalists so stirred up. They refer to it as 'well stimulation.' How's that for your government watching out for the public?"

"Geez, you guys are depressing," Brad said, forcing a smile. "The Delta's being destroyed so Big Ag can make billions planting the desert. And when they can't get enough water from the Delta, they pump the hell out of the aquifer without regulation. Meantime, Big Oil is dumping wastewater from fracking into the same aquifers. State politicians and bureaucrats know all about it and let it happen."

"You got it, Crat Man," Tanner said, clearing his sinuses and leaning over to spit into the fire.

The other men nodded their heads in semi-sober agreement as they stared at the fire.

Brad stole a peek at Dillon, who, surprisingly, still seemed immersed in the discussion. His boy's whiskered and set jaw suggested that Dillon was signing on with his new hunting buddies for a piece of this fight. And the way his son studied him, Brad felt pressured to enlist. The fire crackled in the still morning and shot a brand at his booted foot. He crushed it and raised his head to the assembly.

"I never considered it my responsibility to track these state issues," he admitted. "I've pretty much confined my sphere to the city I worked in. But it's special out here. It would be a horrible shame not to take care of it. I just don't know what I can do to help."

Dillon nodded somberly.

Doc Tompkins leaned over and tapped Brad's foot with a stick. "You have a *lot* to do with how you manage the piece of nature you're responsible for, including how you use the water that comes from this place. All we ask is that you be a responsible steward of the natural resources in your area. Will you do that much?"

Brad glanced around the group and saw everyone looking at him. Dillon seemed especially intent on his reply. "I will," Brad promised. It was not a throw-away, alcohol-induced line. Dillon's mien indicated that his son would not forget it. "This has been a terrific day. I want Dillon to have the same experience with his kids someday. I hate knowing that my generation is turning over such a troubled planet to the next one."

Brad examined his maturing son over his coffee cup and noticed a gaggle of geese on the levee behind him looking their way. Witnesses of his oath? He reflected on the circle of life but cut it short to stay in the present. The grilled sausages called to him, the warmth on his lower body countering the coolness against his face. He took it all in, aware only that something within him had shifted and life was different.

The clubhouse door slammed shut and a tall, stately looking man strode over to the fire. "I'm 85 and hoping to get one of those sausages before I die."

"Shit, you're going to outlive us all," Tanner responded. "Get in line you old fart. Jack Kelly, meet my brother-in-law Brad Jacks and his son, Dillon. Crat Man, you'll have plenty to talk about. Jack's on the Lodi City Council. Brad here is city manager of Santa Ynez, down by Santa Barbara."

"Santa Ynez!" the councilman exclaimed. "The home of Kay Nance?"

Brad was surprised to hear his councilwoman brought up so far from home. "That's the place," he replied. "How do you know Kay?"

"We're on the League's Environmental Quality Committee together," Jack explained. "She's something. Can't say I always agree with her politics, but she sure is one helluva lot of fun at a conference." Jack had said it slyly, implying spicy stories.

"I'll take your word for that, Jack," Brad said, hoping to end it at that. He decided to change the subject. "How's my friend,

Deni, settling in there?" he asked, referring to the newish city manager of Lodi. *Business acquaintance* would have been more apt. People working in professions like to feel connected to their colleagues. Besides, after a double-shot of Jameson, everyone was a friend.

"*I* think Deni's doing great," Councilman Kelly said, "but we have new people on the council and two of them want to fire her already. They were backed by the police and fire unions and we had tough negotiations last year. I heard they're even contacting her former cities looking for dirt on her."

Brad gasped. A sucker punch to the gut just when he was enjoying some rare time in the moment. The councilman continued talking about his city's politics, but Brad was back in another place nearly forty years ago. Surely, it was too long ago for anyone to go snooping around and find out what happened. And, after all, he was just a no-name budget analyst at the time, his first job in city government after graduate school. He was not a visible official like poor Deni from Lodi. There had been no headlines about him. And Marie's name and exact location of the attack had been left out of the papers.

Shortly after the attack, Marie and Brad moved from the East Bay region of San Francisco Bay Area and severed ties to that region. The couple made a fresh start soon afterwards when Brad got a staff analyst job with a medium-sized city in Minnesota. Logic told him nobody was looking for his skeleton today and, even if they went back over his last few jobs, there was nothing incriminating to find. But fear trumped logic. The peaceful mood of the day was hopelessly gone as Brad sunk deeper into the horror of that night and his panic about what would happen if someone ever found out.

CHAPTER 13

The Jacks family spent Saturday morning kicking back at Marie's family ranch. Tanner took Dillon out to the barn to show him how to weld a metal floor panel into the Cobra Mustang he was restoring. Brad spent most of the day lazing on the couch with football on in the background while doing Internet research on the St. Francis Dam in anticipation of visiting again with Lilly who was out of the hospital already.

They left for home following breakfast on Sunday. Dillon drove the first two hours to Harris Ranch, a popular restaurant off Interstate 5. He had a little swagger in his step following the duck hunt and welding experiences. His confidence behind the wheel had grown.

With Marie and Dillon as his captive audience, Brad killed time lecturing them with what he had learned about the circumstances leading to the dam disaster. San Francisco blossomed into a cosmopolitan city after the Gold Rush as Los Angeles languished as a small, dusty pueblo of 10,000. Fred Eaton, owner of the small private water company and his cronies, who were jealous of San Francisco's preeminence on the West Coast, longed for the growth that would put LA on the map. The biggest obstacle was LA's semi-arid climate and being surrounded by the Pacific Ocean and deserts. They needed cheap water for LA to fulfill its destiny. Eaton had a plan.

Eaton knew of the abundant water resources in the Owens Valley on the east side of the mighty Sierra Nevada mountain range northeast of LA. He speculated that it could be transported over two hundred miles to LA by gravity in enough abundance to turn the arid valleys into a metropolis. He recruited a syndicate of wealthy, influential Los Angelinos who fronted the money to kick off the plan. Eaton left the water company to become mayor of LA and pushed the idea of the city buying his water company mainly to raise the money from taxpayers to buy and transport the Owens River water south. He also ensured that his protégé, William Mulholland, became the head of the new city water department to carry out his plan.

"Watch your speed," Marie warned her son.

Brad continued his lecture. Using dummy corporations, bribery, political pressure, and subterfuges that would make a veteran con man blush, the syndicate secretly bought options to all the water rights in Owens Valley they needed. That done, they bought thousands of nearly worthless acres in the San Fernando Valley that would become valuable with Owens Valley water.

"Sounds like that movie *Chinatown* with Jack Nicholson," Marie said, interrupting Brad's monologue. "CHP on the right, Dillon."

Brad smiled at her observation. "Similar," he said. "The Hollywood version got some of the story right: how city officials colluded with the LA Times' and faked a drought, even dumped potable water in the ocean so the paper could run pictures of empty reservoirs, making it appear that the city water supply was in jeopardy. The scare tactics worked. They got the voters to approve a bond measure to address the drought although the money was really used to reimburse the syndicate for secretly optioning the water rights in Owens Valley. As planned, they went back to the voters later for a much larger bond to build the aqueduct. They argued it would be a waste of the taxpayers' money from the first bond measure to not bring down the water they bought."

He paused recalling something. "Hey, that's like how the State Water Project was sold to the voters in the '60s."

"Hard to imagine they could get away with all that conniving," Marie said. "I realize that syndicate had a lot of people with clout. But where were all the other city officials, reporters, and such who should have blown the whistle? Wasn't there anyone brave enough to stand up to the power? Not so close, Dillon."

An image of Planning Director Megan Cain came into Brad's mind. He shifted uncomfortably in his seat. He was getting a headache trying to keep the story sorted out while spying on his son's every move behind the wheel.

"I don't know how they got away with it. The way our City Hall leaks, if I even joked about doing something half as shady, I'd read it in the morning paper."

"Probably a good thing," Marie teased. "Why don't we visit Lilly on the way home and see if she feels up to telling us more about the dam disaster."

The single-story rehab center appropriately projected an aging but well-preserved image. After catching up on Lilly's condition, Marie brought out leftover pecan pie, plastic plates, and forks.

"You two have been so kind to Lee and me," Lilly said.

"We're lucky to have you as neighbors and friends," Brad said. "And that was before we learned Lilly had such an interesting life."

"Yes," Marie added. "And we want you to know how much we appreciated you telling us about the dam disaster. We know that wasn't easy for you to re-live."

"A horrible night," Lilly said, soberly. "My life changed forever, and so did my dad's." She sat up. "Oh dear, about that, Lee told me that when I was rambling in the hospital, I confused you about my father."

"Oh, right," Brad said. "Lee explained that you call your birth father who died in the flood 'father' and his brother who adopted you 'dad', right?"

"Yes," Lilly said pensively. "Dad actually worked for the Los Angeles Department of Water and Power and even worked on the dam."

"Wow! What did he do?" Marie asked.

"He was an engineer," Lilly replied. "He admitted to me that he helped design the St. Francis Dam." She paused. "Dad was so sorry for going along with it. He knew the design was wrong."

Lilly seemed to ponder the story. "Chief Mulholland hired my dad soon after the city took over the private water company at the turn of the century. He was right out of college with a degree in civil engineering from UC Berkeley and worked in Mulholland's office. He got promoted fast, and the Chief put him in charge of planning big construction projects."

"Your dad must have been bright," Marie observed.

"Yes, but he said the Chief resented the college men. The Chief had all this experience and an encyclopedic knowledge of the entire water system going back to when he started as a ditch tender. But he didn't have any formal engineering education himself and didn't tolerate much questioning from his college boys."

"So, your dad never questioned Mulholland about the dam design?" Brad asked.

"Oh, he did—on little things. But after the Chief twice ordered the dam raised without also thickening the base, dad complained to his co-workers how unsafe that was. The Chief found out and hit the roof. The Chief told dad to do what he was told or get out."

"I can't tell you how many times I've wanted to say something like that to my staff," Brad said.

"Oh, I doubt that Bradley," Lilly said, pausing for a sip of water. She stared at the water in the glass and cocked her head. "Dad said that the rock in the canyon walls was unfit for a dam. He said that during a hearing following the disaster, an investigator dropped a piece of the rock from the canyon into a glass of water and it dissolved."

"You know, Lilly," Brad prompted, "I'm amazed at what they pulled off with that Owens project, especially keeping it secret and getting the voters to approve two bond issues under false pretenses. You could never get away with such a scheme today." As soon as he said it, his mind drifted back to the Delta and the state's pushing ahead with the ill-conceived tunnels. His heart sank. *Of course, they can.*

"Disgusting, if you asked my dad." Lilly responded. "I bet he wanted to quit the whole time, but my aunt talked him out of it. It paid well and they liked attending events with the bigwigs of Southern California. He stayed on but wasn't happy."

"Your dad was in a tough spot," Brad said. "It must have been an ethical tug-of-war for him." His stomach tightened.

"To his credit, Chief Mulholland took the blame for the dam break," Lilly said, "but dad admitted to me that he and some of his workmates knew they shared in it. They went along with it knowing it was unsafe. It haunted him all his life. I suspect he stayed on mainly for my benefit. Times were tough and dad wanted to make sure I was taken care of. I often wondered if staying on the job, despite being miserable, was some sort of self-punishment for his role in the dam failure."

"My goodness!" Marie exclaimed. "I'm sure nobody did anything wrong on purpose. Maybe they just didn't know as much."

"That was pretty much the general opinion at the time," Lilly agreed. "The Chief was viewed as a miracle worker who did great things for Los Angeles. Sure, his image was destroyed by the dam disaster, and he never did another project, but people forgave and even pitied him. But dad never forgave himself for going along rather than fighting the powerful interests pushing the project ahead.

"When I was packing for college, he sat me down and told me all about the dam disaster and his personal failings. I'll never forget his words. He said, 'The true measure of personal integrity is whether you'll do the right thing even if nobody is watching - even if nobody will know your sacrifice to do it. I failed that test, Lil.'"

Lilly dabbed her eyes with her tissue. "Dad went to his grave with the guilt from not measuring up to his values and, of course, from the disastrous aftermath. He was very hard on himself."

Marie smiled at Brad. "I know somebody who's too hard on himself, too, Lilly."

Lilly paused and looked directly at Brad. "Dad was never able to forgive himself and move on. I'm sure that in your position, Bradley, you are faced with difficult ethical decisions all the time. I hope that despite whatever regrets you have you'll be gentler with yourself. We all fall short sometimes."

Brad met Marie's soft eyes.

"After a month or so in college," Lilly resumed, "I got a call at the dorms that dad committed suicide."

"Oh!" Brad and Marie gasped in unison. Lee patted Lilly's hand.

"How awful," Marie said sadly.

"I was shocked at the time, but I should have expected it," Lilly said. "They discovered him in a bathtub full of water. He cut his wrists with a razor blade and laid back to die."

"He must have carried a lot of pain," Brad said, squeezing down another stomach cramp.

"I'm sure he did," Lilly continued. "Dad teared up when he talked about the bodies and destruction he saw when he drove the Chief to the dam the morning of the disaster."

"What did the locals do when they saw people from LA there?" Marie asked.

"Dad said there were signs that said, 'Kill Mulholland.' But no violence. Unlike how things are today, Mulholland stepped up and took all the blame, and the City of Los Angeles was credited, even by the victims, for how quickly they came to the aid of the people and paid restitution."

"There's speculation about their true motives," Lee scoffed. "The federal government was planning the Boulder Dam on the Colorado River at the time to bring Southern California even more water for growth. But Boulder had a similar design as the St. Francis dam. The last thing LA wanted was a lot of publicity about that design failing. So they paid restitution fast and the whole story sort of died away. Not many people know about it anymore."

"That's for sure." Brad said. "I'm so sorry, Lilly, about everything you had to deal with in your life. I can't imagine."

"Yes. As terrible as the flood was, the hardest part for me was seeing the pain dad lived with until he couldn't anymore. You see, it wasn't just the design shortcuts that tormented him," Lilly continued. "Southern California Edison was the main competitor to the Department of Water and Power but people at the working level were friendly. I learned that dad used his contacts to help my father get the job that put us all at the Kemp tent camp."

"Geez!" Brad gasped.

"I've seen a lot of misery in my life. But one of my most painful memories is a night I came home from a high school dance. Dad was sitting in his chair in the dark. A half-empty bottle of rye stood next to him. He had been crying." Her words came slowly. "He told me that in the days before the dam broke, he and other department employees and residents downstream worried about leaks coming out of the dam face. The day before it burst, the Chief himself had visited the dam and announced that everything was fine. Father called dad later that day asking if they were in danger. Dad could barely get out the last words he said to my father: 'Don't worry, Walt, the Chief won't allow the damn dam to fail.'"

Brad's smile at the play on words dissolved into a frown as he considered the consequences of abused power. It was then as it is now. He was depressed the rest of the day.

CHAPTER 14

Councilwoman Kay Nance was at Jane's desk when he arrived Monday morning.

"Hi, Brad," Kay said. "How was your family reunion?"

"Glorious," he smirked. "We had a yummy Tofurky roast in your honor." He stuck his index finger into his mouth in a gagging gesture. "What brings you in this morning?"

"Dropping off expenses for my League trip," she said.

Brad smiled, recalling the duck hunting trip when Councilman Jack Kelly commented about how much fun Kay was at a conference. He opted not to bring the topic up.

"How was your trip north?" Kay asked.

"Interesting. I learned a lot about the Delta problems. I can see where you're coming from. Oh, I wanted to ask if you knew anything about those big billboards all along I-5 that say things like, 'Congress Created Dust Bowl?' I'm suspicious. Got a minute?"

She nodded and he led her into his office, plopped his paperwork on the desk, and joined her at the coffee table.

Kay shrugged. "Those signs are a mystery. I have a friend on the board for a nonprofit public interest group that protects the Delta. They've been fighting Astroturf groups."

"Astroturf?" he asked.

"It means a group that masquerades as a grassroots organization, but isn't," she explained. "Fake grass, get it?"

"Clever."

"My friend says these groups are shills for the big water contractors. Their names and websites suggest they're all about protecting the Delta, but they're fully funded to promote big water. Very devious. Some of the billboards at the southerly end of the valley were traced to a big public relations firm in Los Angeles. Not exactly made in family barns."

Brad shook his head. "It's clever how they've framed the issue as a choice between some lowly endangered species like the Delta smelt versus food and jobs for people. I get it that the smelt may not have a lot of commercial value, but my daughter says they're the canary in the coal mine—an indicator species showing us by their near-extinction that the water quality in the Delta is failing."

"Geez, Brad, maybe there's hope for you. You're right. Throw in a shot at Congress that has an all-time low approval rating of around fifteen percent," Kay added, "and the public eats the deception up."

"Despite all their conniving," Brad countered, "the water contractors aren't getting their way on everything. Consider the cutbacks to state agricultural water deliveries."

"Sure," Kay said with a wave of her hand. "We're in a serious drought and government deliveries have been cut. You'd think the growers would fallow their land for the time being. But you couldn't miss the thousands of acres being planted in high-value, permanent crops like nuts, citrus, and grapes."

"Yeah, I guess I never paid attention to all that new planting. I remember mostly dodging tumbleweeds along I-5. Now there are trees and vines as far as you can see. At least that worthless land is generating jobs and tax base."

Kay snickered. "You'd be surprised. Remember, in the southern part of the valley, we're mostly talking about huge corporations with thousands of acres, not small family farms. Everything is more mechanized. There's not as much farm labor as you'd get with smaller farms."

"What about the increased value of all that new production?" he argued. He relished playing the independent thinker with Kay.

"Oh, the land value *has* increased," the councilwoman countered. "But did you know the total value of all the farm production and food processing in the entire state only amounts to between one and two percent of California's gross state product?"

"What?" he exclaimed skeptically.

"Don't look at me with that tone of voice," she said, suddenly smiling. "Isn't it weird how we end up saying the same stupid things our parents said to us? Anyway, check it out yourself, Brad. The vast majority of the water we spent billions of dollars to capture and hundreds of millions to move around the state every year mostly benefits a small number of the largest corporations in the world. Yet it contributes only a small percentage of the state's economy."

"People have to eat, too. It's not only money."

"Don't fall victim to that 'jobs and food' spin, Brad. With all the new almond orchards planted in the Central Valley, California now has over one million acres producing eighty percent of the world's supply. California is known around the world for its excellent wines. Almond value is now two-and-a-half times greater. And we aren't even eating them here. Seventy percent is exported, mostly to China."

"We need more exports to help our trade balance," Brad persisted, still hoping to one-up his boss.

"Yes, but like everything else, it's about balance. The California almond crop uses over a trillion gallons of water a year, and walnuts are even thirstier."

"I can't relate to that," he admitted.

"Try this: it takes one gallon of water to grow one almond and nearly five gallons for one walnut. You could flush your toilet five times with the water from a single walnut."

"Yeah, but I'd have to squeeze it really hard!"

She rolled her eyes. "Very funny. My point is that there's all this emphasis on conserving water in the urban areas while eighty percent of the water used by humans in California goes to agriculture. It's four times the urban use. And, like I said, all that ag water contributes less than two percent of the gross state product. Consider that, Brad."

He was.

Kay continued. "We've lost so much big industry in California. We have thousands of acres of abandoned industrial parks in the urban core that could be putting that water to much better use in terms of jobs, tax base, and community redevelopment."

"Not sure about that," he replied. "There are a ton of regulatory and global economic factors behind the decline of heavy industry. I don't think water supply is high on the list."

"Maybe with heavy industry," she conceded. "But we both know that many of our cities and counties have had to pass up opportunities to recruit wet industry. We are missing out on high-paying jobs and a huge tax base so that a handful of big multi-national ag corporations can sell almonds to China. Almonds alone require twenty percent more water than all the indoor home uses across the state. You can't have a meaningful discussion about managing our water resources and leave out ag."

Kay was on a roll now. She pointed out that per capita urban water use has dropped in the last twenty years, thanks to public education promoting conservation and pricing mechanisms. But the water savings have been used to promote more suburban sprawl, like Green Valley Village, under the banner of economic development. She concluded saying: "Whether you're talking about farming in the deserts of the Central Valley, the future of the Delta, or what we do right here in Santa Ynez, too much power tilts toward money and not to public steward-ship."

Her comment brought him back to the duck hunt and his commitment to the men around the fire to take better care of his city's natural resources. Had that pledge already faded like so many others in his life? What the hell was he supposed to do? He changed the subject. "Kay, can I speak to you as a friend?"

"Yes but be gentle. I'm fragile, you know," she joked.

He chuckled and leaned closer in his chair. "Thanks to you and others I've talked to lately I have a better understanding of the critical water issues we face in this state. But there's also lots of complexity, too. And while you and I may not always be on the same page politically, I like and respect you."

"The feeling is mutual, Brad," the councilwoman responded with a mock tipping of the hat. "Get to the point. I can handle it."

He swallowed hard. "Okay. It's not my role to give you political advice. So, as a friend, let me share my observations from forty years of helping elected officials come to consensus on public policies."

She perked up and folded her hands in her lap like an obe-dient schoolgirl. "Please do."

"It's basic negotiation strategy. If people consider you immovable on an issue, they'll marginalize you. They'll dismiss your points of view and not put any effort into trying to work a compromise with you. You give up a lot of power by taking yourself out of the negotiation process. And most public policy issues are just that—a negotiation among people with com-peting values and interests."

"So, this about you wanting me to play nice with the rest of the council on Green Valley?"

Brad paused, searching for the right words. "Like I said, I'm not trying to give you political advice. Maybe you're satisfied being the tough dissenter rather than winning a position."

Kay laughed. "Been there. Done that."

"I'd ask you to consider whether that role is more important to you than what you might want to accomplish on the council. None of you can get anything done without getting majority approval. And to get majority support, you need to compromise sometimes. That draws people to you and makes them more willing to compromise *their* interests to stay connected to you. If you aren't willing to negotiate on anything, your colleagues have no incentive to give you anything *you* want. It will always be win/lose."

Kay Nance was uncharacteristically quiet. He pressed ahead. "One of my mentors used to quote a Persian proverb, 'The dogs may bark, but the caravan moves on.'"

"Oh, I'm a barking dog, now?" she teased.

Brad was in serious mode. "I'll let you mull that in the context of what you want to accomplish on the council. Remember, the barking dogs don't stop the caravan. You have to be in the tent, engaging with the chieftains, to influence where the caravan goes."

"So, do you have some ideas for me on where to compromise with Green Valley?" she asked.

"No, that's for you to decide," he replied. "You're smart. I'm giving you a perspective to consider. Maybe you don't want to do anything other than let everyone know you're going to fight Green Valley to the bitter end. Or maybe you'll come up with some proposals for changing the plan that will make it more palatable than what it might end up being if you are on the losing end of the vote. Food for thought?"

She gathered her stack of travel receipts. "Diplomatically put, Brad," she said, rising from her chair. "I appreciate the friendly advice and the spirit behind it."

Brad stayed seated as Kay walked to the counter to talk to Jane about her receipts. He waited for the outer office door to clank and closed his office door, giving Jane a wink. She nodded her understanding.

He turned his high, black leather chair around, leaned back, and put his feet up on the wood-veneered credenza that matched his desk. He stared at the large, framed photograph of Mount Shasta hanging on the wall over the credenza, a gift from his wife years ago during his short-lived meditation phase. One of his favorites at the time was a mountain meditation on tape cassette. The speaker had him relax and imagine himself as a huge mountain constantly undergoing forces it could not control: high winds, rain storms, and snow. The mountain stood through the ages accepting whatever came along, at peace majestically alone above the high deserts of upper Northern California.

Connecting with Mt. Shasta was like meeting with an old friend. Brad shut his eyes to concentrate on his body sensations and identified shallow breath, constricted chest, and taut shoulders, hands, and arms. The familiar fight-or-flight response to danger. The Green Valley Village project popped into his mind. He sat with it for a time until it morphed into calmness and a touch of exhilaration. Maybe his candid conversation with Kay would lead to a softer landing for Green Valley thereby lessening his danger.

Following ten minutes or so of quiet focusing, Brad's restlessness took over. He got up, stretched, and opened the door. "Good to go now," he told Jane.

"You don't need me to bring you three envelopes, do you?" she scoffed.

An old joke. The departing city manager leaves three envelopes behind in the desk drawer for his successor with notes containing advice if things go poorly with the city council. The first envelope said, "Blame your predecessor." At the next bump in the road, the second envelope suggested "Reorganize." The third crisis brought this message, "Prepare three envelopes."

"No, not ready for that. Yet." He turned to go back in the office and added, "I've got a feeling everything's going to be all right."

Brad answered the phone in the darkness on the third ring, hoping it did not wake Marie. "Hello," he croaked.

"It's Elaine, Brad. Sorry to bother you so late. Did I wake you?"

His heart raced. There were only a few reasons Police Chief Elaine McLaughlin would call this late. All of them bad.

"It's okay, but Marie is asleep, so I have to be quiet."

"Not anymore," his wife said with a sigh as she turned on her side to face him and scrunched her pillow.

"Who died, Elaine?"

"Nothing that bad, but I thought you ought to know that we seem to have a cat burglar operating and that the mayor was the fourth victim last night."

"Oh, shit." He sat up and shook his head at Marie's questioning look.

"Doesn't look like the perp got much. A little jewelry. Mayor Murray and his wife got home late from a party and must have spooked the guy. The mayor saw the guy through a side window as he was running from the back. When he got to the front door, the perp was hauling ass a half block away. The mayor said he was going to talk to you in the morning about increasing patrol. But frankly I doubt extra patrol is the answer with this guy. He's too smart. We probably haven't seen the end of this guy. He's pretty crafty and bold. We're going to get the word out tomorrow to take precautions."

The chief's words took Brad's breath away. He covered the receiver with his palm, took a deep breath, and barely eked out: "Okay. Thanks for the heads- up, Elaine," before hanging up.

Brad briefed Marie on the incident trying to sound calm. But the thought of a cat burglar again threatening their lives overwhelmed him. He went downstairs to watch TV.

Marie woke up around 3 a.m., surprised that Brad was not beside her. She walked to the stair landing. It looked like every light in the house was on downstairs but there was no TV or other noise coming from below. She walked cautiously down the stairs and around the corner of the kitchen, her heart pounding, and noticed the bourbon bottle on the counter. She walked a few more steps and saw Brad in his recliner. TV off. An empty glass on his side table. Eyes open. Sitting very still.

Marie was instantly alarmed and rushed to him. Brad snapped to alertness and pivoted in the chair towards the threat, his fists raised. She gasped. Brad shook his head and lowered his arms. Marie bent over, holding his head next to hers as she had done on other occasions since that horrifying night.

"You're thinking about that night, aren't you?" Marie prompted.

He nodded, trembling.

"It's okay, Hon," she said softly. "It's just that PTSD. I sure wished you had joined me in those therapy sessions afterwards.

They were painful at first but really help me cope with what happened."

With Marie coaching Brad to stay with the fear rather than trying to overpower it, they stayed up talking about the circumstances surrounding Marie's rape soon after they got married. Their exchange was cathartic with each of them speaking from the heart about what happened then and how it still affected them today. Brad was even able to gingerly admit that it made him feel worse anytime he knew he had let her down, on anything, and she acted like a martyr. They went to bed feeling a renewed bond. Brad could not have anticipated how the strength of that bond would be tested in the coming days.

CHAPTER 15

Three months later, Thursday, late April

"Good morning, Brad." Fire Chief Barry Powell was sitting in Brad's office waiting for him. "I have good news and bad news."

"I'll take two helpings of the good."

The fire chief chuckled. "Remember that fire behind Nettlers' rental yard a few months ago?"

"Sure. You and Hubie nearly came to blows. What's good about it?"

"We have a confession from the arsonist."

"Arson? I thought it was a tossed cigarette from a car."

"That's usually the cause all right. But the sheriff's investigator found traces of an accelerant, probably lighter fluid, on some of the fence boards that burned. He investigated and picked up some decent images off the yard's security cameras. Based on the size and clothing he suspected it might be a kid. It hasn't been a big priority because nobody got hurt and the damage was small. But he's been showing the photos around the local high schools and middle schools."

"I saw my son at breakfast so he's off the list. Anyone I know?"

"That's the bad news. Hank Nettler's teenage daughter."

"Jessie? I know her!"

"Close. Jenny," the chief said. "You've met her?"

"Yeah, Jenny. I met her when I presented at high school a few months ago. She confessed? To torching her dad's business? How'd you nail her?" Brad leaned in eagerly. It was exciting to be in the inner circle of an investigation.

The chief smiled. "Forgive the pun but I guess you'd say we smoked her out. The detective started showing up at lunch time and after school flashing the photos around. He let it drop that we had forensic evidence coming back from the state lab and we were zeroing in on the suspect. Jenny's teacher, a Mr. Heldt, called last evening to say that Jenny wanted to turn herself in."

Brad shook his head. "She was such a bright girl. Why'd she do it?"

"Jenny said the night before the arson she confronted her father about the demeaning way her father and grandfather treat women, especially strong-willed women like her mother and her. He slapped her and she wanted to show him that she wasn't powerless. She only intended to burn his fence."

"Geez. I feel sorry for her. She must have been desperate."

"Oh, as a matter of fact," the chief said, "your name came up in her interview. Jenny said you didn't talk down to her in class and even invited her to intern with you after she gave you a bad time. You were the paragon she measured her father against."

"Oh great! As if I needed another reason for the Nettlers to hate me."

"I'm afraid it gets worse," Chief Powell warned. "Hank's all jacked up that we arrested his daughter instead of allowing him to just quietly pay restitution and put her on a diversion contract with counseling to avoid an arrest record. I told him it's the DA's call now, but he's mad as hell. I didn't tell him, but my guess is the DA will want to throw everything at her because arson's a serious crime and the Nettlers are so high profile. Hank is a wounded animal. Better watch your back, Brad."

Upon returning from the family reunion, Brad mediated a meeting between his public works and planning directors to try to resolve the objections Megan Cain raised about Dee Sharma's analysis of the Green Valley traffic and water impacts. He felt like a boxing referee trying to keep his department heads' blows above the belt. After an hour-and-a-half of counter-punching and mind-numbing forays into the minutiae of multiple thick reports, Brad called the fight and awarded a split decision. He gave round one on traffic to Dee but concluded that Megan had raised some legitimate arguments that Dee might be understating the project's water demand and possibly over-stating the city's reliable supply.

In desperation, Brad ordered them to hire a neutral engineering firm, Payton/Carlisle, for a peer review of the other water analyses. His friend and former colleague, Quinn O'Rourke, had promised a quick turnaround. Brad trusted him to provide effective cover fire in the battle to come.

Now, two weeks later, he was eager for the lunch meeting today with O'Rourke to get his friend's take on the Green Valley water issues. Finally getting off the phone with an angry resident, he raced to Martellaro's, his favorite Italian restaurant, jumped out of the car and fast-walked to the front door, his customary five-minutes late. Quinn O'Rourke stood in the lobby studying the framed celebrity-autographed photographs on the wall.

"Sorry I'm late," Brad panted, as they shook hands.

"Relax, buddy. You're going to blow a gasket. It's only me, remember? Besides, I was enjoying all these photos."

WHEN THE DAM BREAKS

"Yeah, judging by the clothes and cars, many of the visitors had probably been up to Rancho Del Cielo in the Ronald Reagan era."

"What about her?" O'Rourke said, pointing at the framed picture of Bo Derek sitting behind a plate of pasta. She had autographed it for the owners: *Lin & Ricky, your marinara sauce is a perfect 10!*

"What a babe!" the consultant said.

"She lives outside of town," Brad said matter-of-factly. "Has a horse ranch over there. We see her all the time. Lovely lady." Patting his stomach, he added, "Aged a whole lot better than some of us, huh Quinn?"

O'Rourke was a little older than Brad, nearly bald, and still had his prodigious gut, despite his constant experimenting with fad diets. Weight control had been a regular topic of their conversations over the years. They had launched their careers at about the same time and even competed against each other once for a city manager job that O'Rourke got and was fired from within a year. They were comrades in arms.

Brad greeted people at several tables on the way back to "his" table that his favorite waitress, Twyla, saved for him. He had a special relationship with her that started with exchanging wisecracks and soon elevated to Twyla dropping a lemon meringue pie on Brad's head for his fiftieth birthday, all arranged by his assistant, Jane.

Brad and Quinn slid into the red vinyl booth. Brad winked at Twyla. "All right, give him the show then get out of here."

Twyla opted for her flight attendant shtick for the daily specials. "In the event of a sudden drop in the booth's pressure, overhead masks will drop," she said, mimicking the motion of falling oxygen masks. "Put the tube into your mouth and suck down the special Chianti at five dollars a glass until you don't care anymore."

O'Rourke laughed.

With the specials creatively presented and drink orders placed, Twyla distributed the menus and left the lunch companions to themselves. They caught up on each other's lives, compared notes on what was happening with other city manager friends, and reminisced about the old days. Twyla was back with the drinks and took their lunch orders. They chatted a while over their drinks and Martellaro's special fried bread. The aroma of garlic emanating from the hot bread was irresistible, regardless of the calorie count.

Twyla brought their heaping platters, staying in character. "Now, so that we can make an on-time start, please check that your belts are low and snug around your hips." She hefted the plates and switched to the *Jaws* scene, "And you're gonna need a bigger belt!"

O'Rourke clapped and Brad raised his glass to toast Twyla's performance.

When she exited, stage left, Brad kicked off the purpose of the meeting. "So, what did you come up with on the water issues?"

"Patience, Brad. First, you know what they say about the precision of public policymaking: 'you measure it with a micrometer, mark it with chalk, and cut it with an axe?'"

"Hah, love that one," Brad said.

"Listen, I work for an engineering company now. We take some basic concepts and assumptions, create some vocabulary around them, zero in on some data factors, run everything through computer models, and publish thick reports with lots of tables and numbers. It all seems empirical. But—" the consultant glanced conspiratorially over his shoulder, "the reality is that our conclusions are just estimates based on assumptions. There isn't mathematical precision to a lot of it."

"I won't report you for blabbing that."

"I'm giving it to you straight, Brad. All I'm saying is that a lot of this isn't Newton's Law. We're working with probabilities here, not absolutes. Either SoCal or your Kay Nance could fairly argue the assumptions and reach different conclusions."

Brad appreciated his friend's caveat. He doubted there would be comparable candor from another firm. And he was comforted by noting that his friend was plugged into the political context of the study.

"I understand. What's your firm's best guess on the water?"

"It's a mixed bag."

The consultant spent twenty minutes summarizing their conclusions on the Green Valley water demand and the city's water supply. He noted that some assumptions supported the existing engineering studies prepared by public works staff and SoCal's consultant, Western Engineering, while a couple sided more with Megan's opinions.

"You're killing me, Quinn," Brad said anxiously. "Do we have enough water for Green Valley or not?"

"Yes," Quinn O'Rourke said, digging at something in his teeth with his tongue. "Some could argue it's too tight. The way everything shakes out, we came up with a twelve percent reserve after existing uses plus some extra for the undeveloped land in the General Plan and Green Valley added. That's not much. Your city, like most other water suppliers in this state, is going to want to keep scrounging for more supply and supporting any efforts to increase the reliability of the existing supplies so you don't run so close to the edge. But, yes, on paper, you have enough for Green Valley, especially in the likelihood that, if it hits the fan, you could adopt harsher water conservation measures to stretch."

"Perfect," Brad said. "We can show enough water if the council majority wants to. If they don't, we could argue that it leaves us too thin. Perfect."

"Yeah," O'Rourke said, laughing. "And you and public works don't have to take the heat for killing off the project by not having plenty of reserves already stashed for it."

"True, true," Brad agreed. "The general public doesn't understand how difficult it is to get more water these days. Sounds like we'll be lucky to hang on to the supplies we already have. The Delta is a mess and that could reduce future state water deliveries."

"Use what you have wisely, my friend," the consultant advised. "We'll never see more water at those prices again. Desalination is getting more feasible, but it's twice the cost of state water and has its own environmental impacts. At the end of the day, nothing beats getting more out of what you already have."

"That's what Megan and my councilwoman keep saying."

O'Rourke smiled. "Megan is sharp. And a bulldog. I'll bet she's a pain in the ass to you. And your Kay sounds like memoir material."

Brad laughed. "But I have to say, I get a kick out of them both. I'm even beginning to think they're right about a lot of their views, especially on water. I love the passion and dedication Megan brings to the job. I wish I still had more of that myself. Been worn down, I suppose."

"Dedication, good. Passion bad, Kemosabe," O'Rourke warned in Tonto dialect.

"I hear you," Brad responded. "But Megan is more like the old-time city managers, willing to call it like they see it. That's changed. Too many times, city staff hires consultants, especially legal advisors, to do the heavy lifting if something is controversial. Not Megan."

"Yeah, well, be careful that she knows nobody anointed her to be Grand Protector of Santa Ynez. She needs to be reminded that she works for you and you work for the council. If she responds too much to her own sense of what's right, it'll be both of your necks in the noose."

"10-4," Brad said, tossing down his napkin. "I don't know, Quinn. How the hell is this state going to survive with the projected growth coming? All the areas of reform are obvious, but they aren't getting through the politics. Unfortunately, it reminds me of a former mayor's favorite saying, 'When all is said and done, more is said than done.'"

O'Rourke smiled. "Maybe Brad Jacks will be the face of the sustainable development movement like Howard Jarvis was for property tax limitation."

Brad waved him off. "The last guy who bucked the status quo like that got crucified. That's not in my financial plan. I have tuition payments to make."

Brad glanced across the room. "Okay, that's enough 'ain't it awful' for now. Let's get out of here. Twyla is dying to do her goodbye scene from *Romeo and Juliet* for you. Act surprised. Thanks for getting the water study done so quickly, Quinn. I got lunch."

O'Rourke tossed his napkin on the table. "Thanks. Let me leave you this as a tip: you're obviously all wound up about Green Valley, Brad. Realize that from the minute SoCal decided to option Nettlers' property, things were set in motion that you can't control. Santa Ynez won't be the same and neither will your job. Remember your oath of office and trust your experience and instincts."

Brad nodded agreement. "Thanks, Quinn. One more question?"

"Sure."

"Are you hiring?"

CHAPTER 16

Brad strode back through the outer office door around 1:30 p.m.

"Don't you look chipper," Jane observed. "I hope this doesn't ruin it for you." She handed him several phone messages.

He flipped through them. "Okay, I've got to prepare for the meeting with that hotel developer, but mom always said, 'Eat your lima beans if you want dessert.' So, I'll return these first. Would you see if Megan can come over for a couple minutes to talk about the Payton/Carlisle report before my fun meeting?"

Brad stepped into his office, set his briefcase on the credenza, and looked at the pink messages in his hand. The first was from an apparently nearly hysterical, angry mother demanding a stop sign to slow down traffic and a crosswalk at the corner of her street.

He braced himself, picked up the phone, and called the lady. The conversation followed a predictable pattern. Brad patiently explained the process the city must go through to install traffic control devices.

The woman became angrier. "Does somebody have to die before you'll put up the stop sign?" she cried.

Brad tried to console her and made another attempt to reason with her. "I know this'll sound strange," Brad warned, "but accident studies show that if motorists who, by the way, are mostly your own neighbors, believe a stop sign doesn't belong there, they're likely to run it or increase their speed in between the stop signs to make up the lost time from stopping too much. Worse, many will make a 'Hollywood stop,' rolling through the stop sign, rather than coming to a complete stop. This is especially dangerous for pedestrians. Studies also show crosswalks are the most dangerous places for pedestrians."

"Huh?" the woman said questioningly.

"Watch for yourself how people behave in a crosswalk. They may be chatting with each other or on their cell phones. Most aren't paying attention to the traffic at all. It's as if they think they've entered some zone of invulnerability once inside the lines of the crosswalk. Those lines won't hold back a five-thousand-pound vehicle driven by a motorist who doesn't expect a stop sign in that spot, or resents it being there, and exercises a bit of civil disobedience rolling right through it."

"That's interesting," she said.

His logic had hit home. The line remained quiet as he waited for her to process his points.

"So," she said, "do I have to get the whole neighborhood to petition the city council to get that stop sign?"

He gave up and promised to refer her request to public works for further review without any guarantees.

The second complaint involved a property owner's objection to the building permit fee quote he received from planning staff for his granny flat addition.

"Sir, it's a council policy that the cost of processing a development application, a special benefit, should be paid by the applicant, not the taxpayers at large through their general tax contributions."

"These costs are crazy. California is killing business. I'm building a spec house in Texas with my brother. The total permit fee was two hundred dollars for the city to inspect the connection of the driveway to the public street. That's it. No other fees. No building inspections. It's up to the contractor and architects to stand behind their work. They don't have big government watching over them and reaching into their pockets."

Brad tried to explain the rigor associated with setting development fees and their importance in funding public improvements ever since voter-approved tax limitations. The man obviously could not care less. Brad walked him through the process for appealing directly to the council.

Megan Cain crossed the threshold of his office, a stack of papers in her arms. He sighed and got up from his desk to join her at the coffee table. She plopped down the Payton/Carlisle report on the table like it was a slab of rotting meat. It fell open to the first page of the Executive Summary. The page was so chicken-scratched in red ink it looked like she had overlaid complex football blocking schemes.

Brad let out another involuntary sigh. "Your arguments were carefully considered," he offered as a preemptive strike. "Quinn O'Rourke told me that these are judgment calls and even if they didn't side with you on all the points it doesn't mean you were wrong."

He waited for a moment to see if her expression softened. It didn't. "Megan, with peer review, the tie goes to the runner. Payton/Carlisle agreed with you in some areas."

He paused again. Still nothing.

"I appreciate your thoroughness in going through the issues since water supply is such a pivotal issue with the Green Valley project."

Megan sat back in the chair and adopted a more relaxed posture. "I can tell you're fine with your friend's report. I say Green Valley's demand won't leave us with enough water in a drought. It's my duty to make sure that a development project will mitigate its impacts and be a net benefit to the community. I'm not convinced."

He folded his hands and smiled. "I appreciate that, Megan. Like I said, Quinn O'Rourke admitted this wasn't rocket surgery. Reasonable people could come to different conclusions."

Rather than accepting that as a face-saving out, Megan pounded away on the report findings. She talked louder and faster. She began to renew her attack on the public works director's ethics.

"Stop!" Brad shot his hand up like a traffic cop.

Megan recoiled with a jolt.

"I don't see anybody giving Scott or SoCal a pass on this thing, including Dee. Now, like I said, you can disagree with the findings on the facts and the pros and cons of Green Valley. That's okay. But you're out of line to attack peoples' motives because they don't agree with you. Knock that shit off!"

Megan Cain tried to respond, but he cut her off again. "Look," he said tiredly, "what do you want from me? This project is controversial. I'm getting pressure from all sides and doing the best I can to be fair. That's why I ordered the peer review. I trust Payton/Carlisle and never tried to influence their findings. Quinn would've resigned if I'd tried."

She stared at him, blinking rapidly.

Brad tensed, trying to keep his anger from running away with him. "And don't go carrying yourself as some sort of independent guardian of the public interest. You're not. You have some valuable input to offer to this process. I've listened to it and will continue to. But I'll make the call around here on the final staff positions, not you. Understood?"

She continued to stare at him.

"Understood?" he demanded.

Awkward moments passed in silence until she finally nodded slightly. He saw the hurt in his young professional and resisted the impulse to soften his demeanor. Quinn O'Rourke's advice to get control of her rang in his ears—for his own sake, if not for hers.

"Here's what I'd like you to do," he said in a businesslike, nonthreatening way. "I know you want to kick out the Initial Study soon. I'd like you to use the Western and Payton/Carlisle reports and Dee's input as the basis for the water supply section. I'm okay with including a short statement describing the difficulty of being too precise with some of these factors, particularly regarding the well and reservoir reliability. And I'm okay if you want to ask the commission to weigh in on whether the twelve percent supply reserve from the Payton report is sufficient buffer. That's fair, but I want you to have the Initial Study conclude that we have enough water for Green Valley."

Megan remained mute.

"When were you planning to circulate the IS?" he asked.

"It's pretty much ready to go," she said, sitting back again in her chair. "We were waiting for this report to finish up the water section. We'll get it to the planning commission tomorrow."

"Great," he said, pretending everything was hunky dory again. "Let me see the final draft before it goes out."

"Okay," she said flatly, gathering her papers and leaving quickly.

Brad sat by himself a moment then walked out to talk to his assistant Jane. She was talking quietly on the phone and ended the call abruptly as soon as he came through the door. Brad held his curiosity in check and merely asked her to keep after Megan in the morning so he could review the Initial Study first thing.

He spun on his heels, went back to his desk, and returned the call to the city's insurance claims adjustor. The elderly woman who had filed a claim regarding a slip-and-fall at the Senior Center now complained of back pain. Or, rather, her attorney, who would likely get forty percent of any settlement, claimed his client had back pain. Nearly impossible to prove or disprove. Brad thought of Lilly. Had she been the one to slip, she would not have even complained. He approved the adjustor's recommendation to defend the case and caught up with emails.

The meeting with the hotel developer had been exciting. A fifty-room, upscale, boutique hotel with Spanish Colonial architecture and plenty of amenities, including a full restaurant, would be a game-changer for Santa Ynez. The Transient Occupancy Tax on the room rentals, along with the jobs, were reasons enough to compete for it. Beyond that, landing a classy project like that would be a big boost to the city's image. A Realtor in the mayor's real estate office who'd picked up the scent that the developer was scouting Solvang down the road talked him into checking out Santa Ynez. Brad pulled out all the stops to entice the project. The developer was savvy enough to know what the city could and could not do to help. He was not leaving anything on the table.

"I'd really be pioneering with this project in Santa Ynez," the developer said. "What assurances can you give me that the Green Valley Village project will be approved? We need some other high-end projects like that to give us confidence in the city's momentum."

Message delivered. Brad joined the broker in describing the political support Green Valley had already garnered. The courtship with the hotel developer looked promising. Brad could nearly taste the tingling champagne bubbles hitting his tongue at the groundbreaking. He called the mayor afterward with a progress report on the hotel.

"Atta boy, Brad," Mayor Buddy said. "You're doing a great job for us. Nail down the hotel and show enough progress on Green Valley so I can get you that raise soon."

The mayor could be wonderfully charming—if he needed something from you.

CHAPTER 17

"Off to finance," Brad told Jane on Friday morning. "Let me know when the Green Valley Initial Study comes in and I'll hurry back."

"Just called Megan. You should get it soon."

"Yip damn yee. Keep at her if it doesn't come in by ten, okay?"

Brad was far more comfortable getting into budget projections than reading the pending EIR Initial Study. The financials were mostly positive. Nevertheless, his mind kept drifting back to the Green Valley project. He called Jane during the meeting and was annoyed that the IS memo still had not come in. Jane called him back near eleven to say it finally arrived. He hustled back to his office.

Jane handed the report to him as he walked in.

"About damn time," he snarled. He settled in at his desk and leafed through the twenty-seven pages to get familiar with what was inside. It promised to be as fascinating as the tax code. He paper-clipped some key sections for a closer read.

A blue jay swooped onto his windowsill and chirped. It triggered a childhood memory of the time he and his cousin, Ed, spent an afternoon with a borrowed BB gun, trying to hit a bird. When Ed finally did, the brief celebration soured to mournfulness. They buried the bird and returned the gun. Brad's mind wandered to other escapades with Ed until the jay chirped several times and flew off. He sighed and turned the pages on autopilot thinking more about his upcoming lunch with Scott Graves.

Jane appeared at the door, a welcome distraction. "Don't forget, you have lunch with Scott in fifteen minutes."

"Geez, you're scary. I was just thinking about that."

"Sorry to nag, but I need to get that report copied for the packets."

Brad picked up his skimming pace searching for Megan's summary of the water supply issues. He expected to find it under the Public Services section which he read more closely. Not there. He finally discovered it in the last section, Utilities and Service Systems.

Brad checked his watch again. Time to leave. His heartbeat quickened until he found the key language at Section XVIId: *Would the project have sufficient water supplies available to serve the project from existing entitlements and resources, or are new or expanded entitlements needed?*

The "Less than Significant Impact" box had been checked below two-and-half pages of small-font text and numbers in the Discussion section. Brad skipped to the references to the Western and Payton/Carlisle reports and lingered on the phrase "the water assessment indicates sufficient water supply for the project."

Relieved, he dashed out and tossed the report on Jane's counter. "Only a couple edits. Let 'er rip!" He hurried to the car, eager to give Scott the "all clear" on the IS over an Enchilada Grande.

Scott Graves was already at Moreno's by the time Brad arrived. Scott said "howdy" as Brad squeezed into the booth opposite him.

Their relationship had always been collegial since SoCal first entered Brad's life. It became more of a friendship after a party last year at Scott's house—a popular annual fundraiser in early December to buy presents for needy kids in the region. Brad had been "over-served" but Scott intervened to sober him up and even drove him home without incident.

Brad noted Scott's no-calorie iced tea, but the untouched pile of warm, salty tortilla chips and hot salsa made him salivate. He dove in. "How's things on the dark side?"

"Supplying the American dream," Scott responded.

They talked about Payton/Carlisle's review of Western's water supply assessment draft.

"Oh," Brad added, "and I reviewed the Initial Study from Megan. It's fine. It says we have sufficient water supply for your project and lists public utilities as a 'less than significant impact.' I'll make sure it goes out today, so we can keep things moving."

"Thanks, Brad."

They chatted more about the project. Scott showed renderings of new home designs prompted by SoCal's updated market study. They eventually got down to the main topic of the meeting, several deal points that separated them from a final development agreement.

Brad's role was the behind-the-curtain closer. The negotiating teams were stalled, and the city's legal consultant asked him to intervene with Scott directly to try to close the deal.

Scott and Brad leveraged their relationship and linked a couple of tentative trade-offs between the menudo and the last bite of enchilada. They parted like old college buddies.

Brad spent the rest of the afternoon catching up with emails, reading memos, drafting a speech on economic development for the mayor, and returning phone calls. Jane stuck her head into his office to confirm that the weekly packets had gone out for delivery and that the Initial Study was part of the planning commission's folder. Following a year-long mostly behind-the-scenes gestation period, Green Valley Village was about to be officially presented to the public.

Marie and Brad had Lilly and Lee over for dinner that night. Marie's pot roast hit the spot on the cold, foggy night. They saw their neighbors more since Lilly's hip surgery. The ladies taunted the men into a bridge rematch. The card game supplied little drama for the evening until Lee asked how the Green Valley project was coming along. He talked about their interest in leaving their large two-story home on one-third acre for the project's assisted living facility.

"Funny, Lee, I've been thinking about Green Valley, too," Marie said, smiling at Brad. "Maybe we'll still be neighbors."

Brad's jaw dropped. Marie mentioned examining the floor plans Brad brought home a while back. She liked the models with two master suites on opposite sides of the house and a granny flat with kitchenette over the garage. It would be perfect for guests and the kids' visits. The smaller lot with the home-owners' association handling front yard maintenance would free them up for easier travel after Brad retired in a few years.

"You mean you'd be willing to move? Again?" Brad asked incredulously.

"Brace yourself, Brad. I was even toying with the idea of taking up golf. It's something we can do in our old age together. I could take lessons and join a women's group at the Green Valley course. I need to make some more friends here."

He smiled and shook his head. "I've been trying for years to get you to take up the game. That's great!" He set his cards down and leaned on his elbows. "I had no idea you'd even consider another move."

"A smaller house would be better for your spreadsheet, what with Dillon's out-of-state tuition." She raised her glass to toast. "And we'd keep Lilly and Lee as neighbors."

Brad clinked his glass with the others then leaned back in his chair with a tight smile. "It's a great plan but don't go putting any deposits down just yet. Green Valley is a long way from a done deal. And, frankly, I'm getting tugged and pulled so hard in all directions that I'm not sure where I'm going to come down on it. You all may end up being very unhappy with me. And even if the project gets approved, I may not make it to the finish line to move in."

Lee stopped shuffling the deck. Lilly reached over and placed her bony hand on top of Brad's. "I don't know all that you're dealing with, Brad. Yes, we'd like to move, but I couldn't live with myself if I thought you had to sacrifice your principles on our behalf. Something good can come from my dad's suicide if it reminds you to act on your conscience regardless of the consequences."

Marie nodded slightly. Brad registered her stoic support and slumped, recognizing the real possibility of letting his wife down yet again.

CHAPTER 18

Brad ran from the window to the bed and half-dragged Marie out of her sleep down the stairs. They had to get out. The wall of mud and roiling water slammed against the side of the house knocking them against a wall. Through the living room window, he saw Lee and Lilly's stucco house burst apart. He grabbed Marie by the wrist and pulled her to the front door, but hesitated, unsure about fleeing or riding the flood out inside the house. Wouldn't it bob to the surface? The living room window exploded. Black, muddy water spewed in and sprayed shards at them. Marie screamed.

"Brad, Brad! It's the mayor." Marie shook him awake with the phone in her other hand.

Brad rallied enough to realize it was Saturday morning. The dim light through the window indicated it was too early to be awake. He covered the receiver with his hand, cleared his throat and said, "Good morning."

"Not so good, Brad. Have you seen the sign?" the mayor said.

"Sign?"

"They put up a huge anti-Green Valley sign right across the street from the site. Damn, Kay and her crowd aren't even going to give it a fair chance," the mayor fumed. "I want you to get the damned thing down. Now!"

Brad's mind started to engage. He stalled for time. "What does it say, Buddy?"

"'Don't destroy Santa Ynez' with NO written over Green Valley Village in big red letters," the mayor said angrily. "It's like the size of a billboard. They must have been at it all night. Why didn't PD stop them?"

Brad had revived enough to formulate a quick response. "Let me go out and see. If it's on public land, I can have the weekend public works crew remove it right away. If it's on private property, I'll have to talk to the city attorney to see what we can do. It's probably a violation of our zoning ordinance either way but we're treading on Constitutional rights here and we don't want to be too heavy-handed."

"Like hell we don't! There's no reasoning with Kay and her groupies. The project deserves a fair hearing. This is America!" The mayor's sentences were delivered like the rat-a-tat of a machinegun. "You better call Scott and tell him you're tearing it down."

"Like I said," Brad began gingerly, "I'll check it out myself and establish if it's on public right-of-way. I know we adopted a schematic design for street and intersection widening in that area. But I don't remember if any of the right-of-way has been acquired yet. I can't promise we can get it removed today, but I'll also talk to Henry to see what options we have if it's on private property."

"I put my chain saw in the trunk," the mayor threatened. Brad held his breath until the mayor continued. "Okay. Call the city attorney. Get on it right away. But call Scott first. Let him know these are just fringe nuts doing this. Reassure him. We need this project."

Rather than calling the developer immediately as the mayor had directed, Brad took a quick shower and completed his other normal daily preparations. He had a hard time functioning properly until he had showered, shaved, brushed his teeth, and been to the toilet. As he finished his routine, the phone rang again.

"It's Scott Graves," Marie yelled from downstairs,

"Morning, Scott, I was getting ready to call you."

"What the hell's going on, Brad?" the developer asked brusquely. Brad was taken aback by Scott's demeanor.

"Yeah, the mayor wanted me to let you know you shouldn't get too upset. Just a predictable tactic."

"Predictable tactic?" the developer said incredulously. "I was completely sandbagged, and you call that 'predictable?'"

Scott's intense reaction puzzled Brad. "You must have had the same thing happen on some of your other projects. Given the opposition from Kay, weren't you prepared to deal with stuff like this?"

"Hell no, we weren't." Scott sounded angrier. "This came out of left field. I was sure we could count on *you* to make sure it didn't."

"What could I have done about it ahead of time?" Brad snapped back.

"For starters, you could have given me a warning at lunch yesterday about it. Based on your assurances that everything was fine, I sent my weekly report up the chain last night saying everything was coming along. I'm going to look stupid now."

"I didn't know about it at lunch, Scott," Brad responded with exasperation. "I'll do what I can to get it removed. I may not be able to kill it today and may need to get the city attorney involved."

"Why the hell do you need the city attorney, Brad? Why can't you just tell her right now to get rid of it?"

"Hah!" the city manager replied. "I assume you're referring to Kay. You don't *tell* her anything. You know that."

"Kay?" queried Scott. "Who's talking about Kay? I'm talking about Megan!"

"Megan? What's *she* got to do with this? Are you accusing her of being involved?"

Scott paused. "I have to assume it's her handiwork."

Brad recoiled. "I can assure you, Scott, that I didn't know a thing about the sign ahead of time and if I find out that Megan was involved with it, I'll fire her."

"Sign? What sign? What the hell are you talking about, Brad?"

Brad stared at the receiver quizzically. "Let's start over. Didn't you call me about the anti-Green Valley sign? I heard about it a few minutes ago from the mayor and was on my way to check it out."

"News to me," said the developer. "Tell me."

Brad summarized the mayor's report. "So," Brad asked him, "if you weren't calling about the sign, why'd you call?"

"The tertiary treatment language, of course."

"Tertiary treatment?"

"You know, recycled water from your wastewater plant," the developer said.

"I know what tertiary water is," Brad said impatiently. "But what are you talking about?"

"The Initial Study language saying tertiary treatment would be studied in the EIR as a project alternative. Didn't you see that yesterday?"

"No. Where is it?"

"Page twenty-three. The write-up basically says that the studies by Western and Payton/Carlisle show there is sufficient water for the project and the rest of the General Plan build-out, but it goes on to say that the State Water Project is uncertain, and the city may not even be able to count on the thirty-something percent reliability. The city should conserve its current supplies. It says that tertiary treatment for the golf course, common area landscaping, parks, and the residential yards will be studied as an EIR alternative to reduce the project's demand for potable water. You said you read the IS."

"I skimmed it, didn't read every word," Brad said meekly. "I never saw it in the draft I read before we met for lunch. I can't imagine that Megan snuck it in, though. I have my agenda packet right here, but the draft she sent over is at the office. I'll go in later and see if that language was in what she sent me. I promised the mayor I'd check on the sign first."

"The sign is a nuisance," Scott said. "I'm much more worried about this tertiary treatment language. It'll cost millions. If you make us do it, we can't make that work and keep everything we were going to do for you in the development agreement."

"I understand," Brad assured. "First, I'm going to find out how that language got in there."

"We need to delete it fast, Brad. Tertiary could kill the project. I'll get more specifics from our folks and check back with you. This is a much bigger deal than any stupid sign."

Brad's next call was to the cell phone of Public Works Director Dee Sharma. No response. Brad left him a voice mail about the sign asking him to call back immediately. He called City Attorney Henry Fitzhenry to brief him on the problem and get him thinking about the legal alternatives if the sign is determined to be on private property.

Brad drove out to see the sign at close to 7:15 a.m. He was greeted by an attractively painted scene of the rolling hills across the street covered with box-shaped houses that proclaimed, "NO GREEN VALLEY VILLAGE" in large, red letters over the top of the scene. He recognized the two women who marched in front with picket signs that said, "Don't waste our precious water" and the word *NO* in red letters over "Green Valley Village."

WHEN THE DAM BREAKS

Paisley Menezes, an artist who specialized in painting whimsical characters on rocks, and Kalo Debevec, a master gardener, waved to him as he pulled up. Common denominator: both friends of Councilwoman Kay Nance.

He recalled the advice he had given Kay about getting along with her colleagues on the council and foolishly hoped it had hit home with her. He sat in the car a moment and said to himself, "Never let them see you sweat," and bounded from the car.

"Top of the morning, Brad," Kalo greeted him as if passing in the grocery aisle. "Pretty sign, huh?"

"It's sure big," he said, trying to sound casual. "And well done, other than that misspelling."

Menezes and Debevec both snapped their heads around, scrutinizing the sign.

"Just kidding," Brad said. "Got to take a couple pictures to make sure it's not on public right-of-way. Do you want to be in or out?"

"We checked," Kalo said, "we're on private property." The women posed proudly in front of the sign as he took pictures.

"Got to run," he said. "There's a stray dog somewhere in the neighborhood and I'm on call this weekend. See you." He smiled and drove off.

He hoped Kay was smart enough not to have done the sign painting herself or the proponents could force her recusal. No doubt she was already getting notified he had been out.

Brad got to City Hall and rummaged through Jane's piles to retrieve his marked-up copy of Megan's draft Initial Study report. He went immediately to the water discussion. This time he read the water section word for word. He had not noticed the subsection called "Special Mitigation Measures" below a Project Alternatives heading. To his shock, it was just as Scott described on the phone. Not too far astray from what he had directed Megan to write, but she had taken some liberties that he did not like. He read on:

CEQA requires that the EIR consider alternatives for meeting the project's objectives while reducing environmental impacts. Tertiary treatment of the City sewer plant's secondary-treated wastewater effluent for the Project's golf course, set-back landscaping and common areas, parks and residential landscaping will be analyzed as an alternative for reducing the Project's demand for potable water and, thereby, retaining a more comfortable water surplus for the future.

He gasped. How had he missed that? He remembered rushing through the report to meet Scott for lunch.

He called his planning director at home and was disheartened that Megan's "significant other" live-in partner, Dr. Fred Buderi, a biology professor at the nearby community college, answered and went for Megan. Brad considered Buderi intense and priggish. Buderi often wrote letters to the editor or op-ed commentary pieces in the local paper that dripped with haughty, sarcastic prose and usually belittled the city, especially on planning issues. The same people who called her Megan Cain't joked about her relationship with Buderi. Brad recalled one of Scott's parties where Hank Nettler speculated that Megan and Buderi sat around at home on Saturday nights getting stoned and bingeing on fresh veggies and NPR podcasts.

"Hi, Brad, you're at it early for a Saturday," Megan said in a friendly voice.

"Yeah, the mayor woke me up early to tell me about an anti-Green Valley sign that went up last night across the street from the site. I'm trying to track down if it's public or private property and what, if anything, we can do about it." He resisted the impulse to ask if she knew anything about it. One issue at a time.

They talked briefly about the sign and the growing controversy the project would be receiving now that public comment was underway. Brad got down to business. He admitted that he had scanned the draft IS too quickly and was surprised about the tertiary treatment study language she had included.

Megan assured him she was not trying to slip anything by him and defended that what she wrote was consistent with his direction. She had neither remorse nor defensiveness in her voice.

"Right now," he said, "my main concern is getting that tertiary language out of the IS. SoCal is having a fit. How do we do that?"

"But it's only an alternative to be explored. The law requires that we consider alternatives for meeting the project objectives with less environmental impact as part of the EIR. Besides, like I said—"

"Megan!" he interrupted. "I'm not going to argue this with you. Now answer the question. Please," he softened. "How do we get that language out of the IS?"

"Hmmm. Not so easy, Brad. It already went out yesterday to the responsible agencies and public, both electronically and with hard copies. It's a reasonable and common mitigation alternative. If we dropped it suddenly, it'll raise a red flag. We'd need some justification for the reviewing agencies besides the fact that the developer doesn't like it."

Megan tried again to defend the study alternative and yammered on about all sorts of complex water issues involving the Delta and the State Water Project and why the city should be stingy with its water supply. Brad was only partially listening. He was more worried about appearing incompetent for allowing the language in the first place and weak if he couldn't get it out.

"I have to deal with that sign now," he said, cutting her off again. "I don't have time to debate that tertiary language with you."

"Can we at least meet on Monday to talk about it before you decide it has to come out?" she pleaded.

"First thing Monday. But come prepared with a specific strategy for dumping tertiary entirely. I'm sure that's where I'll want to go."

He hung up with Megan and called his public works director again, this time connecting. Brad apologized for bothering him on a Saturday morning and explained that he needed him to go into the office and check the ownership on the sign location. He texted his photo of the sign to Dee's city cell phone. Nothing more to do for now.

Brad locked up the building, stopped at Jiffy Lube for a long-delayed oil change, and then drove to the park for the soccer field dedication. SoCal had built two artificial turf youth soccer fields at Sunny Fields Park where the Nettler family had donated numerous improvements over generations. The mayor would be out of town and asked Brad to handle the emcee duties for him. Brad suspected the mayor viewed him as a safer choice than giving another local politician the limelight.

The day turned dark and blustery, sprinkling off and on. Nevertheless, this was a welcomed event for his city and Brad expected a big turnout. He slumped a little at the wheel and sighed, imagining Scott Graves and other Green Valley supporters jumping him about the tertiary treatment study and the billboard. That worry tripped the "play" button on the tape recorder in his head. He cycled through the familiar themes: his inadequacies, job insecurity, personal financial jeopardy, and general sense of impending catastrophe.

Brad suddenly realized he had no recollection of the last few minutes or miles of driving. His worry was palpable. The rain progressed from a spitting sprinkle to a steady drizzle. Off to the left, a dollop of pale blue broke through the gray, billowing clouds. Shafts of light illuminated his immediate surroundings, showing off the beauty of the oak-dappled green hillsides. Brad leaned forward against the steering wheel for a better view of the vivid nature display. Okay. Okay. I get it. He relaxed and saluted to the heavens.

Pulling into the park's parking lot, he spotted a large anti-Green Valley banner stretched across a section of chain link fence. Dee Sharma called him en route to confirm the billboard was on private property. Brad relayed that to the city attorney who wanted more time to review the Municipal Code to see what the choices were for abating it. City Attorney Henry Fitzhenry did not volunteer to work on it over the weekend. No surprise there.

At times, the city attorney was maddening. Like today. The man could not be moved to urgency. Staff members joked about Henry Fitzhenry's cautious, plodding nature. Some called him Bond, James Bond, in exquisite satire. Brad got along with him fine. Henry left him alone to run the city. He did not meddle on policy matters and was not one to find prohibitive liability risk in every situation. Henry Fitzhenry was competent, just slow.

Brad locked his car and walked to the park entrance. "Hello, again," he said to the picketers he had photographed earlier. They, and a few others with pickets, now stood behind a table under a portable canopy next to a wide banner zip-tied to the chain link fence that matched the billboard.

"Care to sign our petition?" Kalo Debevec teased.

"Oh, rats, I don't have a pen. Let me get back to you on that," he joked.

He took a beeline for the portable podium under the tent where the event organizers were gathering. SoCal's Scott Graves stood with his boss, Jeff Simpson, whom Brad had met once. His stomach tightened.

"Some reception, huh?" Scott said, nodding back at the banner and petitioners. "You remember Jeff Simpson."

"Hi, Jeff. Sorry about that. I didn't know that was going to happen." He offered his hand.

"Seems to be a pattern around here," Simpson grumbled, shaking hands perfunctorily.

Scott quickly changed the subject to the lousy weather and how pleased he was that so many people turned out for the dedication. Brad thanked Simpson for his company's generous donation and excused himself to get festivities underway. Simpson merely stood with his arms crossed.

Brad eventually announced on the portable PA system for everyone to gather around. A Boy Scout group posted the colors under the canopy, and a sixth-grade girl sang the National Anthem to the shaky accompaniment of the Santa Ynez Valley Christian Academy band. A stream of speakers came to the rostrum to extoll the virtues of the youth soccer, the new fields, and SoCal's generosity. The rain picked up as Brad invited Scott Graves to the mic.

Scott was his normal, polished self. He credited his boss, SoCal Communities Vice President Jeff Simpson, for approving the donation of the fields. "I have to tell you that Jeff has been giving me grief all day. I've always argued that Santa Ynez has perfect weather for our active adult community, and, so far, Jeff has been willing to write the checks to make it the first-class project we all want. He reminded me a few minutes ago that this is his fifth visit to the area. Two of the days it rained, one day we were socked in with fog, and another day was so smoky from a wildland fire on those mountains you didn't want to be outside. I keep telling him it's usually perfect here, but he's beginning to wonder."

That brought some snickers from the crowd.

"I told him that the city arranged for the little rain today to demonstrate how much the kids will like playing on these all-weather fields. Well done, Brad."

The crowd chuckled again.

"In fact," Scott continued, "Jeff's wondering if we should use artificial turf for the golf course, just in case."

"Good!" a shrill voice shouted from the back of the crowd that Brad instantly identified as Kalo Debevec.

As everyone else turned, she began chanting, "Save our water, save our water."

Paisley Menezes joined in, followed by three others. The chanters pierced the air with their picket signs, punctuating each word. They did a few more choruses then stopped but kept their picket signs up to shield themselves from the rain.

Scott turned to his boss and said, "See Jeff, I told you the Chamber Ambassadors Committee would be here to welcome us today."

Even the protestors laughed. The tension was broken. Brad got the mic again to wrap up.

"Wait, Brad," Vice Mayor Mullikin beseeched him. "I'd like to say something."

"Make it quick, Tim!" Hank Nettler shouted, his voice like course sandpaper.

The vice mayor grabbed the microphone. "I guess it's all been said, but everybody hasn't said it yet." He got a laugh. "I know if the mayor were here, he'd want to be sure we tell everyone how thrilled we are to have SoCal Communities as a partner in the city." The vice mayor was doing his best to sound mayoral, but he came across as a pretender, a sycophant. The crowd was restless and wanted to get out of the weather.

Brad stepped forward, giving the vice mayor his cue to exit and called the dignitaries to line up twenty feet in front of the west goal facing a dozen eager little kids in every manner of brightly colored jerseys for the ceremonial first shots on goal. At his signal, the adults bunted kicks toward the net which the kids easily blocked.

The rain persuaded most of the people to leave. Brad noted that the two SoCal officials huddled with Hank and Hubie Nettler and Vice Mayor Mullikin under the canopy. Jeff Simpson was doing most of the talking, wagging his finger at the vice mayor. Jeff was a big man with a stern visage.

Brad presumed he was hammering his boss about tertiary treatment. He wished he could have briefed the councilmembers about this latest issue ahead of time. He decided to face the music and approached the group.

Simpson wasted no time and narrowed his eyes at Brad. "What are you going to do about this tertiary treatment crap?"

Jeff Simpson did not seem to be the type who cared about building a relationship. He was all business, so Brad responded accordingly. "It got into the Initial Study without my knowledge. I'm trying to find out what we can do about it at this point."

"Let me help you with that one, Brad," Hubie said sarcastically. "Drive a stake through its heart. Right now! SoCal can't live with that language in the study."

Brad tightened his jaw and braced himself for more blows.

"I have our people working this weekend on a cost estimate," Simpson said, continuing his attack. "I don't have a number yet, but from other projects we've done, I can tell you it runs about a hundred dollars a foot to run a twelve-inch line from the sewer plant three miles to our site. That's around one-and-a-half million. The tertiary plant cost is based on volume. At *least* another million-and-a-half. If we have to run parallel potable and tertiary lines and meters to the golf course and all the landscaped areas, parks, and yards we're talking at least a six-million-dollar hit."

"What we really don't get, Brad," Scott added, with a less biting tone, "is that there's no need for it. Our engineer, Western, who your city has used for years, public works, and finally Payton/Carlisle all concluded you have enough water to serve our project. Megan couldn't let it go at that, could she?"

Brad appreciated that Scott was giving him an opportunity to put all the blame on his planning director. While getting out of Jeff Simpson's gun sights was appealing, he was not prepared to throw his young department head under the proverbial bus.

"She's made a strong case that new water is going to be tougher to get in the future," he said. "She's raising the question about whether we should be giving so much of our remaining supply to uses that could do fine with recycled water. I'm meeting with her on Monday to see what we can do."

Simpson scowled. "That's not what I wanted from you, Brad. Listen, Green Valley is a big project for you, but it's small for us. With everything we're giving away in the damn development agreement, it hardly pencils out at all. You throw this tertiary cost into it, and the project is upside down. I've never lost the company money on any of the projects I've built, and I'm not going to start here. I'd sooner cut our losses now and take it down the road where we can count on the city leadership, and we don't have people with closed minds." He nodded toward Vice Mayor Mullikin. "How would your council like that?"

Brad winced at the vice mayor's scowl. "I think it's a great project and I'll continue to do my best to promote it. I don't know what I can do about the tertiary thing yet. Working on it."

Jeff stiffened and put his fists on his hips, elbows straight out, ready to lash out again. "Bitch wings," the stance was called.

Scott apparently noticed, too, and intervened. "The problem is that in our experience with government agencies, once something gets on the table it's hard to pull it off. And we don't face Megan Cain'ts in other cities. We're afraid that the tertiary treatment will end up being imposed if it's studied."

"You're threatening the whole project," Hubie complained. "Dump that language now so we can get on with the damn EIR."

"I already said I'd do what I could, Hubie," Brad snarled back.

The big man glared back at him. "Some of us question lately how motivated you are to get this project done, Brad," Hubie said ominously. Then, turning deliberately to the vice mayor, he added: "Or maybe he just doesn't have the background to handle tough issues like Green Valley."

Brad stiffened at the word "background." His thoughts returned to the duck hunt and what his city manager colleague in Lodi was going through with her opponents digging into her past. His heart raced. "I do and I'm on it," he said and excused himself with building panic.

CHAPTER 19

Planning Director Megan Cain sat across from Brad on Monday morning, fidgeting like the storied cat on a hot tin roof.

"I'll give you ten minutes to make your case," he said.

She tried. Brad sat mutely. She got the message and wrapped up.

"With all these real threats out there to the Delta water supply, we should hang on to as much water as we can for the existing developed area because I see a reduction of water in our future."

"Megan," he said, "you've given some convincing arguments for better water management. In fact, based on what I've learned the last few weeks, I can't disagree with a lot of what you said. But these are huge, complicated issues. We are a small city here. We can't hold the Green Valley project hostage over statewide issues that we can't predict or influence anyway."

"So, we should keep on approving water-thirsty development without thinking about the long-term?"

Brad shifted in his chair. "Again, you're talking about major statewide policy matters. Santa Ynez is a tiny player. Is this some personal crusade you're on? Are you trying to reenact *The Mouse That Roared?*"

Megan sat back, dropped her chin to her interlaced hands, and looked down at the papers on the coffee table. Moments later she straightened with a determined expression. "Maybe I am. Maybe I want to change how we plan our cities. Maybe I want to make a stand for more sustainable, interesting, and livable residential development instead of sprawl based on car dependency, money, and politics."

"That's Fantasyland, Megan."

"It doesn't have to be. We approve run-of-the-mill developments. Empty calories that fill up space in the General Plan. We can and should do better for the public."

"Run-of-the-mill? Wait a minute, Megan, you can't possibly be putting Green Valley in that category."

"It's nothing special," she scoffed.

"You're selling yourself too short, Megan. The development agreement you contributed to has a lot of pluses for this community and the Specific Plan is extremely attractive."

She shrugged. "It's nothing too different from what SoCal has done in their other developments. That doesn't take any great creativity. It's just another example of converting ag land into low-density residential. It's sprawl. We already know that's the wrong way to provide for population growth. We are destroying our environment and it's costing taxpayers too much to keep doing it."

He stiffened. "What would *you* have us do? You want us to reject Green Valley and change the General Plan so we only do high-rise residential from now on?"

"Frankly, if it were up to me, I *would* reject Green Valley. A high rise in Santa Ynez is ridiculous. But Fred and I talked a lot over the weekend about how boring and wasteful our planning concepts have been for decades. Our subdivisions and neighborhood commercial areas are just like the ones down the road, which are just like those everywhere else. We could take a stand for something more special if the people around here had the vision and courage."

"Like what?" he snapped, feeling attacked.

"Look at Solvang, right next door. A group of Danes settled it a hundred years ago, wanting to create a touch of home with their architecture. People love it. It's so unique for California. Yes, I'd like to see us do something bold like that rather than another sprawling, low-density residential project like Green Valley, with standard house designs painted in blah earth tones. Boring. Since I don't see the will to do anything special here, the best I can do is to try to reduce the project's impacts."

He bristled again. "Sure, downtown Solvang is unique, but most of their residential areas aren't. You want to one-up them by turning Santa Ynez into some sort of movie set? Maybe a blow-up version of Disneyland, with one neighborhood in a New Orleans theme and another like a jungle? Come on, Megan. Get real."

She did not flinch as much as she had to his prior scolding. In fact, she was surprisingly calm.

"I didn't mean to upset you, Brad. I know you're under a lot of pressure with Green Valley. But the more Fred and I talked about it over the weekend, the more I concluded that I *am* being real. The reality is that we need a new paradigm for city planning that puts more value on preserving the environment and creating more intimate, pedestrian-oriented communities where people are connected to their neighborhoods and each other. Sprawling out into prime ag land, where people live behind gates and drive their cars to everything isn't the answer. I'm not going to rail against Green Valley, but the policy makers should at least study the feasibility of tertiary treatment to make it a little less horrible."

Brad paused to mull that point. His mind drifted back to a duck hunt and his solemn pledge only weeks ago. He swallowed hard. "The problem is that if tertiary gets into the EIR, it's going to be hard to not impose it as a condition. I have Dee checking with Payton/Carlisle today on the cost. The SoCal guys told me this weekend it would be in the six-million-dollar range. That's a big hit on top of what we're already getting from them through the specific plan and development agreement. I believe the council majority wants all those benefits more than saving some water, especially with the studies showing we have enough for the project."

Megan shook her head. "How do we know the project can't support that extra cost without dropping things from the development agreement? All we have is SoCal's argument that they can't afford it. Why don't we make them prove it by analyzing their pro forma?"

"The council won't want to take that hard a line with SoCal."

"So, why don't you push them to do the right thing anyway?"

He glared at her, trying to control his anger.

She slumped. "How about this, Brad? Why do anything yourself right now? If you do anything at this point, you're going to put yourself in the spotlight. Why not let the planning commission weigh in? The Initial Study is on their agenda tomorrow night. Let them do their job and provide advice to the city council."

The possibility of kicking the whole tertiary issue to the planning commission gave Brad a wave of relief. Still, he was wary. Megan was the primary staff support to that commission. She had much more influence on the commissioners than anyone else, including him.

"Okay," he said. "We'll let the commission decide what to do with the tertiary study. But I want *you* to stay out of it. If they decide to keep with the tertiary study alternative, I want it to be *their* idea, not the result of your arguments. If you can give me your assurance that you'll do that, I'll stay out of it for now, too, and let the commission decide."

Megan cocked her head. "Wait. Are you telling me I can't talk to my own commission?"

"You can talk about everything *but* the water issues. I want Dee to cover the discussion about water supply and demand, including any questions the commissioners might have about the tertiary treatment alternative. I'll instruct him that he is to present the tertiary alternative as you've written it in the IS. Let the commissioners decide whether they want to proceed with it without a lot of drama. Agreed?"

Clearly, it was not.

Megan objected to yielding such a significant matter to the public works director whom she regarded as biased.

Brad held his ground. "Some people don't think you're giving the project a fair shake. I want to get you out of the field of fire. Let Dee present the water stuff and let the commissioners decide it. Don't you advocate on it."

"But, Brad," she complained, "that would be like you sitting mum while the finance director presents an annual budget you don't support. Your training and integrity wouldn't allow it. You'd want to give the council your best advice. It's unfair to deny me the same opportunity with *my* commission. Besides—"

"It's *the council's* advisory commission, not yours," he interrupted. "Either way this goes there will be controversy. I want it to focus on the issues, not the people. You're too politically hot, Megan. I repeat, you need to stay out of the water discussion."

"I'm prepared to take the heat," Megan responded, ignoring his admonitions. "Fred and I talked a lot about that over the weekend, too. I know that in the total scheme of things in California what we do here in Santa Ynez won't even be a ripple. I may not be able to bring much influence on statewide issues, but I can plant a flag for sustainable planning right here. I don't care about the personal consequences. It's the right thing to do. Let me do it, Brad."

He observed a change in his young department head. The agitation she showed at the beginning of the meeting now looked like determination. He noticed her coral pink sweater, the same shade as the housecoat Lilly wore in the hospital. He thought of the man Lilly called "Dad" and the guilt he lived with for not standing up to power. What a contrast with the young woman sitting in front of him who had the courage of her convictions.

"I respect you for being willing to stand up for what you think is right, Megan."

"But?"

"But nobody anointed you to be the savior of community development in California. I want the staff to be seen as neutral, objective professionals who dutifully carry out the direction of the councilmembers elected to set policy and their commission advisers. Staff shouldn't be pursuing their own agendas. Now, the commission may agree with the tertiary alternative or they may not. Either way, I want the staff role limited to asking the commission about the adequacy of a twelve percent water surplus and whether it wants to study tertiary as a mitigation. Let the commission reach its own conclusion based on the facts Dee presents, not all these other broader issues involving statewide water policy you want to get into."

"But—"

"I know you don't agree with this but I'm doing what I think is best for the overall organization," Brad contended.

Megan glared at her boss. "Best for the organization or best for you?" she challenged. Brad bolted to his feet. "Damn it, Megan!"

Megan hastily retreated, gathered her papers, stood up, and smiled. "I heard you, Brad."

CHAPTER 20

"Did you see the paper this morning?" Jane Stanar asked ominously as Brad walked into the office on Tuesday morning.

"No, I went for a jog and was going to glance at it here. What are our friends in the Fourth Estate up to now?"

"Making trouble for you, I'm afraid," she said, pointing to a front-page article. The headline said, *Green Valley EIR Set for Approval.*

"What the hell?" he cried.

"The article itself is fine. It's the headline."

He stood at her counter and skimmed the article. It noted that the planning commission was due to get a briefing tonight on the Initial Study prepared by city staff to determine the scope of the EIR study. Blah, blah, blah.

"Same old problem," he said. "The people who write the stories don't usually write the headlines. The headline implies that the whole EIR is up for a vote tonight not just a discussion on the scope of study. This is going to stir things up for the planning commission tonight."

"Do you want me to get the editor on the phone for a correction?"

"I guess not. I don't ask for a formal correction every time I see something in the paper that's off. I agree with Mark Twain,

'Never pick a fight with people who buy ink by the barrel.' Besides, the damage is done for tonight. I better alert the council so they can clarify for their groups. Will you call Megan and make sure she knows? She might want to prepare the commission for a crowd tonight."

Brad called Scott Graves later in the morning about the troublesome headline.

"That damned IS is the gift that keeps on giving," the developer moaned. "We're going to have Kay's people all cranked up thinking that we're bypassing the EIR review process and going straight to approval."

"I've called the councilmembers asking them to spread the clarification to their folks. Maybe it won't be so bad."

"Where are we with tertiary treatment, Brad?" Scott asked hopefully.

"Still waiting for a response from the city attorney. Don't know what we'll be able to do about rescinding it prior to the meeting tonight."

"Jeff Simpson's not going to like that," Scott warned. "Between this tertiary business and his perception that Megan is out to get us, he's beyond jumpy about Santa Ynez. SoCal has to take risks, but Jeff expects us to manage them better than it's going here. I'm working on a plan that might satisfy him—and help you too. You need to stay out of it."

Brad was getting ready to leave for the day when Jane put through a call from Councilman Al Landon.

"I just got back from picking up some tickets at the Chamber," the councilman said. "Scott Graves was in a closed-door meeting with his supporters. They clammed up after I opened the door to say 'hi.' I made a little crack about how conspiratorial they looked. Scott said, 'Just doing some risk management to better the odds.' He said you'd understand."

"Hmmm," Brad mused, trying to appear nonplussed. "Wonder what that was all about?"

Brad settled back in his family room recliner and switched the cable box to channel seventeen, the government access channel, a little before 7 p.m. Tuesday evening. The screen displayed a graphic of the city logo that announced the upcoming City of Santa Ynez Planning Commission meeting.

A couple minutes later the screen changed to a rear view of a packed city council chambers. People lined the walls and sat in the aisles. Some waved signs. He suspected the crowd spilled out to the lobby and possibly outside. His pulse quickened. He could see Chairman Parker Fleischman standing behind the dais with Commissioner Jerry Wright, Planning Director Megan Cain, and City Attorney Henry Fitzhenry.

The pow-wow eventually broke up and everyone took their seats.

The sound came on, revealing the background hubbub that comes with a roomful of stirred-up people.

Chairman Fleishmann banged the gavel and called the room to order. "Ladies and gentlemen, welcome to the planning commission meeting. The fire marshal says we have exceeded the room's occupancy limit. However, he will not order a reduction in occupancy if a few rules are observed. First, people are not to block the exit from the chambers to the lobby and from the lobby to the outside door. Second, picket signs that could pose a trip hazard in the event the room had to be evacuated will be picked up. I'm asking representatives from both sides of the Green Valley issue to gather them up now and pile them on the floor in front of the commission dais, so they'll be out of the way of the exits."

Several people popped up to collect the signs.

As that was going on, Chairman Fleishmann continued. "And this point I emphasize, everyone is to exercise proper decorum. No shouting, applauding, or similar demonstration either for or against anything that will be said tonight. Anyone who violates this protocol and disrupts these proceedings will be removed."

"Sieg heil!" someone yelled from the back of the room.

Many in the audience turned around.

Brad stiffened in his chair.

Chairman Fleishmann acted decisively. "That's exactly the kind of behavior that will not be tolerated. The police are on the way and will keep order. Now, it's obvious that most of you are here for the Green Valley Village Initial Study presentation. And maybe by now you understand that the newspaper headline this morning was misleading. The EIR is *not* up for a hearing tonight. We planned to have *only* a staff presentation on the Initial Study tonight. That just talks about what will be studied in the EIR. I repeat, the EIR itself is *not* up for vote tonight. The draft report hasn't even been prepared yet."

The camera showed people in the audience talking to each other. Some acted confused or angry like a fast one was being pulled.

"If my colleagues concur," the chairman pressed ahead, "since we have other action items on the agenda and most of you are here about Green Valley, we will go ahead first with a brief staff presentation of the Initial Study—no public comment tonight on it, then move to the regular agenda. I'd like to propose a special session for this Thursday to receive public comment before we take action on the Initial Study. Is that acceptable to the commission?"

"We're here now! Don't stall!" shouted another angry voice.

Chairman Fleishmann ignored the shout. "Can the rest of the commission make it for a special meeting Thursday at seven for public comment on the Green Valley IS?" All but one member could.

With concurrence, Chairman Fleishmann led everyone through the preliminaries: Pledge of Allegiance, Moment of Silence, Roll Call, and Approval of the Agenda. The Chair got concurrence to take the Green Valley item first, out of agenda order and ahead of the scheduled public hearings and Business from the Floor, the latter being an opportunity for anyone to speak for two minutes about anything not on the agenda. With such a big crowd and emotions already running high, that would be fraught with peril. Thinning the crowd out before getting to Business from the Floor was a wise precaution.

Brad glanced up from his packet to see the rear camera pick up a uniformed police officer enter the room from the rear door behind the dais and huddle with the planning director and city attorney. Brad assumed they were briefing him on the ground rules for the evening. Officer Crombie was a perfect choice for this assignment. He was a big, imposing authority figure with a friendly demeanor.

The Chair announced, "We'll now take up item F."

"Yeah, 'F' for fucked up!" A male voice from the audience left shouted.

Parker Fleishmann nodded at the officer. The rear camera showed him walking up the center aisle, gesturing to the offender to get up, and taking him out of camera view. The chairman waited for the message to sink in.

"We aren't kidding here, folks. We have a full agenda we need to get through tonight. And we'll observe proper decorum. I know some people have strong opinions about this project. But we are all neighbors. Let's respect each other's right to speak without commotion. You'll have a chance to address us on Thursday. I'll now ask the planning director to present the Green Valley Village Initial Study. Ms. Cain?"

Planning Director Megan Cain conducted a PowerPoint presentation of the staff's recommendations regarding the issues to be studied in the Green Valley Village Environmental Impact Report. The audience sat quietly, except for a few unattributed cat calls. Officer Crombie returned to stand behind the staff table, scanning the audience from side to side, all business, but friendly. Brad made a mental note to send one of his formal "Atta Boy/Girl" notes to the police chief about Crombie.

Megan started through the alphabetical listing of environmental issues, touching upon aesthetics, agricultural and forest resources, and air quality.

Chairman Parker Fleishmann interrupted her. "Megan, most of this is standard stuff. And since we are going to be going through it again on Thursday, I'm going to ask you to just hit the main issues."

"Let her talk!" a woman yelled. The camera operator switched from the shot of Megan to a wide-angle view of the audience from behind the dais. The officer was already on his way up the aisle to audience left. A woman stood up and pulled a small picket sign from under her topcoat that said, "Vineyards Not Houses!" She ignored the officer's command to come with him until he squeezed by a few seated people and gently clutched the woman's arm and whispered something in her left ear. She immediately put down her sign and was escorted out of camera view. It reminded Brad of the officer in Santa Paula in 1928 who said something that convinced the mostly Span-ish-speaking crowd to get off the bridge just before the dam break waters destroyed it.

The chairman held a somber visage. "I will clear the audi-ence if we keep having these interruptions. Please continue, Megan."

People whispered to each other.

Megan picked up the pace on the other issues in the Initial Study. She wrapped up the transportation and traffic section. Brad noted that Utilities and Service Systems was next up. He hit "Record" on his remote control. Megan covered the wastewater portion of this section, noting that there is adequate capacity in the city's wastewater plant to accommodate the demand from the project, as well as the build-out of the rest of the General Plan area.

So far, so good.

"Public Works Director Dee Sharma will discuss the water portion of this section," Megan said, without further explana-tion. She flicked off her microphone button and leaned back in her chair, rocking with her arms folded, clearly piqued.

Brad winced and turned up the volume.

Public Works Director Dee Sharma sat at a table in front and left of the commission dais with his back to audience right. He, too, used PowerPoint slides that summarized the Western and Payton/Carlisle water reports.

Scott Graves was in the shot, in the front row, over Dee's right shoulder.

The camera switched from the screen where the slides were projected to a close-up of the public works director. There must have been some audience reaction to his presentation. Chairman Fleishmann hit his gavel and issued another warning off camera.

"In conclusion," Dee said, "we have enough water to serve the Green Valley Village project and the rest of the General Plan area and still have an adequate surplus. There's a comment here that asks if the commission thinks it's necessary to keep an even bigger water surplus. If you do, the possibility of requiring tertiary-treated water for the golf course and landscaped areas could also be studied in the EIR. But only if *you* think it's necessary. It's not a staff recommendation to do that."

Brad squirmed in his chair. That was not exactly what they had scripted.

Dee gave a short description of tertiary treatment. He called it an expensive process, similar to bringing the city's treated effluent water from the end of the wastewater plant up to drinking water standards.

The camera switched to a shot of the full commission. The chairman hit a button in front of him and recognized Megan Cain. The camera operator must have been distracted as the live shot being sent out was still of the public works director, not Megan. Dee, along with Scott Graves, Kerry Fenton from the Tourism Bureau, and Chamber CEO Brian Brando looked warily in Megan's direction.

Off camera, Megan could be heard saying, "I believe what the public works director *meant* to say is that you can reach different conclusions about water supply and demand. These two studies showed there *could* be a surplus with this project, but the staff would like the commission to decide if it's enough of a surplus and to consider studying tertiary treatment to reduce demand. It's a water conservation measure being done all over the state."

The camera showed Dee Sharma frown and shake his head. Behind him, Scott sat up rigidly, staring first in Megan's direction, then at the back of the public works director's head as if trying to bore into his brain. Scott leaned forward and whispered to Dee.

"The water supply and demand figures used in these studies," the public works director responded without asking for the chairman's permission to speak, "came from consultants who are experts in this field. They rely on their lengthy experience and knowledge of industry standards, like they did for wastewater, drainage, traffic, and everything else that gets studied in an EIR. Of course, since we're talking about projections, there's always room for some differences in interpretation. However, the point is that both studies showed we'll have an adequate surplus of water even with this project."

"Bullshit!" someone hurled. The chairman banged the gavel again. Officer Crombie was back in view moving down the aisle on the audience left as a reminder of his presence. His demeanor said, *don't mess with me.*

The camera remained on Dee who stiffened at the outburst and glared in Megan's direction.

The chairman punched a switch on his light panel. "Commissioner Wright?"

Jerry Wright gazed above the audience, as if pondering some weighty matter. "I'm a little confused about your testimony, Ms. Cain," the commissioner opened. "Does the Initial Study conclude we have enough water to serve the project or not?"

The operator switched to the front camera for a side-angle shot of Megan Cain mulling her response as the seconds clicked by. "That question needs to be directed to the public works director," she said in a monotone.

Commissioner Wright leaned forward. "I *will* ask Mr. Sharma, but right now I'm asking *your* opinion, Ms. Cain. This commission relies on your judgment all the time. I'd like to know what *you* think."

More seconds went by.

"Tell him, Megan!" someone yelled.

The chairman rapped his wooden gavel on the dais again.

The camera showed a shaken Megan Cain. She looked down at the papers in front of her, as if reading a prepared statement, and said, "I've been directed to turn over questions about water supply to the public works director."

The microphones picked up the background rumbling of the crowd.

Brad's gut tightened. He had just been brought onto the battlefield by inference.

"Bullshit!" the same male voice yelled again. This time Officer Crombie could be seen walking purposefully back to the rear of the audience and out of view of the camera. People turned their heads to watch him.

Commissioner Jerry Wright still had the floor.

"Sleaze ball!" Brad grumbled to the TV screen. Wright was the reason they had to create the word "smarmy." He was a political operative for hire, always playing the big shot at civic events and giving large donations to popular causes on behalf of his biggest client, the local Indian resort casino, as if the money came from his own generosity. He fancied himself as a smooth PR professional. Brad's assessment was that Wright's only skill was cultivating and hyping his own connections to local businesses and politicians. Brad had been delighted to see Wright get his comeuppance in the last council election when, despite business community backing, he failed to pick off either incumbent, Kay Nance or Claire Schmitz. Wright was rumored to be the originator of the Megan "Cain't" slur.

"Ms. Cain," Commissioner Wright said, "I can see that you are biting your tongue. And I don't want to put you in an awkward position."

"Like hell, Jerry!" Brad barked again at the TV screen. Wright had tangled for years with Megan. His council race included slogans like "Let's make City Hall work for people again," presumably, his clients.

"So," the commissioner continued, "I'm not going to ask you the details about the water issue. I understand that the public works director is the expert in that area, anyway." Wright smiled for the camera. "But Megan, you said tertiary treatment is being done all over. My understanding is that it's such an expensive process, it's only being done where the water supplier doesn't have enough potable water. Isn't that right?"

"I haven't done a survey on it, Commissioner Wright," Megan replied. "But—"

"Oh?" Wright raised his eyebrows in mock surprise.

"But," Megan continued, "I'll stand by my statement that tertiary treatment is an increasingly common practice to conserve water, Commissioner."

Commissioner Wright still spoke to the horizon. "But you don't have any facts to support what you're talking about, do you, Megan? And you haven't disputed my contention that the only places using tertiary treatment are those that don't have adequate water supplies, which both you and the public works director have already said isn't a problem in Santa Ynez. It's obvious there's something else going on here."

The camera switched to the young department head who stared bullets back at Jerry Wright. "I said I didn't do a survey, Mr. Wright, on how many cities have tertiary treatment. But I know it's a growing trend in a state with so many water problems. Planning conferences often have presentations on what other cities are doing with tertiary, desalination, and recharge basins. As to the expense, yes, tertiary treatment would be considered a major condition of approval if it ends up being required. *That's* what's obvious, Mr. Wright," her voice oozed sarcasm.

Applause erupted from audience left which the chairman gaveled down.

Brad slammed the arms of his chair. Stop, Megan!

Commissioner Wright still held the floor. He shifted his attention to Dee Sharma. "Now, Mr. Public Works Director, you are responsible for ensuring that infrastructure like streets, water, and sewer that will be analyzed in the EIR will be sufficient, correct?"

The camera switched to Dee Sharma who sat up. "Yes, Commissioner Wright."

"And I know, Mr. Sharma, that you have been doing this kind of work for Santa Ynez for many years and for other cities for many years prior to that. Isn't that correct too?"

"Yes, sir."

"And, I suspect, Mr. Sharma, that like any other department head, you'd like to have more of everything in a perfect world. Just like the police department would like more officers on the street and the parks and recreation director would like more parks. You'd like more traffic capacity and water too, wouldn't you?"

"Of course," Dee said flatly.

"But it's a matter of balance, isn't it, Mr. Sharma? Somewhere in the design of public services, the taxpayers or ratepayers need to be considered. You don't push for unreasonably expensive service levels or facilities if they aren't needed. It's not that you wouldn't love to have more and better, but you have a responsibility to not overburden the people who have to pay the bill, right?"

"Yes," Dee said again. "It's a balance."

"Hmmm," the commissioner said, looking right and left down the dais. "I apologize to my colleagues for these questions. It's just that this tertiary treatment study seems to be the biggest issue we are being asked about. I understand it is such an expensive option that, if it is required, could kill the project. Before we even start down that road, I'd like to hear from the person most responsible for ensuring adequate water."

"Proceed," said the chairman.

"Now, Mr. Sharma, you said a little while ago that two separate consulting reports concluded we can serve the Green Valley Village project, and the rest of the General Plan area, and still have a water surplus. And I believe that you labeled that surplus 'adequate.' Not 'abundant' or 'excessive', but 'adequate,' in keeping with your responsibility to achieve a reasonable balance. Is that correct, Mr. Public Works Director?"

"Yes."

"If that's the case, then I'm confused, Mr. Sharma. Why are you recommending that tertiary treatment even be studied in the EIR?"

The background noise spiked with angry voices. Commissioner Jerry Wright smiled in a pose reminiscent of a congressman at a nationally televised committee investigation grilling a hapless witness.

The chairman restored order with a few raps of his scarred wooden gavel and said, "Folks, I'm going to bring this to a close. We aren't going to decide anything tonight, and we'll have a public meeting this Thursday where everyone can talk. But since Commissioner Wright asked a direct question, I'll let the public works director respond. Mr. Sharma, the question was: why are you recommending tertiary treatment be studied if you believe the city has adequate water to serve the project?"

The camera switched back to Dee who was reading. He looked up to the commission and said, "To be clearer, the IS doesn't *recommend* that tertiary treatment be studied. It just asks the commission if *you* think it should be."

"Since I haven't yielded the floor," Commissioner Wright pressed, "it doesn't make sense to me, Mr. Sharma, that you'd be asking us that question. You are the professional expert being paid to make that decision, aren't you? Are you asking us because you aren't sure? Or is this issue too controversial and you want the commission to decide it for you?"

Brad braced himself. Commissioner Jerry Wright scored a direct hit to Dee Sharma's most vulnerable spot: defending his position without feeling attacked and coming unglued.

"No, Mr. Wright!" the public works director erupted. "I'm not unsure about anything. We'll have a large enough surplus of water even with the project, without going to the expense of tertiary treatment. The facts support that."

"Thank you, Dee," the commissioner said, with a satisfied smile. And, as if an after-thought, he added, "Gee, Dee, I guess I'm gobsmacked. As our expert in utility capacities why did you even include the idea of a tertiary treatment study at all if you don't consider it necessary?"

"Yeah! Why?" yelled someone from audience right.

"*I* didn't!" exclaimed a clearly exasperated Dee Sharma.

Behind the camera shot of the public works director, Brad saw Brian Brando, the Chamber CEO, nudge Scott Graves with his elbow.

Commissioner Wright affected a quizzical mien. "Mr. Sharma, can you tell us how that tertiary idea got in there and why? Who wrote that part, Dee, if it didn't come from you, our expert?"

The camera switched back to the public works director whose face looked like he had guzzled colonoscopy prep. After a loud silence, he said, "The planning director wrote the Initial Study report and added the tertiary treatment study concept. I suggest you ask her."

The crowd noise spiked again. There were no shouts this time. The camera showed people whispering to their neighbors in anticipation of the drama that was about to unfold. A second police officer joined Officer Crombie.

A short, thin, bearded, middle-aged man with his hair pulled back on top and braided down his back, stood in the third row of audience left pointing at Commissioner Wright. It was Kay Nance's potter friend, known only as "Noble." "You know damned good and well who wrote that, Jerry. She's trying to protect this city from people like you and public works who are in SoCal's pocket!"

Another man Brad knew as a Chamber Ambassador stood up from the other side of the audience, pointed his finger at Noble, and said something harsh that the television didn't pick up. It must have been spicy since other people on both sides of the aisles jumped to their feet. Both officers took up positions in the center aisle, motioned for everyone to sit, and pointed forcefully at Noble and the Chamber Ambassador to come with them. Noble balked. Officer Crombie put his big left arm around to the back of his Sam Browne belt toward his handcuffs and held it there a moment for emphasis. Noble left with him without a struggle.

"Chairman Fleishmann!" Megan Cain's voice came from off camera. "I will respond to Commissioner Wright." She had not waited to be officially recognized. "*I* wrote the section about tertiary treatment. That's the 'who.' As to 'why', it's what I said before. Reasonable people can come to different conclusions about water supply and demand. We had one consultant report that said one thing. We got a second opinion that was more conservative. In *my* opinion, even the second opinion was too optimistic. They came up with a twelve percent surplus with the project, which leaves little room for contingencies.

"I continue to question several of the assumptions about how much water the future residents and landscaping will use along with how reliable our current water sources will be twenty-plus years out. The reports don't even address all of the threats to the Delta where a good part of our supply comes from. We're more likely going to end up with less water than what these studies indicate."

"But, Megan, if…" Commissioner Wright blurted in.

She ignored him. "I *know* that if we were to get an independent assessment of the situation from a consultant who had their finger on the pulse of all the truly troubling problems facing water supply in California, which, frankly, I believe would be prudent for this EIR, we'd be much more interested in conserving what we have now. In that light, using tertiary treatment to retain more of our precious potable water is smart planning. It's being done all over and the developer hasn't presented any evidence that requiring it would be unfeasible. It should be studied."

A mixture of fast applause and hoots capped her comments.

Brad's stomach knotted.

The wide angle from the camera at the back of the room picked up the entire commission dais. Commissioner Wright flicked on his microphone switch. "Commissioners, it's clear that there is an agenda being played out here. It's the same anti-development hysteria we have always seen from planning."

Megan shot forward in her chair and flipped on her own microphone, speaking to the entire audience, not the commission. "*My* only allegiance is to the citizens and businesses of our city, both today, and in the future. If this project goes forward and we end up not having as much water as some people hope, it will impact everyone already here." She swept her arm across the audience. "*All* of you, not just the future residents of Green Valley, are going to suffer the consequences."

She turned her head in the direction of Commissioner Wright with her jaw set and eyes like blue lasers. "So, Jerry, you can try to spin this away from the serious water issues we face in this state and right here in Santa Ynez and try to make this about me. Since that, too, seems obviously to be *your* agenda. I don't care. I'm used to it. But as long as I'm here, I'm going to give this commission and this city the best advice I can, even if it's not what you and your clients want." She smacked off her mic switch, held her head up, and stared straight ahead.

The audience erupted. It sounded to Brad like the loud applause and cheers of the project opponents drowned out whatever the project supporters were yelling. The rear camera showed Commissioner Wright snarling something back at the planning director that couldn't be discerned over the din and the chairman's vigorous gavel-banging.

Chairman Fleishmann shouted into his microphone, "I'm declaring a fifteen-minute recess. There will be no more discussion tonight about the Green Valley project. We will resume our normal agenda in fifteen minutes."

Brad re-played the last few minutes then changed the channel and headed to the kitchen for a bourbon and water.

CHAPTER 21

"Kay's in there to see you." Jane said as Brad trudged through the outer door Wednesday morning.

"Thanks," he said through his hangover, "for the warning," he added with a whisper.

Councilwoman Kay Nance was curled up in some sort of yoga position atop one of the chairs next to the window. Her eyes were closed, and her head upturned to capture the morning sunlight on her housecoat, an Asian-inspired pattern: bright red, with big golden dragons.

"You know she was set up, don't you?" Her eyes were still closed.

"Huh?"

She let out a long breath born deep in her core and continued through closed eyes. "I had a little gathering at my house for the meeting. We decided Scott, Jerry, and the gang knew you had muzzled her on the water discussion. They hatched a plan to bait her into speaking out anyway."

"Interesting theory," he said uncomfortably. "But how would they know what I told Megan to do about that presentation?" Brad asked.

She opened her eyes narrowly and shifted in the chair slightly to face him. "That's what we'd like to know."

He cocked his head and held up his hands defensively. "Wait a minute, Kay. If you're accusing me of plotting against Megan, you're way off base!"

"We know you support the project and are friendly with Scott. And you know how strong-willed Megan is, especially if she's defending her positions. It's hard for us to imagine that you'd expect her to sit there quietly when you knew Dee would soft-peddle the project impacts. Were you pressured into giving Megan marching orders she couldn't ethically obey so you could fire her when she didn't?"

"Absolutely not! Just the opposite," Brad protested. "My direction to her was designed to protect her, get her off the hot seat, not to get rid of her. I wanted the commission to make the decision and gave specific instructions to both Dee and Megan on how to handle it."

"And Dee did what you told him?" she asked.

"No, not exactly. And I'll take that up with him. But he came a lot closer to doing what I said than Megan. I was sick about it all night."

They stayed silent for a few moments. Brad breathed rapidly, getting angrier by the moment.

"I have something for you." Kay reached over her head with both hands and removed her necklace: a leather cord with a shiny piece of metal dangling.

"It's the Chinese symbol of Forgiveness. I made it for you last night after everyone went home. Sliced my finger open in the process." She showed her bandaged index finger. "Fortunately, I had some pain-numbing medicine on hand," she laughed. "I made this amulet to give you if I was convinced you weren't involved in getting Megan. I am satisfied and ask that you forgive me for upsetting you."

He took it from her and examined it as it lay in his palm. In his nearly forty years in public service, he had never received a gift like this from a councilmember. Maybe they considered his annual contract gift enough.

"I appreciate this very much," he said.

"I'm sorry I accused you," she said, gathering her bulk and dismounting from the chair. "I didn't think you'd do that to her, but I promised I'd ask. I hope the power of forgiveness is in you for me *and* for Megan."

He sat speechless as Kay reached the door. Like her amulet, Kay Nance was a piece of work.

The newspaper story this morning about the commission meeting fanned the flames of controversy between the planning director and business community. Brad recalled a mentor who described the press as bystanders who avoided the field of battle and once the carnage was over came rushing in to shoot all the wounded. He took the "no comment" route this morning with the City Hall reporter.

Mayor Buddy dropped in to demand Brad fire his planning director and call Scott Graves to apologize for her behavior. No, he had not seen the planning commission meeting himself, yet. Brad suspected that he got all the information he needed at the coffee shop this morning. The mayor did not care if Megan had been baited.

Brad took phone calls most of the day. He did not need a log to know the anti-Megan sentiment was far more vocal than her defenders. "I appreciate you sharing your views. I'll take them into consideration," was his standard blow-off response.

Councilman Landon came in to watch the DVD copy of the meeting since it had not yet been uploaded to the city's website. He came back to Brad's office afterward. "It's pretty tough to watch, Brad."

"Yeah, I'm disappointed."

"Hubie and the Chamber group are patting themselves on the back this morning that they finally got rid of Megan. It must have been what they were cooking up at the Chamber yesterday. Is it true?"

"It's probably true they're crowing, but it isn't true she's been fired. I haven't even talked to her yet."

Councilman Landon did not attempt to influence Brad. He put a hand on Brad's shoulder and said, "Remember, God is with you as you struggle with this difficult situation."

Brad relaxed slightly and thanked his boss. Two gifts from councilmembers already this morning.

Chamber of Commerce CEO, Brian Brando, called later in the morning. "Any truth that you are letting Megan off the hook?"

"Now where did you hear that, Brian?" These leaks! Brad threw his pencil at the wall. "Here's a deal: you tell me your source and I'll tell you the secrets behind the Warren Commission report on who killed Kennedy."

Silence in the receiver momentarily.

"Listen, Brian, you know this is a personnel matter and I can't talk to you about it, right?"

"Yeah. But as your friend, I wanted to make sure you knew that we've been frustrated dealing with Megan and people are watching *you* now to see what you do."

"Thanks for that, Brian," Brad said insincerely and gave him the noncommittal response of the day.

"While we're sharing rumors, Brian, there's one about last night being a plan that you and Scott and Jerry Wright played out hoping to get Megan fired." He waited.

"All I'll say is that we aren't going to lower the flag to half-staff if you, in your wisdom, decide to send her packing. Hell, you'd probably be a lock for Grand Marshal of the 4th of July parade."

"You helped me decide, Brian. I'm giving her a ten percent raise. Thanks for the call."

Vice Mayor Tim Mullikin stopped in next. That, by itself, was unusual. Mullikin was a frequent visitor to the police department, where he had coffee and chatted it up with the dispatchers and sworn staff where he used to work. He seldom came to City Hall unless he had to. Even though his position on the city council made him part of "the city" instead of "the police department" he was still more comfortable hanging around the PD. The sheriff's department lieutenant designated as the city's police chief complained that Mullikin undercut her authority during his visits. Brad repeatedly counseled his boss about that—gently.

The vice mayor was apparently tasked to deliver today's message, "We're watching *you* now, Brad. Better fire her!"

Megan held her head high, jaw set, as she entered Brad's office. They exchanged crisp hellos, keeping up the pretext that this was a normal meeting.

Early in his career, Brad had to fire a department head. He was nervous and tried to make it as painless as possible for him. Brad hemmed and hawed so much that the personnel director later that day said that the man was shocked when he was called for the exit interview. Lesson learned.

Brad came out from behind his desk and sat across from Megan. "I suppose you know I have to let you go."

"You 'have to' or you 'want to?'"

"I don't want to, Megan. I wish you had done what I asked you and this wouldn't be necessary. You chose to put yourself at the head of the storm. And now your objectivity is irreparably damaged."

"Do you believe that what I said was wrong?"

"Not completely. Where you went wrong was disregarding what I told you about staying out of the water issue. I like and even admire you, but I can't let any department head get away with such insubordination."

"You could give me a letter of reprimand or maybe a week's suspension. After all, this started over the tertiary language in the IS, a very reasonable alternative, which I made no attempt to slip by you. If you had read what I wrote, which was the same as what I talked about before, we probably would have come up with something that satisfied us both." She sighed. "But I suppose you have to deliver my head, don't you?"

He slumped and paused before gathering himself. "Megan, I've taken a lot of heat about you. I've counseled you when I thought you needed it, but generally you kept things between the lines. Last night you obliterated the lines. I told you I want Green Valley and every other matter that comes to planning to receive fair treatment. If there's going to be arguments, they should be about the merits of the project, not the director's objectivity."

Megan seemed resigned to the firing to come. "I was going to let it happen like you said but got fed up with Dee misrepresenting the IS and sweeping the Green Valley impacts under the table. Oh, and by the way, by *his* disobedience of what you told him to say. Seeing the signals passing between Scott, Dee, and Jerry Wright, I guess I'd had it. I've been fighting with some of these people since the day I started here."

Brad nodded his understanding. "I've always told people that the planning director's job is even more difficult than mine. You get it from both sides on any development application."

Seeing that as a tangent from the main point, he recovered. Get it done. "Like I said, I am letting you go, but I'll give you the opportunity to submit your resignation. You can talk about how much you've enjoyed the experience here in Santa Ynez and want to pursue other interests. That sort of thing. I'll do a press release thanking you for your dedicated service to the city. I don't have a bloodlust to fire you."

"Everybody will know I've been fired."

No denying that. He sweetened the pot. "I would also be willing to have a separation agreement, giving you three months' severance pay and continued health benefits until your successor is on board in exchange for your full liability release and assistance to staff on an on-call basis during the transition. But if we're going that route, everything needs to be done by five today. I'm not going to get into a negotiation with some attorney over this. And, frankly, you don't want people on the council getting wind of that offer or I'll withdraw it."

She sat there quietly for a while until speaking softly. "It's like I told you Monday. Fred and I concluded that community development and water policy in California need to change. I'm going to join that battle. I'll sign the agreement and move on."

Brad thought again of Lilly's dad's tragic decision to suppress his values for the sake of keeping his job. The stress and tragedy he had been exposed to for weeks seemed to come crashing down. He fought back tears and barely whispered to himself: "*God bless you, Megan.*"

Brad was reading a report later that afternoon when his assistant, Jane, came to the door.

"Well, this should be interesting," she began. "Jenny Nettler is outside and asked to see you."

"Hank's arsonist daughter? Oh, great. Did you tell her I can't get involved in a criminal matter?"

"I tried to discourage her, but she said she had to tell you something you should know. It's not about her case."

"Ok, bring her in, but I want you to sit in as a witness."

"I know her. It will be all right."

Brad was taken aback by Jenny's entry. She had been a confident, brash, young women in her high school setting, a far cry from the demure girl who now accompanied Jane to a chair.

Jenny looked down at her folded hands. "Thank you for seeing me, Mr. Jacks, I won't take long and I'm not here to ask you to help with my problem."

"I'm sorry that you found it necessary to set a fire, Jenny," Brad said sincerely. "I don't know what drove you to do it. But I was out there that day and can tell you that it could have been a disaster. I hope your confession helps you."

She looked up. "We'll see, Mr. Jacks. But I promised this wasn't about my case. Actually, it's about you. Well, the city, anyway."

"Oh?" Brad glanced at Jane who gave a "search me" shrug.

"That's right. Um, you probably won't remember, but when you came to my government class, I asked you about endangered species."

"I remember it well. You badgered me about a bunch of stuff, but your interest in endangered species really puzzled me. I asked somebody about that and heard nothing has been identified so far. I kinda forgot about it after that."

Jenny looked back down at her hands and fidgeted in her chair. "Sorry. I guess I *was* having some fun with you. But, um, I was—I mean I am, interested in endangered species." She paused, took a deep breath, and shot a determined look at Brad. "Have you ever heard of the Gaviota Tarplant?"

"Nope," Brad said. Jane shook her head, too.

"A professor named Dr. Buderi spoke to our biology class last year and showed pictures of endangered species in the area. I thought one looked just like a flower on our property."

Brad cocked his head. "I know Dr. Buderi. He's close with my planning director. But this is the first I've heard of that plant. Gaviota Tarplant?"

"Yes, sir. It's like a grass but it gets these pretty yellow flowers in the summertime. They look like little sunflowers. My favorite place in the world is a little ravine on our back property that's covered with these flowers. Ever since I was old enough, I'd ride my horse back there. I'd stay for hours, reading, listening to music or just thinking. It was my own private world to escape hearing my mom and dad fight or my grandfather ordering people around." She held up a finger. "Oh, yeah, I have a picture," Jenny said, reaching into her handbag, "it's a selfie I took on my horse at my secret hideaway. See the yellow flowers?"

Brad examined the proffered photo and handed it to Jane. "Very pretty. I can see why this place is special to you. Did you ask Dr. Buderi about it?"

"Yes, sir. Right after the class, I came up to him and said I thought we had a plant on our property that looked just like in his pictures. He opened his laptop again and I pointed to what he called 'Gaviota Tarplant'. He told me the only areas where it's been seen around here are between the Santa Ynez Mountains and Highway 101, not this side of the mountains. Um, but then he said they sometimes discover new species locations, and it was possible that there is an area on our property with conditions that would support the tarplant."

Brad felt rising tension. What was this all about? "Interesting," he said, "go on."

"Well, I told him I could pick a sample and drop it off at his office at the college. He seemed excited and gave me directions. I slid the samples under his office door the next day. It was wintertime and the flower wasn't blooming, so I was only able to leave him grass cuttings and a photo of the flowers."

"What did Dr. Buderi tell you?" Brad asked, leaning forward.

Jenny looked confused. "Really weird. He sounded excited at school about a possible new species sighting, but I never heard from him after I dropped off the samples. I just figured the samples weren't good enough for him to decide anything."

"Hmmm, odd that he didn't call you back," Brad said. "What scientist wouldn't want his name attached to a new endangered species find? Keep going."

"Well, this all happened around the time dad and grandpa were talking about selling our land. I told them about the tarplant and giving Dr. Buderi the samples. They knew the area I was talking about and the flowers that bloom there but they didn't know they might be endangered. Grandpa said he'd look into it and for me to drop it. So, I did. Or at least they *thought* I did."

Brad began fidgeting. "And?"

"I asked dad and grandpa about the tarplant for a couple of days but every time they brushed me off and got mad because I wasn't dropping it." Brad sensed the girl gathering the courage and self-confidence he had seen from her in the classroom. He stole a glance at Jane who must have picked up the change, too, and nodded slightly to him

"I bet, Mr. Jacks, that if I was the oldest *boy* in the house, they would have included me. I suppose I was kinda like a non-entity around the house." The smirk from before returned. "But when you're invisible you hear and see a lot. Dad and grandpa talked business when I was around. They probably thought I was watching TV or wouldn't understand anyway."

Brad remembered the fire chief saying Jenny's motive for the arson was lashing out at how her father and grandfather treated women. "What did you pick up?"

"A week or so after I told them about the tarplant, I answered a call for grandpa at dinner time. Dad said something like, 'Right on schedule.' The caller didn't say his name, but I thought it was Dr. Buderi. He has a funny voice. I was curious. Grandpa got up from the table and took the call in his office. Later that night I went into his office and saw 'mitigation bank' and '$500k plus' on his notepad. I looked it up, $500k means five hundred thousand dollars."

"I know," Brad smiled. "Hmmm, one of the options for dealing with endangered species or habitat on a developing property is to buy credits to replace the habitat at a designated preserve. Your ravine habitat must be large if they got such a big estimate to replace it. All that will be dealt with during the environmental review for Green Valley. Why are you telling me about this today?"

"My dad kicked me out of the house after my arrest. He took my car away and told me I could forget about college."

"So, this is about revenge?" Brad asked.

"I know it looks like that to you. But my dad says and does things like that when he's mad, then forgets about them when he calms down. I know this will blow over with him."

"That's Hank," Jane acknowledged, then added, "I've known your father a long time."

Jenny nodded. "Yeah, I was mad at him at first, but I've calmed down, too. I'm not here out of revenge. Please believe me," she implored. "That ravine is my favorite spot. It kinda looks like the Green Valley plan makes it part of the golf course. I can't stand the idea of destroying it like that. And I have enough Nettler blood in me to fight for what I want. Nobody's going to stop me, not even another Nettler. I'm telling you because I don't trust my family to protect my spot."

"Why not, Jenny?" Jane protested. "From what you said, we can assume your grandpa and dad know about the tarplant but they haven't done anything to destroy it. Right?"

"Not yet." Jenny agreed. "I rode up there yesterday and everything was fine

"That's encouraging, Jenny," Jane said.

Jenny looked confused. "I don't get it. From all the conversations I listened in on between Grandpa Hubie and Dad about Green Valley and in all the reports and letters and things they left lying around, I never saw anything about the tarplant. I know they know about it. And I knew about Dr. Buderi's relationship with Ms. Cain, so I thought sure he'd tell her. But I watched the planning commission on TV last night and read that report, some kind of study, and there was nothing said about the tarplant. I'm here because I think I can trust you, Mr. Jacks, to protect it and not rat me out to my family. They'd kill me."

Brad's face scrunched in thought. "I don't know anything about all of this. I don't know what will happen to the plant or why it hasn't come up before. But tomorrow night is another planning commission meeting on Green Valley and the first time the public gets to comment on what will be studied in the environmental impact report. And you probably know Megan Cain and Dr. Buderi are environmentalists. Let's just say I have reason to believe Ms. Cain will make a big deal out of the plant tomorrow as a private citizen. I'm sure she and Dr. Buderi will make them protect your spot. Don't worry." He stood to end the meeting.

Jenny picked up her bag and gave Brad and Jane a firm handshake. "Thank you, Sir. That's a relief. But I'll be watching tomorrow night."

"I think the whole town will be," Brad said anxiously. "Oh, before you leave, can you show me on the aerial map over there about where your special place is?"

He quickly located the Green Valley site for Jenny on the colored aerial photo on the wall. She got her bearings on the property and pointed to her spot. As she turned to leave, Brad called after her, "And don't worry, Jenny, we won't say a word to anyone about you being here."

City Attorney Henry Fitzhenry was reluctant to even work on the separation agreement with Megan without consulting his clients, the city council. Brad painted a likely scenario for him. A young, dedicated civil servant with annual evaluations that cite her work ethic and competence pushed out in what appears to be a conspiracy that likely involved appointed and elected officials. Even if the city prevailed in a wrongful discharge action, the attorney fees would be far more than the severance payment and councilmembers would be dragged through the mud. Fitzhenry went along.

Near 5 p.m., with the resignation and agreement executed, Brad called councilmembers to tell them what he had done and to expect a press release in tomorrow's paper. A done deal. He was not asking their approval, only letting them know.

The council's responses were uniformly negative for widely differing reasons. He took their feedback respectfully and argued his action as best he could. The most troublesome response came from Councilman Al Landon who called to say how unfortunate it all was. The minister said he would pray for both Megan and Brad, then added, "Maybe there's a lesson in this for you to exert stronger control over your department heads so things like this don't happen."

Brad slammed down the receiver. He had managed to unite his fractured council—against him.

CHAPTER 22

Brad sat in his office Thursday morning reading a long letter from the boutique hotel developer when he heard Jane greet developer Scott Graves. He tried to eavesdrop on their muted conversation but heard only muffled laughter. He tossed the letter onto his desk and went to the door.

"Morning, Scott. Here to see me?" Brad asked.

Scott, who was leaning over the counter, straightened instantly. "If you have a minute." He held a manila folder in his hand.

Nobody ever took a minute. "Come on in."

"Sorry, Brad, I couldn't warn you fast enough to get out through the window," Jane joked.

"You're not as quick as you used to be, Jane," Brad teased and motioned the developer to his office. Then he stopped and turned back to Jane. "I withdraw that, Jane. It was a dumb thing to say, and I apologize."

Jane laughed and waved him off. "Forget about it. If we can't joke around, I don't want to be here."

Brad looked at Scott. "You're my witness, Scott, that I apologized, and Jane took no offense."

"What was that all about?" Scott asked, taking his seat.

"Oh, I was just kidding. But believe it or not, the Older American Act puts Jane in a protected class since she's over forty. I have to be careful about any suggestion of discrimination."

"Geez, Brad. You can't ever let your guard down." The developer frowned looking at the folder on his lap. "I'm afraid this isn't going to relax you any." He opened the folder slowly, pulled out a two-page letter, and handed it across the table.

Brad tensed. "Doesn't sound like fan mail."

"Nope," the developer said. "This is a letter from Jeff Simpson. We went back and forth on it. It's harsher than I wanted, but he's the boss. It's addressed to the mayor and city council directly. It makes official what we've said. Our engineers have penciled out the cost of tertiary treatment at over six million. It describes how the draft development agreement and project feasibility were predicated on unit types and price points from market research and detailed cost estimates that didn't include tertiary. The lawyers say this letter should give you enough to find that tertiary treatment doesn't qualify as a feasible alternative under CEQA, so that you can drop it from the EIR scope right now."

"That *could* be useful," Brad said, neutrally.

"I figured you'd like *that* part of the letter, at least," Scott said. "Jeff also writes how we got into this project to do a high quality project for the community, how we started down the road with the belief that we could make it work if we had the full cooperation of the city. He says the tertiary study threatens the economics and with the way staff sprung it on us he's disillusioned about achieving the necessary partnership with the city staff to make the project successful."

"Ouch!" Brad responded, making a stabbing motion to his heart.

"The letter says that if the planning commission doesn't kill the tertiary language tonight, he wants the council to hold a special meeting to do it. Failing in that, he will conclude that he has neither a feasible project nor a willing partner. He'll do a press release announcing we're pulling out."

Brad winced initially then forced himself to slow his breathing and sat in silence, staring out the window, as he pondered the threat. Suddenly he grinned and turned to the developer. "I see why you'd be nervous about the letter. Elected officials don't like ultimatums."

"I know," the developer said. "Frankly, I argued that your taking care of Megan improved our partnership. I told him that you and I have a close working relationship and I wouldn't want the council majority to zero in on you if they got this letter and blamed you for obstructing the project."

"I appreciate that," Brad said. "But I don't believe you intend to send this letter out. You know that without the mayor you need a 3-1 vote and you can only count on Vice Mayor Mullikin for sure. Councilmembers Landon and Schmitz want the goodies in the development agreement, so you have a chance with them. But if Jeff comes guns blazing with this ultimatum, he'll turn everybody off and may end up 1-3. The letter is just a ploy aimed at me."

Scott's face twitched.

Brad continued. "Besides jacking up my blood pressure, what are you really trying to accomplish with this letter?"

The developer's serious expression became a broad smile. "I won my bet. I told Jeff you were too smart to bluff with that letter. You know, I've been singing your praises to the company. I have more than I can handle already with three projects in the area and another about to launch. I'd like to see you come aboard with SoCal when the time is right. You'd report to me, but it would be more of a partnership like we have here. You wouldn't have to move, and I assure you the compensation package would be attractive."

"Hmmm," Brad said. He thought of Quinn O'Rourke enjoying his life after city management and felt a jolt of excitement. *A safe landing if I get caught in the crossfire over Green Valley. A way to give Marie what she wants: to retire here in Santa Ynez.* Or was this a test of his ethics?

"I'm flattered, Scott. But that's not an appropriate discussion for now. There may come a time, however—"

"Give it some thought, Brad."

"I guarantee I will. Back to the business at hand. What's this letter really about?"

"You're right, it was aimed at you. It's not going to the council. It's a shot over your bow to let you know how close Jeff is to pulling the plug. Trust me, as a friend, he's never been that thrilled with the pro forma on Green Valley Village and he's pretty cranked up about this tertiary thing. We need to resolve this today."

"I'm guessing you have a proposal for doing that besides just relying on that vague language in your phony letter that tertiary isn't financially feasible. You gotta know that won't fly without public disclosure and independent verification of your pro forma. Jeff sure as hell won't want that."

"Right again, Brad. Here's the deal: we'll agree to revising the tertiary study limited to only the golf course if you'll commit to making us whole for the extra cost. I had to fight hard for that compromise. It's the best we're going to do. Jeff is truly ticked about the tertiary thing. He considers it a waste, pardon the pun, and blames Megan for pushing it for her own agenda, even though it's unnecessary. He wants your commitment today or he is going to send out a letter like this to the council."

"I see," the city manager said somberly. "Answer this, if Jeff is so adamant against tertiary treatment, why would he go along with even a more limited study alternative for the golf course?"

"Business, Brad. I convinced him that we should position SoCal as a sustainable development company. Using some tertiary water for the golf course, along with the low-flow and energy-efficient appliances, the photovoltaic panels at the neighborhood center, and everything else we are doing with Green Valley, will help us on RFP's in other cities we are working on. Cities are recruiting green developers. We'd get a little street cred adding a tertiary component."

"And maybe we can throw in a kumbaya party for Jeff and Kay and see if she'd write a letter of endorsement," Brad joked. "What'd you have in mind for the cost offset?"

"We can up our fee credits. There's plenty there."

"Yeah, I figured that's where you'd want to go," Brad said. "You know, I had a hard time selling the council majority on the partial credits we already included for the street improvements. Al Landon argued both sides in closed session and finally went along when I reminded him your streets are going to be private and the city won't have to maintain them. If I have to go back and ask for more credits, I'm going to need solid facts to support it. I can't do it on my own charisma."

"You could make the case for some water credits because the new tank is improving water pressure outside our project. Or eliminate park fees since we are building our own. We'll give you everything you'll need to make the case to the council. I'll get you the votes."

Brad gazed out the window to some distant place.

The developer pushed to close the deal. "Jeff will be okay going forward with the IS if we limit the tertiary to the golf course and I can tell him that you committed to selling the council on the fee credits. That gets the EIR launched now and buys us some time to resolve the cost if the city imposes the condition. Can I count on you for that much?"

"Tell you the truth, Scott, I'm not comfortable committing to anything right now. I don't know where we are legally with all of this. And let me remind you that we don't need your concurrence for what we include in the EIR. It's the city's call as lead agency."

"Now who's bullshitting who, Brad? Don't make me go over your head with this. It's a fair compromise."

Brad exhaled deeply. "Touché. You can tell Jeff I'll recommend pulling back from the full tertiary to just the golf course and that I understand you want a cost trade off if we impose the requirement. I have to figure out how to sell that."

They stood up and shook hands. "We'll work through this, Scott. I appreciate you coming in. I'd love to be able to bring forward a reasonable compromise to ease the tension at the meeting tonight."

"Me too, Brad," the developer seconded. "I enjoy working with you."

Brad accepted the compliment silently. He had an urge to confide in Scott about the studies being done quietly in the wake of revelations about water quality problems at Well 2 but held his tongue, not certain how far that information would travel.

Brad stretched out in his recliner after dinner and closed his eyes, his mind racing about tonight's planning commission meeting that he was now staffing in Megan's absence. She was right. If he had not missed the draft Initial Study language about the tertiary treatment alternative, it would not have become the problem it was now. He would not have had to push her out, thereby displeasing the entire city council either because he let Megan go or because he allowed her a severance agreement. Scott expected him to support a compromise on the tertiary study. Kay and her group would never accept that a compromise on the alternative was necessary, let alone that the city should subsidize the cost with fee credits. What would he say tonight?

And where do the iron and chromium spikes at Well 2 fit into all of this? Brad had asked his friend Quinn O'Rourke from Payton/Carlisle Engineering to check on a few things in case someone was planning to drop that bomb tonight. With Megan on the outside now, anything could happen. He remembered being on the phone when O'Rourke called him back with his report and that he had asked Jane to cover the call. Brad grabbed his laptop and pulled up Jane's emailed notes from her talk with O'Rourke:

- *Confirmed iron and chromium below Maximum Contaminant Levels at Well #2.*
- *Not enough info to predict if probes are recent anomaly or signaling trend indicating sharper decline.*
- *Reverse osmosis to treat chromium ±$1 million per well.*
- *Can't tell whether treatment or new well better, need more longitudinal data, drill test well?*
- *Pub notice reqd only if contaminant exceeds MCL, doesn't apply, (yet).*

He sighed with relief at seeing confirmation that there was no legal requirement to disclose the iron and chromium readings at this point. He had time to get more information and develop a strategy.

Marie came over with a cup of coffee and a plate of his favorite Owl Eye cookies from Madsen's Bakery in Solvang.

"Here you go. This is a reminder of the joys life has to offer. There will be more cookies waiting. And I rented *Midway* for you. That gives you two things to look forward to."

"Thanks, hon. You know, the Battle of Midway was the deciding point in the Pacific Theatre. Admiral Spruance recognized he was going to be known forever as the man who either won or lost the war. Obviously, the stakes are much lower, but I'm feeling like that with Green Valley. It's mine to win or lose."

"Go get 'em, Admiral," Marie cheered. "Oh, and I love a man in uniform. There, that's three things now," she smiled flirtatiously.

"Thanks, hon. I love you," he said, choking up. His wife gave him a peck on his lips and brushed his cheek with her good hand.

CHAPTER 23

Brad got back to City Hall at 6:30 p.m., leaving time to get what he needed from his office prior to the planning commission meeting. The parking lot was already filling up. A fire engine and rescue along with four police cars were parked near the front entrance to the city council chamber. Brad wondered where they dug up all the police cars since PD normally had only two on duty at any given time. But after the last commission meeting, he endorsed the show of strength to set the right tone.

He unlocked the outer door to his office and went to the bank of filing cabinets behind Jane's desk to retrieve the Local Agency Formation Commission Municipal Services Review in case he needed background on water and other city services for the meeting. The cabinets were locked. He opened the top right drawer of Jane's desk to get the key and made a mental note to tease her about her hiding place, the equivalent of putting the front door key under the welcome mat.

The files were organized alphabetically. He could not find the report under the "M's". He tried the "L's" for LAFCo and "W's" for water and struck out and called Jane at home.

No answer. He tried her cell.

"Hi, Brad," she answered on the second ring. "Did you decide to run away or are you at the planning commission?" She sounded happy.

"I'm at the office, unfortunately. I need the Municipal Services Review report but don't know where you filed it. Help!"

"That's a LAFCo report, right?" she said instantly.

"Yeah, but I didn't see it under the 'L's'."

"It would be under the 'S's'," she advised.

"You're saying 'S' as in 'Sam'?"

"Sure," she said. "It should be under SBCLAFCo for Santa Barbara County Local Agency Formation Commission. That is their official name, you know."

"Naturally," he said sarcastically. "Why not under the P's for 'potential annexations'? You're already my right arm. You don't need to engage in such obscure filing for job security."

"Hey, a little extra security never hurt a girl," she said.

"I could use a little security myself about now."

"From what you said this afternoon, since the council majority is for Green Valley, you shouldn't get any heat from them if you get the planning commission to compromise on the tertiary study. You're still going to propose that, right?"

"Yeah, it keeps Green Valley moving forward. I gotta get to the meeting. Thanks for the fascinating insight into your filing logic."

"Have fun."

"Sorry for interrupting your night out or whatever else you're doing."

"Just dishes," she said quickly. There was something funny in her voice. "No problem. Good luck. I'll be watching."

He wondered why she had not picked up her home phone but let it pass.

Brad walked up to the front door of the council chambers and touched base with Sergeant Heather Mahnken who oversaw the police detail. She seemed less perturbed about the job ahead than he was.

He chatted with Chairman Parker Fleishmann, faking a casual pose while constantly scanning the audience. He recognized many of the people. The factions were self-segregating with the supporters again on the audience right behind the staff table and the opponents veering to the left side of the center aisle. Friends of the bride or the groom?

Brad's elderly neighbor, Lee Andre, walked through the lobby door with Dillon on his heels. Their appearance briefly flustered Brad until he recalled Lee and Lilly's interest in the assisted living component of Green Valley Village and that his son was doing a term paper on the development. He cringed as they took seats on the right. He wished Dillon were standing at the back—in the middle.

The chambers buzzed with the normal background noises of laughter, squeaking folding chairs, and yells like "Over here, Sheree."

A scream and angry shouting emanated from outside piercing through the hubbub.

Sergeant Mahnken put her hand to her earpiece, signaled to Officer David Williams to come with her and to Officer Crombie to stay put inside. People in the audience stood at their chairs trying to see what was happening outside.

More raised voices came from outdoors. Officer Crombie shifted his weight from side to side, ready to move.

A few minutes went by without anyone else coming into the chambers. Moments later, the flow resumed, led by former planning director Megan Cain and her partner, Dr. Fred Buderi, who went directly to two seats saved for them at audience front left. Buderi's sweater was ripped and his long black hair disheveled.

Sergeant Mahnken opened the door behind the dais and beckoned Brad over.

"We had a little fracas outside," she told him. "Hubie Nettler got into a shouting match with Ms. Cain and her friend. Supporters from each side faced off, but we jumped into the middle of it and separated everyone. A few people got shoved, but no punches were thrown. We ordered one person from each side to go home or they'd be arrested. It settled down. Nothing serious enough to warrant an arrest. All the same, I'll stick around through the meeting with Officers Crombie and Williams. We'll keep an eye on outside too."

"Thanks, Heather," Brad said. His stomach tightened as he took his place on the semi-circular dais to the commission's right.

After he settled in and organized his papers, he glanced up to see his son directly in his line of sight, sitting in the middle of the "pro" side with Lee. Dillon caught the contact. He dangled a Ziploc bag of Owl Eye cookies and gave him a thumbs up, no doubt on Marie's instruction.

City Attorney Henry Fitzhenry took his seat next to Brad, which calmed him considerably. A friend in the foxhole.

At 7:10 p.m. Chairman Parker Fleishmann rapped the gavel and brought the special meeting to order. He admonished the crowd about decorum and the consequences for those who do not observe it and acknowledged the city manager's attendance tonight in lieu of the planning director. He did not have to explain why.

Chairman Fleishmann followed the process that had been discussed with Brad and the city attorney. He called the Green Valley item and asked for the commission's concurrence with the evening's procedures. Unlike the previous meeting, this meeting would be devoted to public comment on what should be studied in the environmental impact report.

Following introductory staff comments, the applicant, SoCal Communities, had ten minutes to address the commission. Members of the public had a three-minute limit. The secretary had a timer with three lights: green for the first two minutes and yellow to wrap up. At the red light, the chair would interrupt and ask the speaker to sit.

Noble, Councilwoman Kay Nance's artist associate, blurted from the front row, audience left, "How come the developer gets ten minutes? He's only here for the money. This is our town. Give us ten minutes, too."

People near Noble clapped while others nodded their heads vigorously.

Officer Crombie strode toward the man. Chairman Fleishmann intervened. "I'm going to ask the officer to hold back this time. Hear me, people, that's the only freebie tonight. We're serious about keeping the peace and won't tolerate any other outbursts. As to why I'm giving the applicant ten minutes, it's common practice for this commission to let the applicant go first with introductory comments, since they are paying for the privilege. Nothing special here."

He reminded everyone to keep themselves under control and added that the increased police presence here was not to stifle public speech but to make sure everyone had the opportunity to speak without being disrupted. The vibe in the room calmed.

Chairman Fleishmann continued by reminding everyone that the only issue for discussion tonight was the Initial Study for the Green Valley Village EIR. The project itself was not up for a vote yet and will not be for at least a year. The speakers must keep their comments to what should, or should not, be studied in the EIR. "If you stray from that," he continued, "I will gavel you out of order as a warning. I'll allow you to continue, but if I have to gavel you out of order a second time, the secretary will move the timer to a red light, and you'll be told to sit." He nodded to Officer Crombie and let that sink in a moment before moving on.

"Second, please don't repeat something someone else already said, or we will be here all night. For what it's worth, having served on this commission for many years, I can tell you you'll be more impactful with a factual, crisp argument than by trying to wear us down or being emotional. Besides, I'm self-employed, and unlike many of you, I can sleep in tomorrow. Think about it."

Some smiles in the audience. *Good job, Parker*, Brad thought.

The chairman asked for, and received, his colleague's approval of the ground rules. As that went on, Brad glanced at the audience to see his son writing in his notebook. He turned his head right and met the gaze of his former planning director. Megan's expression was not menacing, but unnerving, nonetheless.

Brad heard his name and realized the chairman had turned it over to him. He sat forward and flicked his mic on. "Thank you, Mr. Chairman, it's nice to be with you tonight commissioners." Insincere, polite, bureaucratic throat-clearing.

Brad summarized the main points of the Initial Study, scanning the commissioners and audience as he spoke. He noticed his son was bent over, either making notes or maybe already bored and texting a friend. Megan Cain was still staring at him impassively. *They must have something big planned about that endangered species. Or maybe she knows about the problems with Well 2.*

Brad concluded with the customary, "I'd be happy to answer any questions." Chairman Fleishmann looked at Brad perplexedly then asked commissioners for questions. There were none.

Fleishmann turned it back to the city manager. "Was there anything else you wanted to mention, maybe about the water section, before I open this for public comment, Mr. City Manager?"

The chairman must know about the compromise Brad and Scott worked out, to study tertiary water for the golf course only, and was prompting him. Brad rocked in his chair looking down at his paperwork, his chin resting on his thumb. Someone coughed, and he looked up, aware that everyone in the room was waiting for him to say something.

Brad glanced up at Scott Graves and cleared his throat. "Ah, well, as I said, we have two independent studies concluding that we have sufficient water for the project. I emphasize that these are estimates. Hopefully, conservative estimates. Nobody wants to run out of water."

Brad paused and saw the developer looking back at him expectantly.

Dillon smiled encouragement. Was his son recalling his father's pledge at the duck hunt to be a good steward of his city's natural resources? Was he expecting Brad to actually do something about it?

Lee nodded slightly as if he understood the conflicts racing through Brad's mind like mice when the lights come on. Dam disaster. Government deceit. Lilly's father's suicide. Retirement in Santa Ynez.

Brad swept a bead of sweat from his brow. "Given the uncertainties in forecasting water supplies thirty years or more out, we're asking the commission to consider studying tertiary-treated water for the project in order to provide an even greater margin of surplus water for the future. Since tertiary treatment was described at the last meeting and, I know the commission wants to hear from the public, I'll stop there."

Brad shut off his mic and sneaked a peek at Megan.

She cocked her head and exchanged puzzled looks with her partner, Dr. Fred Buderi.

Brad sensed something was wrong. He quickly replayed his words in his mind. And panicked. Did he just recommend the full tertiary study, instead of simply asking the commission whether they wanted tertiary considered at all? And he forgot the golf course-only compromise. He looked at Scott Graves sheepishly.

The developer raised his eyebrows at Brad and opened his hands in a gesture that conveyed "what the—?"

Chairman Fleishmann turned to Brad and cued him again. "Anything else you'd like to add, Mr. City Manager?"

Brad stared ahead toward his son and got lost in his head. The next generation. Water. The Delta. His pledge. Out-of-state tuition. Dillon was still smiling back calmly. Could his son possibly understand the nuances and ramifications at play here?

"Brad?" Chairman Fleishmann prompted again.

"Oh, sorry. No, Mr. Chairman, I have nothing further at this time."

The chairman seemed puzzled. Resignedly, he invited the applicant to come to the podium and directed the secretary to put ten minutes on the timer.

Scott Graves rose and glared at Brad like a batter getting off the dirt after a brush-back pitch. He managed to pull off cool, calm, and friendly, despite the scores of citizens over his left shoulder who might have tomatoes at the ready.

Scott removed his large gold watch, set it on the podium, and pulled his notes from his periwinkle-blue blazer's breast pocket. He walked everyone through a PowerPoint overview of the development project, emphasizing the high-quality design and community benefits it promised. He completed the last slide, squinted at his watch to see how much time was left, and transitioned to his next bullet point.

"Our company is in nearly complete agreement with the scope of the environmental impact report. There is, however, one alteration that I wasn't sure if the city manager wanted me to address, or if he was planning to later." He pivoted to Brad for some signal.

Brad hesitated and motioned for Scott to proceed.

Scott Graves appeared uncharacteristically flustered. "If I have a little time left, I want to address the water impacts."

The developer praised the city for its foresight in securing multiple sources of high quality, potable water—an enviable position that put Santa Ynez ahead of comparable California cities. He mentioned a city on the coast that had to resort to a new desalination plant at considerable cost to the ratepayers because *they* had not done their job of ensuring adequate water resources. Scott applauded the city staff for getting two independent water studies from reputable firms to be doubly sure.

The light on the timer turned to yellow. Scott shuffled his papers hurriedly.

"As the city manager noted, there are always uncertainties when it comes to forecasting. Most of us are better at 'post-casting.'" The developer waited for a laugh that did not come. His neck muscles strained, and he spoke faster.

"We have provided staff with documentation showing that the cost of tertiary treatment for the golf course, landscaping, and home yards is unfeasible given the costs for all of the benefits SoCal is prepared to bring the community under the draft development agreement. Tertiary treatment is not an acceptable alternative because it will not support the project objectives. Therefore—"

Ping! The timer went off and the light turned to red.

Scott flinched. "May I finish, Mr. Chairman? I only need another minute or two. I thought the city manager was going to cover this last part."

"Time's up, Graves!" Noble shouted. "Tell him to sit down, Parker."

Brad recognized Chairman Fleishmann's quandary. If he gave a time extension to SoCal, how could he deny it to anyone else?

The chairman apologized to Scott, he needed everyone to abide by the ground rules. No exceptions.

Somebody patted Noble on the shoulder.

Brad saw Scott exchange looks with Commissioner Jerry Wright who dutifully hit his light switch for permission to speak. Wright thanked the chairman and asked him to confirm that commissioners would be permitted to ask questions of the speakers. The chairman agreed.

"Thank you, Parker," Wright said. "Now, Mr. Graves, I understand there is an alternative suggestion for the tertiary treatment study that you wanted to propose. A win/win alternative. I believe this commission and the public would like to know about that."

Scott loosened his grip on the podium. "Yes, Commissioner Wright. Thank you. With the commission's indulgence, I want to say again that we are sensitive to the environment. And while the city has done a superb job of managing its water and will have a large surplus even once our project is built out, we endorse studying the feasibility of using tertiary water for the golf course as one of the required EIR alternatives but not for the houses and other landscaped areas which wouldn't be feasible."

Commissioner Wright seized the spotlight again. "Thank you, Mr. Graves. Can you or the public works director give the commission an estimate of how much that would reduce the project's water demand?"

"Over sixty percent, Commissioner Wright," Scott said triumphantly.

"Really?" the commissioner gushed.

"Yes, it is a significant savings," Scott said, apparently going for a deliberate underplay for credibility.

"Fabulous," Wright fawned. "I'm sure we all appreciate your commitment, not only to Santa Ynez, but to the environment. I know that treating the water from the sewer plant to the equivalent of what we drink out of the tap will be expensive. I salute you for being willing to consider that alternative for the golf course."

"Oh, brother," Brad whispered to the city attorney. "It's up to the city, not SoCal, to decide what should be studied in the EIR. And notice that Jerry doesn't ask how the golf course tertiary would be paid for if it gets imposed?"

The attorney smiled as he continued doodling on his agenda. Brad surveyed the audience. The "pro" side seemed impressed by the reasonableness of the revised tertiary proposal. In contrast, Megan Cain and Fred Buderi flipped fervently through materials on Megan's lap like junk yard dogs straining against their tether.

Chairman Fleishmann broke the mental tangent by thanking Scott Graves for his presentation and asking those who wanted to speak to line up in the center aisle. He again reminded them of the ground rules.

7:40 p.m. already. *Let the fun begin.*

Brad had a running $1 bet with the city attorney about who could come closer to guessing the number of "O's" appearing on the agenda handout. They both filled in the "O's" to make them easier to count and to kill time. He and the city attorney might be seen "conferring" during the public testimony when they were more likely comparing their "O" tallies.

After nearly forty years of public meetings in growing cities, Brad could predict the arguments that would be raised for or against a development proposal. Sometimes there were surprises. A city manager colleague told the story of a council hearing on a small residential infill subdivision on a barren two-acre site. One of the neighbors had bemoaned the loss of the habitat and begged the city to buy it for a wildlife sanctuary. She hit the Joanie Mitchell button, "Take paradise, put up a parking lot," and concluded that what was being called improvements for the site were desecrations. "Man can't improve on nature," she pronounced with finality and spun around to take her seat. A contractor's boisterous, busty, bleached-blond wife, of fun-loving notoriety bolted to the podium next and said, "Who says you can't improve upon nature?" With that, she pulled her t-shirt up to her shoulders and proudly announced: "A man sure improved these!"

Brad did not expect such titillation tonight. He sighed, seeing the line of speakers stretch from the first row to the lobby. City Attorney Henry Fitzhenry slipped him a piece of scrap paper with "10:30" written on it. Game on. Brad wrote "11" on the scrap and handed it back. Another buck rode on who came closer to predicting the meeting adjournment. Fitzhenry went first this time. Their rule required that once the first person picked a time, the second person's time had to be either a half hour earlier or later, his choice. Brad's experience guided him to the "over" bet. The city attorney frowned. Brad sighed and wondered if the promised cookies, bourbon, and movie were only a chimera.

The next two-and-a-half hours followed a predictable pattern. Chairman Fleishmann did his best to keep things moving. He wielded his gavel with a surgeon's precision in a valiant attempt to keep people on point and snuffed out spontaneous applause or taunts.

Brad penciled in the "O's" on the commission agenda as he listened, raising his head to the podium occasionally.

Commissioners, seeing the large number of people lined up to address them, self-policed by not asking many questions of the speakers along the way.

As the line dwindled, Dr. Buderi stood up and walked regally to the rear with three speakers still in front of him. Here it comes.

Brad noticed Scott Graves whisper to Kerry Fenton of the Tourism Bureau, who got up and whispered to others on their side of the aisle, who nodded and joined the line behind Buderi.

Brad stopped filling in "O's" and paid more attention. He wished he could have caught Megan and Buderi before the meeting to tell them he knew all about that Gaviota Tarplant species – take some of the wind out of their sails.

The next speaker was a Chamber backer. She said a few words about how Green Valley Village was a dream project for the community.

The chairman gave her a first gavel, warning her to talk about the EIR.

She turned hostile. "I've had to sit here and listen to those people," she jerked her head back and left, "threaten to recall anyone who supports this project."

Chairman Fleishmann raised his gavel for the second time saying, "You are out of order. Please be seated."

She did not move. "I'm telling you right now I've got a lot of friends."

The chairman kept slamming the gavel.

"And we will recall anyone on the council who doesn't support this project."

The chairman was smashing the gavel so hard Brad feared it would break. Officer Crombie went into motion.

"You people are like all the other no-growthers," she said, pivoting left. "You got your house, but nobody else should get theirs."

The officer touched her forearm lightly as the chairman continued banging. She allowed herself to be led away from the podium and out of the council chambers.

The last speaker before Buderi was Pat Kirby, Santa Ynez's "Grievant Laureate." An eighty-plus-year-old former middle manager with the federal Government Accountability Office, Kirby relished his role as the local political gadfly. Smart enough to be dangerous, he lived to comment at public meetings, especially since the city council and planning commission meetings started airing on local cable TV. He always had a front row seat and folders laid on the narrow counter in front of him. Brad had been embarrassed on more than one occasion to find that Kirby was better prepared for an agenda item than he was.

Several people on the "pro" side groaned as Kirby approached the podium. He said "hello" to everyone as if hosting them at his home. The chairman already had his gavel in his hand. Kirby saw the threat and hurried to make himself relevant.

"Commissioners, there have been a lot of questions and comments raised tonight about the EIR," the watchdog said.

Chairman Fleishmann lowered his gavel but kept it at the ready.

"This is a big project—the biggest we're likely ever to confront." Kirby regularly said "we" to include himself as a decision-maker. "And the EIR is probably the most important document we will be reviewing. I know it's getting late and you want to whiz through this meeting. I recommend that you set another meeting, so we can get the responses from staff and have another opportunity to address the commission again based on what they say."

People on both sides of the audience groaned with the mere suggestion of another round of this drama. Brad flashed on C. Northcote Parkinson's quote a favorite mayor often cited, "delay is the deadliest form of denial." The law did not even require a public meeting on the Initial Study. It was approaching cruel and unusual punishment to even consider a third such meeting.

The commissioners allowed Kirby's suggestion to evaporate into the ether. After an awkward silence, the chairman thanked and excused him.

Dr. Fred Buderi approached the podium. "Good evening. My name is Dr. Fred Buderi. As some of you know, I have a PhD and considerable training and experience in the environmental sciences. I have a lot to contribute to your deliberations about environmental impacts, but I can't do it adequately in three minutes. We ask that you extend me the same ten minutes you gave the applicant."

The chairman stepped in immediately. "I explained the ground rules up front, Dr. Buderi. We are following our customary practice." He turned quickly left and right down the dais. "Is there anyone on the commission who wishes to discuss changing the rules of procedure we previously set?"

No motion was forthcoming.

"You have three minutes, Dr. Buderi," the chairman said. "And let me remind you that you are free to send in a letter with any comments you have about the environmental assessment, even if you can't get it all in tonight. I'll ask the secretary to move the timer back to the beginning. Please continue."

Brad squirmed in anticipation. Here it comes. He tried to slow his breathing.

Dr. Buderi's testimony focused on water reliability citing all the factors threatening the city's main supply: the Sacramento Delta. He talked authoritatively but hit so many technical points in such a short time that Brad sensed he'd overwhelmed people. The timer light switched to yellow then red. Nothing about Well 2. More surprisingly, nothing about the

Gaviota Tarplant. Is he saving that for Megan? She must have a doozy of a wrap-up.

Dr. Buderi got in a final lick after the timer pinged. "Please, commissioners, this sprawl and waste of natural resources must stop." He nodded over his left shoulder in Megan's direction. "Some people have sacrificed to expose the myriad problems in California water policy and community development being brushed aside in favor of the moneyed interests. Listen to those brave enough to speak truth."

The anti-side exploded in applause and hurrahs. Chairman Fleishmann pounded his gavel. Angry voices countered from the "pro" side.

The scientist persisted. "Don't give in to the status quo. It's driven by corporate greed. It's bad for California and bad for the citizens of Santa Ynez."

"Please be seated, Dr. Buderi," Chairman Fleishmann ordered.

Buderi grabbed his papers from the podium and turned with a parting shot. "Include a fair and impartial review of our State Water Project supplies in the EIR. You are public officials. Protect the public interest, not the corporate interest."

"Sit down!" Hubie Nettler stood and yelled from audience right.

Officers Williams and Crombie moved toward the middle of the room under the protective fire of the chairman's gavel.

Things settled down, but the queue which had dissipated suddenly regenerated like a severed Gecko's tail, mostly from project supporters.

Two more anti-project people spoke next. One woman talked about the loss of view once the hills and grazing land were developed. This was listed as an unavoidable impact and, in her mind, the suggested mitigations did not diminish the impact. She asked that the water tank being proposed on a ridgeline be undergrounded. Dee was asked to comment on that suggestion and responded that at least partially burying the tank was likely for water quality reasons. The woman wanted it completely buried for aesthetics.

Another man from the anti-side made a valiant but amateurish attempt to endorse Dr. Buderi's comments, whom he twice called "Dr. Berry."

As the final speaker finished up, Brad dared a peek in Scott Graves's direction and saw the developer glaring back. He stole another glance at his son who was still locked on him. Chairman Parker Fleishmann tapped the gavel to end the public portion of the meeting. That's it? Megan never spoke and Buderi never mentioned the endangered species. Brad reflected on all the Y2K doomsday predictions that fizzled when clocks routinely advanced to January 1, 2000.

"Mr. Jacks, is there anything final you wanted to say?" Chairman Fleishmann asked. It sounded more like the priest on Death Row asking him what he wanted for his last meal. Brad's brain was in warp speed, searching for a landing zone in the fog of his conflicting thoughts, emotions, and values.

"Mr. Jacks?"

CHAPTER 24

City Manager Brad Jacks sensed all eyes on him. He had to weigh in. But how? Did his responsibilities require him to disclose now that the water quality at Well 2 might affect the city's water supply? What about the tarplant? Instinctively, he sought out his neighbor, Lee, who was becoming a father figure. Lee was smiling at him with kind eyes. Did his neighbor expect him to support Green Valley because they both wanted to live there? Or was he conveying a reminder from Lilly's dad: "Do what's right even if people won't know."

He looked at Dillon. His son could not possibly understand. Public policy issues are complicated. He would explain to his son that his role is to carry out the wishes of the council majority even if he disagreed with them. Sometimes you have to go along to get along. It is a real-life lesson his son must learn. Or was he selling out like other officials had?

"Mr. Chairman, and members of the commission," Brad began, hoping his opening words would kickstart a flow of cogent comments, "I agree with those speakers who noted that this state has some serious water issues in need of reform. But smart people on all sides of water policy have been fighting about these things for a hundred years. It's unreasonable for the

City of Santa Ynez, or a specific development project, to take on the burden of sorting it all out in an EIR."

He looked directly at Scott Graves to see if he was scoring points. The developer studied him.

Brad would remind his son of the higher cost of out-of-state tuition, unaffordable if his father is unemployed. An adult must make tough choices and sacrifices. Besides, it is nothing like St. Francis Dam where people died. *And God knows I owe Marie a pleasant retirement in Green Valley after all I have put her through.* He charged ahead.

"We've had a lot of excellent comments tonight. And while the chairman has said it many times, it bears repeating. Tonight is only about discussing some preliminary information about the project to determine which issues should receive further study in the EIR. There will be numerous opportunities for the public to stay involved in the long process ahead.

"Now, except for floods, when it comes to water discussions in California, more is better. We can't predict with any certainty what's going to happen in the future. The best we can do is to deal with what we know today and make some reasonable contingency plans in case there is a glitch. I emphasize 'reasonable' is a loaded term. The city attorney might want to comment on this, but it's my understanding that the courts have ruled it's not reasonable to study an EIR alternative that doesn't meet the project's objectives. An alternative that is so expensive as to make the project infeasible would not be deemed reasonable."

Restless crowd noises.

"However, some additional safety margin for the city's long-term water supply would be prudent. Therefore, I recommend the commission adopt the Initial Study with the inclusion of the potential of using tertiary-treated water for the golf course only. Staff estimates that would reduce the project's water demand by over half, at a cost that's only about twenty-five percent of the full tertiary option. In short, it's a good bang for the buck and worth considering."

Brad waited for some reaction from the audience. Nothing. He pushed back an impulse to mention the potential water quality problems that might also have a bearing on the discussion. He opted to throw a different bone to the project opponents, audience left.

"If the golf course tertiary ends up being imposed as a condition of approval, the staff and consultants will be reviewing the cost of that mitigation. I'm sure SoCal will want to negotiate that cost and seek some trade-offs in the draft development agreement." He could not let Commissioner Jerry Wright get away with implying that the extra cost would be donated by SoCal.

"But the golf course-only tertiary option might equate to only about a thousand dollars added to the home prices. We shouldn't lose many of the community benefits we have in the draft development agreement to make it feasible."

The meeting ended with the commission approving the Initial Study for the Green Valley Village EIR, with the golf course tertiary language, on a 5-1 vote. People filed out of the council chambers. Brad stood at his position, fiddling with his papers to give an opportunity for people to come up and chat.

Scott Graves was the first visitor. "You gave me heartburn, Brad," the developer said. "I was wondering if Kay and her crowd got to you and you weren't going to support the compromise we talked about. I had the votes for it anyway. Jerry was all set to lead the charge if you bailed on me, but if you had, I don't know what Jeff would have done. He trusted me that you were committed to the compromise and to helping us with the cost if it gets imposed. I hope he doesn't see the video of this meeting.

Your last-minute qualified endorsement and suggestion that the whole cost can be loaded on the house prices, was, let's say, more than disappointing."

"I know, Scott. Downplaying the cost issue and implying it could be loaded on the houses was part of selling the compromise, that it wasn't a complete capitulation to SoCal. I'm still there with you on working out a trade-off on the costs. You can tell Jeff."

Scott walked off leaving Brad alone with his thoughts. He had tried to be statesmanlike, reconciling competing perspectives and pitching a deal that would work for the developer and the council majority. Yeah, maybe he was a little disingenuous implying in public that the tertiary cost could be loaded onto the project, while promising Scott afterward that he would still support a partial subsidy. But his tactics were not nearly as deceitful as those of Mulholland, Pat Brown, or the promoters of the Delta tunnels. It is always 'shades of gray' in this business, remember? He is an agent of the city council sworn to carry out the majority's wishes.

His reflection was broken by the sight of Megan Cain walking toward him with Fred Buderi in tow. "You had me going for a minute," Megan said ruefully. "I thought there was a chance you were going to do the right thing and recommend the full tertiary study."

The right thing. Megan had a way of cutting directly to his innermost struggles. "Well, I've got to consider a host of factors that you don't have to acknowledge, Megan. I don't see the council majority keeping the full tertiary study you wanted, and they sure wouldn't have imposed it later. But we can get the golf course tertiary done. Half a loaf is better than starving, in my book. And speaking of 'had me going,' you two sure faked me out. I held back waiting for you to come in with blazing guns over endangered species."

Megan cocked her head. "Huh? Why would we?"

Megan did not know about the tarplant! Buderi never told her. Brad thought of his source, the young Jenny Nettler, and felt a jolt of panic. He had to protect her. He shrugged casually and addressed Megan. "Oh, I just meant that I was kinda braced for you to drop some blockbuster like in those Perry Mason trials to sandbag the EIR process."

He changed the subject to how rowdy the crowd was and that he needed to check in with Sergeant Mahnken about what was happening outside. The pair walked off with a "this isn't over, it's just starting" salvo.

Brad chatted with the sergeant on the way out and shut off the lights to signal it was time to leave. He stood outside by the door pretending to read the top paper on his stack, hoping some of the Green Valley supporters, his friends, would come over and shake hands. Nobody did. He spotted a cluster of project proponents in the parking lot listening intently to Scott Graves. Another smaller group of opponents nearby laughed loudly.

Nobody came up to Brad or beckoned him over. He had made no friends in either camp tonight. He was like a man without a country. Worse, he could not shake the image of Lilly's uncle. He felt like he had acted deviously and feared he had disillusioned his son who likely expected him to act on his commitment at the Delta.

Brad faked a nonchalant air and headed to his car slowly, still hoping someone would befriend him along the way. A few did say "good night" but they weren't the right people.

Nearing his car, his cell phone vibrated. He pulled it out of the holster. The screen showed: "Jane Stanar."

"Glad you called," Brad said, "I can use a little propping up right now."

"…have been worse," Jane said.

"You watched the meeting?" Brad asked.

"…screwed the pooch" he heard a man in the background say. Something familiar about that voice.

"Jane?"

Brad could make out only muffled conversation. He pulled the phone away and stared at the screen, confused. Definitely Jane. He put the phone back to his ear and heard a man's voice, but with cars starting, horns, laughing and other commotion outside it was impossible to pick out the words. Brad figured it out. Jane had pocket-dialed him by mistake.

"Jane!" he yelled.

He heard her say, "At least he finally recommended that compromise. And he fired Megan."

His heart raced. She was talking about him! Who was she with? He jammed the phone hard against his left ear. A small group, several cars away, erupted in laughter. He glared at them, inserted his car key, hurried inside, and closed the door softly. He missed some of the dialogue in the process.

The male voice said, "Wimp."

"He's getting tugged from all sides," Jane said.

He picked up bits and pieces of the man's response. The man said something about "the well" then "chromium." That voice. Who is that?

Brad pressed the phone to his ear so hard it hurt. The man was doing most of the talking. His tone was harsh but Brad couldn't track the words at first. He heard some rustling noise through the phone and the man's voice suddenly got louder and clearer.

"…raped up north," the man said.

Brad gasped and immediately poked the red circle on the phone, ending the call, and killing the unmistakable, gravelly voice of Hank Nettler.

CHAPTER 25

Brad sat in his car bathed in the dim yellow light from the pole above feeling like the last man on earth. A few diehards yucking it up in the parking lot fed his misery. His chest pounded.

Hank Nettler knew about the iron and chromium! I trusted Jane with the confidential information about the water quality problems. And everything else. She sold me out. How blind could I have been? Jane and Hank Nettler! Thought she might be seeing Scott. All those leaks. It was Jane, not Dee after all.

The shock of those revelations paled in comparison to the hysteria gripping him from Hank's reference to Marie's rape. Brad could not believe that anyone, even the Nettlers, would ever dig into his past like that. Not after all these years. How much did they know? Images of that night sprang forward. This time Brad resisted the impulse to repress them. He remembered Marie's urging to control his breathing and pay attention to the changing emotions as he relived the worst night of their lives.

The Jacks became aware of the infamous East Area Rapist shortly after they were married in 1978 when they lived in Diablo Terrace, an unincorporated area of Contra Costa County, east of the San Francisco Bay. The rapist had attacked several times in the dead of night in that area after forty rapes in the greater Sacramento area between 1976-1978. Despite the entire Sacramento community being on full alert and the all-out effort by law enforcement to catch the serial rapist, he remained elusive. Descriptions from the victims generally matched: white, around twenty-five years old, about 5'10", 165 pounds, athletic build, and light brown or blond hair. He was said to have a small, narrow penis.

Investigators later told the public that the East Area Rapist started as a prolific cat burglar, silently breaking into homes while occupants slept. He switched to stalking and raping single women in their homes at night until becoming increasingly brazen. He then preferred the thrill of striking homes occupied by a couple, sometimes with children and even large guard dogs that inexplicitly did nothing. Dog behaviorists, who were consulted about the unwillingness of even trained protective dogs to engage the intruder, theorized that the dogs sensed and were afraid of the criminal's psychopathology just like people instantly were.

As the attacks increased in number and viciousness, the rapist began taunting law enforcement in the local media, further adding to his reign of terror. Sacramento felt like a community under siege. People bought guns, boarded over their windows, kept lights on all night, and dreaded the approach of nighttime. The rapist hit ten times in Contra Costa County after Sacramento, the last time within a mile of the small house Marie and Brad rented shortly after their wedding. He was later connected to murders in Southern California and was also dubbed the Golden State Killer or Original Night Stalker.

Considered one of the worst serial offenders of all time, the psychopath suddenly stopped in 1980 for reasons that experts can only speculate about. But the investigations never stopped. Finally, using groundbreaking DNA ancestry data, he was arrested, tried and convicted in Sacramento County nearly thirty years later. He admitted or plead guilty to thirteen homicides, thirteen cases of kidnapping/robbery, fifty rapes, and hundreds of burglaries.

Victims gave heart-rending testimonies at the rapist/killer's sentencing hearings of the pain they still carried from their attack. Brad remembered their courage as he sat alone in his cold car, ready to face the horror of that night in full.

Brad awoke to a blinding light. A ski-masked face hovered above him.

"Don't move. No sound," the mask said in a voice loud enough to wake Marie who let out an involuntary cry.

"Feel this," the mask said.

Brad felt pressure on his neck.

"I have a knife on your neck. You're both gonna do exactly what I say or you're both dead."

Brad grimaced as he felt the knife slide slowly across his throat. The masked man pulled the knife up momentarily and shone the flashlight on it so Brad and Marie could see the blood.

Marie stifled a scream. Brad lay there completely still, looking up with wide eyes filled with terror. He knew who this was and what was about to happen.

So did Marie. She whimpered but did as she was instructed, getting out of bed quietly, instinctively pulling her cotton nightshirt down tightly as she rose in a feckless attempt at modesty. With the knife still on Brad's throat, he was commanded to roll onto his stomach and bring his hands behind his back. The rapist gave Marie what appeared to be boot laces and instructed her how to tie her husband's hands and ankles, which the attacker then tightened further. He then tied the ankle bindings to the bed footboard as Marie stood shivering helplessly. He ordered her to go to the master bathroom to get towels and warned that if she tried to escape, he would catch her and kill them both. He cut the towels into strips, which he used to blindfold and gag Brad. He then took Marie away for a short time and they both came back to the bedroom with a stack of the couple's dishes and cups that Marie was forced to place on Brad's back. The attacker stuck the knife point in the back of Brad's neck. "If I hear the plates rattle, you're both dead."

Blinded, muted, and immobile, Brad had only his hearing to speculate on the horrors befalling his wife. He knew from press accounts that his wife's hands would also be bound before being raped. His teeth ground into the gag as he gingerly tried his bindings, being careful not to overturn a plate or cup balanced precariously on his back.

From what sounded like the squeak of a wood floor, Brad judged his wife was now in the family room at the back of the house. He could not help but imagine the scene. Suddenly there was a commotion followed by a scream that seemed to be quickly muffled. Unidentifiable noises. A scraping sound. The coffee table being moved? Then silence.

Brad tried counting seconds to keep track of time and get his mind off what was going on down the hall. But he quickly lost count. After what seemed to be a long time, maybe a half hour or more, he began to think it was all over. The rapist had left. Then there was a noise. Glass bottles clanging in the refrigerator. A kitchen cupboard hinge squeaking. Things hitting the tiled kitchen counter. Eventually, the kitchen noises died down, too. Brad listened hard for any sounds of the attacker leaving.

Nothing. His shoulder blades pinched behind him, spasmed. He tried shifting his position slightly to get relief from the cramping.

"I'm going to kill you," came the voice out of the silent darkness. Brad felt the knifepoint again at the back of his neck, then the damp warmth of his urine. He braced for the final pain. Then nothing. Was he gone? Or was he standing over him, waiting for him to move again? Taunting him?

Brad had no concept of how long he lay there waiting to die. It seemed an eternity. How was Marie? Silence. Then rustling noises from all over the house. Brad could make out doors being opened and drawers dumped followed by another sudden, long silence. He could not be sure the attacker had left this time, so he continued to lie motionless despite the agonizing cramping. For much of the silent time, Brad convinced himself he was acting bravely by taking the pain but not giving the attacker a reason to kill them both. The psychopath might be in the room with him at this moment. But after another long silence, the truth could not be squelched. Brad was too frozen by fear to attempt to break free. He lay quivering in his urine and sobbed silently for Marie.

He heard something! Movement in the hallway. *Coming for me.* He had an image of the ski-masked attacker and his knife at the doorway.

"Brad," Marie cried softly.

Brad jolted and began rubbing his blindfold vigorously up and down against the mattress. The clatter of dishes was deafening. He succeeded in pushing the blindfold up slightly and twisted from his stomach onto his right hip. Out of his peripheral vision he could make out Marie slumped against the door jamb, her left arm covered in blood, her yellow night shirt a mass of crimson. He struggled against the gag, his hands still bound behind him and his legs hog-tied to the footboard.

He heard Marie collapse to the floor just out of his sight. He struggled against his bindings, on his right side, trying to see her. He was startled moments later by breaking glass right behind him. He twisted onto his left side and saw Marie on the floor holding a shard of their dishware in her right hand, her left arm hanging limply. She put the piece of glass on the bed, barely hoisted herself to her knees and hacked at the boot laces at Brad's hands.

With her last bit of strength, Marie was able to cut one of the laces before crumbling to the floor. She had little time left. Brad frantically tried to break loose. When he finally unraveled the binding from his hands, he winced from the cramping in his shoulders. Still hog-tied, he ripped his gag down, stretched painfully over to his nightstand, grabbed the small marble golf trophy, and hurled it with everything he had through the single-pane bedroom side window.

Gene hefted his sample case into the spacious trunk of his new company car, a silver '78 Olds Cutlass. Having a stylish, comfortable car to drive was the least the company could do to compensate him for all his travelling, especially today when he had to leave at 4 a.m. for his monthly visit to a big account in Bakersfield. He reached up to close the trunk lid when the quiet darkness of the morning exploded. He whirled his head around in the direction of the noise across the street and saw curtains flapping in the lighted entry walk at the Jacks' house.

Gene had been enraged about the recent rapes and the affect they were having on his neighbors, especially his wife and Marie. He had frequent fantasies about chasing down the East Area Rapist and snapping his neck with his bare hands, as he had been trained to do in Viet Nam. The noise signaled that the psychopath could be nearby. Gene never gave a thought to calling the police. He pushed his sample case aside, pulled a softball bat out of a dirty, black canvass bag, and ran across the street. He stopped outside the broken window of the master bedroom at the front of the house, his muscles taut around the bat.

"Brad? Marie?" Gene yelled frantically.

"In here, break the door down. Quick." It was Brad.

Gene threw his strong frame against the front door. The hinges burst off the jamb so easily that the momentum took him to the ground. He scrambled up and dashed down the hallway. His first sight was Brad contorted on the bed working on some sort of cord around his ankles, a piece of cloth wrapped around his forehead and another around his chin.

Brad pointed down to the floor next to the bed. "Help Marie," he cried.

Gene scurried over and found Marie in a heap. Her pallor and all the blood nauseated him. He saw a partially torn towel on the carpet and applied it to the laceration on her left arm.

Brad cut himself free with the shard of glass and started to get out of bed.

"Call 911," Gene screamed.

Brad raced to the kitchen wall phone but was back in moments. "Line's cut," he shrieked.

Gene paused a moment, still applying pressure to Marie's wound. "My phone. Living room by the couch. Keys in the car. Hurry!" Brad took off running, wincing from leg cramps.

Brad had only vague recollections of what followed. Waiting forever for help. A cacophony of sirens, radios squawking, flashing red lights, and even TV lights. Marie looking close to death when they got to the hospital. Sedation, transfusions, bandages.

By late morning, Marie was stabilized and moved to a private room for observation. It was their first time to talk privately. Prior to then, Brad had way too much time to list all the ways this was his fault. The landscaping was overgrown providing too much concealment. After Marie's third request, he did trim the oleanders enough to allow more light from the streetlight at Gene's house into their front yard. She asked Brad to put up outdoor security lights as well. Even though Brad was willing to pay for the lighting himself, the landlord's property manager required him to fill out paperwork so she could submit it to the owner for approval. Brad hated paperwork anyway and this application was total overkill. It required photographs of the locations for the lights, measurements, copy of the installer's contractor's license, and other details. Brad got angry every time he picked it up to work on it. Marie wanted him to just install the lights and deal with the paperwork later. But he did not want to make waves since the property manager was a friend of Brad's boss, the city manager. As he sat in the hospital room, Brad realized that the film with the photos showing the light locations was still in his camera.

Marie also thought they should put plywood over the side bedroom window, which they both reasoned was their most vulnerable entry point. Their neighbors had done the same thing. Brad intended to do that but did not have a way to transport the 4' x 8' sheets. He said he would ask Gene to borrow his pickup. But he never got around to it. The sheriff's investigators later declared that the point of entry.

And then there was the attack itself. Marie had tried to claw the monster's eyes out when he got her to the family room. He slashed at her with the knife. She instinctively tried to block the knife with her left forearm and instantly felt the searing pain from the blade. The attacker then hit her squarely in the temple, subduing her enough to tie her securely. But Marie had fought while Brad lay in his own filth, paralyzed by fear.

He held her right hand at her bedside and cried with her over the terror they had been through and how he had let her down. Why hadn't he taken some of the precautions she asked for? He had good excuses. He was busy working late, being the go-getter in his first job in his selected career field. And there were hoops to jump through to get the plywood and install the security lighting. But he knew the biggest factor was the power struggle he and Marie were engaged in at the beginning of their marriage, as they sorted out their new relationship. Brad considered home security his domain and resented Marie's constant imploring to do more. She never let her disappointment in him show. She did not have to.

They left the hospital after a two-day observation period, but Marie could not go back to their home. Their neighbor, Gene, took the lead in working with the property manager to fix the broken door and window and clean the blood stains from the floors. In the meantime, the Jacks lived with Marie's mother on the ranch outside Stockton, an hour-and-a-half away. She felt safer there and her mother and Brad gave her good care.

In the evening of their first night there, Marie began to complain about pain in her arm. Brad gave her a pain killer and advised that what she really needed was sleep. He slept on the couch to not disturb her. When he went into the bedroom to check on her late the next morning, the pain had worsened, and her arm smelled like rotting meat. Brad gingerly pulled back her bandage and nearly vomited from the sight of large purple and black blotches. They rushed back to the East Bay hospital. He wished later he had taken her to the closest hospital. "Necrotizing fasciitis" was a term they would never forget, a fast spreading, flesh-eating bacteria that can enter the body at the site of a cut or burn. Brad would never forget the anguish as his young, beautiful wife tried valiantly to hide her grief when the surgeon told her the choice was disfigurement or death. Marie consented to the amputation at her left elbow.

A horn nearby brought Brad back to the present. He sat in the car at the City Hall parking lot a while longer and took stock of himself. He had relived that awful night, faced the pain, and was calming down now. Then Jane's betrayal recaptured center stage. The Nettlers were close to discovering the secret Marie and Brad kept since the rape. The threat the Nettler clan posed now escalated beyond his survival as city manager of Santa Ynez. His family was imperiled.

CHAPTER 26

Nobody was downstairs when Brad got home. He took off his coat and tie, kicked off his shoes, poured a tall bourbon on the rocks, and collapsed in his recliner to sort everything out.

"That's kinda loud," Marie complained, coming down the stairs, pulling her floor-length blue fleece robe tighter.

"Sorry," he said, reaching for the remote.

She spotted the distinctive brown bottle on the kitchen counter. "Must have been a doozy of a meeting."

"You didn't watch?" he said incredulously.

"Bridge at Lilly's tonight. Remember?"

He nodded and took another swallow of bourbon. Marie sat on the black leather couch and pulled on a colorful afghan. "Tell me about it?"

Brad summarized the commission meeting and the inadvertent call from Jane afterward.

Marie listened impassively until Brad got to the part about the rape.

"Oh my God," she groaned. "They know! How?"

"I've been thinking about that. A lot of powerful people in town have badgered me the last couple years to get rid of Megan. Obviously, I didn't do it until recently. And, as we saw with the Megan set-up, even some of the people I've considered friends are fully capable of hatching a plot to get what they want. I don't know whose idea it was, but with so much money on the line with Green Valley Village, I can see the Nettlers paying a few thousand dollars for a private investigator to look for dirt on me. If they found something, you can bet they'd have no qualms about using it."

"That's blackmail," Marie cried.

Brad shook his head. "Maybe so but nobody has tried to coerce me over the rape. No crime yet. I'm sure Hank Nettler has no idea what I heard on that phone call. If I confront him now about the investigation while he's mad about his daughter, Jenny, getting arrested, he could leak what he's found out of spite. You know, teach me a lesson."

"Vile, for sure" Marie said, "but I see your point. Probably not illegal."

Brad leaned forward. "Regardless, if they know about the rape, we should assume their investigator will eventually put two and two together. We can't let the Nettlers hold that over us. As awful as it is, I think it's time to do what we've feared all these years. How do you tell your daughter her biological father is one of the worst monsters in criminal history?"

"Oh, no, Brad! We can't. We just can't," Marie sobbed. She was trembling more than he had ever seen her since the night of the rape.

Brad moved to the couch and clutched his wife's right hand. "We've protected Kris for all these years," he began softly. "But it's time. They're too close. She's a grown woman now. She can handle it."

Marie pulled her hand away and frowned. "No! There's no need to put this on her now, or maybe ever. Look, they know I was raped and we moved shortly after that. So what? Nobody back there knew I got pregnant. We moved into the cottage at the ranch until you got that job in Minnesota a couple months later. I didn't even start showing for a long time after we got there. As far as anyone knows, if anyone cared to think about it at all, Kris was conceived in Minnesota. There's no need to burden her with any of this."

Brad pondered that, then shook his head. "True, we don't know if Nettlers will probe further now that I fired Megan. Maybe that's all they were after anyway. But if they keep digging it wouldn't take much to discover our blood types and that Kris couldn't have come from us. We've been through this. You and Kris are "O". The father could have been A, B or O. That's like 95% of the population. But it leaves me out. I'm AB. Remember how I had to lie about my blood type when she was doing that project in biology? Then investigators released that the rapist is Type A."

"Yes, but how can they get all of our blood types? We checked and it's not on our birth certificates."

He shook his head again. "Yeah, but blood type shows up in all sorts of other places, like hospital records, which we all have. Or blood donation records. I don't know. But whether or not Nettlers find out, I'm exhausted carrying the weight of this secret from our daughter and the rest of our family."

"And I'm not?" Marie cried, her eyes tearing up. "Think about what this would do to her. You know Kris. She won't just shrug it off. She'll do research. She'll find those studies that show a link between DNA and criminality. And we're not talking here about a common drug addict who robs or even kills to support his habit. We're talking about one of the most diabolical serial criminals ever known."

"Yeah, but isn't DNA thought to be only a factor, not a guarantee of criminality?" Brad responded. "Shouldn't Kris be aware of the risk and take action if negative tendencies appear?

And, besides, weren't those studies just about boys? We don't know if she'll ever have kids, let alone a boy. That problem might not even arise."

"Trust me on this, as a mother, if we tell her and she has a boy, Kris won't bond with him like she would normally. Is that fair to her or her baby?"

Brad sighed. "I just don't know. But I'm learning to pay attention to my gut and trust that things will work out somehow. Blame yourself for that," he smiled.

Marie smiled tightly but tears still streaked down her cheek.

Brad pressed ahead. "Regardless what the Nettlers learn or do with the information, we're both tired of carrying this secret. If Kris ever learns about it in some manner other than our talking to her, like stumbling into the mismatch on blood types, she's going to be even more upset…at us. I think we should drive up there this weekend and tell her."

"No!" she shouted, slapping the arm of the couch.

Brad's demeanor became resolute. "It's clear to me now, Marie, that it's the right thing to do." He looked at her with anticipation.

Marie buried her head in her hands and sobbed deeply, her chest heaved as she gasped for air. He moved closer to her on the couch and put his arm around her.

"It's okay, hon. Don't you see we have to do this now?"

She gathered herself, straightened, and looked him in the eyes. "There's something you should know." She glanced back down at her hands.

Brad tensed. "What? What?"

"Just because your blood type and mine couldn't produce Kris, it doesn't mean she's the rapist's daughter. There's another possibility. Another person…"

He recoiled from her words and the inference. "What?"

She raised her eyes again to his. She, too, seemed to have reached a point of resolution.

"It was a one-time thing that happened a long time ago. It meant nothing and I knew it would send you into a tailspin if you found out. As much as I wanted to tell you, I worried even more that you wouldn't be able to process it. I kept it to myself. For us."

"Come off it," he snapped. "I'm not going to let you make some affair my fault."

"I think we share the blame." She turned to face him more fully. "Do you remember how, before the attack, I kept asking you to put up outside lights, board up the side window, and things?"

"Of course, I do. I've lived with the guilt of not doing those things ever since."

"And do you remember that a week or two before the attack you went on a golf trip to Scottsdale with your brother and some buddies?"

"Yeah, I remember that."

"We had a fight about your leaving so soon after the rapist hit our neighborhood without making the house more secure."

"I know. I know. Get to the point."

"I was freaked out living in that house alone. The back and side yards were so dark. I was on the phone for hours every night you were gone, talking to Mom and Tanner just to have a lifeline. I had the feeling I was being watched. And, as it turned out, I probably was. I heard a noise in the side yard but was too scared to look out the window, afraid of what I'd see. The only people we knew in the neighborhood were Gene and Jan across the street."

"Gene! It was Gene?"

"Let me get this out. I called Gene because I was scared. He came over with a flashlight and baseball bat and walked around the yard. I didn't want him to go home so I invited him in for a glass of wine. I was still scared and kept pouring wine to keep him there. He told me he and Jan had separated two weeks before. And, well, it went too far. I don't know, maybe some of it was because you and I seemed to always be arguing back then and I was mad at you for leaving me vulnerable. It happened once and never again. I've regretted it ever since."

Brad removed his arm from around Marie and lowered his eyes.

"Wait," she implored.

He held up his hand in a "stop" gesture and stared down to his lap. Thoughts and feelings cycled through. Shock. Disbelief. Anger. Then, curiously, relief. Gene, not the East Area Rapist, could be Kristen's biological father? Finally, compassion. He knew what it was to carry guilt for forty years.

"What's Gene's blood type?" Brad asked flatly.

"I don't know. I never called to ask him. He would have figured out why I was asking, and I didn't want any further entanglements with him. And, like you just said, there was a 95% chance he had a type that would be compatible with Kris and me. It wouldn't have settled anything. Not knowing Gene's blood type allowed me to believe that he was the father, not that creep. Besides, regardless of whose seed it was, *you're* Kristen's father. You've always known that."

Brad mulled that. After a few minutes of reflection, his awareness came back to the present. His head still downturned, he noticed Jane's prosthesis in his field of vision and turned to her. She leaned toward him slightly, with a questioning expression.

"I love you, Brad. You need to know it meant nothing. Can you forgive me?"

And in that moment his guilt and resentment of his wife's long-suffering stoicism was swept away by a wave of love beyond anything he had ever felt for her. Marie, too, had suffered her own guilt all these years. "Can *you* forgive *me?*" he begged.

They embraced and cried from the relief of off-loading so much emotional baggage. With *Midway* playing in the background, they stayed up late talking about what the future held and what to do about their daughter. By the time Admiral Spruance made his fateful decision to launch his aircraft at the enemy carriers instead of holding them back to protect his fleet, Marie and Brad made their own command decision concerning Kristen.

CHAPTER 27

Friday morning broke like too many others lately. Brad Jacks hit the alarm more tired than when he went to bed. He pivoted to the side of the bed, groaned, and rubbed his throbbing head. Too much bourbon last night. He thought about calling in sick, a common practice for many on Fridays. Brad had so much sick leave on the books, he could stay home until Independence Day. He swore to himself, plodded off to the bathroom for his daily ministrations, popped two aspirins, drank a smoothie, and left for the office.

Brad approached the glass panels of his outer office and was relieved to see that Jane was not at her desk. Maybe she would call in sick and he would not have to deal with her today.

He dropped his briefcase on the credenza and went back to the outer office to make coffee. Brad stood by the coffee maker and slowed his mind enough to enjoy the gurgle and pop of the machine and the pungent aroma.

A baby wailed somewhere, and he glanced up from the coffee maker through the glass wall to see Jane at the City Hall entrance, uncharacteristically late. He wanted to make a hasty retreat to his office, but the coffee maker acted like an aging diva—in no hurry to lose the attention. He pivoted quickly to avoid contact and grabbed a water conservation brochure from the rack next to him, pretending to read it. The door opened behind him.

"Good morning," Jane mumbled.

Something was wrong with her. Brad did not care. With all the revelations of the prior night, he did not have a plan for how to deal with his once-trusted assistant. Ignoring her for now seemed the best course.

"Good morning," he replied coolly, without turning around. He kept his head bent to the brochure while glancing impatiently at the coffee pot. Jane walked slowly to her desk, retrieved the filing cabinet key from her not-so-imaginative hiding place, unlocked the master latch, and began opening the file doors, her back to him. Brad quickly poured a cup and walked briskly through the low swinging door by her desk into his office without a further word. This would not work. How could he ignore her all day?

Brad sat at his desk staring out the door to the corner of Jane's desk where she sat in silence. No phone calls, shuffling of papers, or computer pings. Nothing. Her chair squeaked. He saw her come around her desk toward the outer door. The lock on the door clanked and Jane appeared at his door a moment later.

"Got a minute?" she asked.

Brad noted her matted hair, smeared make-up, and puffy face. Her left cheek was a little red.

"I guess," he replied guardedly. He stayed in his chair behind the desk watching her take a seat at the coffee table.

She looked down at her folded hands for a moment and broke the silence. "Something happened last night. I wasn't sure if I was going to talk to you about it or not. It's embarrassing. But I have to tell you."

"Uh-huh?" He rested his chin on his pointed index fingers and waited.

Jane gathered herself and peered up at him through blood-shot, hazel eyes. "The Nettlers know about the problems with the well. You know, about the chromium and iron. And they know about the discipline process underway at the water plant."

"Of course they do," he exploded, "you told them!"

"What?"

"Oh, save it, Jane. I know all about it."

She was on the verge of tears. "But—"

"How do I know?" He leaned back and smirked. "You ought to be a little more careful with your cell phone."

She cocked her head and stared at him.

"Okay, you accidentally called me last night on your cell. I didn't listen long but long enough to hear you tell Hank about the wells."

"No!" she protested.

He picked up a paper clip and began pulling it apart. "Get off it. I heard what you said to him. I never expected you to stab me in the back. Hank Nettler! Explain!"

Jane trembled. "We've known each other since school days but the relationship changed at a party Scott threw last spring. Hank and his wife had separated. He's been living on the ranch in the main house with Hubie. There's not a lot to choose from in this town. I don't have much time away from work and raising the girls to, um, socialize. I sure didn't want to do the bar scene in a gossipy small town. Just wanted companionship. And Hank's been so sweet and generous to me and the girls.

"I'll bet," Brad scoffed.

"Well, Hank came over for dinner and brought some wine. I couldn't get a sitter, and he wanted to watch the planning commission meeting, anyway. So, we stayed home, drank wine, and watched the meeting."

"With you providing the background commentary on the problems with Well 2, it sounded like."

She sat rigidly, shaking. A tear escaped down the side of her nose. "No. I didn't. You have it all wrong. What did you hear?"

He clenched his jaw, threw the paper clip into the waste basket, and smacked the top of his desk so loudly that the picture frame of his family fell over. "I heard you tell Hank about my going along with the tertiary compromise and firing Megan, and then you talked about the well problems."

"No," she cried, shaking her head slowly. "Hank's the one who brought it up. He knew all about it. I was defending you." Jane looked down to her lap.

"I'm sorry, Brad, but he also said something about Marie being raped a long time ago." She slumped, dropped her head into her hands, and broke down.

Someone jiggled the locked outer office door. Neither moved to open it. Brad sighed, got up from his desk, and handed Jane a small square box of Kleenex in a green floral pattern from his credenza. She blew her nose. Brad took a chair across from her and waited impatiently for her to compose herself.

"I want to know *exactly* what he said about that."

"I don't remember exactly. We were pretty drunk. I remember Hank saying you were supposed to propose having the EIR look only at tertiary water for the golf course. He told me the family gets two hundred-thousand-dollars from SoCal once the EIR is launched. Hank was afraid that after what you said last night, SoCal may bail before they get that big payment."

"Go on."

"He called you a wimp, waiting to make your recommendation after you felt safe. And, forgive me, how you didn't have the balls to push the project along. He said you couldn't even protect your wife from getting raped."

"I see," Brad said dolefully. "What happened next?"

"He said something about having you by the balls. I think he meant because he knew about Marie. I yelled at him about using that and told him it would backfire on them. We had words and he slapped me."

"I'm sorry, Jane. The Nettlers are bullies and can't take it when anyone, especially a woman, stands up to them."

Jane caressed the red spot on her left cheek. "That's for sure. I'm sort of glad he hit me. It knocked some sense into me and I made him leave. Brad, you have to believe me. I never told him anything I shouldn't have last night...or ever." She collapsed back in her chair beginning to sob again.

Brad no longer saw a backstabbing turncoat before him. Jane was again his trusted, now vulnerable, ally who had been wrongly accused. "I do believe you, Jane. Now, at least. Can you remember anything else? Like how he knew about the well problems?"

She crushed her tissue and peered up to the ceiling a moment. "My impression is that the family has been taking their own water samples at the well and knew about the chromium and iron. It didn't seem to worry him. In fact, he laughed that it won't be a problem for his cows."

"For his cows?" Brad asked. He remembered Hank saying something at Rotary a while back about the family expanding their beef business and maybe opening a dairy. Strange.

Brad leaned back in the chair and rested his lower lip on the steeple of his raised index fingers. "Let me sort this out. The Nettlers are eager to have the Initial Study approved so they get a big option payment. They're worried that SoCal will bail without making the payment if they don't get the golf course tertiary compromise. But they don't seem to care about the well problems. Why not?"

"Maybe they have something in their agreement with SoCal that protects them," Jane posed.

"Their agreement…" Brad mulled. He tapped his chin with his fingers, deep in thought. "Nettlers are smart. They know we aren't going to want to stick that treatment cost on our current residents and businesses especially, if we can show we have enough water for the existing customers without that well. We'll be more likely to impose the obligation on Green Valley to pay for the treatment. Given how nervous SoCal already is about their pro forma, that condition might kill the whole deal."

Brad stared out the window. "The family likely makes a ton of money with the land sale to SoCal. Why would Hank not care more about the well problem? And what did he mean about not bothering his cows?"

"I don't get it either, Brad. And, come to think of it, he seemed like he was taunting me, like he was dropping a few hints about some devious plan they had but wouldn't tell me."

Lost in thought, Brad let her statement sink in a while before straightening up and wagging his right index finger in the air. "Devious, huh? Hmmm…"

"What, Brad?"

He nodded his head slightly, narrowed his eyes, and turned to face her. "When he talked about a dairy, do you think he might have meant on the same property they optioned to SoCal? Instead of Green Valley?"

"Don't know."

Brad held his index finger to his lowered forehead and closed his eyes. They sat in silence for a short time with Brad occasionally nodding his head or furrowing his brow. Eventually he opened his eyes again with a sly expression. "What if the Nettlers never intended to sell the 550 acres for Green Valley Village at all?"

"What?" she protested. "But you said yourself they probably will make a killing selling that land once the project is approved."

"True, but we don't know how much they stand to net from that sale after taxes. Their basis would be like zero."

"I don't follow you, Brad."

"Maybe, after taxes, they're better off long-term with the cash flow from a dairy or expanding their beef business instead of selling to SoCal. Besides, have you ever known Nettlers to sell the family's land? When you mentioned their agreement, I remembered Scott telling me about it at Rotary a while back. It had all kinds of nonrefundable progress payments tied to milestones in the approval process. You said they're getting a couple hundred thousand dollars once this EIR gets underway. Approval of the Initial Study launches the EIR. Maybe that's their whole scheme. String the city and SoCal along and collect as much as they can in progress payments, then scuttle the deal and build a dairy on the property. They don't care if the whole deal blows up at the end over water quality costs or anything else so long as the process drags out long enough to hit more milestones."

Jane sat back in her chair. "You think? How does that tarplant figure into it?"

"Only a theory. Let's go through it. Didn't Jenny tell us she learned about the tarplant from Fred Buderi a year ago or so?"

"Yes. She remembered it was the same time that the family was negotiating the sale with SoCal. And she thought it was Buderi who called Hubie about a five hundred-thousand-dollar mitigation cost."

"And Jenny said she was just up there and saw that the habitat hadn't been disturbed."

"Right."

"So, if the Nettlers were worried about the cost of dealing with the tarplant messing up the sale, don't you think they would have destroyed it by now?"

"Yeah," she agreed. "They have all the earthmoving equipment they need and could probably scour the entire area in an hour with nobody knowing. Jenny was worried they would do just that. I wonder why they didn't?"

"You can bet it wasn't because of their deep, abiding concern about protecting the habitat or complying with environmental laws."

"No doubt."

Brad tapped his chin trying to dislodge a memory. "Back to the agreement. If I remember right, there was no extensive review of the site for endangered species or hazardous materials when they signed, but Nettlers are on the hook if something comes up later in the EIR process." Brad's look of concentration suddenly changed to a big smile. "Aha! *Or* Nettlers can terminate the deal! That's it, Jane! That explains why they wanted such an unusual option agreement. That's why Nettlers have been pushing the process so hard. That's why they're willing to do anything to remove any obstacles, including obstacles named Megan Cain or even Brad Jacks."

Jane leaned in expectantly. "You're way ahead of me."

Brad rocked silently a moment, his smile getting larger. "I think I see what's happening with the whole tarplant thing." He paused and looked at the ceiling before continuing.

"What? What?" Jane implored.

"The sonsabitches are playing us all. The Nettlers never intended to sell to SoCal at all. Scott said they weren't interested at first but then changed their stance and wanted to make a deal. My hunch is that during that period Jenny told her family about the tarplant and they devised a way to use it to their advantage. They insisted on a complex deal with multiple milestones to accomplish and nonrefundable progress payments along the way. The tarplant is their way out of the deal."

"They could terminate their agreement?" Jane asked.

"Based on what I remember Scott saying, yes. I think he said Nettlers would have to reimburse a hundred thousand dollars of SoCal's development costs if they terminate."

Jane waved her hand. "Probably chump change compared to the payments they hoped to get. And they've been sitting on the well problems to avoid SoCal freaking out and canceling too early."

"Maybe. Or maybe they were going to have the lab tech start reporting the problem when the time was right. Now that I think of it, it's going to take months to determine the magnitude of the well problem and develop a solution. And because water supply is the most critical go/no-go issue facing the development, there's no point in spending time and money on all the other studies described in the Initial Study until the water is assured. The biological survey that will discover the tarplant gets put on a back burner until the water problem is fixed. Who knows how many more progress payments Nettlers will get by then?"

"It all sounds so devious," Jane said then frowned. "But it all fits and I hate to admit I can see the Nettlers doing it. Poor Scott. And all those people counting on Green Valley Village. If what you say is right, we're all being conned and will never know. But how could Hank and Hubie think they could keep the tarplant a secret when Jenny and maybe Fred Buderi have known about it for so long?"

"Right. Buderi. I was baffled why neither he nor Megan brought up the tarplant last night. It's not like Buderi would have forgotten about it. What scientist wouldn't want his name attached to a new endangered species sighting? He must not have told Megan or she would have used it last night herself."

"Do you think Fred…"

"That's exactly what I think. Buderi scouts Jenny's spot and confirms her discovery of the plant and calls Hubie to alert him.

That's when Nettlers hatch the scheme to structure the progress payments with the species as their out. Buderi wasn't officially engaged to do a survey, so I doubt he'd be violating any laws by selling his silence. Sure, he made some negative comments about the project at the commission last night because for him not to would have looked odd. But I remember thinking last night that he was fairly milquetoast with his presentation."

Jane nodded agreement. "Looks like the doctor 'has some 'splaining to do.' Are you going to ask him about it?"

Brad shook his head. "I can't without him realizing Jenny told me about him knowing."

"Oh, Jenny! She's right. God knows what they'd do to her if they knew she told us. She really is a sweet kid."

Brad nodded concurrence. "You heard Jenny. Hank and Hubie apparently don't recognize her spunk. They don't give her enough credit to even be a threat. She's in the clear now and we need to protect that. We better keep you out of this too, Jane. You have your kids to consider. I don't know if I'm going to come out of this whole Green Valley thing intact but there's no sense in your going down, too."

Jane cast a worried expression. "There are a lot of people counting on things in the Green Valley development agreement. People aren't going to be happy if the project folds. They'll be looking for somebody to blame and City Hall is always an inviting target. The Nettlers could complain it was your mis-management of Megan and the water plant that first started to turn SoCal against the project. Oh, and I hate to remind you, you have another public disclosure quandary with this tarplant situation and the whole thing with Marie."

"Yeah, as the dinosaur said, 'I wish I had a bigger brain'. I need some alone time to think about this."

Somebody rattled the outer door again. Jane nodded toward it. "Hold calls and visitors a while?"

"Yes, thanks. You read my mind, Radar. No interruptions, please. And Jane, thanks for coming to me with this. I'm sorry I doubted you. I appreciate you."

Alone in his office, Brad felt the weight of the world. He picked up another paper clip, bending it into different shapes, as his mind processed the situation. Having accomplished only a fair likeness of a right triangle, he tossed the clip on the desk. There were too many factors to hold in his head at the same time. He scrawled a list:

- *Green Valley dead, won't happen*
- *Community torn apart for nothing*
- *Nettlers playing SoCal/city? Just pushing project for progress payments*
- *How to block Nettlers without implicating Jane/Jenny?*
- *My duty*

He scrolled down the list several times trying to formulate a strategy. Each time, his pen lingered over the last item and added another underline to it.

Brad exhaled slowly, turned his chair to the wall, leaned back, put his feet on the credenza, and stared at the photograph of Mt. Shasta. He shut his eyes and concentrated on his breathing. After about ten minutes, he slowly opened his eyes to a plaque just below the Mt. Shasta photo. The International City/County Management Association's Code of Ethics sat in a frame on his credenza largely unnoticed for years. He scanned it now, twelve tenets calling members to the highest ideals of public service.

Tenet Four jumped off the page. *Recognize that the chief function of local government at all times is to serve the best interests of all of the people.* Interesting. He read it again. That's odd. Typically, when facing a difficult policy recommendation, he went with his expectation of what the council majority wanted. He read the tenet again and had an "ah ha!" moment.

Somewhere along his lengthy career path, his role morphed from protecting the public interest to doing the bidding of the council majority. Had the pressures of a mortgage, retirement planning, and kids' college turned him into Lilly's father? Going along with the powerful people rather than questioning? He certainly found it less complicated and safer to count three votes than to muck around with a vague concept like the public interest.

Brad closed his eyes again to let this new insight settle in. *What is in the public interest with the whole Green Valley controversy?* His stillness manifested as palpable fear when the answer he was looking for arose: *I have to kill the project.* After his recent face-off with the East Area Rapist stress, he found it easier to sit with the fear a while, breathing in and out fully, to see where it would go. He soon felt the tension in his gut, chest, and arms starting to give way to a tingle. Exhilaration. Then a sense of power. He had a plan that might stymie the Nettlers and keep him employed. It felt right. Scary, but right.

Brad smacked his desk with resolve and walked over to open his office door. "Jane, what time will the packets get delivered to the council today?"

"Around three."

"Good," he said. "May give me just enough time."

"Time for what?" she asked.

"A few more things I need to do today." He closed his door again.

CHAPTER 28

Former planning director Megan Cain answered on the third ring. They chatted a while about how she was doing. Brad volunteered to write her a letter of recommendation for which she thanked him.

"Megan, how would you like to get even with the Nettlers and kill Green Valley Village in the process?"

"Sounds like fun," she said eagerly. "Tell me more."

"First, I need your solemn oath that you won't talk to anyone about this, especially, and I repeat: especially, Fred. If you do, he and some innocent people will be in serious trouble. Trust me on that. And don't speculate how I know what I'm about to tell you. Digging into that will hurt people."

After being satisfied with her pledge of silence, he told her he had good reason to believe that there was an endangered species, Gaviota Tarplant, habitat on the Nettler property, the Green Valley site. He told her where on the property and what he wanted her to do. Megan was all in.

Brad then called Marie to tell her Jane did not know any more about the rape than that Nettlers had discovered it. He briefed her on his plan and admitted anxiety over what he'd set in motion. "I'm like a picador who is about to stab and weaken the bull. Megan understands that she is the matador who will be the primary target for the bull's rage and will deliver the fatal thrust. Neither of us better miss."

"Jane, bring your pad, would you? Let's do this thing." Brad said resolutely.

She settled in at her normal spot at the coffee table as he got into dictating position: pacing.

"This is a council agenda memo," he began, "Subject: Reconsideration of Planning Commission Approval of Green Valley Village EIR Initial Study."

"Oh, Brad, are you sure you want to do that?"

"Hell no, I'm not sure! I hear a voice saying, 'prepare three envelopes.'"

"But it's so unusual for you to appeal an action by one of the council's commissions. And you'd be appealing your own recommendation to them. You're going to make yourself the target."

"I know, but the planning commission approved the IS and that's the end of it unless somebody appeals it to the council. We have to act fast, so I'm it. If I don't do this, Scott will rely on the commission's approval and make that big progress payment. Nettlers win. Everyone else loses. I think the public interest is best served by stopping it before this entire community becomes even more divided for no good end. It's my responsibility to do it."

"But the Nettlers and Green Valley supporters will come after you," she warned.

"Ah, but consider the upside," he smirked. "Maybe Hank will give me one of his juicy T-bones to nurse the black eye he'll give me."

"That's not even funny."

"Gallows humor. Remember? An occupational hazard."

"I'm sorry for anything I may have done to put you in harm's way."

"Nah. I put myself in harm's way when I chose this career and took the oath of office. There may be a better way, but this is the best plan I've come up with on short notice to protect you, Jenny, and, ultimately, the entire city. I have to play this straight, like I have a legitimate issue involving the project and not let on that I have any inkling the project has been stillborn from the onset. The water quality problems at Well 2 are about to come out in the disciplinary hearing before the council pretty quick anyway, so making some general reference to them isn't a stretch."

"Why do *you* have to be such a Boy Scout?"

"Everybody finds forks in the road that make them question their sense of right and wrong. I recently heard a very sad story of a principled man who didn't act on his values and it literally resulted in disastrous consequences. The guilt killed him. It's been on my mind a lot lately."

"I expect all of us have skeletons in our closets," Jane said quietly. "One of mine is named Nettler."

"I'm not proud of some of my decisions, either Jane. But maybe your devil is my angel. If it hadn't been for your relationship with Hank, the accidental cell call last night, and our talk this morning, I would have been left with regrets over how I handled things at the meeting last night. And Marie and I would still be carrying around some old, heavy baggage that we finally dumped last night. You gave me a chance for redemption on a couple levels."

Jane nodded, not prying further. "You're quite a guy, Brad."

"Just another flawed human being trying to get better. Let's finish the memo before I get cold feet."

He labored over the words as he paced around the room, making constant revisions. After finally finishing, Brad added, "Oh, let's keep this confidential for the time being, right?" he said.

"Sure, Brad. I've never betrayed your confidence."

"I know. Would you go ahead and finalize the memo, but don't send it for copying yet in case I decide to make some changes? And please ask Dee to come down."

Brad briefed his public works director on his decision to ask the council to reconsider the commission's action on the Initial Study and to do the *full* tertiary water study, not just limiting it to the golf course. Dee Sharma began to repeat all the reasons that was unnecessary and even foolhardy. Brad held the course and cut the meeting short, telling Dee he needed to get on the phone immediately to inform the council about his revised recommendation on the IS before the packets went out.

Brad busied himself the rest of the morning with paperwork and returned phone calls. He put the finishing touches on his counterproposal to the boutique hotel developer and gave it to Jane to prepare for his signature. He looked at his watch. Nothing yet. Should not be long.

He thumbed through the police department's year-end crime report, killing time. A paragraph heading in eighteen-point bold type screamed, "Auto Theft Up 50%." He read closer and grinned. Just as he thought. Six last year, four the year before. Got to love living in Santa Ynez! How much longer would he have the pleasure? He read that property crimes were up sixteen percent, but the totals were still small. Violent crime dropped. He knew what to expect in the text and found it. The drop in violent crime was tied to the police department's aggressive community policing initiatives, while the property crime increase resulted from broader economic and social trends beyond the PD's control. He smirked and tossed the voluminous report aside.

Brad checked his watch again and scrolled through his emails. His phone buzzed and he scooped it up.

"Scott Graves," Jane announced.

Brad grinned. "Scott! You beat me to it. I was getting ready to call you."

"Afternoon, Brad. It sounds like we need to talk."

"About what?" the city manager said coyly.

"About your revised recommendation on the IS, of course."

"Boy, do you have a bug in my office, Scott? I haven't even sent the memo out yet."

"You know how politicians talk. You should be glad people worry about you doing something you'll regret."

Brad sniggered. "I'm grateful to have that kind of support. Who on the council should I call to thank for watching out for me?"

"Nice try, Brad. The important thing now is for us to talk this through. You better understand the ramifications."

"Talk away. I owe you that much, Scott."

The developer took a deep breath before proceeding. "You should know I've spent a lot of time defending you since the commission meeting. People aren't so sure they can count on you to drive this project over the finish line."

"Oh?" Brad responded, matter-of-factly.

"Yeah. I told them you did what you thought was best to get out of the full tertiary study gracefully even if you hedged on the cost offset and weren't as forceful as we'd hoped. But now, if you change course and recommend the full tertiary study, I don't know what to tell people anymore. And Jeff Simpson? You have to know, he'll be pissed…at both of us."

Brad savored his victory.

"Brad, are you still there?" Scott asked.

"I'm here, but you also should know something. First, there are only two people who know about my revised recommendation. And I told them different things. I haven't even called the council yet. Second, despite what Dee told you, I'm not recommending the full tertiary study."

Brad sat smiling as he waited for his prey to realize he had been caught in the trap.

"Busted," the developer finally admitted. "Don't be hard on Dee. He didn't call me. I called him about turning over maintenance at the soccer field and we got to talking about last night. He sounded upset and I dug it out of him. He hoped I'd have some influence on talking you out of it. He was protecting you from yourself."

"I suspect he was more worried about protecting himself," Brad cracked.

"So, you're not asking the council to go with the full tertiary study?" Scott asked hopefully.

"No. I'm asking them to do what government agencies do best: postpone action. It'll give us time to figure out what, if any, impact the Well 2 problems will have on our water supply before we start the EIR."

"Postponement of the IS? Damn it, Brad, that's even worse than what I thought! You should have consulted me first."

Brad noted that the developer did not ask about what he meant by "the Well 2 problems." "I have your interests in mind, Scott. You better know where we are with water before you spend more money for—things." He caught himself before warning Scott about further option payments to the Nettlers.

"If you're talking about the iron and chromium problem," Scott said dismissively, "we know all about that."

"You do? You told me you have a big, nonrefundable payment due to the Nettlers after you accept the Initial Study. Don't you want a better handle on the water issues before you make that payment?"

Scott sighed into the receiver. "I guess I shouldn't have expected you to understand," Scott said glumly. "You live in a world that puts the emphasis on process and avoiding risk. If a developer did that, we'd go broke. You have to take chances to make real money."

"I get that, Scott," Brad said. "It even drives me crazy sometimes. I'm more like the old school city managers who want to see things coming out of the ground. But I've come to understand that sometimes running roughshod over public processes hasn't turned out. I may not like it either, but it's best to have a little more process in this case."

"Not in this case, not at all," Scott said pointedly. "As I started to say," the developer continued, "we don't have the luxury of time or doing things sequentially to minimize risk. We have to run concurrent processes, make educated guesses, and take big chances."

"But you'd be running a helluva risk proceeding without certainty about our ability to supply your water."

"Sure, it's a risk. Everything we do is a calculated risk. And, by the way, we've beat the issue up and down for months. Dee didn't tell me about the iron and chromium problem. Nettlers disclosed it. We brought in our engineers. They said it probably won't require taking the entire well field out of production. It may eventually require some additional treatment, but it's doable."

It took a moment for that to register. "Wait, you've known about this for a year?" Brad exclaimed.

"Sure. Nettlers' lawyers probably warned them that it would likely come out eventually that they had done their own testing, so they better disclose it to us, or we could nail them big time later. Nettlers may not be pleasant people, but they have lawyers who cover their butts like Desitin. We agreed to just sit on it for the time being. There was no point letting that information out now and give Kay and her group more ammunition against the project before I've built more popular support."

Brad quickly thought of a more devious Nettler strategy: disclose the well problems to appear to be negotiating in good faith to make SoCal more comfortable that everything was on the table during the due diligence period while holding back on the tarplant. But he was confused. "You guys were bitching so much about tertiary treatment for only the golf course. Aren't you worried about a big bill on additional treatment for the chromium? Reverse osmosis is expensive."

Scott sighed again. "Like I said, it didn't serve our interests for there to be any question about water supply. Yet. Let it come out later in the process after we have everything figured out and our supporters solidly in place. And as for the cost of the additional treatment, that's a cost you'll have to spread to the entire customer base, you can't stick it on our project alone. The water quality problems are an existing condition. We didn't cause it, and we won't be the only ones to pay to fix it."

Brad massaged his throbbing temple. "But you and Jeff kept saying you can't absorb any other costs," he protested.

"Oh, come on, Brad. It's a negotiation. Our pro forma includes a contingency for our fair share of the water quality problem, but nothing for tertiary. Despite what you said last night, we can't blithely add that to the house prices. The studies show we are already pushing the market as is. We usually don't get this far in a new project without projecting a much higher return. I've been able to convince Jeff to keep going based on our cost estimates and lots of local support to get everything done quickly and minimize our risk. That's why I needed you to come out strong for the tertiary compromise and cost offset."

Brad's victory lap from finally exposing the City Hall leak had been cut short. "I see," he said. There was no point arguing the matter.

"Let me put it this way, Brad: you manage a city. Most of the time, it doesn't matter much if some decision comes now, or months later. Or if a capital improvement project is built now or next year. In our business, timing is critical. We have Green Valley programmed in our plans to begin construction in two years. To do that, we have to hit our milestones. If you are talking about the EIR on hold until we drill test wells and decide how to resolve the water issues, we miss the construction season we've targeted."

And I'd be doing you a favor… Green Valley is as dead as disco, Brad thought.

The developer continued his protestations. "If we miss that construction window, *everything* is up in the air. We always have other projects moving through stages and competing for our time and money. I've told you that Green Valley isn't a big homerun for the company. It's a small project with barely adequate returns. It's been left in the pipeline to keep our people busy. If the delay you want puts us off schedule, Green Valley goes back into the pot to compete with other projects we scheduled to come online later. And I know it won't be competitive."

"I see," Brad mumbled. *This is a waste of time. Tell him what's really going on.*

"I know you were trying to do the right thing. But, to be honest, I'd rather you had proposed the full tertiary rather than a postponement. I can get the votes on the council to kill the full tertiary, but how do I mobilize against a city manager who says publicly he's worried about his water supply and possible carcinogenic contamination and wants more information prior to committing to a big new development? Where you come down makes or breaks this project."

"I can see your point, Scott. And yes, I didn't intend to make this more difficult for SoCal. Just the opposite."

"But it's not too late, right?" Scott said, sounding hopeful. "You haven't talked to the council yet and you said the memo hasn't gone out, right? Don't bring everything to a grinding halt. Let the commission decision stand. We'll deal with the water stuff later. We'll indemnify you."

Brad sighed and threw in the towel. He was tired of trying to manage so many things he neither totally understood nor controlled. "Scott, I agree with what you said at the beginning of the call: 'we need to talk.' Just you, me, and Jeff Simpson. In Pasadena. As a friend, trust me that it's important not to tell anyone else."

Friday afternoons were normally quiet. Not this one. Brad placed calls or left voice mails with the councilmembers and Planning Commission Chairman Parker Fleishmann to inform them of his decision to place the Initial Study on the council agenda, with a recommendation to postpone circulation pending further water study. They all wanted to know the details behind such a turnabout in his recommendation from the night before. He used the confidentiality of employee disciplinary rights to say little more.

Mayor Buddy stormed over from his real estate office, panting through his tirade. The mayor insisted on knowing the sordid details. Brad gave him a little more about the investigation at the water plant without getting too graphic about all the goings on or talking about rising chromium and iron levels at a well. He advised that he had to keep the mayor's independence for the disciplinary hearings to come and did not want anyone spooked about water quality prematurely. He wanted desperately to tell him the whole story.

The only supportive call came from Councilwoman Kay Nance late in the day in response to the voice mail he had left her.

"So, you're still there," the councilwoman joked when she called back later in the day. "They haven't run you out of town yet, huh?"

"No, but I smell hot tar and am nervous. Resurfacing the parking lot isn't in the budget." He gave her a little more background on why he recommended the postponement, being careful not to tell her more than he did the mayor.

"You earned some points today," Kay said. "At least with my side of the aisle. I appreciate that you're trying to do what's right and are likely taking shots over it. Speaking of shots, if you and Marie need a place to hide out tonight, come on over. I can probably dig up a bottle of Tequila for you."

He laughed. "Yeah, Kay, hanging out with you is sure going to help my image right now. But we second your idea of getting out of town."

CHAPTER 29

Brad was standing in the ticket line at Universal Studios in Hollywood Saturday afternoon when City Attorney Henry Fitzhenry called.

"Henry! What's the good word?" he asked sarcastically.

"Hi Brad. Sorry to bother you on the weekend."

"I imagine you've been pestered a lot since yesterday. Everything copacetic back home?" He chuckled, relishing the image of the city attorney having to work Friday night and Saturday on the mess Brad left behind.

"I wanted to let you know that the council asked me to advertise a closed session for Tuesday evening prior to the council meeting to evaluate the city manager's performance. They want you to be available in your office on stand-by. And, if the press calls you about it, say that annual evaluations are part of your contract. Nothing else."

"Oh, I see. Was the meeting called by Buddy alone or are you following a majority of the council?"

"I'm afraid the majority, Brad. Sorry to have to call you like this." He sounded sincere.

"It's okay, Henry. I'm not exactly shocked by the news. Thanks for the heads-up."

"Oh, and Brad," Fitzhenry's hesitated. "You didn't hear this from me. I'm sticking my neck out here. Okay?"

"Sure, Henry," he chuckled, imagining the city attorney's angst compared to what he was going through. "I promise I'm not recording this."

"All I want to say is that although a majority went along with setting a meeting, I don't read it that there's a majority to fire you. So, don't go driving off a cliff or anything."

He ended the call and wiped the grit and sweat from the creases in his neck. Weird to be so hot and miserable in spring. Out of season Santa Ana, "devil winds," were blowing hard, scouring Southern California with hot, dry, sandy air from the deserts to the east. Fire departments worked to exhaustion trying to prevent localized flare ups in the hills from becoming conflagrations. Fine sand penetrated every crack and orifice. Everyone's skin crawled. Nerves fired. Tempers flared. Not a time to get bad news or be in a ticket line with scores of other grumpy tourists and their kids trying to keep things nonviolent. He studied the colorful, cool, blue sign above and smirked at the irony. He hoped the Water World venue would not turn out to be another California mirage.

Brad yawned. They had an easy two-and-a-half-hour trip that morning to Pasadena, the home office of SoCal Communities. Marie visited her sister in Glendale while Brad drove on to the lion's den to meet with Scott Graves and his boss, Jeff Simpson. The meeting started tense, with the developers attacking Brad's decision to recommend postponement of the Initial Study.

Brad explained that he could not go into details about his suspicions without putting vulnerable people at risk, so he asked the developers to keep an open mind. "What if the Nettlers never had any intention of selling to you under any circumstances?" he posed. "What if their game plan all along had been to push Green Valley ahead to collect progress payments then kill the deal at some point? What if they have a different idea planned for the property? What if we're all being played?"

Jeff Simpson mostly stared at Brad during the "what ifs." Brad suspected it was the seasoned developer's pride preventing him from imagining he had been had by these country bumpkins. "That's a lot of nothing, Brad," he finally said. "You have to give me more facts before I call that bastard Hubie Nettler and accuse him of something."

"Like I said, Jeff, I have to protect my sources. But I have a suggestion to see for yourselves if the Nettlers are being up-front with you. First, Scott mentioned that you have to make Nettlers a big progress payment when the Initial Study is approved. And I think your contract has a reopener on haz-mat or endangered species mitigation that allows either party to terminate if you can't settle."

"That's right," Scott confirmed. "But don't forget, if Nettlers terminate, they have to pay us a hundred thousand."

"I remember. My action to put the IS on the council agenda was to stall for time to have this meeting with you and convince you not to make that payment."

"Go on." Simpson said anxiously.

"I will. But only if you commit to not dig into my sources and to act based only on public information."

"Alright, alright," Simpson snapped. "Get to the point."

"I'm going to rely on your word about that. And, if I'm right, I think you'll see you owe me at least that much." Brad leaned forward. "Check the Sunday Santa Ynez Reporter tomorrow. I have reason to believe there will be a story about an endangered species find that should make you want to revisit that reopener language. Maybe you'll even offer to help with the mitigation cost with Hubie. Pay close attention to his response in light of my 'what ifs.' That should tell you whether you are working in good faith with the seller or being scammed. But act fast. I may not be around after Tuesday to help you."

The meeting had accomplished its goal. The developers had been alerted. They would talk again after the weekend.

Brad yielded to his curiosity and read the on-line versions of the local paper Sunday morning. It had three big stories that began on the front page. One was a short article announcing a closed session of the city council scheduled for Tuesday evening before the normal city council meeting for the purpose of evaluating the city manager's performance. The city attorney attempted to downplay the gravity of the meeting, saying it was common practice for the council to conduct such evaluations this time of year. Brad snickered when he read that the reporter asked the city attorney when he last received *his* council evaluation. Henry was quoted as saying, "I don't remember exactly."

The bigger article carried the headline: "City Manager in Jeopardy?" It speculated on the true purpose of the meeting, replete with unattributed, off-the-record statements. Councilmembers were officially "no comment," although Brad suspected some of them were sources. Councilmembers had to take care of their relationships with the local press after all. The article quoted "veteran City Hall watchdog" Pat Kirby who called the city manager competent and fair. But the slant of the story got it right, Green Valley Village supporters were on the warpath over Brad's handling of the EIR Initial Study and he was taking their slings and arrows.

The most disappointing comment came from his friend, Chamber Exec Brian Brando, who said that while the Chamber has had a cooperative relationship with the city manager in the past, even if they have not always agreed, the Chamber stays out of city personnel issues as a matter of policy. Brad swore at the computer screen.

The third article was perfect. The headline said: "Rare Species Found on Green Valley Site?" It included a photo of a cluster of people with Megan Cain, dressed in hiking gear, standing next to a sheriff's car talking to a deputy. Brad also spotted an obviously angry Hubie Nettler on the other side of the deputy.

The story described that former planning director Megan Cain, now a private citizen, and a teenager named Martin Irwin, had come on Saturday morning to do some reconnaissance of the Green Valley Village site. "I'm no longer leading the environmental review for the project," the story quoted Megan, "and I don't know when a full protocol-level survey of the site is going to be done, or when my replacement will be on board. I came to get a baseline of existing conditions to ensure that nothing is disturbed in the meantime."

The teen flew his drone over the property zooming in and taking pictures of areas of interest to Megan. They had been at it, working from a county road, for several hours when Megan spotted what she believed could be a growth of Gaviota Tarplant grasses, a state and federal endangered species. The story included a small photo of the tarplant credited to Megan Cain and some background on the plant, endangered species in general, and what the discovery could mean to Green Valley, all attributed to Megan.

"We have excellent zoomed images to confirm the species," Megan said. "It appeared to be a significant habitat. We were in the process of mapping the area when we heard a rifle shot and the screen went dead."

The story said that landowner Hubie Nettler admitted shooting down the drone, but it was unclear which side called the sheriff's department. A sergeant later confirmed that no arrests were made. "This is a civil matter," he said.

Brad spent Saturday and Sunday morning dodging calls from the press, preferring a "could not be reached for comment" over the spin he was told to give.

They opted to take the long way back from Hollywood to Santa Ynez Sunday evening, via Highway 126, the path of the Saint Francis Dam flood of 1928. Brad had his iPod hooked up to the car's USB port, playing his 60s playlist. Judy Collins came on singing about looking at clouds from both sides now. He offered his hand and Marie reached across her chest with her right hand. She smiled back at him.

"Nice of Kay and Claire to call you," Marie observed. "From what you said, it sounds like they're busy getting public support for you."

"Yes," he agreed. "But frankly, I wish I'd get a call from Al Landon. He would be the swing vote if it ever came to that. Actually, this whole dust-up about firing me is more interesting than scary. If this all goes the way I expect in the next day or so, it will settle out and provide me a pretty good barometer of where I stand in town and with the council."

They drove on listening to the music and enjoying the scenery along the undivided highway. Marie could see Brad's mind was still churning. "What are you thinking?"

"Megan played her matador role well. I'll bet she loved sticking it to Hubie and Hank, stumbling upon the tarplant prematurely, sort of. The Nettlers see red anytime Megan comes to mind so it will be easy for them to conclude this was all just Megan being Megan, meddling in their business. Hank never talked to Jane about the tarplant the other night and Jenny's not on their radar screen at all, well, at least not related to the newspaper story. They're in the clear. And I hope I will be soon."

Brad looked at his navigation screen and noticed that they were approaching the imaginary line separating Los Angeles and Ventura counties. He saw the train tracks. "Right about in here, I think," he said, pointing out his side window. "This must have been about where Lilly was when the flood hit their camp."

Marie looked left and right. "Imagine that wall of water and debris barreling through here in the dead of night."

"Yeah, ninety-plus years ago Lilly was clinging for her life on those hills over there as her parents washed out toward the ocean. Think of it."

He held her hand tighter as they drove on towards Fillmore and Santa Paula.

Brad glimpsed the early moon above the darkening horizon and his mind drifted to the vastness and order of the cosmos. He had not felt this connection to nature, or God, or whatever, since the duck hunt.

"It's so beautiful!" he said solemnly.

Brad marveled at the precision of the dark green rows of orange and lemon groves passing beside them. The quartering moon made its appearance in synch with the vast universe as it had from the beginning of time. The tall sycamore trees swayed gently in the warm, spring breeze, sturdy limbs silhouetted against the clear purple sky. Brad imagined his neighbor, Lilly, blissfully riding her hobby horse, Brownie, in those fields. Beauty and horror live in this place. Life itself is unpredictable, offering no guarantees other than change. He remembered a lyric from an old Roger MIller song: "Good ain't forever and bad ain't for good." Resiliency. That's what you needed. And faith.

Brad mulled what may be ahead for them as he drove on. He sneaked a glance at Marie and instantly felt a warm glow melting his anxieties. He smiled at his wife then slapped the steering wheel and blurted: "Bring it on!"

Epilogue

I understand now that the saying, "May you live in interesting times" is a curse, not a blessing. Brad and I would have gladly opted for our predictable routine over what we came home to that Sunday evening. Our answering machine filled with reporters pestering Brad for a comment on his potential termination and friends offering ideas to help him. Brad kept his nose to the grindstone Monday and Tuesday. He never talked to the press but did call his friends to thank them for the support and asked them not to do anything. He did not tell them about his ace in the hole.

Late Tuesday afternoon Scott Graves delivered a letter to the City Council from Jeff Simpson, Vice President of SoCal Communities. The letter announced that they were withdrawing the Green Valley Village application citing a contract dispute with the sellers. It apologized for not being able to fulfill the community benefits it was hoping to bring to Santa Ynez and that the company would look for another opportunity to come back to the area where they had made so many friends. It closed by thanking the city councilmembers for all their help and named Brad Jacks one of the best city managers they had ever had the good fortune to work with. I have never been prouder.

The closed session to evaluate Brad went ahead that evening before the council meeting. Brad was never called in. From what City Attorney Henry Fitzhenry told him later, Mayor Buddy and Kay went at it because of the way the mayor called the meeting, creating such uproar in the community. Councilwoman Claire Schmitz agreed and added that she hoped Brad did not start looking for another job because of worrying about his job security. She was followed by Councilman Al Landon who said that the SoCal letter today made it obvious that Brad was not to blame for Green Valley Village going away. Clearly, he was a seasoned professional doing his best for Santa Ynez. Landon reminded them of the boutique hotel Brad was trying to land for the downtown. Mayor Buddy Murray counted to three and must not have wanted to appear weak by being on the losing side of the majority's positive evaluation of the city manager. Vice Mayor Tim Mullikin did not want to be on any side that did not include Mayor Buddy.

Brad said that the entire council seemed tense when they came out of the closed meeting to open the regular council meeting. Councilwoman Kay Nance gave Brad a wink. The mayor announced that the council met in closed session regarding the city manager's performance evaluation. Brad was stunned when he went on to say the council approved a five percent salary increase for Mr. Jacks. People in the packed council chambers were not sure what to make of that. Some had come to show support for Brad, others hoping to see a public hanging.

The council approved Brad's recommendation to pull the item about the Green Valley Village Initial Study from the agenda because SoCal had withdrawn their application. Brad's able assistant, Jane Stanar, who doubled as the City Clerk, had copies of SoCal's letter for anyone interested. Most people on both sides of the issue were stunned. The packed council chambers erupted in cheers from the Green Valley Village opponents, again, audience left.

The council took a five-minute recess to let the chambers clear. Kay came up to Brad and said, "See, I listened to that advice you gave me. I compromised to get what I wanted: you. My motion was for a ten percent raise but Al Landon's up for reelection this year and was worried about doing too much. I'm guessing you're happy with five, considering where this *was* headed."

Scott Graves came in to see Brad the next day. He volunteered that he and Jeff Simpson met with the Nettlers on Monday about renegotiating that reopener allowing Nettlers to terminate with a one-hundred-thousand-dollar payment rather than agree on a sharing of the species mitigation costs. When the Nettlers declined all of Jeff Simpsons overtures about an amicable settlement, SoCal had all the proof they needed that Brad's "what ifs" were reality. The Nettlers were just milking SoCal for the progress payments and never were going to sell.

Scott said that Hubie claimed the family wanted to do more research on the mitigation alternatives and, in the meantime, expected SoCal to make the next progress payment for the Initial Study. Hubie threatened Jeff Simpson that if they didn't make that next payment, SoCal would be in default. Simpson understood this was Hubie's way of trying to get out of the one hundred thousand termination payment they owed. Scott paraphrased a Jim Croce song: "you don't pull the mask off that old Lone Ranger and you don't mess around with Jeff." Scott said that Jeff gave Hubie both barrels. After cussing out Hubie, Jeff threatened to hire private investigators to prove Nettlers knew about the tarplant all along. He would sue them for fraud and end up getting back all of SoCal's costs, and then some. That must have spooked them. Brad suspected that the Nettlers piled into their pickups and paid a visit on Dr. Fred Buderi who no doubt swore he never said anything to Megan about the tarplant. Through their lens, nobody can be trusted, so they could not count on Buderi's silence. Brad and I secretly savored the idea that SoCal turned the tables on the Nettlers with that private investigator threat.

In the end, the parties ended up with a settlement agreement and SoCal got its termination payment from the Nettlers. Small consolation, but something. Scott admitted he had ghost-written the tactful letter to the city council and convinced Simpson to sign the settlement agreement. SoCal still had projects in the region and did not want to burn bridges in Santa Ynez. Scott thanked Brad for watching out for them and repeated his interest in adding him to the SoCal team—when the time was right. He handed Brad a package: a framed color photo of the Gaviota Tarplant which now hangs in our bathroom.

It has been four months since the eventful council meeting and the fallout from losing the Green Valley project. The council supported the termination of the lab tech who falsified the readings at the well. By then, Public Works Director Dee Sharma had announced his retirement. Brad's press release thanked Dee for his service to the community. Insiders knew the full story.

Brad had the new public works director prepare a comprehensive report on the iron and chromium problems at Well 2. It included an analysis by Payton/Carlisle Engineering assuring that there was no current risk to public health and describing pro-active alternatives including the impact of taking that well or both wells offline entirely. It described the conservation measures residents and businesses would have to take if the wells are closed. The council accepted the staff recommendation to keep monitoring the water quality and to develop a contingency plan that would involve the water fund borrowing from other city funds to add more treatment with pay-back over time from modest, phased-in rate increases.

With the Green Valley Village dead, things have become calmer in the Santa Ynez body politic. Everyone is excited about the announcement of a new hotel coming to downtown. At Brad's request, the developer revised his plan to include retail space on the ground floor for uses like a bakery, deli, and coffee shop.

Megan Cain joined a sustainable development company that seeks small in-fill residential projects. She and Brad have been working closely together on her first project, live-work townhouses a block from the new hotel site. She plans to open an office on the ground floor and live upstairs. Local accountants, attorneys, hair stylists, and others have also expressed interest in the benefits of a live-work project. She is no longer with Dr. Fred Buderi.

Brad's status seems secure enough. But, as he warns, you cannot look beyond the next election. Candidates have lined up for the November council election. Mayor Buddy, Vice Mayor Mullikin, and Councilman Landon are up this time. Rumor has it that planning commissioner Jerry Wright wanted to run on a ticket with the mayor and vice mayor. The pro-development bloc preferred to throw in behind a more predictable supporter to replace Al Landon but considered Wright too polarizing. They convinced planning commission chairman Parker Fleishmann to join their slate. The Green Valley opponents countered with Megan Cain, artist Paisley Menezes, and master gardener Kalo Debevec. Both sides were officially neutral toward Councilman Al Landon, hedging their bets.

So far, the Nettlers have not come at Brad with anything about my attack. Maybe Jane's warning to Hank that bringing it up would backfire on them hit home. Or, more likely, with

Green Valley gone, they do not need to try to control Brad so much. They are probably focusing their scheming ways on county officials as they pursue a use permit for a dairy on the old Green Valley site. They lost a lot of their Green Valley supporters with that one. People are stirred up against the smell so close to town.

We have not said anything to our daughter about the attack and the question of her biological father. That sleeping dog can just lie there. Or go to hell as far as we are both concerned. If it rears its ugly head, we will deal with it honestly in confidence that Kristen will cope.

Brad is more at peace. He is not drinking as much. Surviving the Green Valley ruckus brought relief. But I know the bigger factor is our stronger relationship. It would be nice to have a delete button to clear the past. We each lived with the guilt from our mistakes related to the damned rapist for far too long. How I wish we both had had the courage to own up to them. I hate that we gave that son-of-a-bitch so much more power over our lives all these years. At least we finally cleared the air.

As for me, I am enjoying golf lessons at the public course in Buellton. It is easier to keep the club on path with my prosthesis swinging a left-handed club. Brad tried to instruct me, but it was too much like our failed attempt at wallpapering together early in our marriage. Too bad there will not be a nice, private course at Green Valley Village. But there are other golf course communities elsewhere if we end up moving again before Brad retires. Who knows?

The reality is we do not know what will happen in the next minute let alone an election cycle or two. Look at all those victims of the St. Francis Dam disaster. How could they have prepared for that? Our neighbor, Lilly, reminds us that even if a catastrophe hits, you can survive. We are so pleased that she and

Lee are doing well. I have my faith and that is enough. I remind Brad to focus on all our blessings, especially family, friends, and our health.

We are fine. Brad's not so sure about California, though. He continues to gather more evidence of the state's mismanagement of water and arrogant disregard for the public interest. Sometimes he sides with all the political pundits who have concluded that California has irrevocably lost its way and is ungovernable. Other times he gets excited about ideas for making a difference. I cannot predict where it will lead. But, after almost forty years of marriage, I can tell you that Brad is not the type to stand on the sidelines.

About The Author

John P. Thompson had a 30-year career in local government including 20 years as city manager of two California cities before becoming a partner on commercial development projects. He holds a Bachelor of Arts in Political Science from the University of California, Santa Barbara and Master of Arts in Urban Studies from Occidental College. He has founded and served on numerous nonprofit community-based organizations and is the current president of a local social service nonprofit. Thompson lives in Northern California with his wife of 45 years, Diane. They enjoy travel, friends and family and especially their 5 grandchildren.

Made in the USA
Middletown, DE
06 November 2021

51269196R00194